SORROW LEDGE

KENNETH ARBOGAST

All rights reserved. Published in the United States by Vigilant Newf Books, 3820 London Road, #210, Duluth, MN 55804.

Cover art by Mariah Mason.

Cover design by Rita Kogler Carver.

Nautical Chart of Maine by U.S. Light House Board, 1900.

ISBN: (978-1-7348721-0-1) (eBook)

ISBN: (978-1-7348721-1-8) (Paperback)

Library of Congress Cataloging-in-Publication Data has been applied for.

❄ Created with Vellum

DEDICATION

PROLOGUE

MAINE
JANUARY 1880

Thursday morning
  15 Jan.

My dear Fanny;
   Yesterday was another Round Top; although few knew of it. The bitter attack on me in the Bangor Commercial *calling me a traitor, & calling on the people to send me speedily to a traitor's doom, created a great excitement.*
   There were threats all the morning of overpowering the police & throwing me out of the window, & the ugly looking crowd seemed like men who could be brought to do it (or to try it). Excited men were calling on me – some threatening fire & blood & some begging me to call out the militia at once. But I stood firmly through, feeling sure of my arrangements & of my command of the situation.
   In the afternoon the tune changed. The plan was to arrest me for treason, which not being a jailable offence, I should be kept in prison while they inaugurated a reign of terror & blood. They foamed & fumed away at that all

1

evening. Mr. Lamson kindly came to me & said he would be the one to sue out a writ of habeas corpus & have me set at liberty again.

That plan failed.

At about 11 p.m. one of the citizens came & told me I was to be kidnapped – overpowered & carried away & detained out of people's knowledge, so that the rebels could carry on their work. I had the strange sense again – of sleeping inside a picket guard.

*T*he pen paused. With his other hand, the writer reached for the ceramic cup of coffee, now as cold as spring water, where it sat on the wooden desk.

Major General Joshua Lawrence Chamberlain sat alone. He had never felt more so.

Frost covered the windowpanes. Through the icy crystals, he watched the shimmering street lamps. Earlier that evening he had observed the march of orange flames as the lamplighters progressed along the streets of Augusta while twilight crept in from the northeast.

Holding the blue mug in both hands, he settled back on the embroidered pillow that rested against the chair's spindles. In a soldier's life, there is plenty of cold coffee. Meals are often little more than a thin, weak brew and hard biscuits. That evening he had hungered for a satisfying dinner but resisted venturing out into the city. In all likelihood, one faction or another might have prevented his return to the hotel. Perhaps in a very violent manner.

The edges of the paper where he had been scribbling a note to his wife curled gently upward. Perhaps he had been writing more forcefully than he imagined.

Just ten days ago, Governor Garcelon had dispatched orders to Chamberlain at his home in Brunswick. The major general was instructed to mobilize the state militia to maintain peace in Augusta. The voting in November had not decisively elected a new state legislature or governor. Weeks of wrangling between the political parties had failed to certify a replacement for Garcelon. The state Supreme Court was reluctant to take up the matter. By early January, all sides anticipated the political dispute would dissolve into partisan violence, as each side summoned angry supporters to the Capitol in case the election would be settled by knife and club.

Earlier that afternoon, the general had stood at the bottom of the magnificent stairway in the foyer of the State House to confront an angry mob. Calm as a clock, Chamberlain positioned himself two steps above the floor so that he had a strategic view of the growing and restless crowd. His left hand rested atop the finial of the balustrade. With his right hand, he opened his heavy blue woolen overcoat to show he was unarmed. By doing so, he once again proffered his chest as a target, this time to men from Maine. He harbored no doubt that a least a few among them had once wore a blue uniform similar to his own. If they were intent on murdering him for political purposes, he would prefer to be shot openly in daylight than slain by an assassin skulking in the dark. He met their angry stares with a level gaze.

"Men, you wish to kill me, I hear," he called out. "Killing is no new thing to me. I have offered myself to be killed many times. Some of you, I think, have been with me in those days. If anybody wants to kill me, here I am. Let him kill!"

His greatest fear at that moment was not for his own safety but instead for his Fanny. While he was away in Augusta busy being dubbed "A Lawless Usurper" and "The Most Dangerous Man in Maine" by the state's newspapers, Fanny waited anxiously at their Brunswick home. Would villains dare kidnap her and demand that the general accede to their treasonous demands? Perhaps such a crime might simply further rouse this growing maelstrom in the state. He picked up his pen to add an assurance for Fanny that no one would think of troubling her, but he carefully spelled out: *"If you are afraid, send word to the selectmen to have the police keep an eye on you & the house."*

Just fifteen years earlier, Chamberlain had been hailed for bravery in adherence to orders during a different civil war. Now when he was once again in a blue uniform, Chamberlain defied orders from a superior, for perhaps only the second time. Despite the governor's direction, he instead came alone on the train to Augusta. A show of martial arms might provoke, rather than deter, violence amongst certain factions.

He glanced back at an earlier page on which he had written to his darling Fanny: "sleeping inside a picket guard..." Together with the cold coffee and sparse supper on a third night, he thought that he could as well be camped in Virginia again. Upon added reflection, he concluded that he might very well be safer, and no doubt find better companionship amongst his army comrades, bedded down across the fields from the Army of Northern Virginia. The rebels mostly obeyed the conventions of warfare. However, a vigilante mob might be pressed into any rash action in the last few remaining days before the state's high court was expected to finally consent to take up the matter of Maine's failed election.

Once Chamberlain had knelt on a grassy battlefield, supporting his weight against his sword planted six inches deep in Virginia soil. He shouted at the troops following him, "Break ranks to pass obstacle!" His sweaty, cursing men pushed past the obstacle – him – in the deadly assault on the rebel defenses at Fort Mahone. His men. Then he had felt a sense of esprit de corps amidst a rush of hurrying soldiers in blue uniforms; charging forward to smite Bobby Lee – for glory, for Old Abe, and maybe even for God. He remembered once again the searing pain of that Confederate shot that nearly killed him as it girdled his waist in much the same fashion a Maine logger uses to fell a great white pine, the bullet tearing a course around his waist along both hips and exiting through his groin. The newspapers of New York City reported that he had succumbed. Neither his doctors nor the generals in his brigade believed he could survive such a grievous wound. All had urged General Grant to expedite the promised promotion so that Chamberlain might cherish the rank of general for whatever time he had left on this Earth.

As he confronted that angry crowd in the statehouse rotunda that afternoon, a fellow veteran came to stand on the step below Chamberlain. The gray-haired man hobbled on a cane, no doubt courtesy of his own wound inflicted during the Recent Unpleasantness. Just moments before, that same man had been a part of this bloodthirsty mob. Now he raised his voice in Chamberlain's behalf and shouted, "By God, General, the first man that dares to lay a hand on you, I'll kill him on the spot." This outburst seemed to blunt the mob's anger. After a few moments of rankled confusion, the chastened throng drifted away like an ebbing tide. Chamberlain was sure that he saw tears on a few of the weathered faces as the crowd dispersed. He prayed these were not tears of pity for him.

The general rose stiffly and limped over to peer out the ice-covered window. The once-white lace curtain was now yellowed by age and tobacco smoke. Chamberlain knew the odor well. Many fellow officers in the Union Army expressed considerable pleasure when their marches and raids throughout the tobacco states uncovered a trove of aromatic stogies.

Above the flickering street lamps and the shadows dancing through adjacent windows, darkness settled. Southwest winds rattled the windowpane where Chamberlain kept his vigil. He wondered if this foretold a January storm that might chill the heated rhetoric among the men on the streets and in the pubs. Instead of a Union Army camp, Chamberlain was living now in the austere comforts afforded by a boarding house – the third such accommodation in as many days. If the plotters conspired to kidnap or kill him to achieve their tyrannical objectives, he intended to thwart them by sleeping in a different location each night. From his lookout on the second floor, he observed through his field glasses only the competing flocks of pigeons and seagulls on the slopes of Weston Hill where the State House was situated.

The Major General shook his head slowly. He considered it ironic to think that some of the same men who once fought beside him were now ready to kill him for no more reason than the result of an election. Abruptly he chortled aloud at that thought. Of course, this occasion was not the first when he had donned a uniform to preserve the outcome of an election. Lincoln's inauguration had prompted southern States to bolt from the Union in rapid secession. He smiled at his own pun.

Remembering that he was quite literally a target of ire to many ornery citizens in Augusta that night, he retreated from the window and settled into a well-worn corner chair. Given his political campaigns, four terms as governor and many public appearances, most people in Augusta knew his face. That flamboyant mustache now graying but still unmistakable, he was perhaps among the most recognizable men in the entire state, behind only the inestimable Senator James G. Blaine. Chamberlain understood without instruction that by complying with the Governor's order to report to Augusta to intercede in these matters politic that he had earned the Senator's lifelong enmity. That concerned Joshua, not a whit.

A convulsive shiver racked his body, and the Major General pulled his blue great coat up tight around his shoulders. Cold coffee was cold comfort that night.

His roving eyes came to rest on a pastel drawing of Portland Head Light House that adorned the wall opposite the window. Chamberlain knew personally many of the light stations that were fixtures of the coastline Downeast. These he had observed on his official voyages and during those sweet summer days aboard the yacht *Pinafore*, in which he held part ownership. As he pondered his many travels and travails, Chamberlain remembered a discussion with his brother Tom back during the war about a light house keeper.

INSTRUCTIONS TO THE KEEPERS OF LIGHT HOUSES WITHIN THE UNITED STATES

1. You are to light the lamps every evening at sun-setting, and keep them continually burning, bright and clear, till sun-rising.

2. You are to be careful that the lamps, reflectors, and lanterns, are constantly kept clean, and in order; and particularly to be careful that no lamps, wood, or candles, be left burning any where as to endanger fire.

3. In order to maintain the greatest degree of light during the night, the wicks are to be trimmed every four hours, taking care that they are exactly even on the top.

4. You are to keep an exact amount of the quantity of oil received from time to time; the number of gallons, quarts, gills, &c., consumed each night; and deliver a copy of the same to the Superintendent every three months, ending 31 March, 30 June, 30 September, and 31 December, in each year; with an account of the quantity on hand at the time.

5. You are not to sell, or permit to be sold, any spirituous liquors on the premises of the United States; but will treat with civility and attention, such strangers as may visit the Light House under your charge, and as may conduct themselves in an orderly manner.

6. You will receive no tube-glasses, wicks, or any other article which the contractors, Messr. Morgan & Co., at New Bedford, are bound to

supply, which shall not be of suitable kind; and if the oil they supply, should, on trial, prove bad, you will immediately acquaint the Superintendent therewith, in order that he may exact from them a compliance with this contract.

7. Should the contractors omit to supply the quantity of oil, wicks, tube-glasses, or other articles necessary to keep the lights in continual operation, you will give the Superintendent timely notice thereof, that he may inform the contractors and direct them to forward the requisite supplies.

8. You will not absent yourself from the Light-house at any time, without first obtaining the consent of the Superintendent, unless the occasion be so sudden and urgent as not to admit of an application to that officer; in which case, by leaving a suitable substitute, you may be absent for twenty-four hours.

9. All your communications intended for this office, must be transmitted through the Superintendent, through whom the proper answer will be returned.

Fifth Auditor and Acting Commissioner of the Revenue

TREASURY DEPARTMENT
Fifth Auditor's Office
April 23d, 1835

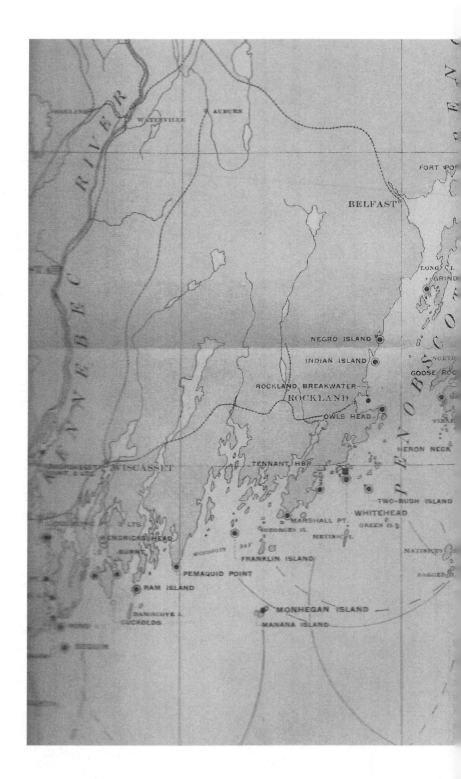

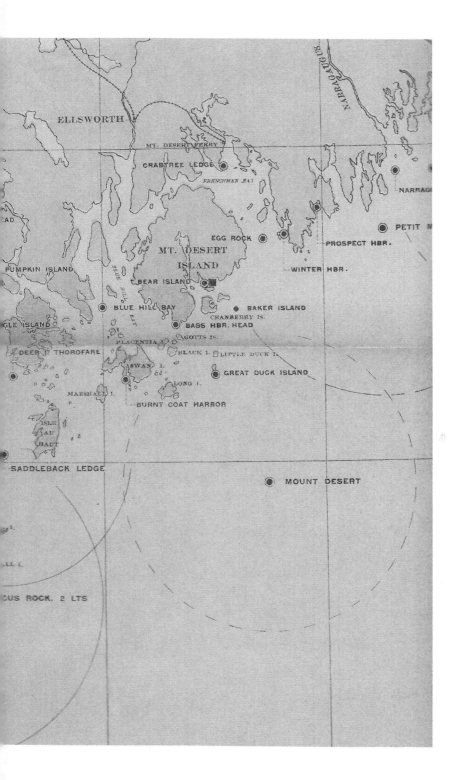

PART I

MAINE
JANUARY 1880

Sound the deep waters: –
Who shall sound that deep? –
Too short the plummet,
And the watchmen sleep
Some dream of effort
Up a toilsome steep;
Some dream of pasture grounds
For harmless sheep.

White shapes flit to and fro
From mast to mast;
They feel the distant tempest
That nears them fast;
Great rocks are straight ahead,
Great shoals not past;
They shout to one another
Upon the blast.

— *Christina Rossetti*

CHAPTER 1

*B*en woke early from a brief, fitful sleep. He felt in his joints and scars the approach of a winter storm. The gale had begun to build during the mid-watch, first blowing out of the west but gradually breezening up as it came about to roar strongly from the south-southwest. In the early dawn, he lay listening to a symphony the winds played against the quarters: the light percussion of rattling windowpanes, a haunting bassoon whispering down the chimney and the shrill flute whistling under the eaves.

The prior day had been unseasonably warm and clear along Maine's coast in January. Sunlight sparkled across the gentle wavelets. Seagulls squawked and fished on the placid leeward waters north of Sorrow Ledge. During the noon watch, the girls read their books outside, wearing light sweaters. Rebecca warned that such a day was a breeder. Many folks Downeast claim that unusually good weather foretells an impending storm. Ben, too, grew up along the coast. As a boy, he had lived at a series of light houses where his father served as the keeper, from Boon Island north to Penobscot Bay. Yet Ben had never quite learned how to distinguish a day of simply good weather from a weather breeder. Until the war. His body now bore so many remembrances of the Southern Rebellion that he sometimes felt his aches and pains were as accurate as any weatherglass.

Ben crept gently down the stairs with his eyes closed. Wearing only socks on his feet, he felt his way along to reduce the noise emitted by each step, hoping not to disturb those still sleeping above. After 30 years ascending and descending the same stairway, he knew each loose tread and riser. Ben came into the kitchen and found only the black dog waiting for him. The big animal's jaw rested on the bare tabletop, jowls spread wide across the wooden surface. Its brown eyes followed Ben's movements closely. Raising its massive head to greet Ben, the dog revealed a syrupy puddle of drool roughly the same size and shape of a skillet.

"Man alive, Bosun! If the missus ever catches you slobbering where she serves the meals, she'll settle your hash but good." Ben's fingers raked the fur atop the dog's head, which reached just above the waistband of Ben's trousers. "Time for your morning constitutional, I suppose?" Ben aimed the animal's snout toward the door. Bosun, too, seemed to be feeling the weather change in its bones. After standing, it craned its head upward and then leaned heavily on its forepaws while inelegantly raising its arse on wobbly legs. When Ben pulled the outside door ajar, the Newfoundland moseyed slowly out, leaving in its wake a small cloud of loose fur and the lingering odor of flatulence. Astride the doorframe the dog stopped, seeming to hesitate as the wind riffled through its shaggy mane.

"Go on now, Bosun," Ben coaxed. "You'll not want to go out when the weather comes on." Instinctively Ben glanced to the top of the granite tower to ensure the light house was still in service. When he tried to close the door, he was surprised to find the dog still standing athwart the threshold. "What's gotten into you?" Ben asked, as he prodded the dog's flank with a knee. "Go on. Your ancestors were from Canada. I'll wager it's a mite colder in Newfoundland this morning than anywhere on Penobscot Bay."

The black beast stepped gingerly down the stone stairs. Shivering on the stoop, Ben watched as the animal ambled about 70 yards beyond the fenced garden to a place on the north slope of the island that served as its personal latrine. While the Newfie completed its morning duty, Ben used the time to finish his daily meteorological observations. Overnight he had watched the barometer drop steeply. With dawn, his prediction was confirmed. In the last moments, as the eastern horizon dipped toward the sun, the sky above was already painted a dark reddish hue. To the south and west, night remained dark. East by southeast, Ben observed a veil of thin, misty fog and clouds through which a partially obscured full moon appeared within a bluish halo.

Bosun returned. Nosing past Ben into the kitchen, the big dog headed for its blanket near the hearth. There it would wait until served the tailings of the family's breakfast. In warm weather, the dog lounged on the cool stone that paved a covered passageway from the keeper's quarters to the light house tower. As winter came on, it spent longer lulling on the kitchen's brick floor that was warmed throughout the day by a Franklin stove built into the old hearth and the nearby cook stove that occupied the center of the kitchen.

With the Newfie and its thick tufts of fur settled at a safe distance, Ben set about getting a fire started in the iron cook stove. Snapping a thumbnail against the tip of a matchstick, Ben ignited a page ripped from an old edition of *Harper's Bazaar* and tossed it in atop the wood. The fragrant sulfur reminded Ben of campfires and musketry. As the flames spread from the kindling to the larger split wood, he removed the old gray, woolen blanket draped over the pump and filled the steel kettle with water from the cistern. Ben considered covering an indoor water pump unnecessary. However, while she was growing up in Rockland, Rebecca's family often woke to a caught pump when the mercury dropped overnight without warning late in the fall or early in the spring. If such a mild precaution quelled any concern in his wife's mind, Ben was not a man to quibble.

The rattle of the pump handle roused the dog to gather its bulk and haul itself to a corner where the girls kept a large tin bowl filled with water to satisfy its needs. Finding no refreshment, the dog pawed at the bowl noisily until Ben came to his assistance. Ben placed the kettle on the stove and retrieved the dog's basin. When the bowl was filled from the pump's spout, Ben laid it back down on the floor. The dog drank so fiercely that the metal pan rattled against the bricks nearly as loudly as when Bosun first pawed at it empty. "Gently, dog, gently," Ben hissed. "Show some concern for the sleeping beauties upstairs, please." Thirst quenched, Bosun next went to stand near Ben, water from its jowls raining across the kitchen floor. The dog butted its head into Ben's slack hand until its master was forced to pet Bosun's massive skull and scratch behind its right ear.

"There's a blow coming on, Bosun," Ben said. "You'll watch the girls, won't you?" The dog gave no direct answer but rubbed its snout across Ben's trouser leg, leaving behind a wide swath of slobber. Ben patted the dog's thick trunk. "You may leave the washing of my clothes to my wife; thank you kindly."

"Always leaving the work for me, eh?"

Ben turned in alarm as Rebecca came into the kitchen, surprised that he had not heard her approach down the staircase. A thick green flannel robe was drawn up close over her nightgown. Her auburn hair hung loosely under a white kerchief drawn across her forehead and tied at the back of her neck. She rubbed the lingering signs of sleep from her face with the back of one hand. The other hand clutched tightly closed the collar of her togs.

"Coffee?" he asked.

"Yes, I'd be happy to brew a pot for you."

"No, I meant would you like coffee? I've already put the kettle on the stove."

"And I'll magically transform that water into coffee." She stepped next to him and raised herself on her toes to kiss his cheek. "Now go sit. You hardly slept after you came down from watch for all your tossing and turning. It's a wonder you're standing upright now."

As she turned away, Ben inhaled deeply to savor the distinctive fragrances about her. She recently had begun to wash her skin with a soap product new in her father's general store in Rockland, but she continued as she had done for years to rinse her hair with rum. Rebecca often dabbed lavender-flavored water around her person, so she smelled a little less like the lye with which she cleaned the house.

"Thank *you* kindly as well, then." He settled in the kitchen, wiping the dog's drool from the tabletop with his handkerchief before Rebecca noticed. Bosun came immediately to sit next to him. The dog's jowls brushed wetly against the sleeve of Ben's flannel shirt.

"So then, I suppose the dog and I are equal in your affections?" Rebecca asked from near the stove. She waved the palm of her left hand over the kettle's spout. "Don't my many years of fidelity and servitude grant me any advantage?" She appeared barely able to contain a laugh.

She opened the stove door and stirred the flames with an iron poker. A wisp of wood smoke escaped and hung between them. He could no longer detect the scent of her rum-washed hair but suddenly felt a desire to hold her again. Now he thought to soothe over their playful spat before a wrong word irritated her. "My darling wife, throughout this land of steady beliefs who could ever be your equal in my affections?" As she started to turn toward him, Ben raised both hands, palms forward in a gesture of surrender. "But I'd prefer that you answer me after breakfast when I might have some dite chance of engaging your wit."

"So, I've no equal in your affections in all New England, then?" She began again, relentlessly. She turned her back toward him; he could no longer see whether there was the same mischief in her eyes. "How about down South where you spent those years? Or perhaps misspent. Marching, you were? Fighting for a noble cause, you were? Don't think for one minute, Mister Grindle, that I'd not heard of the low women what comforted our brave soldiers, even in the nation's own capital. Or was it the charms of the Southern women you found so irresistible?"

Ben smiled grimly at Rebecca's jesting. How could any human creature be so lively so early in the morning? Of course, he knew, she was all in a humor. She would never say such things when the girls were up and about. He also understood there was at root a question she did not wish to ask directly for fear of the answer; whether he had, in fact, visited one of Washington's many famous bawdy houses or gone off with some painted drozzle tail? He knew too that if she wondered still, so long after the war had been concluded in McLean's parlor and Old Abe was back home in Illinois, that Ben's simple words of denial would sound like a lame claw-off. Remaining quiet, he put a hand through the open collar of his cotton shirt. He rubbed at the ache in the long scar on his shoulder. A souvenir from a rebel bayonet.

Ben watched his wife fuss over the coffee grinder and again agitate the fire with the poker. The flames flared in the stove door, illuminating Rebecca's face with a reddish glow. Though he first saw her nearly 30 years earlier, he still enjoyed the simple pleasure of watching her. It was not always so. When he first spied her in her father's dry goods store in Rockland, he thought her clumsy and annoying. He and his father were there on important business for the government; she was merely childish. On later visits, he granted that she was at least cute and sometimes funny, if unintentionally so. After his father died, Ben alone made those trips from the island to the mainland for supplies. She had grown, too, and he started to think of her as almost pretty and even sweet when she helped him complete an order and cart it all down to the dock. It did not seem more than a year later when he realized that she was growing into a lovely young woman with a mind nearly as clever as his own. Just a few years later, Ben spoke with Rebecca in a corner of her father's store. Amidst the wooden barrels filled with flour, sugar and salt to bear witness, Ben asked if he might call on Rebecca socially when he returned from Mr. Lincoln's War. She actually snorted. "Why Ben Grindle, isn't that why you've been buying here all these years? Surely, you know you could have much better prices over at Lovejoy's. I'm simply what my father calls 'window dressing.'"

Since becoming her husband, Ben sometimes wondered if this was how painters felt, watching a sketch turn to great art before their eyes. Of course, he had no hand in the creation of her beauty and had added no brush strokes at all save the creases of worry at the corners of her eyes.

"And in addition to your coffee, sir, what else would you have for your breakfast?" Rebecca asked, now sweetly. "If you're all in a rush, I'll fetch a couple of eggs and fry them up right quick. However, if you don't mind the wait, I'll fix hash for you and Seamus. With the storm coming on, the pair of you might need something more substantial in your bellies."

Rebecca's mention of the weather brought Ben out of his youthful revelry. As for breakfast, Ben knew there were loaves in the buttery baked fresh the day before. He relished the thought of dipping soft bread into the wet yokes of two or three fried eggs. He also knew Rebecca was right about what the coming storm might bring. A goodly portion of corned beef hash blanketed generously with ketchup could carry a grown man a long distance across the Arctic. He went around the stove and hugged her after she had finished adding more firewood to the stove. He could no longer smell lavender on her, but instead only the familiar odors of an army at dawn – burning wood and coffee. "Before I came down last night, the barometer took a dropped steeply, so I believe you're correct about the coming weather. I won't be surprised if we're sounding the fog bell on the noon watch, and I can't guess when we may stop. I'll rouse the girls to help you because I think we may all need a hearty breakfast, both the eggs and hash you so generously offered, and perhaps some flapjacks, too."

"Any other requests?" Rebecca asked as their embrace lingered.

"Would you please make the hash with beef and not salt horse?"

She drew herself away from his hold when the kettle began to whistle. "Have I ever served you a meal of embalmed beef?" She clearly remembered his stories of the horrid victuals supplied by army contractors, that caused even the hungriest of soldiers to question the source of the meat they were served and, on occasion, its species of origin. Turning from the stove, she encountered Ben looking at the ceiling and rubbing his chin like a man lost in contemplation. She swatted his elbow with a free hand. "You just stop now; do you hear me? Did you lose all your manners touring the Potomac?"

He kissed her cheek, humming aloud the tune to "Hard Times, Come no More," but recalling in his mind the lyrics of the soldier's parody, *"Oh, hard crackers, come again no more."* Turning to go upstairs to dress for the day, he knew he had not merely misplaced all civil niceties while tramping along the Potomac. Instead, Ben was certain that his good manners, along with many other social graces, had been deliberately cast away on Virginia soil. During a December afternoon along the banks of the Rappahannock, his regiment, the 2nd Maine, had interceded – in a most chivalrous manner, of course – into a brawl between the 22nd Massachusetts and the 118th Pennsylvanians. The regiments had been attempting to march through sheer mud until the entire Army of the Potomac, horses included, was sunken knee deep in a morass that reminded Ben of a good-old Maine bog. Then the well-intentioned General Burnside approved issuing a ration of whiskey to the rain-soaked and mud-sodden men. The result was the same as pouring kerosene over last night's campfire – one ember became a spark that ignited a forest fire. Soon more than 1,000 men of at least three different regiments from as many states were embroiled in the world's largest fistfight. Ben smiled as he recalled that the Maine men had emerged from that quagmire as the undisputed winners, an event later referred to somewhat reverentially as the Mud March.

The pleasance of his reminiscence faded as he climbed the stairs toward their bedroom, and he peered out a window with a southern exposure. Between blue calico curtains, he watched the churning breakers. The waves battered themselves against the long, low strand that marked the southwestern foreland of Sorrow Ledge. In the distance, a misty fog hung in the air between the heaving ocean and the darkening skies. Ben could not yet tell whether the mist was oncoming rain or snow but concluded it mattered little. Snow or ice would melt away quickly. The greater danger lay in the ranks of white-capped waves surging toward the light station from the southwest horizon. A high tide could easily lift the breakers to reach the light house. The added effect of a coming full moon only increased the danger. Twice before, surge tides had completely swept away Rebecca's vegetable garden. Both times, Ben had hauled barrels of dirt from the mainland to replace what was washed away. Without the fresh soil that Ben labored so hard to import, little would grow on that rocky outcropping in the Atlantic apart from seaweed and seabirds.

From the ancient maplewood armoire in the corner of the bedroom, he gathered his work clothes, starting with warm undergarments. Over a worn cotton union suit, he pulled on gray woolen trousers and a red flannel shirt. Next, two pairs of woolen socks. As he laced a leather boot, he closed his eyes to listen.

From their room just beyond an adjoining door, he could hear Molly and Phoebe whispering and giggling as they dressed for their morning chores. In the kitchen, Rebecca sang a popular ballad, *"The smiles that once you gave to me, I scarcely ever see them now, Though many, many times I see, A dark'ning shadow on your brow."* Again, he heard outside the tempest laying siege to the stone fortress called Sorrow Ledge. At times, a deep thunder shook the glass windowpanes, as does the echo of field cannon before an infantry attack. At other times, he heard a high-pitched whistling in the eaves of the living quarters that mimicked the shriek of a passing Minie ball. There was another noise too, a low rhythmic rumble at a slow tempo that Ben could not easily name. Other sounds around the living quarters changed as the girls went down to breakfast and Rebecca shooed the dog away from their plates. The cadence of that slow drumbeat did not falter. At last, he recognized the rhythm of gravel churning under the breaking surf on the shoreline. He saw in his mind the frothing, tumultuous waves approaching, a prolonged, steady assault as the ranks of an endless army might march forward in step across a battlefield to assault an enemy position.

"Did you not hear me calling you to breakfast?" Rebecca asked from the doorway. "I thought you were going to dress and come back down right off. Molly and Phoebe have already had their oatmeal porridge, though I think any of the hens could eat more burgoo than both girls together. And Molly is carrying a plate up to Seamus now." She began to draw up the bedsheets on the side of the bed opposite where Ben sat. "If you ever decide to make me the happiest wife in Maine, I ask only for a feather mattress. I believe I could die happy on down pillows and a feather tick."

Her voice sounded far away, as though she was speaking into his deaf ear. Since Gettysburg, he was unable to hear on the left side. He remained sitting on the edge of the bed. Still. One foot rested on the stool. The laces of the brogue were only half done. "Ben?" she asked and then again, "Ben?" She came slowly around the foot of the bedstead, repeating his name as she did. His hands were on his knees, clenched fingers twisted in the cloth of his trousers. She sat gently next to him and wrapped her arms around him, careful of his back. "Ben?"

25

She hugged him tighter. "Come down, now. Come eat. You hear the storm. Just the weather. It's not the elephant. Not the war today. I promise you, not the elephant." He felt her head against his shoulder as they rocked gently. The bedstead creaked as they swayed. In a soft cadence of her own, she whispered again and again into his good ear, "Not the elephant. Not the war. Not the elephant."

CHAPTER 2

*C*oming down into the kitchen, Ben inhaled deeply the many aromas of the breakfast Rebecca had cooked over the stove: flapjacks with sweet maple syrup tapped just last spring; hash covered with thick ketchup that the girls had cooked at summer's end; eggs sprinkled generously with ground pepper alongside bacon cut thick and fried in grease to be sopped up with fresh bread. Settling at the table, he realized he had more of an appetite than he first guessed. Relishing a bite of corned beef hash, Ben glanced up and caught the dog staring at him through drooping eyelids. Seamus, Rebecca, and the girls were already finished with their breakfasts.

"My darling? Has Bosun had a bite yet this morning?"

Rebecca chuckled. "That moose can eat whatever's left when you're finished. The dog isn't what I consider to be my first duty." She, too, was now dressed for the expected weather of the coming day. She wore a white cotton blouse under a knit wool sweater, with a long linen skirt and ankle-high boots. Her long hair was wound up in a chignon at the back of her head, held by a knitted cap.

"I suspect it may disagree with you," Ben said.

"He, Ben. The dog is a he," Rebecca corrected, with feigned exasperation. "For the millionth time, a dog is mammal not mineral."

Despite her insistence, this was not a point Ben was yet ready to concede. Compared to their prior Newf, a gentle female, Bosun exhibited the charm and grace of an army pack animal. Years had not tempered Ben's disposition toward the beast.

Without lifting its chin from the floor, the dog tracked with its brown eyes each forkful of Ben's breakfast from plate to mouth. After taking his final bite, Ben left the last morsel of bread along with a helping of hash, a few strands of bacon and some egg on his plate, which he set on the puncheon floor. For a big animal, the dog was soon devouring the remnants of Ben's meal with surprising speed. Ben patted Bosun's long back. "I hope you'll be as quick if it comes to rescuing me from the briny sea." Ben turned to Rebecca. "And may I be excused from your table, madam? I hope you won't think I'm ungrateful to gulp down breakfast and dash off, but I'd better get onto the chores now."

"But of course, sire," she demurred as she curtsied before him, drawing up her skirt with both hands. "What purpose do I serve upon this rock but to satisfy your every want and need? And please don't get me started on his lordship in the tower. Expecting his meals to be carried up to him just like a royal."

Ben tried his best to ignore her theatrics and said plainly, "Please have the girls fetch in today's fresh eggs and stock the firewood, but beyond that, I think they should stay indoors. You'll occupy their time well? This blow will come on before evening."

"So you now believe my prognostications yesterday as to the weather today?" She abandoned her performance and began to gather the plates and mugs from the table into a neat pile that she carried into the kitchen. "You know I'm always grateful for any efforts you make to save my little garden."

"Well, ma'am, I don't believe that the protection of dirt is enumerated among a light-keeper's daily duties."

"I see, and do these regulations permit you to maintain a wife? Or burden her with the duties of all cooking and cleaning? Or the counting of seagulls? I'd like to see this list of 'daily duties' because I believe there might be amendments I would make." She turned toward him.

He again raised his hands in a gesture of surrender, a posture that was more common between them than he would willingly admit to his former comrades in arms. "Could that discussion be saved for another time, in better weather? June, perhaps?"

She smiled and came toward him. When their lips touched, a slight static charge shocked them both. She pulled away and smiled, touching a finger to her lips. "I still get such a thrill from you."

Ben snickered. "I saw you get just such a spark while brushing Bosun's fur last week. So, the dog and I are equal in your affections, then?"

Rebecca chuckled as she stepped back. "Very clever, sir." She bowed slightly. "Very clever, indeed."

Ben started out through the kitchen door, trailed closely by the Newfoundland. He stopped and pointed back inside with his arm. "I asked you to keep an eye on the girls today, Bosun. To your post." When the dog did not budge, Ben stooped to lift the dog's thick snout with his hand and stare into its brown eyes. "Bosun, you watch our girls now." Seeming finally to comprehend both the impending danger and its duty, the black dog turned abruptly and trotted back inside, barking sharply as a buck sergeant might issue orders to an unruly command.

On clear days, the light was extinguished from an hour past sunrise to an hour before sunset, the exact times of the celestial events determined each day from the almanac. On those days when the weather was clear, the lamp was not attended throughout daylight hours, allowing the two keepers time to complete larger work projects and perhaps even rest. On overcast days and during storms, the beacon remained illuminated around the clock and was attended continually. This constant vigil that Ben and Seamus kept in shifts could go on for days at a time. As keeper, Ben had the privilege of setting the light station's watch rotation. Ben had decided during poor weather that splitting four watches per day of six hours apiece with his assistant was reasonably fair. Ben planned to relieve Seamus in the lantern room at noon. The afternoon should give the lad a decent rest before his evening watch began. However, that meant Ben had only three hours to secure the light station and fully batten down all structures. He was not sure how much time remained before the storm brought its full fury to bear on the island. As the son of a wickie and now one himself for two decades, he had weathered many gales, and he knew instinctively how to prepare. Except for two years as a soldier, Ben had spent his life in dutiful service to keeping Sorrow Ledge. He knew the nineteen dry acres of the rocky island better than any person still alive.

Sorrow Ledge lies on the southwest navigational approach to Penobscot Bay, referred to as Two Bush Channel. The rock is flat and wide, barren of all vegetation because it was thrust from the ocean depths without any soil for roots to take purchase. Seagrasses and weeds common along most coastlines instead die in the harsh sunlight if they venture too far above the low tide mark on the Ledge. Nearby islands provide nesting grounds for the myriad seabirds that range along Maine's northeast coastlines. The rocky crags of Sorrow Ledge are best suited for the burrowed nests of puffins. Harbor seals sun themselves on the wide flat ledges that skirted the dry land. Early Maine settlers learned from native Abenaki elders that the island was long considered cursed; no tribe or clan ever laid claim to the little isle of stone.

Long before Ben was born, the dry rock of Sorrow Ledge was home only to transient seagulls and the nesting puffins that sought refuge in the rock's fissures. For vessels coming on a northeasterly tack from Boston or Portland, as many in the coasting trade did, the flat island appeared as a bright ridge on a calm, sunlit day that became hidden in heavy seas, obscured at night and turned wholly invisible in a storm. This illusion made the rock a deadly obstacle easily overlooked by watercraft approaching Penobscot Bay, the waterway into Rockland and Bangor. Crews aboard ships passing the rocky ledge would occasionally report observing flotsam in the vicinity: timbers, barrels, sails, and cordage. Those accounts were never accompanied by the rescue of survivors. Over time, those unnamed shipwrecks suggested a name appropriate for the barren ledge where so many ships and sailors met with sorrow.

Prior to construction of the first light station, the highest elevation on the island was occupied by a pile of rocks that even passing mariners could see was manmade. Few early sailors had ever attempted to go ashore to investigate the monument. The island's solid rock coastline was treacherous to approach, and it was apparent the barren ledge contained nothing of value. Local lore held that Vikings had built the stone cairn there during their early visits to Maine for future explorers to navigate a safe entrance into Penobscot Bay.

So many ships had foundered upon Sorrow Ledge that the legislature of Maine petitioned the federal government for a permanent light house nearly as soon as President Monroe signed its statehood into law. Construction of the first light house was completed in 1823. The surveyor selected the exact site of the mysterious monument for the base of the new tower because it was situated at the island's highest elevation. Workers who removed the historic cairn did indeed find an ancient mariner, though not quite as old as a Viking. The skeletal remains belonged to a man of less than average height. The barrel of an antique pistol and a brass buckle were the only possessions of a British sailor that remained after nearly a century exposed to tide and time. The remains were respectfully re-interred after the stone pyramid was reconstructed on the north slope of the island.

Ben thought Sorrow Ledge resembled nothing more closely than a bird in flight. The light station sat atop a high stone bluff that formed the avian's body. Its pointed head was a collection of boulders that narrowed into a low, gravelly beak aimed southwest. Two long gray ridges jutted outward like wings from the main body of the island in opposite directions – southeast and northwest. Toward their outer span, the stone wings tapered gradually into the ocean. In the northeast, the elevation of the body descended toward a fanned tail of smooth stone that sloped gently toward the rock's leeward waters in Penobscot Bay.

As he began preparations for the coming gale, Ben was reminded that the quarters where his family now lived was already the third building erected on the same site within just 30 years. Two earlier stations had been swept away entirely in the winter storms called nor'easters. Like winter hurricanes, nor'easters come north along the Atlantic coastline, gathering moisture and then speed as they churn for hundreds of miles across the open expanse of the Gulf of New England. When such a storm arrives at Sorrow Ledge, the surging waves and howling winds had twice shown themselves capable of carrying away light towers, quarters and families as easily as Bosun might brush aside Phoebe's paper dolls with its thick tail.

Ben's father had been appointed as the new keeper at the woebegone post in 1852, in the wake of the tragic loss of the whole light station along with the second keeper and his entire family. During reconstruction of the tower, Ben had camped with his father under a canvas tarp stretched across the crumbled walls of the former keeper's quarters. Amidst the debris they had swept out of the ruins, Ben found a dozen playthings that belonged to the prior occupants – metal figurines of soldiers painted red and blue, rag dolls, a wooden wagon, a toy Jacob's ladder. The storm had not spared the children, only their toys.

Light houses at the time were constructed under the auspices of several government agencies; funds and architectural design came from the Treasury Department, engineering provided courtesy of the U.S. Army and logistical support from the Revenue Marine. Local contractors supplied materials and manual labor. The third tower at Sorrow Ledge had been constructed of granite, unlike the earlier wooden structures. The young army engineer assigned to the project initially favored New Hampshire granite but soon located a quarry just across Penobscot Bay. With strict direction to limit costs, Lieutenant William Clough was both surprised and relieved to discover the quality of the granite on the nearby island of Vinalhaven. He repeatedly praised a pair of quarrymen there, Webster and Bodwell, who proved capable of bringing the cut stones to Sorrow Ledge well below the estimates provided by the Light House Bureau. The cut stone had been shipped to the northeastern shore of the island where the prow of the barge was run up on the gentle slope of the coastline. The four draft horses that dragged the granite across the island on a wooden cart were the only mammals, apart from keepers' pets, that had ever trod upon Sorrow Ledge.

The keeper's quarters faced southeast, toward the light tower and dawn. A wooden passageway joined the quarters to the tower permitting the keepers to come and go without being exposed to inclement weather. In preparation for the pending storm, Ben began to batten down the wooden shutters on the southern side of the passageway near the tower, working in a northwesterly direction toward where the keeper's quarters sat. The glass panes on the southern exposure of the passage were already quaking against the southwesterly wind. At times, the ferocity of the gale hampered his efforts to bring the shutters out of their dormancy and turn them toward each other. Using a long boat hook with a brass gaff at the end, Ben set the upper catches. The lower hooks he was able to reach with his gloved hands. He continued to move in a clockwise manner along the exterior of the quarters. At the southwest corner, he ducked under an elevated sluiceway that carried away the household's daily effluent. This wooden aqueduct was a creation of Clough for the convenience of the quarters' residents because digging an outhouse latrine or septic tank into the rock would prove impossible without explosives. From inside the quarters, the family could dump dishwater and the contents of chamber pots into a steel tub that drained onto a copper-lined channel buttressed by a framework similar to a railroad trestle. This contrivance carried the sewage away to a crevice that emptied out on the cliff along the island's southern exposure. Clough recommended flushing the system with a bucket of hot water and lye every few days or whenever the system froze in the cold winter air.

Even as the granite blocks were erected for the Light Tower, another crew built the keeper's quarters using less-expensive fieldstone, hauled by barge from the docks in Rockland. The blocks of the tower were set using fast-drying cement brought up from Portland; the house was assembled with traditional mortar. Similarly, the first floor of the boathouse, which shielded the station's dory, was built with fieldstone. The second floor above the boat, where government stores were kept, was cobbled together with heavy planking from the state's white pine forests. A pair of steel rails, called ways, ran from the big double doors down to the water on the island's northwest flank. A pulley system enabled one man to draw the station's small boat up the ways into the boathouse. The remaining buildings on the island – the quarters for the assistant keeper and the fuel house – were both situated on the north-east portion of the rock bird's left flank. Apart from the light house, the next sturdiest building constructed on the island was the stone bunker that stored fuel and gunpowder. Reflecting its relative importance – or lack thereof – to the Light House Bureau, the assistant's quarters had been hammered together on an oak frame with pine for both joists and planks.

With the family quarters secure, his next task would be moving the chickens to cages in the upper deck of the boathouse. During the first winter Ben and Rebecca had spent together on the island, the high tide of a December storm had washed away their coop entirely, taking 15 laying hens and a rooster. It was a hard lesson. A storm the following year carried off Rebecca's first attempt at gardening as well as her small terrier, a gift from her parents. The little dog panicked at the height of the storm and escaped the family's quarters but could not outswim the surging tide. When Rebecca recovered from her grief at the loss, she insisted that all future dogs on the island would be natural swimmers. Bosun was their second Newfoundland – a breed of water dogs known among sailors to rescue from drowning the occasional unfortunate sailor gone overboard.

As he came around the corner of the quarters, Ben found Rebecca already sprinkling dried corn across the rocky ground to attract the poultry. When that was done, it would be easy to collect them individually. She wore her heavy winter coat cut from a wool Hudson Bay point blanket, with its three indigo stripes across the hem. Her hair was wrapped in a heavy reddish scarf that prevented her from hearing when he hailed her. She jumped in surprise when he touched her shoulder.

"What the tunket?" she exclaimed, turning toward him.

"You speak that way where our girls can hear you? Though I suppose I look like the very devil."

"Ben, please," she said, raising her hand to the left side of his face. "I did not mean ...." Her voice failed her.

"Why are you out here?" he asked. "If I can handle Bosun, I can surely round up a dozen biddies."

"I know you're laboring today with the storm. You didn't hardly sleep, and I saw you grappling with the shutters. Is it your joints today?"

"Weather flows and ebbs like the tide. No need to blame what's only natural," Ben said, not wanting to discuss the physical challenges he carried home from the war. "I prefer to think I'm still as independent as a hog on ice."

"I'm not saying you can't stand upright, but wouldn't this be easier and quicker with two of us? Especially covering the garden."

He accepted her assistance, though remaining grateful and resentful by turns. Each chicken was accorded a cage built high up in the loft of the boathouse where the government supplies of dry goods were kept. From that perch, the chickens were more than 15 feet above the hard rock surface of the island. If the surge tide reached that height, it was unlikely that the Grindle family would be alive to enjoy eggs again from any source. They each made the trip three times, with a chicken firmly clamped under each arm. Once the biddies were gathered and removed to safer ground, the lonely rooster willingly surrendered himself to Rebecca's grasp and went quietly along to his own cage at the higher elevation.

Next Ben hauled the station's dory up the steel trestle into the boathouse and bolted shut the big wooden doors at top and bottom. The vessel was a uniquely Maine design called a Quoddy boat, a double-ender equipped with oars, as well as a jury-rigged mast that could be erected. As an added precaution, Rebecca retrieved from a storage cabinet five cork vests that were stowed into the boat. This would save precious time in the event it became necessary for them all to leave the island in a raging tide. He secured the brass oarlocks into place and lay in both pairs of oars in position – the primary and a spare set. She held the wooden rudder while he bolted down the iron braces that held the steering arm in place to be used whether the boat was under sail or tow. As an added safety measure, he stored under the transom in the stern of the boat a tin box containing a set of Poston flares. There was no need for a compass or charts because the most obvious destinations in an emergency would be the lighthouses at Matinicus Rock or Two Bush, depending upon the prevailing wind.

Before leaving the boathouse, Ben secured to the bow of the boat the end of a seapainter, a long line with a shackle on one end. At the other end of this hawser was an eye about two feet around, which he had long-ago braided then carefully enclosed and bound with soft doeskin. Many times, he and Rebecca had discussed and practiced this emergency procedure. If neither Ben nor Seamus were available to assist, she was to roll the cart on which the dory rested down the ways to water's edge, careful to use the handbrake so the tram did not get loose and set the boat adrift. With the girls secured in the boat, she was to put the noose around Bosun's neck and command the dog to take her and the girls "to port." Molly would assist with the oars while Phoebe kept lookout. Given several years of practice, Ben did not doubt that the big Newfoundland would tow the boat to safe refuge at the dock on Owls Head or give its life in the effort.

"I pray we shall never need to do this," she said with a shiver.

"Better to be prepared than surprised," he said, quoting on of the sergeants who organized the picket guards who maintained watch when the 2nd Maine camped close to Confederate troops.

Together they gathered two dozen hefty stones from the beach below the boathouse in two steel buckets and hauled them to the edge of their most recent effort to establish a vegetable garden. He was ever mindful of her dire warning: Without her fresh produce the island's inhabitants – spare the dog – might well perish from scurvy. From the boathouse, he carried out a large square of sailcloth. The white canvas was in remarkably good condition for a bit of flotsam that had drifted ashore three summers past. As he unrolled the sheeting, a strong gust got underneath and lifted it like unfurling a topsail, nearly pulling Ben off his feet. They stretched the canvas tarp draped over the brown dirt in which Rebecca toiled spring and summer to produce the only fresh vegetables known to the island. He stooped to place a heavy stone along the edges of the canvas sheeting to prevent wave or wind from carrying away either the sheath or the underlying soil.

He felt a hand on his back. "Would you please let me do that? You don't need to be stooping like that. It's no sin to accept help."

"Isn't sloth one of the deadly sins?"

Rebecca laughed. "Slothful? Isn't your stubbornness more from pride? Which I believe is also a sin."

He smiled at her and recited a quote from his favorite book: "'I am not proud, but I am happy; and happiness blinds, I think, more than pride.'"

"You're going to make me read that book someday, aren't you? As some test of my fidelity?"

"Endurance."

"You don't think raising two girls and handling that dog are a daily test of my endurance? Speaking of, I should go check on their safety." She stroked his cheek and headed off to the quarters.

Despite nearly six decades of effort and experiment, the challenge of growing fresh fruit on the island went unmet. The stone dome did not admit the roots of apple trees or other fruit-bearing shrubs no matter the depth of soil Ben had layered above. Throughout the summer, Ben hauled back from Rockland bushels of any fruit in season. To carry them through the winter months, Rebecca and the girls would spend two weeks each autumn working in her mother's kitchen back in Rockland to jar whatever produce was available. Ben referred to this task as "jarring and jawing." He knew the ladies were engaged during the hours they worked with catching up on all the news they had heard about neighbors and strangers alike. During the year, Rebecca's mother and sister Anna curated gossip as scrupulously as Boswell. Along the coast of Maine, women shared tittle-tattle nearly as reverently as reading the Gospels, because such talk provided a moral education based upon the foibles, follies and even tragedies of modern times and often local settings.

The morning sky overhead darkened like those days rendered sunless by the dense smoke of an artillery barrage. Ben shuttered the windows on the boathouse and lastly the assistant keeper's quarters where Seamus lived alone. Finally, he trudged out to the far north end of the island to where the fuel house was located. The birds of yesterday that frolicked and fished in the leeward waters of Sorrow Ledge were gone, flown off to other shores and other waters. Ben's approach scared up a solitary brown mallard that flew away, screeching an angry "bwaaack" as it launched itself into the air.

The fuel house was located at the farthest distance possible on the island from the inhabited structures while still above the reach of high tide. Lieutenant Clough had insisted upon this location. While surveying the island with Ben and his father, the lieutenant had carefully explained the need for this precaution. Clough's concern was the dangerous mix the warehouse would contain – fuel for the lamp, mineral spirits for cleaning, and powder for the fog cannon. Given the combination of explosives, Clough speculated that an accident might blow down every structure on the island. To address his unease, the officer designed a two-room vault, with its common wall fabricated of brick to separate the combustibles. For additional protection, he directed the construction of a semi-circular, free-standing wall around the fuel house using blocks of stone that had been damaged so severely in transit from Vinalhaven that they were no longer useful for the light tower. Clough explained to Ben that the granite bulwark would divert the force of any explosion upward toward the sky rather than outward across the rocky promontory. Clough also admitted that so using the stones allowed him to reimburse Webster and Bodwell for the imperfect granite blocks that were no longer suitable for the tower structure itself.

Every three months the skiff of a contractor's supply ship delivered a cargo of kerosene and other supplies to a small wooden pier at the northern terminus of the island. The kerosene was hauled to the fuel house in large barrels, where it would be pumped into 5-gallon kegs. From the fuel house, the keepers hauled the kegs two at a time across the barren island. The load was suspended from a hand-carved yoke, approximating what an ox might wear. The yoke was just wide enough to distribute the weight across the wickie's shoulders and still fit through the doors of the fuel house and lighthouse without forcing the carrier to make an awkward sidestep. The prior keeper had carved that same yoke some 25 years earlier out of a timber washed ashore from yet another unnamed shipwreck.

As Ben pumped the kerosene into the smaller kegs, he thought about the many changes since his father had painstakingly whittled the rough wooden spar into that smooth yoke. While Ben was a young boy, the common type of fuel used in lanterns was spermaceti oil. Extracted by whalers from the heads of giant sperm whales, spermaceti oil did not emit the awful odor that kerosene did. Soon after his father's tenure as keeper ended, the light had been converted to colza oil. When American farmers failed to produce a sufficient supply of colza oil, the Light House Board ordered lanterns converted to burn lard oil and still later to kerosene, a switch that Ben regretted deeply. Kerosene smelled acrid to Ben, too much like the residue of gunpowder that lingered in his uniform no matter how many rainstorms or stream crossings washed his clothes as the 2nd Maine marched along. Kerosene also created more smoke than spermaceti oil, significantly increasing the amount of time that Ben and Seamus spent cleaning the many surfaces of the Fresnel lens.

Ben understood precisely why the Light House Board had mandated the transition. By the time Ben went off to war, the whales were well gone from the North Atlantic. He recalled only a few rare sightings as a child – a great solitary beast rising out of the water just at the farthest range of his father's looking glass. These were solemn occasions. Three earlier generations of Grindle men had gone whaling. Ben's father finally gave up the family trade because the search for whale oil and corset stays took him ever farther and longer from home. On his final voyage, the elder Grindle had spent two months icebound aboard a whaling ship in the Bering Sea, not far from the Pribilof Islands. The decision to tend a remote light house off the Maine coast made sense to anyone who heard the tales Ben's father told of those 64 desolate days, listening to the ship's wooden hull groan and shriek under the pressure of the ice floe.

As Ben hauled the kerosene out of the fuel house, he glanced at the only remaining structure on Sorrow Ledge, one that did not need to be secured during his round of storm preparations. On the northeast flank of the great stone bird sat the rock cairn, moved and rebuilt to make its original location available for construction of the light tower. The unfortunate sailor was reburied along with the little evidence of his life that remained. When he was just 15 years old, Ben had placed a second corpse there. He wrapped the remains in a canvas tarp pulled up from the foamy tide years before. Then he set about careful reconstruction of the rock monument, placing each stone by hand. Not even his siblings knew of this secretive burial. On the blustery morning of the 15th of January in 1880, only Ben and one other person alive knew about that second internment.

The light tower itself was squat and rounded, only 78 feet from the rock surface to the peak of the ventilation ball. The stone tower's design was furnished by a famous Boston architect named Parris. Under strict instructions from the Light House Board, Clough spared every unnecessary expense. He demonstrated a remarkable innovation in using the tower's natural features. After weeks of numerous observations at different times of the day, the officer determined that the island's prevailing wind came out of the west southwest, predominantly between 240 and 245 degrees. The lieutenant next laid out the foundation so that the center of the exterior door entering the tower's base was set at 243 degrees. The few windows in the tower that the budget permitted were then spaced at 45-degree angles to that baseline, following the upward sweep of the interior stairs in a clockwise fashion. By opening the door and windows on clear but breezy days, the lieutenant predicted, the wind itself would create a natural current to push heat and moisture up the tower and out through the windows. This natural ventilation, he explained to Ben, would force fresh air throughout the structure and reduce the constant interior sweating that stone buildings experienced.

Ben and his father had spent many cordial evenings with Clough, a New Yorker. The army officer was the only person apart from the two Grindles who remained on the barren rock after the workday finished each night. The quarrymen returned to Vinalhaven. The construction crews headed into Rockland an hour before dusk and returned an hour after sunrise. Rockland offered decent lodging, meals, and beverages. Despite the so-called Maine Law of 1851 that brought prohibition to the state, the workmen had little trouble locating stouts and whiskeys bootlegged from Canada. This was the normal routine through 1852 and during the Spring of 1853 until May, when a massive inferno burned down many of Rockland's businesses, including six dwelling houses where the men had lodged. Construction progressed much more quickly through that summer as the labor force remained on the ledge rather than going into Rockland each evening, allowing for longer work days.

After carefully closing the portal that separated the chambers that housed fuel and powder, Ben hoisted the yoke to his shoulders. As he adjusted the weight, he felt the pressure build in his back and hips. He exhaled deeply to push out the pain and set off walking across the uneven rock. To the southwest, thrusting into the sky like a gray mountain range, cumulo-nimbus clouds hung in thick masses over white-capped waves. The density of the storm front reminded him of an angry-looking blizzard that amassed over Mount Katahdin. He had gone north one year with cousins from Castine to hunt a moose whose meat the families would share for the coming winter. By the following autumn, he had become the primary light keeper.

Each evening during the first summer while the tower was under construction, Ben had listened as his father and Lieutenant Clough talked for hours about their military experiences. For two men with such different backgrounds – one a career army officer and the other a light keeper – they soon discovered an unusual connection. Both had served under General Winfield Scott, though in very different wars. Over time, the two men sounded to Ben like comrades in arms as they shared their individual war stories.

Fresh back from the whaling trade with no work prospects ashore, Ben's father had been among Governor Fairfield's volunteers who marched up the Aroostook Valley to push the Canuck timber thieves back into New Brunswick. Fearing the worst, President Van Buren in 1838 sent Scott to prevent vigilante Americans from invading Canada in retribution. General Scott managed to keep a lid on tempers so well that Mainers dubbed the conflict the Bloodless War. Eventually, these border issues were resolved by treaty in 1842.

The Aroostook War lasted far longer for Ben's father, who continued for years to take umbrage at the slightest mention of the events of 1838. The name of an unfortunate volunteer, Hiram Smith, had become synonymous in Maine with bad luck of the worst possible odds when a fable got around that Smith was the only fatality of the Bloodless War. Poor Hiram failed, even, to die in combat; instead, tales claimed variously that he was drowned, frozen, poisoned or run down by a supply wagon. These legends gave rise to a common expression in Maine, "to have the luck of Hiram Smith." Whenever Ben's father heard the axiom, he flew into a rage, ranting that other good men had endured the hardships of winter in the Aroostook Valley and that Hiram Smith wasn't worthy of their memories. More than once, Ben watched his father chase a man down the streets of Rockland, screaming and cursing at the victim who had mentioned hapless Hiram. Ben eventually realized that his father's zealotry was motivated only in part by his desire to set straight the history of his Bloodless War. Ben suspicioned that a measure of jealousy was at the root of the elder Grindle's outsized anger.

Not long after Ben's father visited the northern border on General Scott's orders, the army lieutenant served on Scott's adventure across the southern border. He had served as an engineer under Lieutenant Robert Lee during Scott's siege of Mexico City in 1847. Outside the city's walls, Clough's horse had been knocked down by a cannon ball, and the rider's knee was crushed. Afterward, the young officer endured enough time as an invalid in an army hospital that he begged to be returned to active duty or discharged from service. The engineer was then assigned to build harbor breakwaters and light houses in Florida, an assignment in which he worked with another engineer and fellow veteran of Mexico, Lieutenant George Meade. Those light towers were a completely different type of construction because they were built at sea. Each required building large wooden cofferdams and pumping out seawater in order to drill into the hard rock below. Sorrow Ledge had been Clough's first construction project with a foundation above sea level.

Ben was just a boy of 13 when he watched the construction crews rig an elaborate system of hawsers and pulleys to haul the lens up the side of the tower to be installed in the new iron lantern room. Approved by the Light House Board a year earlier, and installed in 1853, the second-order Fresnel lens was among the first in the nation to replace the old Lewis-style light that had been the agency's primary lamp for 40 some years. With its beveled glass and highly polished brass fittings, the lens glittered in the sunshine as the crew raised it into the air. As a witness to the construction work, Ben had learned much about engineering and history, as well as many expressions he would not hear again until the midst of battle.

At an impressionable young age, Ben imagined that the new Fresnel lens had been assembled from the magnificent jewels discovered by Edmund Dantes on the island of Monte Cristo. In his traveling trunk, Clough carried a two-volume set of the French novel, which he gladly loaned to Ben at the end of the work season in 1852. The boy had devoured its contents over the cold Maine winter. The officer never returned to reclaim his books.

Through the door at the base of the light tower, Ben turned to the right and navigated his way to a storage cabinet under the stairwell. Breathing a sigh of relief, he settled the burden of the kerosene kegs gently on the floor, then detached the leather straps from the wooden yoke. He hung the yoke itself on an iron peg tapped for that purpose into the cement between two granite blocks. On an upper shelf of a steel cabinet was a three-gallon can to transport the fuel up the tower. Ben refilled the smaller container and shut the two larger casks inside the locker. Against the opposite wall was a steel box filled with gunpowder packed in canvas bags ready for use in the fog cannon.

With the fuel can in hand, he started up the steps to the watch room. He moved carefully, one hand gripping the single handrail along the inside curve of the steps. Ben knew that if he tripped, he could easily tumble down the entire elevation and land on the stone foundation below. At least such an impact would likely ignite the kerosene, so he might best be incinerated immediately rather than lay about crippled for years, every bone in his body shattered.

The black stairs spiraled up the tower, following the course of windows as they traversed the external wall. Below each window casement was situated a wide landing that provided a way station for men carrying burdens to the peak, though comfort of the keepers had never been the objective of the Light House Board. The landings served as workstations when it was necessary to survey the granite blocks or repair the cement grouting in the tower's exterior. From these platforms, workers could pass supplies to a man suspended on a boatswain's chair dangling along the outside of the tower.

Above the ground floor, there were 12 such landings, each separated by 10 individual steps that spiraled up toward Sorrow Ledge light. As a boy, Ben was grateful for these rests as he climbed up twice each day to relieve his father on watch. When the tower was first completed, he stopped at every other window ledge, but within a year, he was managing to make the whole ascent with only three rests. After his father died two years later, the speed of his progress again slowed when he inherited the duties of primary watchstander and the mantle, both figurative and literal, of hauling fuel up the tower. On these long, sweaty climbs, he tried many distractions to keep from focusing too much on the pain in his back and legs. He sang but soon discovered that only exhausted his breath more quickly. He hummed until the daily exertions exhausted his small repertoire of hymns. He recalled his father's tales of whaling, but these often involved barbarism of the same type that had put him in this situation as the primary watch-stander. When he set out for Bangor in 1861 to join his newly forming regiment, he was relieved to leave behind this duty to his younger but sturdy brothers.

Upon returning from service and marching to hell and back, Ben one day tried using a cadence call to keep his tired legs climbing upward. Ten steps – landing. Ten steps – landing. Ten steps – landing. Sometimes he would even close his eyes and feel his way along with just the memory of the routine climb. After a few weeks, he began to measure the ascent in the terms he now knew best – marching and fighting. Step, step, step, step, step, step, step, step, step, step, battle. The ground floor was Bull Run, followed by ten steps to Yorktown. Ten more steps carried him to Hanover Court House. Another ten steps onto Beaver Dam Creek. Then ten steps to Chickahominy River. Ten steps: Malvern Hill. Ten more steps: Groveton. Ten steps: Second Bull Run. Another ten steps: Antietam. Ten steps: Fredericksburg. Ten steps: Chancellorsville. Ten steps: Gettysburg. Ten steps: New York. That last step brought him into the watch room, one level below the lantern room. Naturally, each daily ascent required a later return descent to terra firma.

When he reached the watch room, he placed the kerosene in a safe location under the work bench where the can was unlikely to be toppled. He gathered several cloths used for wiping down the lens that were lying on the workbench and put them in the steel bucket where they would wait to be washed. He called out to his assistant working in the lantern room overhead.

"Ben?" Seamus answered. "You've come a tad early, aren't you?" His voice registered surprise.

Ben climbed the vertical ladder into the light room itself. He squinted in the luminous glow of the Fresnel lens. The light generated enormous heat. The assistant keeper had shed his wool jacket and wore only a white cotton shirt, with the upper buttons at his neck undone and the sleeves rolled up to his elbows. Beneath both arms, the shirt was yellow with sweat stains.

Even the most casual observer could guess that the young man was of Irish extraction. His red hair was wild and uncombed; a large cowlick dangled across his forehead. Every bit of exposed skin was covered with freckles of many hues. His nose was reddened by the low January sun, and bits of skin were peeling away. Yet by far his most astonishing feature was the lad's mismatched eyes; one iris was emerald green while the other was a startling shade of bright blue with reddish streaks through the white field.

"Has somethin' gone awry?" Seamus asked, with the lingering touch of the County Kerry brogue Ben first heard at Gettysburg in 1863.

"No, there's no trouble. I'm sorry, but I'm not here to relieve you just yet. I brought up a few extra gallons of kerosene." With his handkerchief, Ben wiped sweat from his forehead, remembering too late that the cloth was already quite damp from sopping up the dog's drool from the kitchen table that morning. "Just a precaution against this storm. If it doesn't blow over, we may be operating 'round the clock for a few days."

"Do you think we'll have a hard time of it?"

"Well, I think we'd be fools to take this storm lightly. We've rarely seen a nor'easter come during a full moon. The tide tonight may have us scrambling for higher places." Seamus nodded but did not seem much comforted, so Ben continued to describe the preparations he had already completed. "The island's battened down tight. I've secured the catches on all the shutters, in your quarters as well as ours. The chickens are safe up high. The dory is ready to run out on the double-quick. Sure, we may see hard winds or high tides, but I hope nothing worse than we've come through before."

Seamus walked around the light to where two mugs and a small steel kettle sat on a simple wooden stool. "Care for a mug? Molly brought it up not long ago so I guess it may still be warm."

45

"No, thank you kindly. I've got a few more chores left, and I'm hoping to have a little nap before I come back up. Can you wait to sup 'til I relieve you, or should I ask Molly to bring you a plate as soon as Rebecca has dinner ready?"

"There's no need for the darling nimbsy to make yet another trip up the tower today on my behalf. My stomach'll hold a few extra moments." Seamus sipped from his newly refreshed mug of coffee. "Rebecca sent up a prodigious breakfast this morning and a nice luncheon as well."

"When you come down, get what rest you can. It won't surprise me if we're ringing the fog bell before supper. If she continues to blow hard into the night, we may need to fire the cannon instead. We'll be busy from then until this tempest blows over." Ben began climbing the ladder back down to the watch room then stopped. "Wait. I've nearly forgotten. We should draw the oil before I go back down."

The duties performed daily by light house keepers and their assistants were outlined in *The Instructions for Light-Keepers of the United States*, a document prepared by the Light-House Board and approved by the Secretary of the Treasury. Strict adherence to the Instructions was mandatory. "The breach of any of the foregoing Instructions will subject the offending light-keepers to the serious displeasure of the Department, and, in the absence of extenuating circumstances, to dismissal," the document concluded. Item 16 required that: "The principal light-keeper shall daily serve out the allowance of oil and other stores for the use of the light-room. The oil is to be measured by the assistant in sight of the principal light-keeper. The light-keepers are, on no account, to leave the turning keys attached to the cranes of the oil cisterns after drawing oil, but shall remove and deposit them on the tray beside the oil measures, or hang them up in some safe convenient place." With more than 15 years of experience completing this task as a team, Ben and Seamus made short work of the assignment. Seamus scratched notes as they proceeded, which he would later transcribe into the quarterly journal. The Instructions were clear on these points as well. Item 17 directed light-keepers to update the journal books as events occurred and "on no account" trust their memories.

Another of the routine duties the keepers performed throughout their watch was trimming down the burnt wick within the lantern inside the lens. From this task, keepers were commonly dubbed "wickies."

"Seamus, we should test the alarm as well."

The assistant nodded. "We haven't had the need of it for as long as I remember, so it'll do no harm."

"Give me time to get back into the house, and then give it one good tug. If the bell doesn't sound, I'll try to sort out the problem."

As he worked his way back down the iron stairway, Ben's eyes followed a continuous cord that was strung through a series of eyehooks traveling down the southernmost wall of the tower. The cotton line connected a brass handle on the floor of the lantern room to the clapper of a bell in the kitchen of the keeper's home. If there was trouble in the lantern room, the wickie on watch could readily summon help from those down below in the quarters with a tug of the handle.

In the nearly 30 years he had spent on the island, Ben knew of only one occasion when the bell had been wrung other than while being tested. While playing war in the tower cupola, his younger brothers had accidentally pulled the alarm, which enraged their father. That day was a lesson that Ben never forgot.

CHAPTER 3

osun raised the alarm before anyone else on the island. The big Newfoundland was resting on the wooden floor in the kitchen when it suddenly sat erect and barked sharply. Rebecca was preparing a thick beef stew for supper, and Ben thought a stray ember from the stove had landed on the dog. As she reached her hand to console it, Bosun yapped fiercely in an outburst that frightened her. Ben rushed from the parlor where he was reading a Hawthorne novel.

"Bosun! What has gotten into you?" he demanded. He glanced at Rebecca, concerned.

"I don't know what's spooked him!" She looked from her hand to the dog's snout in disbelief.

"Did it snap at you?"

"No, I don't think he meant to bite me."

The dog stood stiffly with its tail erect and flared. Ben heard a low growl emanate from the dog's chest. The ears on its large head were raised in suspicion. Then it barked four or five times more in quick succession.

At that instant, the alarm from the tower sounded, clanging fast and loud. Ben stared dumbfounded at the lead clapper as it swung wildly within the brass bell. When the noise stopped abruptly, he lurched toward the door as if suddenly awakened from a trance. Then he brought himself up short.

"Get the girls dressed and ready," he told Rebecca. "Don't go to the boathouse yet. Try to eat and get something into the girls, too. I'll be back as soon as I know what's alarmed Seamus."

"Ben, please ask for help tonight," she said. "Don't get hurt."

Ben smiled at her. "A little late for that." He chuckled.

"Ben, please."

Snatching his blue woolen army uniform tunic from a peg by the kitchen door, Ben opened the doorway into the passage connecting the structures. He turned suddenly and went back to where Rebecca stood with her sweater pulled tightly around her. "First Bosun, and now Seamus has raised the alarm. Please be careful tonight, too. Whatever comes." He kissed her cheek, hugged her gently, and went into the tower passage before she had time to say a word.

As soon as he stepped out of the quarters, the wickie felt the air temperature drop significantly. The gale's winds shrieked in the eaves of the wooden passageway like the howling of coyotes skulking among the dead on a battlefield at midnight. A shiver of memory racked his body. The storm thundered against the passage's southern wall. Despite the shutters, the windows there shook violently. He ran through and began to climb the stairs toward the beacon on the quick-step. Ten steps and battle; 10 steps and battle. In the darkness of the tower, he simply closed his eyes and followed without hesitation the upward sweep of the stairs that he knew as well as Rebecca's face. In the watch room, he first heard the terrible ruckus overhead: wild shouting and loud thudding. Heart racing and breathless from running up the stairway below, he climbed the vertical steel ladder into the blazing white light of the lantern room.

Emerging from the darkened watch room, Ben was immediately blinded by the intensity of the Fresnel lens. He shielded his face with a forearm and topped the ladder. At first, the heat radiating from the lens warmed him, but he soon felt a strong cold wind blowing through the gallery. Had the blizzard breached a window of the cupola? He called for Seamus as he made his way around the lens. An unbearable racket of screams and screeches filled the lantern room. All around him, the glass windows shuddered as if they hammered from the outside by unseen fists.

Though his eyes were shaded by his sleeve, tears streamed down his cheeks at the lantern's brightness. Still unable to see clearly, Ben shut his eyes tight again and navigated around the circular deck in a clockwise manner toward the violence ahead. To his right, heat radiated off the Fresnel lens; on his left, the rushing wind chilled the air in the cupola. Glass crackled under his feet. He stumbled over objects lying on the floor. Blocking his face with his sleeve still, he glanced down and saw several dozen carcasses of birds strewn amidst the shards of glass on the lantern room floor. Mostly seagulls and mallards, but also grouse and even a puffin. More birds cawed loudly as they flopped about, half-dead or half-alive. A kingfisher struggled to right itself with a broken wing.

The angry tumult did not subside. Now Ben could distinguish the elements of the cacophony around him; furious winds wailing, birds screeching, and one human voice screaming. Through the broken window, he saw Seamus on the catwalk at full whee-up, swinging wildly at the dark night sky with a straw broom. His attack was so violent that Ben feared his assistant might topple over the railing and fall to his death. Ben reached through the broken window and grabbed Seamus by the suspender to haul him back inside the cupola.

In the harsh beam of the lantern, Seamus looked a bloody mess. Streaks of red ran down his flushed face; the front of his shirt was soaked crimson. Shirt and trousers were torn. The back of his hands bore open gashes where birds had attacked with beak and talon. He leaned heavily on the broom and gasped for breath.

"I'm sorry, Ben," Seamus said finally. "First a few birds hit the windows. Then that big mallard crashed through a panel. More came in right after. It's like they're out to destroy the light itself." He continued to huff several minutes longer, struggling to regain his breath.

All around them, the thuds and thumps shook the windows as more and more birds hurled themselves against the glass panels. Ben rested his hand on the younger man's shoulder. "It's a blind flight. Birds get lost in a storm and fly at the brightest thing they see."

"I was about to trim the wick when..." Seamus stopped abruptly and jumped aside. At that moment, a large merganser came through the broken window and slammed headfirst into the glass of the Fresnel. The bird squawked once and fell to the floor. The smell of burnt feathers filled the lantern room.

"Quick, wipe the lens!" Ben ordered.

"Can we board up this window?" Seamus asked as he ran his bunched linen apron across the bloodied spot where the bird had struck.

"I don't believe we have the time," Ben answered. He glanced at the mess of shattered glass and bird carcasses all around him. His eyes were drawn to the blood on Seamus and the reddish streaks down the beveled glass of the lens. The air was acrid with the burnt feathers and blood from the bird strikes against the lens itself. "We'd have to haul lumber up from the boathouse." Ben took up a linen rag, doubled it over and rubbed at a bloody stain on the light. Even with the added thickness of the cloth, he felt the heat stinging his fingertips. As soon as the smear disappeared, he pulled his singed hand away.

"What else can we do?"

"Extinguish the light," Ben said

"Are you certain?" Seamus gawked at Ben. "What about the First Instruction? Won't there be trouble?"

"Probably. But I don't see an alternative. If the birds keep striking the lens, their blood and oil will get on the glass. When the moisture heats up, the lens will crack. If the light goes darkened, perhaps they'll fly somewhere else."

Seamus nodded and paced deliberately around the lens to the access panel. He reached inside and turned the knob that allowed the kerosene to feed the wick's flame. Within a few moments, the lantern went dark. From standing in a light so intense that it made a man sweat, Ben and Seamus were now engulfed in dark and cold. The lantern room filled with the scent of unburned kerosene. Bitter winds through the shattered window whistled around the cupola.

Although the lantern was extinguished, the incessant thudding of the winged creatures against the remaining windows continued unabated. In the darkness, the rattling of the panes sounded even more ominous. Ben wondered how much weight a bird must carry or how fast it must travel to shatter glass.

"I can't see anything," Seamus whispered as if his voice might attract even more avians to assault the windows and lens.

"Stay where you are. I'll bring up a lantern from below." Ben closed his eyes and inched his way back toward the ladder down into the watch room. Finally, his foot touched the open hatch. Holding tightly to the rungs, he clambered below. With his feet on a solid deck, he was able to navigate through the dark compartment from memory. On the workbench sat a storm lantern. In the drawer directly below it, he located a box of sulfur matches by touch. With a burning match in one hand, Ben could see well enough to open the lantern's weather guard and turn the wick upward. Soon the watch room was brightened by the lantern's small flame. Ben carried the light back up the ladder. He paused just before he entered the lantern room and called to Seamus.

"Do you still hear birds striking at the windows?"

"Yes. Less, but still a few."

"Let's wait a few more minutes then. If we restore the light too soon, we may draw them back."

"You've been through this before, then?" Seamus asked. "I don't recall what I've ever heard of a blind flight."

"Not me personally, no. But my father told me about times his lights were struck. A blind flight struck Matinicus Rock while he was there. And Owls Head was hit just before he took charge. Those each did a lot more damage than what I think we'll find that needs fixing." Ben still hung on the ladder, one hand dangling below to keep the full glow of the storm lantern from illuminating the lantern room. Then he added somberly, "At least, I hope."

"Did I do something that drew the birds?" Seamus wondered aloud.

"I can't imagine what you could have done to attract them or should have done to ward them off. My father said it was just a pure random thing. Like lightning. You can't predict when lightning might strike a tower."

For a while, both men were silent. Waiting in the gloom, they listened to the howling winds and crashing birds, accompanied by their cries and screeching. Ben wondered why the creatures still came at the darkened light. Were they drawn by the heat?

"Come here, Seamus," Ben said. "I'll give you the lantern to see your way to get the fog cannon ready. I'll wait here a while longer before I ignite the light again. We can't risk any more damage."

Just as he finished speaking, a bright green light flashed in the sky, arcing high above the tower and illuminating the white snowfall like the fireworks of artillery lighting the gun smoke fog of battle. Caught by surprise, Seamus twisted to watch it pass. In the darkness, he may have stumbled and reached out a hand to catch himself, only to place a palm on the hot surface of the Fresnel lens. Seamus yelped in pain. Ben knew instinctively how his assistant had been hurt, even in the pitch black of the Maine night. "Quick, double up your apron and wipe the glass where you touched it! We can't risk any more cracks tonight."

Seamus did as he was told but was clearly distracted. "Ben, that was a flare! A ship's run aground! I didn't see which direction it came from." The burn on his hand went unexamined, and Seamus did not mention the pain again.

"Aye, we'll have to go find her. Suit up warm, then put on your oilskins and cork vest as quick as you can. Would you search the northwest side of the ledge, down the windward side first and return on the lee side? I'll have Rebecca go to the southeast. I'll go out on the strand. As soon as I get below, I'll have Molly and Phoebe start ringing the bell. Send any survivors you find back in this direction. Be careful, Seamus, the rock will be slick tonight."

"Ben, what about the light?" Seamus asked. "We can't leave it dark."

"As long as the birds are striking the glass, we can't risk putting the lens in danger. I'll need you to help search, and we must put rescuing any survivors before safeguarding the light. I can't leave you here to fight off birds with a broom."

Ben dropped to the floor of the watch room, but Seamus did not follow him immediately. Ben knew why his assistant hesitated: violating the Instructions of the Fifth Auditor had gotten more than one light keeper relieved of duty. Ben also knew the flare likely meant survivors. Those poor souls must be the priority.

"Seamus, come on now. I'll deal with the Superintendent when it comes to that."

The assistant scrambled down the ladder, and they went at the double quick down the twisting stairs of the light tower. In the dark stairwell, with his eyes closed, Ben descended much more quickly than Seamus, who was younger but relied upon the light of the storm lantern to find his way. When Seamus reached the bottom of the tower where their storm clothes were stored, Ben was already inside the quarters, providing instruction to his family.

CHAPTER 4

*B*efore going into the living quarters, Ben opened the exterior door of the tower and leaned out. A harsh wind raised tears in his eyes, reminding him of a common Maine observation on storms, "Blowing fit to make a rabbit cry." The mild sleet of the afternoon had transitioned first to light hail as night brought colder air. The combination of ice, hail and snow would make walking across the exposed rock of Sorrow Ledge utterly treacherous.

Inside the warm, bright quarters, Ben found Rebecca and their daughters gathered at the kitchen table, eating a bit of summer sausage and cheddar cheese. On the stove, the beef stew still steamed. All three were dressed in warm clothing. Their scarves and mittens rested nearby on the tabletop. The girls were nearly the same height, though Molly was almost two years older. Both looked very much like Rebecca, with her piercing blue eyes and thick auburn hair. Ben saw little of himself reflected in the girls, and he was not at all unhappy with that outcome. Bosun sat wedged between Molly and Phoebe, closely inspecting each bite they ate. The dog's ears were still erect, as if it was eavesdropping on a distant conversation.

"Seamus and I spotted a flare not more than five minutes ago. There'll be a shipwreck somewhere along the ledge. Girls, get your coats buttoned up because I'll need you to ring the fog bell the way we've practiced before. Rebecca, please take Bosun and cover the southeast ledge. You'll need to wear my old oilskins because what's coming down now is turning to a mix of ice and snow. I've asked Seamus to scout up the northwest wing. I'm going down to look at the strand. For God's sake, remember it's January. Trust no step even if you've made it a thousand times. Thin ice is just as dangerous as heavy ice."

When Rebecca gave him her usual smile of apparent meekness and batted her eyelashes at him, Ben realized that he sounded more like a newly minted officer commanding veteran troops than a father seeking help from his family. Nudging the Newfie aside, he hugged the sitting girls together in his arms. "Come on, let's get you dressed for the night."

Then he stood and gently kissed his wife's cheek. "Please help me," he whispered at her ear. "And please be careful." Then, in a loud voice, he announced, "Ok, Bosun, patrol." Bosun went straight to the kitchen door, its usual exit.

"Just so I'm clear," Rebecca asked, "who is it that's in charge? The dog or me?"

Ben smiled at her and caressed her cheek with his fingers. "I'm partial to you, but the dog works for scraps."

Bosun barked abruptly and stalked back to Rebecca before returning to the door. After pulling over her shoulders a rigid water-proof jacket of oilskin large enough to fit Ben, Rebecca accepted the storm lantern that he had lit for her. At the threshold, she turned and brought the gloved fingers of her right hand to her forehead in an obedient salute. She smiled at Ben and then disappeared wordlessly into the night and storm. She followed the Newfoundland outside on the leeward side of the quarters. When the girls had donned their thick mittens, Ben led Molly and Phoebe through the dark passageway to the light house. They went into the base of the tower then back outside into a small foyer beyond the main entrance where a large brass bell hung on the exterior wall. The foyer was not shielded by an exterior door; however, the enclosure would provide the girls a modicum of shelter against the wind. Dangling from the bell's clapper was a thick line that ended three feet below in a large rounded knot called a monkey's fist.

"Listen, girls, it's very important that you keep ringing the bell constantly," Ben told them. "Take turns. Don't let your arms get tired. Keep your faces toward the tower so your skin doesn't get frostbite. Whoever isn't ringing the bell can stand inside the tower to stay out of the wind. Understand?"

The girls nodded together.

"If any survivors make it here, send them into the passageway. They won't be warm, but at least they'll be out of the winds. I'll be back as quickly as I can." Ben turned away.

"Wait, Daddy!" Molly caught at his elbow. "What if there's trouble?"

"You're right, Molly, good question." Ben paused, realizing that the girls would be alone at the tower while Seamus, Rebecca and he were off searching the shoreline. "Ok, here's what I want you to do. Stop ringing the bell and count to 30. Ring it for a count of 10, and then stop again for a count of 30. Keep up that pattern. I'll hear you and return as quick as I can. Do not leave the tower under any circumstance until Mother or I return. Be brave, girls."

When they nodded their heads in unison, Ben turned his head into the gale and left them to their task. More than once his own father had left Ben and his brothers to handle just such a job in a dire situation at even younger ages. Ben had not his father's stern hand that demanded strict obedience from the boys. Not because his own children were female. More simply, he felt the discipline of a whaling ship was not suited for a home, even though that home might be connected to a light house.

Ben's trek took him directly against the storm, leaning forward as he walked straight into a predominant headwind. Hail pelted his face. His ears stung from the biting cold. He squinted as the gale caused his eyes to weep. The tears froze on his cheeks. Finally, Ben simply closed his eyes. Unlike Seamus and Rebecca, Ben did not carry a lantern. Once he'd been blind for a week and walked nearly 250 miles in that time. Now he often preferred to trust his other senses to navigate the dark night. Knowing that the blow came out of the southwest, he could maintain the correct direction by keeping the howling wind steady on both cheeks, his own personal approach to dead reckoning.

Just 100 paces out from the tower, Ben no longer heard the clang of the bell where Molly and Phoebe labored unless he stopped and turned toward that direction. This storm blew as hard as any other he could remember during his tenure as keeper. The wind's roar was almost deafening, but still he heard the pounding surf somewhere ahead in the night, as well as the same dull rumble that he had recognized earlier that morning. He even believed once or twice that a clap of thunder rolled over Sorrow Ledge; however, no flash of lightning brightened his closed eyelids.

A burst of freezing rain dampened his trousers below the hem of his oilcloth jacket. As his garments froze, movement became more arduous. The accumulating snow provided little traction across the ice-covered rock. He counted his paces. If his direction bore true, he had only another fifteen feet or so before he reached the edge of the sheer precipice on the island's southwest coast. An iron chain was strung there on stanchions across the crest of the headland. Initially the Light House Board had balked at this extravagance but relented when it was reported that a keeper had stumbled to his death in a heavy fog. Two earlier deaths by the same cause – the first wickie's young son and a mason during construction of the third tower – had not been so persuasive.

Ben slowed to a shuffle. If he moved too quickly, he feared slipping on the icy surface at the peak of the cliff. He also worried that if he reached the chain barrier with too much momentum, he might topple over it. In addition, his joints were starting to ache from the cold. During the war, army doctors called it rheumatism and attributed their ailments to the troops sleeping afield on chilly nights and waking covered with frost. The troops themselves said their aches and pains came from wearing out their joints marching every damned place they went.

His outstretched hand touched the barrier first. The chain was encased with a thick coating of ice like sausage links. As close as he was to the light station, the darkened tower was invisible in the dense snowfall. When he turned back, he heard only faintly the fog bell his daughters rang. The windows of the living quarters shone dimly through the freezing drizzle, providing no useful light to guide him down the steep cliff. Ben knew that the chain fence had a gated opening at the start of a natural passage that led down the face of the promontory. He turned to the right, feeling his way along for the stanchion where the chain was joined together with a clasp. The descent down this narrow path was guided by a cotton hawser strung between two cement anchors, one at the top and another far below. If his boots slipped in the ice and snow while making this descent, Ben still might grasp onto the rope before he fell down the sheer face onto the boulders below.

Just as he reached for the chain's clasp, he opened his eyes and looked off in each direction toward where Rebecca searched first and then Seamus. To the southeast, he saw only a foreboding darkness obscured by the blowing snow. In the opposite direction, he was shocked to see a wavering white light. He left the clasp shut in place and followed the frozen boundary chain toward the hazy brightness, which he soon recognized as a storm lantern. As he slowly made his way toward the northwest, he finally realized the lantern was moving toward him as well.

"Seamus?" he hollered. "Seamus?"

His assistant keeper came within calling distance and held the lantern high above his head. "Ben, I found her." Seamus was also cloaked in ghostly white. The oilskin he wore shimmered with an icy glaze, and small drifts of snow sat atop his shoulders and hat.

"Is she aground?" Ben asked, trying hard not to look directly at the lantern Seamus carried and thus become blinded in the darkness.

"Aye, hard aground." The assistant was winded again, probably from coming back up the long ridgeline in the deep snow cover.

"How many souls aboard?" Walking along the windward edge of the island, Ben felt the cold creep into his toes and fingers.

"I spoke the captain. Nine aboard her. Three crew, the skipper and the rest passengers. Bound into Belfast and then onto Bangor."

Ben waved his arm back in the direction from which Seamus came. "Let's move before we freeze in place. Is she damaged or will she refloat at high tide?"

"Ben, her keel is resting solid maybe 10 feet above the surf. If she floats again, it will be flotsam. I told the skipper I was coming to find you, and we'd bring everyone off together."

Briefly, the keeper considered exactly how the Light House Board would respond to the report of a vessel wrecked on Sorrow Ledge during a winter storm, likely while the tower was darkened. He tried hard to push this thought aside and focus on the tasks at hand. He hoped when they reached the tower that he would find Rebecca and their daughters safe inside the quarters and preparing to welcome the survivors.

"Let's get those folks off while the hull is intact," Ben shouted over the wind. "Hopefully we'll have no injuries and get everyone up to the quarters safely. Listen, Seamus, you're to keep a safe distance and only talk as necessary. We don't know who these people are or where they may come from. There could be claims and lawsuits for the wreck. Understood?"

His assistant nodded in affirmation. Holding his storm lantern aloft, Seamus led Ben back down the slope along the perimeter chain toward the northwest wing of the island. The storm's high winds were abating, but the snowfall was now accumulating more rapidly. In places, the thicker snow cover made for better footing, but in elevated spots, the wind had blown away the snowpack. There a thin crust of snow covered the sheer ice below, and the two men alternately slipped and fell. Gradually, Ben began to discern the silhouette of a grounded hulk. First, he saw three white lights in a triangular pattern. One glowed about fifteen feet above the other two, probably hung high up in the ship's rigging. The lower lights would be on the foc'sle and the aft deck. In time, he could see the large murky shape of the ship itself, a two-masted packet boat. He paused for a moment, dumbstruck. Still on a northeasterly tack, the vessel's hull sat athwart the descending ledge, though now canting hard to starboard. Both masts and her rigging seemed intact, looming toward him out of the night and storm. Ben had seen other wrecks aground in Penobscot Bay, but now he felt a certain awe as this vessel emerged from the gloom. He agreed with the estimate Seamus gave. It was stranded nearly two fathoms above the pounding surf, as though lifted and placed there by an enormous hand. The way the hull rested on Sorrow Ledge reminded Ben of a toy boat abandoned on the beach. A big toy for a boy giant.

Ben estimated the vessel's length at sixty feet, with a full thirty feet or more of its keel resting solid aground on stone. Smoke belched from a narrow stack amidships, probably emanating from a Charley Noble connected to a coal furnace or a stove in the galley rather than a steam engine. The exposed stern showed no propeller, and Ben assumed the hulk was among the dwindling commercial fleet that relied wholly upon canvas. She looked to be a simple baldheaded schooner, bearing no topsails unless perhaps they had been neatly carried away in the gale. Strung out from the stern as far as Ben could see was a tangled mass of cordage and canvas, probably the crew's effort to drag a sea anchor to reduce their speed. Overhead the sails were reefed. Clearly, the skipper had been trying to slow the rate at which wind and wave were driving the vessel along before the wind until she collided in the darkness with Sorrow Ledge.

By the time the two wickies reached the wreck, her crew was already attempting to get their passengers ashore. A ship's Jacob's ladder hung from the hull's waist. Two men clung to the bottom of the rope ladder to anchor its movement from the gusts. On deck, a dark shadow was shouting indelicate encouragement at a bulky figure climbing down the rope ladder.

"Damnation, Missus Skevold, tha starm'll blow inta Nover Scosha before ya get to ground!" a voice screamed. "Ya aran't tha only one be needin' to git ashore at this port o' call."

"Fan! I no young girl longer." Ben did not recognize the woman's language that followed, but by the hasty delivery and harsh tone he guessed she was privately cursing back at the crewman.

Ben counted the survivors he could see. A rather portly woman dangled halfway between ship and shore. Two crewmen steadied the Jacob's ladder from below. Another crewman stood on deck barking uncouth orders, perhaps the captain. If nine souls were aboard, Ben could not account for five. As Missus Skevold set foot on the snow, Seamus took her by the arm and led her to a safe distance up the slope of the ledge in case the wreck collapsed onto its starboard side. Ben stepped past her and climbed quickly up the ladder and onto the deck amidships.

"Skipper?" Ben hollered to be heard above the winds. "I'm Ben Grindle, the light keeper here." He extended a hand toward the man at the top of the ladder. "You're aground on Sorrow Ledge."

The man accepted Ben's outreached hand. He shouted to ensure he was heard as well. "First mate. Billy Pendleton, outta Stonington. Skipper's astern. He'll be along." The mate's grip was strong and his hand well calloused from working aloft in the ship's rigging. He wore a slicker that covered down to his knees. An oilskin cap topped his head. Beneath the floppy brim, Ben saw only the black coils of a coarse beard and lips drawn tight.

"My assistant said you had nine aboard. There's only three ashore. You and your skipper make five. Who's left?"

"Passengers!" Pendleton voiced disgust. "Got a family of three – parents with a lass. I thought there'd trouble with the *lady*," he nodded his head toward the ladder, "so I left them all snug and warm in the galley 'til *her ladyship* was safely ashore. Expect the gentleman'll demand we pipe 'im ashore."

Ben chuckled at the vision of this first mate rendering formal side honors. Ben shook his head in confusion. "The family makes eight. Are you missing anyone?" Ben asked, leaning close to hear the mate's response.

The first mate chuckled grimly. "None that I'd miss, no."

Ben was now confused. "Who's the ninth person?"

"A deadhead. Skipper took him aboard as a favor to a friend. Last favor he'll do, I'll wager."

The fierce wind through the rigging created a loud vibration, which reminded Ben of the noise created by a curious wooden instrument his father brought home from Australia that he had called a didgeridoo. The deck was snow-covered. Ben realized that all the railings, the masts, the deckhouse walls, all the vertical surfaces were iced over, as if painted on thick with a brush. Small icicles dangled where the lines hung slack overhead.

"Have you a length of cordage nearby?" Ben asked. "I'd like to run a guideline when we take everyone up to the light house to be sure we don't lose anyone."

As he turned, the mate clasped Ben's arm for balance. "Aye. I got somethun that'll work." Taking a new handhold on the railing before each step, Pendleton then scrabbled forward on the slick listing deck. Ben looked back toward the quarterdeck. The ship's wheel spun wildly in the wind. Where were the captain and the remaining passenger? In a matter of minutes, Pendleton was back with a coil of three-strand hemp line.

"Mister Pendleton, let's bring your other passengers ashore now," Ben shouted.

Gripping a handrail along the superstructure with both hands, the mate pulled himself up the sloping deck and opened a narrow door into the cabin. He leaned in and yelled something that Ben could not hear. Soon three people emerged, two adults and an adolescent. The slender girl looked to Ben to be only a few years older than his own Molly. Her parents held her tightly between them as they came down toward the gunwale. The trio slipped and slid across the frozen deck in unison, reminding Ben of skaters on a pond. Their shoes were better suited for a Portland theater than the deck of a listing vessel aground in Penobscot Bay. They did not speak but appeared to regard the first mate with a certain disdain.

"Time to get over the side," Pendleton growled.

Ben stepped toward the family. "Sir, if you'll go first, you'll be able to help your wife and daughter land safely. There's nothing to worry about at all. It's solid ground below."

In the dim light emitted from the deckhouse, Ben could see that underneath their cork vests the family wore fine clothing. All three were clad in heavy woolen overcoats. A dashing bowler sat atop the gentleman's head that matched the shade of the fur pelt along his collar. The women wore velvet bonnets rimmed with lace ribbon.

"Gently. Take your time," Ben called as the father clambered across the rail and turned to face the vessel's hull. He began climbing downward slowly. On the third step down, his foot slipped between the rungs, and he dropped several feet unexpectedly. Fearing the man was in free fall, Ben lunged forward and grasped the man's fur collar. The bowler flew off and tumbled away into the snowfall. With Ben's assistance, the man managed to haul himself back up to stable footing and continued climbing downward.

Much to Pendleton's obvious dismay, the family went over the side and down the Jacob's ladder at no greater speed than Missus Skevold had proceeded just minutes earlier. With Ben and a young girl nearby, the mate didn't offer his brand of encouragement. Instead, he showed his impatience by dramatically groaning at importune times and spitting tobacco juice onto the deck with a practiced ferocity.

When the family was safely down the ladder and ashore, Ben turned to Pendleton. "They wanted their baggage ashore, did they?"

Pendleton threw back his head and guffawed. "Yeah, damn 'em. I've been at sea since I was a boy. First aboard my dad's fishin' trawler. In the war, I blockaded rebel ports. Then whalers and frigates all ovah the globe. I'll be nobody's god-damned porter."

Ben laughed, too. "I don't know what you said to them, but I believe you convinced them not to ask for anything from you ever again."

"I served under the meanest bully boys you'd ever hope to meet. I can make a man regret a question before he's all done askin' it." Pendleton's grin exposed gaps in his upper jaw where two incisors and a canine tooth went missing.

Nearby hatch covers and the ship's superstructure now showed at least two hands of snowfall. Ben began to worry about safely moving the ship's complement to the light station with the new accumulation on top of the ice he had encountered earlier.

"Mister Pendleton, is there any way you might speed your skipper and the last passenger along?"

The first mate went to the rail and pulled out a belaying pin. He wrapped the dangling loose line from the ship's rigging around the nearby railing. As he passed Ben, Pendleton flipped the pin so that the heavy bulbous end protruded from his fist. Ben had been aboard enough ships to know that a belaying pin was equal to a New York copper's billy club for ability to persuade a man to cooperate, or at least to stop resisting. Pendleton stalked aft along the railing and disappeared into the storm.

Ben climbed back down the Jacob's ladder and approached the other two crewmen. They were hunched over, huddled together with their backs against the gale. Ben motioned them toward him. Both wore rain slickers over thick wool sweaters, with watch caps pulled down to their eyebrows. Their beards were clumped ice chunks. The smaller of the two was also older and thinner, with a black tattoo of a long-tentacled sea serpent prominent on the side of his neck from ear to collar. Weather and sun had etched his face with lines and furrows like the cracks and crevasses on the stone surface of Sorrow Ledge. The younger man was tall and gangly; his sparse beard was scraggly but long. His face was pocked by long-past smallpox. Ben introduced himself.

"Aye, aye. Name's Gerty," the wizened sailor said. "The boy's Tommy."

"The skipper'll be along with the last passenger, momentarily I would guess," Ben explained. He handed the rope to the seaman who appeared more experienced. "Can you make a guideline? Nothing fancy. Just ten coils to drop over their shoulders. Run them about a fathom apart or so. If someone falls, I don't want them to pull down the whole group of us. Understand?"

Gerty nodded. "Just ten loops? Sure, now? We carried four souls plus our crew. Add you and your friend. Don't that make eleven?"

"Make it an even dozen then, but I doubt that your last guest will walk up to the light house on his own strength," Ben said, wondering whether the remaining passenger would even be upright when he came off the ship given Pendleton's attitude and apparent intent with a belaying pin. Perhaps it would be necessary to lower the unfortunate fellow from the deck in a cargo net.

The sailor quickly found the bitter end of the line and tied a simple bowline large enough to loop over a man's trunk. He pulled the line taut across his outstretched arms as a rough measure of a fathom. Then he doubled up the line and knotted an end to make a simple loop. He continued measuring and tying until he reached the other end. He shuffled the line back through his hands, counting the knots. "Twelve loops, cap'n" he said, showing a mostly toothless grin.

"Thank you. Give the lead to my assistant over there. His name's

Seamus. Help him get the passengers strung together. Tell Seamus he's to take the lead. Then two passengers. Next either of you. Then two more passengers, and next whichever of you is left. This won't be a cake walk because your passengers are wearing their Sunday best shoes. When the skipper and your mate come off, we'll follow up the rear. Clear?"

"A question, sir." Tommy, the younger sailor, spoke up. "Just where the hell are we, beggin' your pardon?" He then spat fiercely.

"Sorrow Ledge. Do you know Penobscot Bay? We're ten miles off Owls Head. What's the name of your vessel?"

"The *Gideon*. The skipper was a Navy man during the war. When he bought her, he renamed her for Secretary Welles."

The crewmen set off to assist Seamus in preparing the passengers for the trek up the snow-covered slope. The cluster where Seamus stood with the other passengers was distant enough that the falling snow obscured them into bulky shadows. Ben turned toward the listing hulk in time to see three men coming forward along the starboard rail toward the ladder. Pendleton came first, struggling to haul what looked to be a large sea chest. From Ben's vantage point, it appeared the last man had his hand hooked in the middle man's arm to keep his balance. Where the ladder hung over the gunwale, Pendleton quickly knotted a line through the handle of the large trunk and lowered it to Ben's feet. When Ben tried to move the baggage away from the hull, he was shocked by its heft. Before the wickie lugged the weight just 15 feet, the three men had already descended the Jacob's ladder. Pendleton moved away slowly from the vessel. Ashore as onboard, the other two men remained close together. One was an older gentleman with an obvious nautical air about him, an impression firmly created by his weathered face, thick pea coat and woolen watch cap. The younger man was dressed in a sack suit of all black, including both vest and necktie. He wore neither scarf nor hat, a small pinched face framed in a swirling pompadour of black hair. A thick, drooping moustache obscured his mouth. He carried a large black valise by a strap over one shoulder.

Finally, Ben realized why the two men stood so closely together.

The younger man held a short-barreled pistol shoved into the sailor's ribs.

"My name is Ben Grindle." Ben called out. "You're aground on Sorrow Ledge. I keep the light house here."

The younger man hooted abruptly. "It appears that you didn't keep it so good tonight." His Irish accent was distinctly more pronounced than even when Ben heard Seamus speak for the first time. Ben wondered if the man was from the home country.

"We had a bird strike. A mallard crashed into the cupola. Other birds hit the lens. That's not good because the oils in their feathers get onto the hot glass of the lens, which leads to small cracks..." Ben gave this dry recitation of obscure facts while desperately trying to think how to handle this stranger with a gun. He had been in battle with rifle, bayonets, knives, fists ... "We had to douse the light to save the lantern."

The gunman's arm suddenly pointed into the air, and a single gunshot sounded. "I don't care about your damned light! It's getting cold, wickie. Help the mate carry my baggage."

Pendleton struggled to hoist the smallish trunk alone. Ben stopped the mate and leaned in as if to help with hoisting the load. "Do you know what this is all about?" he whispered.

"Didna' know about the gun. Skipper don' like 'em aboard ship except his own." Pendleton grunted as he lifted the valise. "I carried men weigh less than this bag."

"It's all right, just help me get it balanced on my back," Ben said. "You're nobody's porter, remember?"

Pendleton supported the trunk until Ben indicated the weight was well distributed across both shoulders. The brown crate was dressed out in good leather with thick canvas straps wrapped around so tightly that Ben was unable to slip even a finger inside to achieve a better grip. Although awkward for Ben to carry because of its size, he calculated that it weighed nearly the same as the usual load of kerosene he carried from the fuel house to the tower.

"Can I help?" Pendleton asked in a whisper.

"Keep an eye on our friend there. And get the passengers moving."

A second gunshot sounded in the storm. "I'm sure we'll all be somewhat warmer socializing at the light house. Let's move along, shall we? Now!"

The quartet of stragglers joined the line of survivors roped together by Gerty's handiwork. Seamus was at the head, followed by the passengers and other crewmembers. Tommy and Pendleton walked ahead of Ben; the skipper followed behind. The gunman wasn't connected to the rope line. He walked about six feet behind the skipper; the barrel of his pistol barely protruded from the sleeve of his black topcoat. At first glance, the bluish muzzle reminded Ben of a Webley Bull Dog, which fit nicely into a man's coat pocket and sold popularly for exactly that reason – it was less visible than the long-barreled Colts. Perhaps that was why the skipper had overlooked it when his passenger came aboard. If Ben's guess was correct, the Irishman had four bullets remaining before he would need to reload.

Suddenly the many problems that troubled Ben just an hour ago – the shattered window in the tower, the oils from bird feathers transferred onto the Fresnel lens, the darkened light, the likely ire of the Fifth Auditor – all were nearly forgotten. For the first time in many years, he was confronted by people unknown to him – at least one who presented a clear danger. After a respite in which he had lived a mostly solitary existence, alone with his family and Seamus, he did not relish this intrusion. During the war, he had seen enough combat that he immediately disliked and distrusted any man whose initial greeting was to fire a weapon. As if caring for these survivors and reporting the incident to the Light House Bureau were not troubling enough, Ben also worried – because he did not know from where they came – that the passenger with an Irish accent might recognize Seamus.

The procession of passengers, ship's crew and wickies was now moving slowly toward the station. Seamus seemed to take extra precaution for the safety of the three women. He carefully snaked right or left to avoid steeper grades on which they might slip. This gave Ben an idea. If the coffle veered sharply in either direction, he might have the opportunity to run straight back at the gunman. With enough momentum from moving down the slope, he could heave the case, hit the Irish lad with its deadweight and get the gun. At Gettysburg, Chamberlain had used the tactical advantage gained by rushing the 2nd

Maine downhill toward a rebel regiment from Alabama. Here Ben would have the benefit of darkness and heavy snowfall, creating surprise in a place he knew better than anyone yet alive. Still he hesitated. The gun. No matter how unlikely, he had to consider the possibilities. Perhaps the man carried a second weapon. If such a surprise attack failed, Ben knew that he would not be alive to protect his family. That was the unacceptable risk. He grimaced, remembering the grievous wound he had endured in that victory over those Alabama troops.

The heavy wet snowfall was blowing from the southwest at a nearly horizontal angle to the surface of the island. Ben tried to gauge whether the gale's velocity was greater than when he first left the tower. That knowledge might help him determine whether the nor'easter had peaked or worse weather was still yet to come. However, there was another high tide coming after midnight, with an even greater chance of a surge tide caused by the full moon.

As he carried the deadweight burden on his shoulders up the slope toward the light house, Ben smiled. After surviving the horrors of the battlefields, some combat veterans he knew began to feel a vague sense of invincibility. Ben felt this now. Within the past twelve hours, Sorrow Ledge had endured gale winds, a blind flight, a blizzard, a shipwreck, and now a castaway with a gun. What else could go wrong?

CHAPTER 5

The first indication that the parade of survivors approached the light station was the sound of the bell ringing from where Phoebe and Molly were posted at the base of the tower. Through the dense shroud of heavy snowfall, Ben watched the keeper's quarters come gradually into sight, signaled by the illumination from the windows. The tower itself remained unlit and therefore invisible to his eyes. Had the barrage of birds against the light finally ceased? Then he thought for the first time about how long he had been away from his primary duty. At the very least, he anticipated a stern rebuke from the Superintendent, if not the Fifth Auditor himself, for the shipwreck and any damage to the light house itself, though especially the Fresnel lens.

Seamus led the snow-caked caravan to the entrance of the tower, where they could shed their handhold on the rope. Molly stopped ringing the bell when Ben arrived. From where she stood at the tower door, Ben saw that her face betrayed a look of awe at seeing so many people emerging from the storm. Through the doorway, he saw that Phoebe was already leading the women passengers down the corridor toward the quarters. Once inside, he stopped and turned toward Pendleton. Together they lowered the heavy leather case from Ben's shoulders to the floor. Gerty gathered up the unneeded rope and faked it down in a tidy coil, which he laid near the tower stairs.

At first Ben thought it natural that at such a moment he should issue a few commands to bring order to the station, starting with lighting the beacon itself. He intended to send Seamus up to the lantern room. Then he would ask Phoebe and Molly to make the survivors comfortable in the quarters. He stopped himself, realizing at that moment that he was no longer in sole command on Sorrow Ledge. The skipper and the Irishman shook off the accumulated ice and snow from their clothing. Ben stepped forward. He raised his hands. "I want no trouble," he said to the armed man. "There are a few things I need to do. My younger girl took the women into our living quarters. We have blankets, biscuits and coffee. We may have stew left over from dinner. For now, I'd like my assistant, Seamus, to go put the lantern back in service. He'll need to carry up some planks to cover a broken window. Perhaps the crewmen could help him?"

The Irishman pushed the captain ahead of him and came closer to the center of the tower. "Seamus? Which one is Seamus?"

Ben tensed. Seamus had remained in residence on Sorrow Ledge for more than 15 years to avoid any such questioning. The assistant wickie raised his hand, careful to keep the brim of his oilskin hat covering his face. "I'm Seamus. Seamus O'Dwyer."

"Where's your home?" The Irishman took a step in the direction of Seamus.

"Here."

That the examination came from a fellow Irishman was doubly troubling. Ben noticed that Seamus made no effort to step forward, out of the shadows in the tower.

The dark-haired man snorted. "Where does your family come from back in Ireland?"

"County Cork. I've got cousins in Ballyvourney still." Ben noted that Seamus made no mention of the fact that he was born a Dinneen in New York City or that never in his life had he stepped on Irish soil.

Suddenly the gunman seemed to lose all interest in Seamus and his genealogy. "All right, go put a light in the tower. It wouldn't serve purposes to have anyone else run aground here tonight." This last statement was said with a special menace.

"Molly, go boil a few wallops of water to make coffee and tea, then have Phoebe open the relief stores and break out the blankets." Ben turned back to the Irishman. "And the lumber, too? Can the crewmen help Seamus bring the wood out of the boathouse to keep the birds from coming through the broken window?"

From where Ben stood, the Irishman appeared to be mulling over his choices. His pistol was now wavering. The muzzle no longer targeted the *Gideon's* skipper but seemed to roam at random among all the men standing in the base of the tower. In the shadows cast by the storm lantern that Seamus had hung near the doorway, their faces appeared fixed and fearless. Ben knew this was all bluff; no man with any sense could disregard a loaded gun aimed at his heart. Finally, the gunman spoke. "Yes, fix the windows, too. Just remember the women folk in there. You wouldn't want to do a thing to endanger them."

The skipper's voice expressed a clear resignation. "I guess we all get your meaning."

Ben turned to Seamus. "Fetch the lumber stored in the boathouse. Cover the windows that were shattered. Then place the remaining planks in the middle of the other panels to reinforce them. With luck, the extra support will be enough to keep the other glass from shattering. And be certain to wipe down every place on the lens that a bird struck before you light the lantern. We can't risk cracks. Use a clean apron and good linens, with plenty of mineral spirits."

His assistant was more red-faced than usual, perhaps the result of windburn and exertion. He looked at Ben in confusion. "But the display? I mean the signal. Won't we change...?" Seamus clearly understood that the placement of wooden panels would obscure the light's regular pattern of illumination.

"Yes, we must obey Instruction Number 9," Ben said, hoping Seamus would remember the phrase, 'all your communications to the 5th Auditor.' "As long as we start the light," Ben continued, "any vessel in the vicinity will steer clear, and even folks ashore will know the light's status." Ben was now looking directly at Seamus, hoping his meaning was now well and fully understood.

Without further question, Seamus nodded and pulled the hood of his blanket coat up to cover his head and left the tower, followed closely by Tommy. Gerty seemed to linger at the doorway, unsure whether to leave his skipper and first mate. Pendleton acknowledged the crewman's show of loyalty with a casual salute but then motioned toward the door with his arm. After Gerty left, Ben watched the Irishman shift the aim of his weapon toward Pendleton. Ben wondered where this new drama would lead; he did not need to wait long. The gunman pushed the skipper toward Pendleton and Ben.

"Gentleman, I apologize for imposing upon you in this manner. However, I must deliver this parcel to Augusta tomorrow, or the next day at the very latest. Our destination was Belfast. I planned to take the stage or a sleigh from there to Augusta. So tell me, what options I have to accomplish this mission."

His choice of the word "mission" struck Ben as somewhat curious. The word sounded like there was a military objective in its intent, but Ben guessed that even on a remote island off Maine he would know if America was now again at war with Canada or Great Britain. Pendleton and Ben exchanged glances. The skipper seemed to remain cowed by having a gun barrel in his ribs for so long. The silence lingered.

"I don't think I've made myself clear, gentlemen. You *will* help me. Eventually."

Ben spoke up first. "I have a dory in the boathouse. You're welcome to it."

"And will it get me as far as Belfast in time?"

"In a dory, with these waves and the coming tides?" Pendleton's laugh revealed equal parts skepticism and ridicule. "You'll be lucky to reach landfall alive."

"If I'm unlucky, then you will all be unlucky, as well." The Irishman smiled and leveled his pistol, aiming at the captain. The weapon exploded in a fiery burst. The skipper screamed in pain. Pendleton reached the captain first, while Ben placed himself between the wounded man and the gun barrel.

"I hope you'll now be understanding how important the mission is." The Irishman's voice became suddenly more menacing. The weapon was pointed at Ben.

"I don't understand what you want from us," Ben said quietly. "The *Gideon* may refloat at high tide in the morning, but I wouldn't bet hard money on it. I believe that leaves you only two choices. You can take the dory from my boathouse or try to float the *Gideon's* small boat." Ben turned to where the skipper leaned against the tower wall, his face screwed up in pain. "Where's the Gideon's skiff?"

Pendleton turned from his attention to the skipper's wound. "When we got inta tha thickes' of tha blow, we lowered away and towed it aft should we be needin' ta take off the womenfolks. We'd probably dragged it across the ledge when we ran ashore. I'd bet it's driftwood now."

Ben nodded as he turned back toward the Irishman. "I didn't see it on the ledge. I saw the sea anchor in the surf but nothing else. I suppose that means you have only one choice. The dory's fitted to run out, ready with oarlocks in place and cork vests stowed."

"Where's the closest port on the mainland?" the Irishman asked. "How long would it take to row there?"

"The closest dock on the mainland is Owls Head. There's no livery or railroad, and it would be unlikely that the road has been broken out by anyone with this storm still blowing hard. You'll be hiking in knee-deep snow for miles." Ben did not want to appear to be withholding any information and risk getting someone else shot, especially as the muzzle was aimed now at his own heart. "Your best bet would be Rockland. I don't know what the train schedule is this time of year. Several of the hotels in Rockland operate liveries where you could hire horses or a sleigh, perhaps. It's no more than 60 miles to Augusta, but in this weather, there's no way to tell the condition of the roads. If your horse or team is first breaking out the route, it'll be a slow, hard go of it."

"And is there any hope to find a Catholic church in Rockland?"

"Yes. Saint David's. Corner of Broadway and Park Street."

"Indeed? I had heard there were troubles for Catholics in Maine."

"Years ago. Before the war," Ben said. "I was just a boy when the mob burned the papist church in Bangor and put tar and feathers on a priest, back in maybe '54. Maine was a bastion for the Know-Nothing Party back then."

"So, when did Maine become so charitable toward Catholics?"

"Not so long after. I watched the construction of Saint David's whenever I went ashore for supplies. It wasn't long after my father died."

The gunman looked back and forth between the three of them as if trying to decide which one to shoot next. Finally, he said just, "Thank you." He motioned with the barrel to herd them up through the passageway toward the living quarters. "Leave my bag here. Shall we go see what the others have been up to all this time?" Then he put his gun into the hip pocket of his jacket.

The skipper pressed a handkerchief to the gunshot wound on his arm. A crimson spot soaked through. When Ben reached to offer his own handkerchief from the pocket of his trousers, he discovered it clumped frozen from the dog's drool and his own sweat. He shoved the rag back into his pocket. Ben then led the three men through the passageway, stopping only to leave his wet oilskin jacket hanging outside the quarters to dry.

Inside, the men found a bustle of activity in the bright kitchen. Phoebe was placing mugs, bowls, and spoons around the table where the three female passengers sat together. Identically patterned wool blankets were draped over their shoulders. The design and material Ben recognized instantly as coming from the locker thoughtfully provided by the Women's National Relief Association just for such unfortunate guests on such dire occasions. Wearing a blue gingham apron over her gray frock dress, Molly was at the stove, fussing over the kettle and a big pot, suggesting that fresh coffee and the stew remaining from dinner were forthcoming. Strands of the dark hair she proudly kept in a neat bun at the back of her head most times now hung loosely around her face. Her forehead and cheeks were moist with perspiration.

Around the kitchen table, the women sat folding coats and scarves. The male passenger, still wearing his overcoat, was seated on a deacon's bench near the old hearth where the Franklin stove was situated. His black shoes were off and pushed up close near the hearth to dry. One leg was up across the other knee, and he busily massaged his stocking toes in his hands.

As Ben entered, he pulled off the wide-brimmed oilskin cap that he had worn out in the blizzard. Missus Skevold shrieked. The other two women at the kitchen table turned toward where he stood at the doorway, and both gasped as well. For the first time in many years of relative solitude on the island, Ben felt embarrassed by the lingering gift of battle.

"Ladies, I apologize. I should have warned you. I understand that my face can be shocking." He said this in a friendly manner, hoping to sound cheerful and not offended. "On this island, I see only my family and Seamus, who have all become somewhat accustomed to my appearance." Each morning in the mirror, Ben confronted the face he wore home from the war. His injury was all too common in a war fought primarily with black powder muskets. More than 15 years later, Ben's face remained scarred and scarlet.

The three men following Ben pushed past him into the quarters. Pendleton and the skipper settled on a bench along the wall between the kitchen and parlor. The Irishman proceeded into the next room. He paced there for several minutes, examining the sparse furnishings before he settled on a wooden rocking chair in a far corner and draped a quilt from its upright back across his lap. Although the young gunman's eyes soon closed, Ben saw that he had carefully situated himself so that no one could approach without disturbing his thoughts or rest.

"I hope you have all settled your differences outside," the elegant gentleman from the wreck said. Ben was relieved that the Irishman either did not hear him or perhaps merely chose to ignore the comment. Apart from a slight smile, the gunman did not seem to react at all.

Remembering the 5th Auditor's instruction to "treat with civility and attention, such strangers as may visit the light house under your charge," Ben set about making certain that he maintained the peace until he had a better understanding of what was afoot. "My name is Ben Grindle. I've been the keeper here since the end of the war," he announced, loudly enough that his voice would carry as far as where the Irishman sat. "These are my daughters. Molly is your cook. Ask Phoebe for anything that you need, even another blanket if you'd like. You may be our guests for a day or two until we catch the attention of a passing vessel. Please let us know what we can do to make you comfortable." Ben walked into the kitchen where the girls were busy with food preparation. "Molly, please put some hot water in a bowl for me. Phoebe, I'll need scissors and some clean cloth from your mother's notions basket." Ben went to the bench where the skipper sat with Pendleton.

In the light of the quarters, the ship's skipper seemed much older than Ben had guessed initially. Streaks of yellow and brown marred the captain's gray beard around his mouth and chin, suggesting a man fond of either snuff or chewing tobacco, or perhaps both depending upon availability. "Captain, let's clean that wound. Would you move over to the table? Could I ask you to make room for the captain, Missus Skevold?" Ben asked. "Am I pronouncing your name correctly?" Ben hoped Rebecca would return soon because she was so much better at these social niceties than he could ever dream of being. Her years waiting on customers at her father's store in Rockland fostered an ability to be friendly even with those she found disagreeable. Ben's own social skills, on the other hand, were perfected almost entirely in the isolation of Sorrow Ledge, except a two-year sabbatical spent studying the art of war.

"Ojda, Mr. Grindle. I'm sorry I … shouted earlier." Her accent sounded decidedly Scandinavian.

"No need to apologize, ma'am. I've heard far worse. Where were you destined when Sorrow Ledge interrupted your travels?"

"I a'going to a place by the name of Eastport. My husband runs sawmill there 10 years." Out of her heavy winter coat, she looked much younger than when Ben first saw her out in the storm. Ben realized there had been a stark change in her girth since she teetered on the ship's Jacob ladder. Then he saw a hefty pile of neatly folded sweaters and skirts stacked on a chair behind her. Ben imagined the scene when Pendleton had informed the passengers in his gruff manner that they could carry off no baggage after the *Gideon* grounded. There was little doubt that Missus Skevold had simply dressed in as much of her wardrobe as she could fit beneath her winter coat. She now wore a smart black woolen dress with a neatly pressed white lace collar. Ben assumed the outfit was her Sunday best and no doubt did other duties such as funeral attire and travel wear. "Thank you for this care, Mister Grindle. Your girls very nice and so pretty, ja?"

"Please, you may call me Ben." With a quick glance, Ben observed that both Phoebe and Molly had blushed.

Phoebe brought the scissors along with swatches of cotton and linen from Rebecca's sewing kit. The skipper took away the improvised bandage from his injured bicep, and Ben helped him slide his arm out of his coat. Swett's clothes emanated a strong odor of tobacco. Then Ben carefully pulled up the sleeve of the skipper's wool sweater and trimmed away the frayed edges of the shirt to reveal the wound. Suddenly Ben realized that all conversation around them had stopped. His ministrations had become the focus of attention. Ben did not want his guests to think too long about the skipper's wound, and then the gunman and thusly grow more anxious.

"Molly, how's the water coming?" While she checked the kettle, Ben stood and went to where the male passenger sat near the furnace, rubbing his hair dry with a towel. "I apologize that I don't know your name at all, sir." Ben approached and extended his hand.

The nattily dressed man rose to stand in his stocking feet and shook Ben's outreached hand. "I am Professor Arthur Russell. This is my wife, of course. And my daughter, Elizabeth. We are, well we were, of course, traveling up to Bangor." The professor had been coiffed recently in a barber's chair. His cheeks were shaved, but a thin beard traced the underside of his chin. His hair was parted from the center of his head, with strands framing both sides of his face equally. Ben noticed the scent of aftershave about him. The jacket and pants of the professor's suit were cut from identical wool cloth. Ben saw the flash of a diamond stickpin on his silk necktie.

Molly brought a half-full bowl of steaming water to the table, and Ben returned to where the skipper waited. Dipping a piece of linen into the water, Ben knelt and dabbed at the wound. Wiping away the blood, he saw that the bullet had grazed the skin, leaving a bloody crease but not penetrating to any worrisome depth. The skipper did not wince. Instead, he watched Ben's ministrations with almost bemused detachment. Again, Ben wished for Rebecca's return, knowing how many times she had tended to his aches and injuries.

"It's not actually Bangor, Father, it's called Orono," Elizabeth announced.

When Ben looked at Miss Russell, she appeared to be somewhat irritated with her father. She was, just as he first guessed, only a few years older than Molly. Probably she would be marrying soon. Ben could not imagine her parents approving the sort of suitors she would entertain in Orono, which prior to the establishment of the State College was best known as a lumber town. Miss Russell, too, wore her hair in a Boston style, pulled back tightly from her face but cascading down the back of her neck in thick ringlets. She was dressed simply in a dark burgundy gown with a black velvet collar and cuffs. What impressed Ben most about the young lady's appearance was the flawless complexion from her widow's peak to the discreet hint of décolletage.

"I believe the school is located on Marsh Island, of course, not Orono," her father responded, in a tone that struck Ben as peremptory.

Missus Russell inserted herself abruptly. "My husband is going to teach at the Maine College of Agriculture and the Mechanical Arts." Unless Orono had changed significantly since his last visit, Ben thought, Madame Russell would find herself at the vanguard of fashion there, or perhaps even the forlorn hope. She was a handsome, trim woman. Her hair was swept up in an impressive pompadour. She sat slightly forward on her chair at the table because of the large bustle that hung from her waistline in the rear. Over the bodice of her dress, she wore a matching jacket that reached just to her waist.

Ben smiled. "An expert in agriculture, then? My wife would greatly appreciate your advice on her gardening."

"I'll be of little help in that department." Professor Russell sat back down. "I'm a civil engineer."

Ben recognized the imperious tone and turned his attention back to wrapping the wounded arm. "I'm sorry, skipper, here I am acting like a surgeon, and I haven't asked the patient's name."

"Ed … well, Eddie … Swett. Cap'n Swett, to most, I suppose."

"Are you from Maine, Captain?" Ben asked.

"Aye. Waterboro."

Ben paused a moment in reflection. "Any relation to Josiah Swett, perchance?"

Captain Swett looked up from watching the bandaging and smiled broadly. "You know my family, then? Yes, Josiah Swett was my uncle. I sailed as the cabin boy on the first ship that he ever built. My cousin Billy was captain."

"Wow, you sailed on the actual *Northborough*?" Ben whistled in astonishment.

Professor Russell spoke up. "I'm curious, of course, sir. What was so remarkable about the *Northborough*? Was it an unusually innovative ship design in its day?"

Ben glanced at the skipper before responding. "If I may? From what I've heard, it was a simple two-masted brig. It wasn't the ship itself; but rather it was the shipyard that was so unusual."

Eddie Swett burst into a guffaw. "Gawd, that's well said. My uncle built the ship on the side of Ossipee Mountain. Took the entire family more than two years to build her. Then when she was ready to be run out, we hauled her nearly thirty miles into Kennebunk and put her to sea."

Russell sat forward on his seat. "Really?" the engineer asked. "How did you transport a ship that distance on dry ground?"

"With oxen. Fifty of them, all told," Swett said. He was suddenly the center of attention in the room, a role he seemed to relish. He spoke louder so that all could hear. "The hull was cradled in two giant wooden sleds. On the first day, we dragged her as far as Shaker Pond. Then we hauled her straight through Alfred Village and Kennebunk. Sure made the people stare. I'll bet those cranky old sea captains in Kennebunk were scratching their whiskers to see us dragging a two-stick hull right past their big manses."

Professor Russell now turned his chair to face the two mariners directly and began a lively conversation about this feat of amateur shipbuilding and transportation. Though he was not there himself, Pendleton had obviously heard the tale so often that he had no trouble providing many of the details that now escaped Captain Swett's recollection. If Ben's memory served him correctly, the *Northborough* had been launched about 1820. If Captain Swett had shipped out on her first voyage as a boy, he was now almost 70 years old. The skipper was being quite stoic for a man of his age who had been shot so recently.

"It's not much of a wound," Ben whispered as he finished tying off the bandage.

Swett replied quietly. "Big as I am and close as he was, he must not be very handy with a pistol."

Ben leaned closer and lowered his voice even further. "No, I think he's a very good aim. If he intends to leave this island, he can't afford to kill any able-bodied seaman. And should he end up in the dory, he'll need men who can use their arms. Consider that a warning shot across our bow."

Swett nodded. "Understood."

"Phoebe, could you dump out this water and put your mother's notions away?"

Ben left the skipper and walked to the doorway leading into the parlor. "And you, sir, where are you from? What should I call you?"

The Irishman's eyes opened and stared at Ben. There was no other movement that Ben could detect. "You may call me Mr. Green." The eyes closed again.

Ben turned back toward the kitchen and heard the ongoing conversation there. Phoebe was offering bowls of stew around, while Molly carried mugs of steaming coffee. In the Ladies' Relief cabinet was an assortment of dry crackers and tins of sweet cookies. These would need to be rationed carefully to keep the survivors well fed so it would not become necessary to break into the family's foodstuffs. Nine additional mouths could consume a large quantity of the staples set in to last only five people for the entire winter. Ben wished Rebecca would return soon to monitor how quickly their unexpected guests were consuming the available edibles. He now realized that she had not returned from her search out on the southeast ledge.

In the kitchen, Ben took Molly by the arm. "Have you seen your mother's storm lantern outside? She should be back by now."

Her brow furrowed. "No, Father, I've seen nothing in that direction, and I haven't even heard Bosun barking either."

What had delayed Rebecca's return? In an instant, Ben was angry with himself that he had become so preoccupied with his attention to these survivors and the Irishman that he had not realized how much time his wife had been outdoors during one of the worst nor'easters that he could remember on Sorrow Ledge. Just as he reached for his oilskin cap, he stopped and turned back into the parlor.

"Mr. Green," he called loudly. "My wife went out earlier to look for a grounded ship after we saw the flare. She's not back yet, and I need to go search for her. The ledge extends to the southeast only a few hundred yards. I won't be gone long."

Green sat up stiffly. "Very well, go. If one of your daughters can help, take her, too."

Ben placed his hand on Molly's shoulder. "I want them to stay safe inside. I know the island better than anyone. I'll find her." He stopped and walked back to the parlor door. "Mr. Green, this isn't any trick. I'm going into the tower to tell Seamus where I'll be. Then I'm going out along the southeast ridge. I'll return as soon as I find her."

"Yes, I believe you will," Green said rather coldly as he looked at Molly. "Go on."

Ben turned and gathered his oilskins from the passageway. He stopped only to light a storm lantern with a sulfur match before heading out the same door into the passageway they had entered just a short while ago. Only halfway to the tower did he realize that Mister Green had not offered to allow one of the girls to help in the search out of any sense of decency or generosity. Green was telling Ben to leave one daughter behind as collateral. Because Ben failed to fathom the Irishman's motives, now both girls were hostage. He ran on toward the tower on the double quick.

CHAPTER 6

*I*nside the light tower, Ben closed the door that led back to the quarters and lifted a brass boatswain's whistle from a peg on the doorframe. He held his fingers away from the buoy and blew hard. After the high-pitched call echoed upward through the tower for a few seconds, he cupped his fingers over the hole. The whistle's tone dropped. Ben waited and then repeated the call.

Soon Seamus peered over the railing at the top of the stairs. "Ben? Is everything ok down there?"

"Come down as fast as you can," Ben called loudly. "Meet me halfway."

The younger assistant had the benefit of age and gravity. Ben barely reached the Beaver Dam Creek landing when Seamus met him. Seamus was excited to give his report. "We've got the broken windows covered and placed most of the other lumber you wanted. We heard no birds the whole time we've been in the lantern room. I was preparing to fire the lantern when I heard your whistle."

"Go ahead then," Ben answered. His voice lowered, and he leaned toward Seamus. "Once you finish topside, get back to my quarters. Rebecca hasn't returned yet, and I'm going to go search for her. You'll go back to the light room as soon as I return."

"Ben, I'll finish and get inside, but I don't understand what's happening. Who is this wild man with the gun?"

"I don't know yet. He says his name is Green. Otherwise, he says little. Talk to him if you can. He seemed to be curious when he learned you're Irish. Chat him up all nice. Just don't talk New York. And don't get so close as to give him an opportunity to study your face. You'll need watch over everyone inside, too. We can't allow foolish yip to irritate Green. He's not afraid to shoot off his gun for no reason."

"It's been more than a dozen years. But I'll tell you, Ben, I've not been so afraid since that day before the asylum."

"Do you believe that the boys helping you know Green? Could they be working with him?" As he asked this, Ben drew his handkerchief from his trouser pocket and wiped the sweat from the back of his neck.

"Not judging by the names they call him. They've used some language that I haven't heard since that day in New York either."

"Be careful, Seamus. We don't know these people, or who we can trust amongst them," Ben said. "I've got to go find Rebecca. I hope she hasn't slipped and twisted an ankle."

Seamus turned back toward the tower peak.

"Seamus, don't forget to wipe the lens as best you can."

"Already done." He continued back up the stairwell.

"Thank you kindly." Just as Ben prepared to return his hankie to his pocket, he saw that the white cloth was crusted and dark from wiping his neck. He raised his hand up to the lantern and studied the black dirt – fine crystals that glittered slightly under the torch. Coal dust? He started back down the stairway. The steel of the lower flights was wet with the ice and snow that Seamus and the crewman had tracked in on their boots as they carried the wooden panels up to the light room. Ben slowed and took measured steps. Still, his mind puzzled over the coal dust. No stove or furnace on Sorrow Ledge had ever burned it. His father disliked the smell and soot that he had encountered at other light houses that relied upon coal for heat. The Superintendent was happy to oblige his father's preference because firewood was plentiful in Maine and much easier to deliver to a remote island.

At the base of the tower, Ben buttoned the collar of his oilskin and reached for the doorknob. He hesitated, then returned to the Irish-man's luggage. He lifted one side so he could read the label that identi-fied the maker as the Henry Likly Company of Rochester. When he laid it on one side, he saw that the backside was black with dust, like soot on the base of a camp skillet. Quickly he undid the silver buckles of the two leather straps that held it tightly closed. There was no lock on the trunk itself, only a matching silver clasp that released when a finger pad was depressed. Ben lifted the lid slowly so that the contents did not shift or spill.

His eyes widened when the lantern illuminated the interior of the Irishman's case. What he saw shocked and then further confounded him, but he realized that he did not have time to investigate. He took the smallest specimen he could find and shoved it into a pocket of his inside jacket. Then he closed the case and affixed the exterior straps in their proper place.

The cold air outside helped focus his mind. The bizarre events of the past hours hurtling past left him confused and feeling physically dizzy. In the night, he closed his eyes, took a breath and set out at a steady pace toward the southeast. In Ben's mind, alone in the howling blizzard where he could think, he designed a plan. Two years afoot in Maine infantry regiments had taught Ben many lessons about strategy, some smart and others imprudent. First Rebecca; he must find her and lead her back to the quarters. Then he needed to understand the puzzling cargo that the equally mysterious Mister Green was intent to deliver to Augusta. Why would any man need to carry more than 100 pounds of coal across Maine in a leather valise? Why this urgency to reach Augusta in January?

As he walked out from the lee of the tower, Ben felt the rush of wind on the right side of his face. Then he heard the thunderous surf where it pounded the rocks below the light station. The snowfall had tapered to flurries. Instead, he felt cold moisture settle on the exposed right cheek above his beard. The drifting mist smelled of seawater. While watching for foot and paw prints in the snow, he also listened for any noises distinct from wind and wave that might reveal the loca-tion of Rebecca and Bosun. He shuffled on through the snow, cautious with his own footing. The slope of the ledge began to fall away more steeply. Ben opened his eyes to take his bearings. The beacon was flashing, just as Seamus promised. The added vertical boards in each window altered the visual pattern of the light's signal. Given the tower's range of visibility in clear conditions, Ben hoped there would be many who would observe the sudden change. Perhaps someone would come to investigate. He expected that among the first of the inquisitive visitors would be a Revenue Marine Cutter on patrol.

By the height of the tower, he gauged that he was about halfway to the extreme southeast point. He held the storm lantern as high aloft as he could. Then he began to call out for them.

"Rebecca! Rebecca!"

"Bosun! Bosun!"

The sound of his voice seemed to vanish in the wind no sooner than the words cleared his mouth. On his right, the roaring waves grew louder and more threatening as he traveled farther down the slope toward the water's edge. Ben closed his eyes and began moving forward again. After listening over 10 feet, he continued calling.

"Rebecca!"

"Bosun!"

He moved on. His right ear was numbing, while his toes and fingers ached. Ben wondered if Rebecca and Bosun had sought warm shelter from the howling blizzard in Seamus' tight quarters. He thought he might even find them resting comfortably atop the stone cairn.

Just as he inhaled to call out again, he heard an unmistakable "woof." He shouted the dog's name and heard a clear response. The bark came from off to his left, down a particularly steep section on the northeast shore. Ben knew of treacherous crevices in the stone there, some more than a foot deep. He opened his eyes and held the lantern lower to the ground. As he moved down the slope toward the northeast, Ben continued to call their names. Only Bosun answered. Suddenly in the flat white of the snowfield, he saw the black of the dog's broad chest. The thought flashed in Ben's mind that the Newfoundland embodied the old Maine expression, *cold as a dog and the blow northeast*, by which they described a small dog waiting outside for its master amid a nor'easter.

When Ben reached Bosun, he was surprised that the Newfoundland did not move, not even to come toward him. The dog yipped and whimpered but remained stock-still. The dark fur on the animal's back and flanks was obscured almost entirely by the thick mantle of white snow. When Ben tried to sweep clear the snow from the dog's pelt, his hand disappeared entirely into the slush. The snow along Bosun's spine was nearly two hands deep. The icicles dangling from the dog's jowls glistened as the beam from the light house came around. Soon Ben realized that the dog was standing over a dark shape, as if on guard. Ben knelt and held the storm lantern down lower. Beneath Bosun, he found Rebecca on her back. Ben spoke her name, but she did not respond. Her cheek was cold where he rested his palm. Unlike the Newf, she was not covered with snow because she was sheltered by Bosun's massive body. He could not reach and lift her because of the dog's stance over her; two front paws on either side of her head and its rear paws at her hips.

"Ok, Bosun, I've got her now. Help me take her up to the tower."

Bosun yelped but stood its ground. Ben reached under the dog's snout for its rope collar. Even as he tugged, the Newfoundland growled slightly and stood rigidly still. As he petted the dog from shoulders to hips, his hand felt only ice.

"Oh, Lord! You're frozen solid, Bosun!"

Ben stripped off both his oilskins and wool jacket to lay them over the dog's pelt. In the dark, he struggled to figure out what he could do even as he came to realize what had transpired. Probably Rebecca had tripped in a crevasse, or perhaps they had been swamped by a high wave. Unable to bring Rebecca back to the quarters, Bosun had tried his best to protect her. As they remained together in the cold – waiting for rescue, waiting for Ben – the mist, the sleet, the snow of the storm had settled over the dog's thick coat of fur in sheets until the animal became frozen like an ice sculpture. Ben knew that he had to breach the dog's frozen shell to reach Rebecca, like knocking free the runners of a sleigh anchored to the ground after being left out overnight in the winter.

He knelt at the dog's head and lifted a drooping earflap. "You're a good dog, Bosun. You watched our girl. I've got nothing to break the ice off you: nothing but Sorrow Ledge. I'm going to come at you hard. If I can knock you down, maybe that'll shatter the ice off your hide. I'm sorry to hurt you, but I must get our girl inside the house so she'll get warmed." Ben had two goals in mind with this little chat. He knew his voice would calm the dog before Ben struck him a fearsome blow. He also thought the warmth of his own coats would melt some of the ice and snow encasing the Newfoundland, and this speechifying gave that thawing more time without the dog becoming increasingly agitated. Finally, Ben stood and thought about exactly how he would hit the dog. He had never freed an icebound animal before. Ben worried that striking it in just one place might break both ice and bone. Finally, he settled on a two-pronged pincer strategy. Such movements rarely worked for Union forces, but unlike Bobby Lee's army, Bosun was anchored in place.

Ben went to Bosun's left side and cleared the snow from the smooth rock surface with his boots. He walked around to the dog's right side to where he sat on the snowy bank and removed his shoes. Then Ben rested one socked foot on Bosun's shoulder and the other on its hip. With a deep breath, he thrust both legs out straight with all the strength he could muster. The big dog toppled onto its flank, yelping and writhing together at once. Ben felt certain he had heard the tinkling of ice shattering on the stone. Before Ben reached Rebecca, Bosun shoved its snout in Ben's face, nosing and licking at his cheek and neck, seemingly to direct Ben toward Rebecca. As Ben knelt over his prone wife, the dog barked fiercely and stalked toward the light house, still shaking loose snow and chunks of ice from its pelt. When Ben did not move quickly enough, Bosun returned to bark close to Ben's good ear. Rebecca had not yet moved or responded to Ben's touch.

"I understand, Bosun," he said. "I've got her now. You lead the way. Take us home, Bosun."

After slipping his feet back into his boots, he did not stop to lace them. Ben scooped Rebecca in his arms, briskly chilled when her cold, wet clothing came against him. Bosun still wore Ben's outer garments draped over his spine. There was no time now to worry about that. Ben held Rebecca to his chest and began moving back up the slope, edging along cautiously because of the snowpack and sheer ice beneath. He trusted the dog's instinct to lead them back to the tower; however, he kept his bearings with the regular flash of the beacon. To preserve his night sight, Ben was careful to close his eyes when the beam of light tower passed over him. He rushed Rebecca back to the quarters as quickly as he could with the dog charging through the deep snow ahead of him.

CHAPTER 7

*B*osun preceded Ben up the icy ledge to the quarters, barking all a biver the entire distance. As the dog cantered homeward, it howled but then lowered its snout into the snow as if taking a refreshing sip of cold water on a hot day. Reaching the tarp-covered garden, Ben thought he heard a chorus of loud male voices coming within the quarters. The dog's echoing bark brought two young faces to the kitchen windows, and the girls hurried to open the door. The Newfoundland bounded directly inside. Trailing a few feet behind Bosun, Ben heard a shrill scream that brought an abrupt halt to the heated discussion amongst the men.

As he reached the granite steps, the wickie saw through the doorframe young Elizabeth Russell backed up against a wall, staring in horror at Bosun. "Bear, bear, bear," she stammered.

"Don't be scared," Phoebe announced. "That's just our dog. He's a Newfoundland." She explained this patiently as she removed her father's coats from the canine's back and hung them near the door.

Just then Ben came through the doorway, sidestepping to avoid bumping Rebecca's head against the door jamb. She lay slack in his arms, head hanging loosely and eyes closed. Her arms hung limply down from her shoulders. The matted mess of her hair dripped water on the floor.

"Ladies, I very much need your assistance. Her clothes are soaked completely. We've got to get her into dry nightclothes and a warm bed. Would one of you please come up and help?"

All three women from the *Gideon* rose nearly as one and started toward him. He knew it might cause hurt feelings to choose between them; however, Missus Russell directed Elizabeth to remain with her father. Ben paused briefly to issue more orders.

"Molly, fill the kettle and get it on the fire. Put a few towels in a bucket and pour warm water over them. Phoebe, go fetch the bed warmer from your room." Both girls ran to their tasks. "Seamus, please haul in two or three loads of firewood. We'll need to heat the quarters well tonight."

The way up to the bedroom took Ben and the ladies through the parlor to the stairs at the far end. Mister Green had not moved while Ben was off searching. Now he stood and shoved his rocker far out of their path. The two men rendered passing honors by merely nodding their heads in the direction of the other. They did not speak. The women helped him carry Rebecca up the same stairwell where Ben had paused that morning to watch the storm's march toward Sorrow Ledge.

He held Rebecca in his arms a few moments longer while the women prepared to assist. Missus Russell brought two extra blankets from a small trunk in the corner. One she lay across the bottom of the bed, and then she went to the armoire to find dry nightclothes. Missus Skevold made quick work of getting the knots undone in Rebecca's oilskin and hair ribbons. Missus Russell struggled to untie her boots because of the ice clotted in the knots. Ben handed to her a pocket knife that he kept with him always, and Missus Russell simply cut the laces away.

With Rebecca's ice-covered outerwear dumped unceremoniously on the floor, Ben gently laid his wife on the dry blanket at the foot of the bed. He and the ladies then set to work unbuckling, unbuttoning and untying every garment she wore. This task, too, was complicated by the frozen state of her clothing. When Rebecca was stripped to chemise and stockings, Missus Russell put a hand on Ben's arm. "Perhaps we should finish, Mister Grindle," she said in a tone both prim and tender. "We shall examine her for injuries and dress her warmly. Shouldn't you check on the progress of your girls?"

Ben did as she suggested, understanding that her concern was for their own embarrassment rather than either his or Rebecca's. He went back down the stairs. At the foot of the steps, he heard the raised voices of the men in the kitchen again. In the parlor, Ben stopped next to Green's seat. "What's got them bickering at each other?" Ben asked.

"Just a disagreement over Maine politics," Green said quietly. Then he closed his eyes and resumed gently rocking in the chair.

Just as Missus Russell suggested, Ben went to see how Molly and Phoebe were doing with their urgent tasks. He hoped this work would occupy their minds and hold their worry at bay. For a while at least. As he listened to the heated discussions among the men in the kitchen, he gathered that a usurper was planning to overthrow the state's government. Alternatively, in the opposing case, one man was all that stood in the way of utter anarchy in Augusta.

"Here, wickie, you're from Maine, aren't you?" Mister Russell asked. "Isn't it appalling that Chamberlain plans to turn the state over to the Democrats and Greenbackers?"

At the mention of that name, Ben stopped in his tracks. "I'm sorry. I haven't any idea what you're talking about. Are you referring to General Chamberlain?"

Swett stood and came teetering toward Ben, showing the slight stagger common among seamen unaccustomed to being ashore. "It's the damned fouled-up election. The professor here believes that Governor Chamberlain will install a Fusionist as governor or maybe name himself a king. I say the man wants only to keep the peace."

Ben was befuddled. "I hope you'll pardon me, gentlemen, I haven't seen a newspaper in nearly three months. By the time we learn of current events here on Sorrow Ledge, most people ashore consider them ancient history." He proceeded into the kitchen to where Molly was waving her palm over the kettle spout, just as Rebecca would do. With a jerk of his head, he motioned for Phoebe to join them. She closed the half-filled brass pan of the bed warmer and placed it behind the Franklin stove where no one might be burned by it. Already Bosun had settled into its customary position, monitoring conversations and movements with just the gaze of its brown eyes. The Newf's chin rested flat on the floor, and its front legs laid parallel to his snout. Growing puddles of water formed at each flank as the snow melted from its fur.

Ben pulled both girls close to huddle together. "I want you to listen carefully now. Your mother fell on the ice, and I think hit her head. She's also very wet and cold. The ladies are getting her into warm clothes. Phoebe, finish loading the bed warmer. Molly, take these warm towels up now. Then I'll need you both to help again. When we get everyone settled down for the night, you may both go up and be with Mother. Understand?" The two girls nodded eagerly and went about their separate chores, but he sensed their natural concern lay with their mother.

While Missus Russell and Missus Skevold were topside with Rebecca, the men remained in the first floor of the quarters. Green remained in the rocking chair in the parlor. The Professor of Civil Engineering and Captain Swett continued debating politics across the tabletop over mugs of coffee. Pendleton sat by the skipper at the kitchen table, puffing an ornate pipe. Tommy sat alone on the floor near his skipper. Finally, young Elizabeth interrupted their angry debate in what Ben sensed was an attempt to divert her father's obstreperous nature. "Is the *Gideon* the first ship that you've lost, Captain Swett?" she asked.

"No, girl. There's been a total of five decks that sank beneath my feet." This answer seemed to stir a shocked response from everyone present, save Pendleton. Swett appeared to notice the disquiet in the room and reacted immediately. "Well, you'll need to understand the times. The first two were intentional. Just after the war started, I skippered two hulls in the stone fleet. We sailed out of New London under Commodore Rice. We would load up a vessel with stones and sail her into rebel waters. We'd scuttle the ships in rivers and harbors to block rebel shipping."

Pendleton spoke up. "The stone fleet probably blocked more

Confederate shipping than all those Navy ships running the actual blockades."

Swett smiled at Elizabeth. "Under old Commodore Bony Rice, we took two separate fleets south. More than 20 ships in all, each loaded with fieldstone. They were stripped down to only the rigging and canvas we needed to make way. While in port, we augured holes in the hull, which we plugged. Once we were on station, we knocked the plugs loose and abandoned the hulls as they sank."

"I've never heard of any such thing as a stone fleet," Professor Russell said, in something of an accusatory tone. Russell sounded akin to Ben's own father, disbelieving anything he had not witnessed himself.

Professor Russell's daughter interrupted. "With the *Gideon* tonight, sir, that would make three," Elizabeth said pleasantly. "Didn't you say there were five?"

"Yes, miss, I did. I lost a paddle-wheeler, the *Nathaniel Greene*, on the Mississippi in '64. Her boiler exploded."

"And the other sinking?" Elizabeth asked, rather sweetly. Ben thought she was intentionally steering the conversation away from her father's purview.

"I wouldna' say it sank," Pendleton observed. "She kinda broke up under our feet."

"Aye, the *Kennebec*," Swett said. "The mate and I were stranded in ice north of Point Barrow back in '71, along with more than two dozen other whaling ships. That's the proper Arctic. The Eskimos tried to warn us that the ice was moving, but we were there following the whales and be damned, if you'll pardon me, that we begged off because of a little ice. The whole fleet got caught up, and every few days the hull of another ship would be crushed like an eggshell. The unlucky skipper would auction the hulk, and the winner would send his sharks in to scavenge what they could, but in the end, not a ship escaped. We rowed and dragged the skiffs across the ice field with more than a thousand people exposed to the elements. I don't like to think how many men we lost, to the whales, the accidents, the ice, the cold. Most of the captains there with me left whaling to pursue another trade if they were able. Some of them swam to the bottom of a bottle and were never able to claw their way back out."

Ben felt relief at how the rapt attention given to the skipper's sea stories distracted everyone from the man with a gun sitting in the next room. Neither Swett nor Pendleton betrayed any intention of approaching the Irishman. Ben hoped that when the other two crewmen came inside that they, too, would refrain from any confrontation that might provoke Green into using his weapon again.

Still wearing his oilskins, Seamus returned with a bushel basket full of firewood, followed by Gerty who carried a load in his arms. Ben knelt to help Seamus transfer the split logs into the wood box in the kitchen.

"Any chance to chat with Mr. Green while I was gone?" Ben asked.

"Not much time. And not much information, either. He's from County Limerick. He arrived in New Orleans three years ago. Spent some time in Tennessee and Virginia then before going up to Boston. He's been in Boston for six months now. After a stop in Augusta, he's traveling toward New York."

"That's all you learned?" Ben asked, with a chuckle. "Nothing about his lousy tailor?"

Seamus did not seem to ken Ben's jesting. "He's not an easy man to converse with, but I did learn that he's got kin who are O'Mahony. They're from Killarney." Seamus lowered his voice to a whisper. "They were Young Irelanders when my family lived in County Kerry. When the lads moved to America, they joined the Fenians."

"He told you all that?"

"Not all. Just the first bits about his travels. However, my mother, God rest her soul, used to say that whatever you want to know about an Irishman, the answer is likely in New York. She prided herself on knowing the ancestry of nearly the entire Celtic population of the city. I learned a great deal from her."

"You said Fenians? The Fenian Brotherhood?"

Seamus nodded. "Yes, Fenians back in Maine, I'm afraid."

Looking toward where Green sat in the rocking chair, Ben said, "Only one. Not seven hundred this time. Still, be careful to keep a distance from him and never look him in the eyes. We've no real idea who he is and what business he's about in Maine." He stood and went to the stove in the kitchen.

Molly was back from upstairs, heating the kettle for more coffee. "Will Mother wake tonight? I think Phoebe will be most upset if Mommy doesn't come to say good night."

"Tonight, I'll need you both to go say goodnight to your mother at her bed. So, you'll tuck your sister in, right?" Molly nodded. With a finger, he wiped a tear from her cheek. "Don't you fret. Your mother has endured me many years now. Surely she can endure a little storm such as this."

While Molly turned her attention toward the whistling kettle and percolating pots on the stove, Ben asked for a mugful. As she poured, she whispered to him. "Where will all these people sleep tonight?"

"That, my darling, remains to be determined." Ben settled at the table opposite Pendleton, discovering too late to be polite that the skipper and the professor were still wrangling about the future of democracy in Maine. First Swett, then Russell, and around again and again.

"I tell you the real culprit is Blaine. He's a senator. He should be in Washington, not inciting riots in Augusta."

"It wasn't Blaine that called Chamberlain up from that two-bit college he runs. Garcelon came third in the votes, so he manufactured the so-called 'irregularities' to discount the Republican votes."

"Garcelon won't be governor again, but Blaine wants to play king-maker. If enough people are beholden to him, Blaine'll be president someday. That's why Blaine doesn't want Grant for another term."

"Or maybe he knows the country won't survive another four years under Grant."

As the two wrangled on, the wickie turned toward the first mate. Pendleton had situated his seat such that it was turned so that he could casually watch Mister Green. "This fellow Green. You said he was a deadhead," Ben said. "Who asked that he get free passage on your ship?"

"Skipper's friend." Pendleton's manner was rather nonchalant considering the events of the evening, as if they were sitting in a tavern sharing war stories over ale.

"Where'd he come aboard?" Ben asked.

"Boston."

"The skipper said you were running from Boston into Belfast? Is that *Gideon's* regular inter schedule?"

"No." The mate's unhappiness with the arrangement was evident. When he furrowed his brow, a long scar just at his hairline became pronounced.

"Another favor, then?"

"Likely."

"Pendleton, I need to understand this arrangement. Will you help me?"

"If I can."

"Let's say a man is traveling from Boston to Augusta..."

"Okay." Pendleton shifted in his chair.

"Quickest way would be aboard the Boston and Maine Line to Portland..."

"Maybe." He drew a drawstring pouch of tobacco from a pocket.

"And then the Portland and Kennebec into Augusta."

"Sure." Pendleton dipped the ornately carved ivory bowl of his pipe into the small satchel.

"So why take a two-stick hull, no offense, ..."

"None taken." With a thumb, he tamped the loose tobacco into the bowl.

"... to a remote pier that even seagulls avoid in January?"

"My guess?"

"Yes." Ben's voice betrayed a certain exasperation.

Pendleton didn't seem to notice the wickie's impatience. "Pinks."

"Pinkerton's men? You mean detectives?"

"Sure." With a match from his pocket, Pendleton leaned toward the floor and struck a flame against the stone hearth.

"On trains between Boston and Augusta?"

"Likely."

"Are you capable of saying more than one word at a time?" Ben's voice was nearly a growl.

"Green's eyes." Pendleton inhaled deeply on the stem, causing the embers in the bowl to grow orange.

"Damn his eyes," Ben muttered an angry swear.

"... are open." A cloud of Virginia aromatic escaped Pendleton's lips. "I believe you told me to keep a watch on him."

"Gentlemen! I hope you've resolved your political issues for one evening." The Irishman stood, throwing off the quilt from his lap. He strode into the kitchen with all the drama of a stage actor in Boston. "I believe it is now past midnight. If Mister Grindle would be so kind as to provide bedding, perhaps we should find places to rest. Tomorrow may be a long day for a few of us."

Ben stood. "I'm afraid I don't have much more comfort to offer. All that I have are the blankets from the Ladies' Relief closet. We have no barracks or bunkrooms. It's just my family here and Seamus in his quarters. I was planning to have the ladies sleep upstairs. There's plenty of room for the seven of us to sleep on the floor down here."

The Irishman seemed displeased. "Seamus, how many can sleep in your quarters?"

"It's no big room inside. We could fit four, I suppose. Three will be on the floor."

Their conversation was interrupted when Bosun went to scratch at the doorway leading toward its usual latrine. "Molly, please let the dog out," Ben called.

Molly complied and opened the door. She screamed.

Seamus was first to reach her. "Ben! Tide's up! Nearly at the stoop!" he shouted. He turned back to the room. "If the high tide reached the threshold here, then my quarters are half underwater."

Ben turned back toward Green. "I'm sorry, but you've picked a terrible time to visit Sorrow Ledge. Between high tide, a full moon and the storm's surge, it appears we'll have unusually high water tonight. If you wish to sleep dry, you'll need to be well above the ground. There are six women upstairs now. You men can sleep on the steps of the light tower or in the loft of the boathouse, which I would recommend for comfort. Seamus will lead you there."

Green hesitated. "No tricks, Grindle?"

"No, but I'd ask to keep the skipper here so I can clean his wound again before he sleeps. I've seen bullet wounds develop gangrene quickly."

"Infantry in a Maine regiment, were you?" the Irishman asked. "Did you see the elephant?"

"At least a dozen times. Not just the elephant. I believe I saw the entire menagerie." Suddenly, Ben thought it wise to change the subject. "You'll be sleeping directly over the dory. If high tide has reached us now, the *Gideon* is most likely gone already. The dory will be your only choice to leave the island." He stopped and tried to assess Green's mood. "I'd like to make one more request. After Seamus leads you to the boathouse and gets you settled, I'd like him to go back to the light tower. If we have another blind flight of birds, he'll need to extinguish the light to save it."

Green's eyes went slowly around the room as if calculating where each man would be for the night. "All right, Grindle. Seamus may go up the tower. What time do you normally switch out the watch?"

"Just before six in the morning."

"And who'll stand the next watch? You or one of the girls?"

"Only Seamus and I stand watch unless there's a dire emergency."

Green laughed heartily. "Tarnation, wickie. If a shipwreck in a blizzard isn't a dire circumstance, what would you call dire?"

Ben considered this challenge for a moment. "Three million men trying to kill each other."

"Fair enough, I suppose. Come, gentlemen, get your togs together." Green moved forward with his arms spread, as though herding the men toward the door. "Don't go up the tower in the morning until we speak. You must get me off the island at first light. Do you know what time is sunrise locally?"

"Seven minutes after seven." Ben was uncertain whether to be offended by Green's insult or astonished at his ignorance. A wickie works and sleeps according to the movement of the sun. Such a question would be like asking a sailor if he could point toward north. "Seamus, can you stand the light until after sunrise in the morning? You've stood watch twice already today, so it seems unjust to ask you now to stand the graveyard watch as well."

"Aye, aye." Seamus touched his fingers to his eyebrow in acknowledgment. "I believe I can lend-a-hand."

"Then I've another favor to ask," Ben said. "Would you start writing out a form for the district inspector to report a shipwreck? Enter as much as you know, and I'll complete the rest tomorrow." Item 18 of the Instructions to Light-Keepers stated that: *"The light-keepers are also required to take notice of any shipwrecks which shall happen within the vicinity of the light-house, and to enter an account thereof, according to the prescribed form, in a book furnished to each station for this purpose; and in such account they shall state, if practicable, whether the light was seen by any on board the shipwrecked vessel, and recognised by them, and how long it was seen before the vessel struck."* Already Ben had begun rehearsing in his mind the language with which he would explain the blind flight and the darkened light in a manner that would placate the district inspector and ultimately the Light House Board.

"Thank you, wickies. You're both quite accommodating hosts for an island called Sorrow Ledge," Green said, speaking in an expansive voice. "Gentlemen, let's go get some rest. A few of you are going to need it in the morning."

"Just a moment," the professor interrupted. "I would prefer to stay with my family."

Suddenly appearing as if by magic, the barrel of the gun flashed in Green's hand. "I would prefer you to stay quiet and follow this good fellow Seamus. Now!" The gun disappeared into his pocket again. "I shall see you in the morning, Ben Grindle."

As he distributed blankets to the men, Ben whispered to Pendleton, "Make no attempt on Green that might endanger the women." The mate accepted his bedding and winked an acknowledgement.

CHAPTER 8

*W*ith Phoebe's assistance, Ben loaded the five men headed for the boathouse with all the remaining blankets from the Ladies' Relief chest, as well as several tins of biscuits and cookies. The men were in ankle-deep water when they left the stoop outside the quarters. Through the kitchen window, Ben and Phoebe watched their progress down the backside of the island. The light from the tower illuminated the men's wet and dangerous walk, as the water quickly rose halfway to their knees. Bosun also went out on a personal chore, but soon returned dripping water.

"Why did that man ask you about seeing an elephant?" she asked.

"It's what some men call war."

Phoebe looked at him in puzzlement. "Why?"

"I suppose because elephants and armies are alike," he said. "They are big and when they fight, they hurt everything around them." He wasn't at all certain he'd answered her question, but with everything on his mind it seemed the best he could muster.

No strangers to the flooding the storm brought, Molly and Phoebe placed tightly woven rugs across each threshold and shoved hard to close the doors atop them. Ben stoked the fires and filled both furnace and stove from the extra wood that Seamus and Gerty had provided. If he heated the interior space and walls sufficiently, perhaps the tidal flooding might not put too great a chill into the stone structure. Ben sent the girls up with a basin of warm water to wash and change for bed. Then he climbed the stairs to his own bedroom.

Rebecca rested in their bed; her eyes remained closed. Her skin looked paler than the white pillow casing. Elizabeth Russell sat on the edge of the bed, leaning against the headboard with her own eyes shut. The other women were asleep, snuggled together on the floor in a corner with Ladies' Relief blankets pulled up over them. The young sylph stirred when Ben entered.

"She seems to be sleeping comfortably," Elizabeth whispered to Ben. "My mother listened at her chest, and she said your wife seems to be breathing well. Mother says she heard no cough or choke or rasping. Mother knows a lot about medicine; she was a nurse during the war."

"Has Rebecca opened her eyes?" Ben asked.

"Not yet. I've seen her lashes flutter so I expect she will at any moment. But not yet."

"Has Phoebe come to visit?"

"Yes. Such an angel. She said her good nights and left on tiptoes."

"Molly will be in soon, as well. Please say little to upset her."

Elizabeth nodded. "Mr. Grindle, I promise I'll say nothing to trouble your daughters." Her voice dropped to a whisper. "And thank you for dealing with our situation. Mr. Green, or whatever his real name is, hasn't been very pleasant on this voyage. He agreed with everything my father said about what's happening in Augusta. But still, they argued all through dinner." She paused, obviously debating how much to reveal. "I was so looking forward to my family's new adventure in Maine. As you might imagine, my parents can be difficult. My father knows everything. Mother believes he knows everything. They have contempt for anyone who won't agree with them."

Ben tried to stifle a yawn of exhaustion. "Do you recall anything in particular that Green said to your father about Augusta?"

"I don't remember it all, but he was angry that when General

Chamberlain was governor, he tried to bring settlers from Scandinavia to Maine instead of from Ireland. He seemed upset because many Irish fought for the Union and some even served under Chamberlain. He said they deserved first consideration."

The veteran nodded, knowing that the State of New York itself had mustered ten regiments that marched under green flags. There were many sons of Ireland who served alongside Ben in the 2nd Maine; yet he knew that Chamberlain would have been aware of the Irish legion who planned to invade Canada after the war.

"So, do you think he treated Missus Skevold badly because of that?" He wondered how Missus Skevold had reacted to Green's complaints about immigrants from northern Europe.

"Goodness, no. He was very kind to us women. Just never let a man cross his path."

"Anything else that you recall he said?"

Elizabeth shook her head.

"I'm sorry we weren't able to bring your baggage off the ship. I think you're a little too tall to wear one of Molly's nightgowns, so please help yourself to one of Rebecca's in that old hutch over there."

"Thank you, but I feel warm enough in my clothes, and I'd hate to get a chill now. It's taken a little while, but even the hem of my skirt is finally dry."

"I'm going back down to attend to Captain Swett. Molly should be in soon to say goodnight to her mother." He paused at the door and looked back. Elizabeth was leaning over Rebecca, patting a towel against her forehead. "I do appreciate your care around my daughters, as will her mother when she awakes. Good night, Miss Russell." He started down the stairs.

"Good night, Mr. Grindle," Elizabeth called after him.

After quietly treading back down the stairwell, Ben then went through the darkened parlor into the kitchen. Along his way, he doused the candle he carried and a lantern. Captain Swett sat hunched over a mug of coffee at the kitchen table, with a wool blanket drawn up close around his shoulders. The flames burning in the stove illuminated the skipper's shadow against the white kitchen wall. Ben went to the stove to refill his coffee. Bosun remained in its favorite position near the hearth. The puddles on the stonework the dog had left earlier from the snow and ice melting off the its pelt were now completely dry.

The skipper extended a calloused hand, and Ben shook it. "Do you smile? I don't suppose a place such as this would have anything stronger than black coffee? A spot of boozefuddle would be much appreciated. I always stow a little extra when I come Downeast for account of the cussed liquor laws, which seem to change with each full moon. Last I heard, they had outlawed even hard cider. Unfortunately, I didn't have much opportunity to carry my own nip ashore this evening, but I could sure go for a jug right about now."

"I may be able to find something." Ben went back into the far end of the pantry. On an upper shelf, he located a bottle behind sacks of flour and sugar. He carried the whiskey back to the table. "Curiously I found this floating in the tide a few years back. Thank goodness I've got it available for times such as these – well, strictly for 'mechanical and artistic purposes,' just as the law allows." Ben pulled the cork stopper and poured a generous shot into each of the two mugs already half filled with coffee that sat on the table before the men. Swett took a long swig. Ben placed the whiskey at a corner of the table farthest from the skipper's reach. "Can you help me understand what's going on? Let me hear what you know about this Green, and then maybe we'll find a way to deal with our guest."

Swett settled back on his chair and pulled the blanket forward around his shoulders like an old woman's shawl. "Well, I was moored in Boston harbor toward the end of December. I had a message from a fellow skipper, an old acquaintance of mine, asking me a favor for an acquaintance of his."

"You'd never met Green before then?"

"No. He came aboard with a letter of introduction from my friend."

"What did Green ask of you?"

"Just passage from Boston to Belfast. As I said, it was to be a favor to a friend. Since Green wasn't offering to pay passage, I posted an advertisement to take on passengers. That's how the professor contacted me, about carrying his family up to Bangor. A simple run

Downeast, I figured. A cabin boy could navigate from Boston to Belfast and then on to Bangor."

"If Green's real destination was Augusta, why did he want to run down to Belfast by ship? Seems taking the trains would have been much quicker, either straight from Boston or down from Bangor." Ben sipped from his coffee to give Swett a chance to ponder this conundrum.

"He didn't avoid the train for lack of money. And he complained the entire voyage about the quality of the grub and the state of the accommodations onboard. I suppose he was expecting better meal service than lobscouse thrice a day."

Ben chuckled at Swett's apparent resentment of any criticism of the *Gideon*. "By the way, wherever did you find this *Gideon*? No offense, but I think your uncle built finer ships on a mountainside sixty years ago."

"Lawyers, dammed rotten lawyers. I had a quarter stake in the *Kennebec* when I took her to Alaska that last time. We'd already sent home a considerable load of furs before we sailed away from Dutch Harbor, heading after the whales. When she was crushed in the Arctic, I calculated that when the insurance paid out that I'd make out all right, maybe even clear gravy." Swett paused to sip the medicinally adulterated coffee. "Well, the other shareholders found an admiralty lawyer who squeezed me through a ship's bullnose. They accused me of negligence in losing her so far north, so they charged off all the expenses against me. The value of her hull, the cost of the rations aboard when she went down, all crew pay after the last day of whaling, the costs to carry the crew back to Seattle. No, the *Gideon* wasn't much; she was neat but not gaudy. But those bastards intended to leave me less money than it costs to buy a sturdy rowboat."

"Was the *Gideon* insured?" Ben asked, proffering another tip of the bottle.

"Oh, sure. Thank you." Swett extended his mug. "Well, yes, she was insured, but I tell you here and now that I don't relish the thought of wrangling with more lawyers and insurance men any more than a Nantucket sleigh ride at my age."

"I'll write out a statement to your insurer. I'll make it clear that the tower was dark in a storm."

Swett waved off the suggestion with both hands. "Nah, the insurance agents wouldn't pay at all then. They'll tell me to file a claim against the government. From what I hear, the government's still reviewing claims from First Bull Run. I haven't got enough time left on Earth to wait twenty years for a Washington clerk to settle my accounts."

Ben knew personally that this was true. A few years after the war while on a rare visit to Bangor, he had encountered an officer he had served under in Company B, the Castine Light Infantry. On the advice of Lieutenant Wardwell, who had been discharged after being wounded at First Bull Run, Ben submitted a claim to the War Department for wounds incurred during the war. Now years had passed without any communication on Ben's application apart from the occasional letter requesting additional witness statements from fellow soldiers of the two Maine regiments in which he had served. Ben had long since given up every hope and come to regret submitting any claim at all. He knew far more comrades who had made the ultimate surrender to the despair of pain than the number who were surprised by the government's generosity in awarding either pension or recognition, even 15 years after the war ended.

"What do you know about Mr. Green?"

"He's an *aggravatin'* cuss and an awful pain in the arse. And if he'd made eyes at Miss Russell any more blatantly, I believe Pendleton would have keel-hauled the mick on principle."

"A lad with an eye for a young lass doesn't seem so unusual. Come now, your eyes are good enough to see for yourself that she's a bit of a dingeclicker."

Swett cocked his head and gave Ben a harsh look of disdain. "Aye, she's a good-looking lass. And I expect your girls will grow into lovely young women as well. That gives no man the right to ogle Miss Russell or your daughters like they were harlots, now does it?"

"No, skipper, I don't think that. But if your mate was so concerned about Green's attention to Miss Russell, why didn't her father feel the need to speak up?"

"I suppose for all the same reasons back in the war we had copper-head Democrats, draft riots and simple skedaddlers." Swett drank from his mug and then sat back in his chair. "When it comes right down to it, most men are cowards. Oh, they'll whine, all right; some will complain, and some might even squeal. Yet when it's time to put their own hide on the line, nine out of ten will balk. I saw it in the war. I saw it in my whaling crews. I've been at sea for sixty years now, and I haven't seen where coin, rum or lash ever gave any man more courage than he brought aboard with him."

Ben smiled to acknowledge that he had also learned during the war the harsh truth of Swett's words. "Well, skipper, I don't yet know how we'll deal with Mister Green, but let me tell you my only goal." He leaned forward to where he could lower his voice so that no person upstairs could hear him speak. "On this island tonight are six ladies and seven men. I don't give a tinker's damn if any man survives, but I surely intend that every one of the women lives through this ordeal."

"Aye, I apologize. You've given me no reason to doubt your intentions. So how can I help?"

"I know Mister Green provided you with rather little personal information, but were you aware that he sells coal by the box load?"

Startled, Swett set back in his chair and stared at Ben in bewilderment. "Now I don't follow you."

"After I carried his case from the *Gideon* up to the tower, my neck was covered with something that looks much like coal dust. I opened the valise and found nothing but chunks of coal. Here, I've taken a piece." He walked to the rack near the kitchen door where Phoebe had hung Ben's wool jacket and oilskin that Bosun had worn back from the ice-covered slopes. Returning to the table, he handed the black rock to Swett. "Felt to me like about a hundred pounds total in his baggage. Who carries a valise full of coal all over God's creation?"

Ed Swett turned the rock over and over in his hand for several minutes. "Would you loan me a pocket knife and bring us a good lantern?"

Ben complied. He left Swett alone for several minutes while he returned the medicinal whiskey to a high shelf and replaced the sacks of sugar and flour as a screen. When Ben came back to the table, a small pile of coal dust sat on the table cloth. In Swett's hand was a shiny orb with a large dark spot.

"What is that?" Ben asked.

"Not coal, that's for damned sure. I've handled a lot of coal on steamers. Seems to weigh a lot for coal. And I don't recall that I ever saw coal rust. On the contrary, I've known many a ship's carpenter who laid coal next to their steel tools to prevent rust."

Ben looked carefully at the object Swett held. He observed the patchwork of corrosion across the surface just as Swett indicated. "Back to my last question then, what is it?"

"Ever hear of a coal torpedo?"

"Not that I recall."

"No, I suppose not. You were infantry, right? No reason for infantry to hear of such devilish things. Rebel spies created it. Made just like a cannonball, but they were cast to look like a lump of coal." Swett handed the object over for Ben's inspection. "Feel sticky? That's because they dipped it in wax before they rolled it in coal dust to disguise it."

"What is this thing supposed to do?"

Swett took the hunk of iron back and began to work the knife blade into a soft spot in the orb. Soon he was turning the knife handle and removing a stopper.

Glancing back toward the Franklin stove, Ben saw the brown eyes of the Newfoundland fixed upon him. Ben stood and walked back into the pantry and opened one of the tins that held strips of jerked beef. Ben gave the dog a morsel. Although its fur had been drying for hours, Bosun continued to emanate the distinctive odor of a wet dog. "You did good work tonight, Bosun. You're a good dog. Mostly." Bosun began to chew the special treat, slowly and lugubriously.

Ben sat down back at the table. When the plug was finally out, Swett upended the torpedo, dumping what soon amounted to a large pile of black powder on the tabletop. Ben recognized its odor instantly.

"Well, that's something I know a little bit about. Must be at least a pound," Ben observed, running his fingers through the small pile. "So why go through all the trouble of making it look like coal?"

"Clever boys, those rebs. This ain't like a normal torpedo that you let float around until the enemy runs into it." Swett took another sip from his mug. "Everybody in the world knows that the most dangerous vessel built by man is a steamship. Whoever thought that putting fire in the belly of a wooden ship was a clever idea? Valve sticks, boiler overheats and ship explodes. Boiler rusts or pops a seam, fire on deck, fuel catches fire and ship explodes. Sparks out the stack set the deck afire and ship explodes. A Mississippi catfish farts too close to the hull, and the ship explodes."

"Well, so long as you've formed a reasoned opinion on the topic." Ben wondered if he had erred in giving Swett a second dollop of whiskey.

"There's just no reason when it comes to steam on ships. My uncle often said that the papers should stop reporting all the accidents and report only when a steam kettle reached its destination harbor safe because that was actual news."

"So how do these things work?" Ben asked, motioning toward the hunk of fake coal.

"Well, the rebs knew a boiler is a dangerous and unpredictable thing, and it just takes a little poke to make one blow. So you place an explosive into a boiler to poke it. Don't need a big explosive, just enough to burst a steam line, dislodge a valve or rupture a seam. And the rebs figured why risk their spies to do it; why not just put the explosive into our own coal supplies on our own docks with our own guards watching them? Who can spot one fake lump of coal when we're loading by the ton? These bombs had Admiral Porter worried enough that he gave special orders that we were authorized to shoot dead any stranger who approached our coal piles on the docks."

"Did the rebels ever succeed in destroying one of our ships with one?" Ben asked cautiously. "Did you lose the *Nathaniel Greene* to a coal torpedo?"

"How would anyone ever know for sure? Steam kettles exploded all the damn time." Swett shook his head slowly. "I don't think even the rebels would have known. Once you throw a coal torpedo on a pile of coal, you couldn't keep an eye on it to see which ship was that loaded it."

"Well, let's hope these were just a clever failure."

The wickie gathered the mugs and refilled them from the kettle. He decided against adding anything extra from the top shelf.

"Well, thanks for helping me see what we're really dealing with here," Ben said. "Though I'm not sure now what to think. Our friend Green seems to have a full trunk of coal torpedoes, granted. I'm sure he wouldn't need a hundred pounds to sabotage the few steamer ships that run up the frozen Kennebec to Augusta in January."

After some time, Ed Swett grimaced and rubbed his bandaged bicep with his right hand. "I been thinking 'bout what you said. You're probably right that he winged me just the way he meant to."

The sound of deep snores reached Ben's ears. Snack finished, the dog had rolled on its flank and gone to sleep, all four legs stretched in one direction. The Newfoundland looked like a narrow table toppled on its side. As he briefed the skipper on what Seamus had learned from Green, Ben saw in the firelight that Bosun's paws were twitching.

"The Fenian Brotherhood?" Swett asked in alarm when Ben finished speaking.

"Yes."

"Wasn't somebody called O'Mahony behind the mess up to Campobello after the war?" The dread in the skipper's question was apparent.

"Yes, but not this lad. I suspect our Mister Green would have been getting his first slingshot at the time, not planning to invade Canada."

"You're right about one thing, for sure. No one carries a hundred pounds of coal torpedoes around unless they plan to put them to use." Swett tossed the empty shell of the coal torpedo into the air with one hand and caught it in the other.

By the clock on the kitchen mantle, Ben saw the time was after midnight. According to the almanac, the high tide was long past, and probably any surge flooding that accompanied the storm. He stood and peered through one of the kitchen windows. From what he could see in the illumination from the light house, the foundation of the quarters was awash in ocean water. He could not see as far as the garden or the chicken coup, but he knew there was little chance either had survived the peak flooding. He smiled briefly at the thought of

Green, sleeping in the loft of the boathouse, being awakened before dawn by the crowing of the rooster and the cackling of the hens.

"Ben, would you kindly bring that bottle back?" Captain Ed Swett called. "I may have an idea of Green's intentions. If I'm correct, I believe we'll both need something strong to chart a course through the coming storm."

CHAPTER 9

*W*hile the skipper mused over a mug of coffee comingled with whiskey, Ben went upstairs to look in on Rebecca. On this visit, he found Missus Russell on watch. She had removed her jacket and wore an ivory blouse with an intricately brocaded front piece unbuttoned at the neck. Apparently, there had been a new discussion about accommodations after he had left Miss Russell. Molly and Phoebe now slept, rolled up close on either side of Rebecca. Miss Russell and Missus Skevold were not asleep on the floor; now the two were probably abed in the next room where the girls typically slept. "I apologize, Mr. Grindle, that we did not discuss the change in sleeping arrangements with you," Missus Russell said.

"I have no complaint so long as Rebecca and the girls get their rest. Tomorrow may be a long day."

"There's no better way to warm a body than to trundle them up with children. According to Missus Skevold, that's how the Laplanders in the Arctic stay warm all winter, by the family huddling together."

"Has Rebecca wakened at all?" Ben asked.

"No, she hasn't yet. However, I wouldn't give up hope. I saw many men during the war who recovered after the doctors pronounced their injuries completely hopeless."

"I may well have been one of those. The regiment's surgeon wasn't certain that I would ever see again." Ben looked up at Missus Russell. "Your daughter said you were a nurse in the war."

"Well, not a real nurse, no. I spent just a few months of the '62 campaign helping Miss Barton as a volunteer. I worked in the field hospitals after Second Bull Run and Antietam."

Ben nodded in understanding. "I saw Miss Barton once. I was helping move the wounded from Manassas Junction to Fairfax. My regiment lost more men at Groveton Heights against Jackson than we did in any other fight."

"Really? I was there, too. With Clara. Hundreds of wounded men laying in the sun and rain for days, nothing to eat, little to drink, no doctors anywhere to be found. We did what we could. Between us, we had only a couple of buckets, a few dippers, and a single lantern." Missus Russell paused. Suddenly her eyes shimmered with tears in the dim light. After a long few moments, she spoke again. "I don't mean to trouble you."

"Don't worry, ma'am. Little troubles me about the war now, except when people who weren't a part of it call the war the Recent Unpleasantness. I suspect you'll agree that what you saw in the hospitals was a good deal worse than unpleasant." Ben's eyes watched Rebecca intently. The only movement she betrayed was that her bosom rose and fell in a steady rhythm. Her eyes did not open, and her eyelids did not flutter at all.

"Oh, yes, what I saw was so much worse than I could ever have imagined. I went home after Antietam. We treated so many boys; some barely older than Elizabeth is now. Boys were going home without a leg or an arm." She hesitated again, tears now coursing freely down her face. "Before that day, I thought I could follow Clara's example and be steady for the men. I held the hand of so many men as they died: gut-shot, bled-out, head wounds. I couldn't stay to see what another battle wrought. Were you there? At Antietam?" she asked as if seeking a compatriot.

"Yes, ma'am. I was in the 2nd Maine. But we were held in reserve and didn't see any fighting that day."

"But then you still know of the carnage." Her weeping became so intense that she shuddered at what she remembered. "I went out with the stretcher boys in the evening. We walked the cornfield and along Sunken Road to carry out the living and wounded. Mostly we found the dead. I hope never to see the likes of that again."

"I think you saw just about the very worst of the war," Ben said earnestly. "And you did what you could to help. There were many in this state who didn't lift a finger to help us win the war, and some who were even opposed to Mr. Lincoln."

Almost as if she had not heard anything Ben said, Missus Russell continued, "After Antietam, I went back to New York. My parents were thrilled that their prodigal daughter had returned home at last. However, I wasn't really that same little girl anymore. I think that fact became clear to them when Mister Brady opened his gallery in the city that fall. I went most days the show was open. Have you ever seen his photographs of the war?"

"No, ma'am," Ben said somberly. "I never felt the need to see the war again."

Though tears still streamed down her cheeks, she smiled at him. "No, I suppose not. But I was haunted. I can't believe the harm people do each other." She dabbed at her eyes with an intricately brocaded kerchief.

"That was war, Missus Russell. We say it was for a good cause. I like to believe that." He paused, taking a breath before trying to change the subject. "But we're not at war here, so I am trying to understand why Mister Green shot at the skipper tonight. Did you hear him say anything in particular about the skipper during the voyage?"

She brushed her cheeks dry against the palms of both hands. "No, I don't recall whenever they saw much of each other. The skipper stayed on deck, battling the storm. I don't remember when that nasty man ever left the, uh, mess deck, I believe it's called."

"That's right. Why do you call Green nasty?"

"I believe he would argue with a rock if no human being was available. My husband agreed with most of what he said, but that wasn't good enough for *Mister* Green." She said the word with an obvious contempt. She paused for a long moment. "And I don't like the way that man stares at my daughter."

Ben wanted to clarify what she meant by that last comment. Did she agree with Swett's opinion of Green's attention toward Elizabeth? At the same time, he didn't wish to alarm her. Ben wondered whether Green had looked at Elizabeth as a possible lover or a potential hostage. Ben decided not to pursue that line of questioning with Missus Russell.

"Well, no matter," Ben said. "He wishes to be off the island, and I have no intention of holding him here. So let's hope we'll be free of him in a few hours."

"I pray it will happen so easily."

With a last look at where his family lay sleeping together, Ben crept slowly and quietly back down the stairs.

CHAPTER 10

"*I* want to be clear about this," Ben said, sipping the thin, cold coffee. "You believe Green has come to Maine because of the election chaos in Augusta?" If he tried to cover the skepticism in his voice, he failed.

"I know you ain't heard about it before, being out here and all, but this kerfuffle in Augusta is a big deal, all the way down in Boston, New York, and maybe even more so in Washington. It was in the Boston papers every day. Everyone knows Blaine will run for president soon. And here's the governor of his state calling out the militia to settle an election in the right direction just like elections occur in Mexico and places south. However, Chamberlain's in charge of the militia and defies the governor's orders. He goes up to Augusta alone. Now there's turmoil in the capital, with one group and then another threatening violence." As Swett spoke, he was carefully brushing gunpowder from the tabletop into the palm of his hand. With his fingers cupped to his palm in the shape of a funnel, he slowly shook each scoop back into the iron device.

"Skipper, I'm not sure the second drink was a good idea, let alone a third."

"It'll take more than three little licks of skulch to make me go all gorming. Listen, you said that your helper Seamus thinks Green is really called O'Mahony?"

"Yes, Green told him that he was somehow related to O'Mahony's."

"And we're both fairly certain that it was a feller named O'Mahony who put together that Fenian army up at Campobello after the war, right?"

"Well, Green might be related to an O'Mahony family, not necessarily to that particular O'Mahony. Related back in the old country." Ben began to worry that Swett's excitement would rouse the women upstairs.

"But the young Russell girl said Green was angry about Chamberlain bringing in immigrants who aren't Irish?" Gunpowder cleaned from the table, Swett carefully screwed the plug back into place. He set the explosive directly in front of Ben.

"Sure, but that doesn't mean that Green is connected to those who were at Campobello."

Swett thrust himself back in his chair and gripped both hands on the edge of the table. "Do you have a better explanation for a Fenian roaming Maine with Confederate munitions tonight?" he demanded angrily. "If he shoots me through the heart next time, would that be more convincing?"

"Skipper, please don't wake the women." Ben raised both palms toward Swett. "I just don't understand the connections you're trying to make."

"I'm not certain either, but we've got to make some guesses. In just a few hours, that madman will be up and asking to be taken to Rockland with his case loaded full of those damn torpedoes. You're right, I don't know a lot of things for certain, but we can make reasonable guesses, can't we?"

Now came Ben's turn to rest his temples in his hands. "Ok, ok, just give me a minute to think." He closed his eyes and tried to recall in detail everything that had happened that night.

Swett reached past Ben's arm and took the now half-empty whiskey bottle. He removed the stopper and drank a long slug directly. Ben heard this but chose not to react. Ben also heard the dog roll itself into another position; the slow tick of the clock on the mantel; and the patter of freezing graupel against the windows of the quarters.

"Listen, Ben, I don't believe you understand how desperate times are. There's chaos in Augusta; that's what I was trying to explain to Professor Russell tonight. There's men with guns marching around the State House. Chamberlain won't bring the militia in to Augusta so that a loose trigger finger doesn't start a blood bath, or they'll all blame that on him. Chamberlain's back is against the wall. The wolf packs are smelling his blood. And I'll promise you this, Ben, if something happens to him, regardless of what the papers say, there'll be war in this state like no one's seen since the British invaded back in '14." Swett's indignation suddenly waned, and he stared intently at Ben with bloodshot eyes. "And do you recall what the Brits called Maine after they captured Bangor? New Ireland! Think of that. For almost a year when I was a boy, fully half of Maine was called New Ireland. By God, that made the men of my family furious."

Hoping to bring the subject back to current events, Ben spoke quietly. "I just cannot fathom how our Mister Green and his 100 pounds of fake coal play into this. Chamberlain's not fighting a naval battle in the streets of Augusta."

Swett rested his forehead against the shanks of both beefy hands. His fingers – yellowed from tobacco – were knotted into his hair. He seemed mired in thought for a long time, though he grunted once or twice. Finally, he raised his eyes to meet Ben's. "By God, it wouldn't work just on a ship. Any coal-burning furnace that heats a steam boiler. Like most large buildings nowadays."

"Like a state capitol? Is that what you're thinking?"

"Sure enough. On a ship, all you'd need is to provide the spark. All the fuel you need to burn it to the waterline is right aboard. But in a brick or stone building, you'd need a tremendous force to bring it down before the fire teams arrive. So you load the furnace with as much of a blast as you can manage to create."

"By God, I fear you may be exactly right." As a man who personally had felt the effects of gunpowder, Ben sat upright in his chair, grasping the full nature of the threat to the state, if not the exact reasons behind it. "But why? I don't understand how this helps the

Fenians. It's been years since their last attack on Canada. I don't recall where the Fenians have taken any action since that debacle up in Manitoba?"

Swett looked baleful, yet surprisingly sober. "The micks have been fighting the Brits for nearly a century. They aren't likely to give up all polite and mannerly because the Canucks rebuffed them." He took out a handkerchief and blew his nose fiercely. "Maybe it's just revenge. Sure you've heard the expression – an Irishman forgives his enemies when he drinks his last pint ... because that's the day he dies."

"Well, let's say Green makes it ashore in the morning and hires a team to get him to Augusta. What then? What good does it do his movement? What does it gain the Fenians?"

The captain looked at Ben with tired, bloodshot eyes. "What did it gain the Confederates for Booth to put a bullet into the President after Lee had gone and surrendered the entire rebel army? Or someone to blow the *Sultana* to hell? Or Texans to fight the Union Navy for another five months after Appomattox?" Swett stood, unsteadily. "The Fenians, or micks under some other name, will be fighting a hundred years after you and I have turned to ashes and dust." Swett leaned forward, gripping the edge of the table for balance. His stance brought him so close that Ben reclined back to look into the skipper's eyes. "Here's what I know. This Green may or may not be a Fenian, but he's willing to fire a gun as he pleases. And he's carrying a case of munitions that serve no purpose other than to blow things apart. I don't know his reasons, and I don't know his target. But if he leaves this island in the morning, there'll be people killed, whether they be Americans or Canadians. Where or when that'll happen, only our darling Mister Green knows for sure. Do you agree?"

Ben only nodded.

"Well good, cause I'm tuckered out. I'm hope to sleep." Swett stood and limped toward the parlor. Then he stopped and came back to the table. He extended his right hand toward Ben. "I'll be seventy-three years old come spring and getting over in my book, you know. I feel the years more and more at the start of each day. I don't know what help I can lend you in the morning when it comes time to deal with our Irish trouble. I'm not the spry lad I was when I shipped out on the *Northborough*. But my crew is good and true. They won't fail you."

Ben relinquished the skipper's hand, and the old man hobbled past him into the parlor. He settled gingerly on the rocking chair where Green had sat earlier, even draping across his body the same quilt that Green had used. In the few hours of the evening, Captain Swett had transformed from a seaman stoic after being shot to an elderly sailor struggling with even the simplest movements. Within just minutes, Ben heard a second snore competing with the raspy drone of the sleeping Newfoundland.

When he was satisfied that Swett's slumber would not be disturbed, Ben rose and stepped quietly to the stove. With great stealth, he opened the iron door and shoved in as much firewood as would fit. He removed his boots and climbed gingerly up the stairs to the bedrooms above, careful to avoid the creak of each step. In his daughter's bedroom, two sleeping forms lay under the blankets, both too large to be his daughters. In his own bed lay Rebecca, flanked by their sleeping daughters. He thought about how much more comfortable Rebecca would be resting on feather down rather than the mean straw mattress where she now lay. Missus Russell sat nearby on the bedstead, her head against the headboard, eyes closed. Ben wished not to disturb anyone and turned carefully to retreat downstairs.

"She stirred a little earlier," a gentle voice called to Ben. He went back to where Missus Russell was rousing. "She pulled the girls tight up against her. She didn't speak, but she snuggled both to her side. I have heard that a mother can do almost anything for her children. Perhaps in your wife's case, that will mean fighting off whatever injury or fever struck her out on this God-forsaken rock."

Ben smiled down on his girls. He tried not to take personally the insult to the stony outcropping where he had spent so many years and was the only home he and Rebecca had ever known together. "Thank you for good news. I suppose Missus Skevold had the right idea."

"Yes, I guess that's true. I believe the fever has broken. She's not as hot to my touch as she was earlier. Now I think she's just exhausted."

"I appreciate all that you and your daughter have done tonight. And I am truly sorry for all you've gone through. I hope we can get you back on your way to Orono in a day or two," Ben said, as he went to the doorway. "Thank you kindly, and good night."

"Good night, Mister Grindle, and thank you for listening to my ravings earlier tonight."

"You gave me no thoughts I haven't already met. I would be pleased, as a fellow witness to the horrors, if you would call me Ben."

"Then I would like very much if you would call me Hortense, at least when Professor Russell is not within earshot."

Ben nodded and then quietly retraced his way down to the kitchen, once again cautious of the noise created by the stairs. Captain Swett still snoozed in the rocking chair; his gray-haired head drooped heavily over his chest. No further sound came from the ladies upstairs. When Ben cleared away the last mugs and flatware from the table top, the dog opened its eyes and raised its massive head in expectation. Ben went into the kitchen and with his fingers fished a large chunk of beef from the pot of cold stew sitting on the stove. Ben tossed the hunk of meat toward the dog. Catching the morsel in its jaw, the dog set to chewing it with gusto. Ben placed Green's coal torpedo on a high shelf in the pantry where it wouldn't be likely to get tossed into the stove by accident. As a last measure of housekeeping that Rebecca normally completed herself, he raised the handle of the kitchen pump and draped the heavy quilt around the thick body of the pump itself to prevent it from freezing during the night.

Ben retrieved his newly dried wool coat from the line of hooks along the wall near the kitchen door. He laid his body longways across the kitchen table, his legs pulled up so that his feet were curled tightly to his thighs. He draped the coat over himself, with the collar at his chin. He stared at the flickering flames where they glimmered among the shadows across the wall. On a regular one-minute interval, the harsh light from the light house beacon illuminated the dark interior of the kitchen.

Ben Grindle thought hard as he lay on his side, feeling the ancient discomfort along the ridge of his spine. What should be done about Mister Green?

A few years after Ben returned home, Ben had followed closely the reports of the attempt by the Fenian Brotherhood to organize an attack against the Canadian mainland from the northeast corner of Maine in 1866. From Rockland to Eastport, folks talked about little else that summer, and each day Ben heard scuttlebutt from local lobstermen or other passing vessels. The rumors and gossip claimed that more than 700 Americans of Irish extract were encamped on Campobello Island, many of them former Union soldiers. The War Department sent General George Meade to quell the uprising, which he did by preventing the invaders from receiving the hired boats necessary to invade Canada by water.

On his return trip to New York, Meade had stopped at Sorrow Ledge long enough to come ashore and share a lunch of steamed lobster and roasted corn with Ben, Rebecca, and Seamus. Meade remembered the late Lieutenant Clough from their service together in Mexico and Florida, and he paid many kind compliments to Clough's handiwork as he toured the light station. For Rebecca, his visit was a rare opportunity to host a guest – the first and only since she had arrived on Sorrow Ledge as a newlywed. She later shared with Ben a letter she had written to her mother that described having an Army General in her parlor, especially one who had helped Lincoln and Grant defeat the rebels. Here he was making a social call on her husband. Somehow, Meade's visit made Ben's tales of war seem so much more real to her.

That day Ben had shown Meade the granite wall that Clough had designed around the fuel building. A half circle of blocks that stood nearly 12 feet high. The general remarked that he had never encountered such a barricade at any light house before. Meade said he understood Clough's intent to protect the other buildings on the barren island. Channel the force of an explosion upward rather than outward, Clough had said. Moreover, Meade approved. After so many years, Ben thought that he finally understood. The only way to protect the women and girls on the island was to redirect Green's violence elsewhere.

Despite years enduring his father's torment and torture, Ben had never understood the cause. Instead he learned not to ponder what he could not know. Watching the dancing flames in the fireplace, Ben concluded that he could not understand Green's politics. Neither could he permit the Irishman to carry his coal torpedoes and murderous intent onto another vessel, into an unsuspecting town or all the way up to Augusta. Ben realized that he must do all he could to deaden the way before Green. Any ambition Green held, any threat Green posed, any desire for revenge Green nurtured must end – as so many dreams and lives had ended before – on Sorrow Ledge.

CHAPTER 11

*F*riday looked early to be dreary and bitterly cold. The storm had passed, but ugly clouds lingered overhead. The beacon from the light tower illuminated the kitchen on its regular rotation, signifying that Seamus remained diligently on duty. As he did all mornings, Ben stretched and strained every limb to ensure that each was awake and alive. Some days one or more extremity did not immediately respond, and he then spent some time working at errant fingers or an uncooperative leg. On this morning, his right hand was not sufficiently nimble. Because he favored his right in most activities, this might prove troublesome should he need to handle a tool – or a weapon. After pulling on his wool coat, Ben opened the kitchen door to find snow flurries alternating with freezing sleet falling lightly through the fog. Offshore the pride of the morning hung over the turbulent waters, further reducing visibility in all directions from the island. He whistled softly for Bosun to join him, but the dog stayed obstinately near the hearth, though watching closely each move Ben made. Despite its reluctance to venture outside, the dog's odiferous farting betrayed a definite need.

"By God, that's a foul animal," Swett murmured, as he was half awake yet still half asleep in the rocking chair. "I cannot imagine how you live with that smell in your home."

Ben thought it best not to respond to this comment because he might be provoked to point out that the most offensive stench on the island that morning probably emanated from the *Gideon's* own crew of whom all evidence indicated they had gone unbathed for several months. He was relieved when Swett's head slumped forward in pursuit of further slumber.

For his first task of the day, Ben needed to take an inventory of the damage inflicted by the blizzard and high water. The flood tide had washed away all the snow that had fallen the night before, leaving a dangerous thin sheath of ice over the smooth rock. Ben elected to conduct his survey from a stationary position on the stoop just outside the kitchen door rather than risk roving across the glaciated surface. With his left hand, he held fast to the doorframe. The most apparent damage was closest to home. As he expected, all trace of Rebecca's garden had been washed away, as well as his futile attempts to cover it in canvas. The chicken coop, too, showed visible signs of damage, as it listed hard to starboard because two support beams on one side had snapped. Luckily, the chickens themselves were still safely high up in the boathouse. Ben was grateful that all the island's other structures still stood, even the flimsy house where Seamus quartered. With a telescope that his father had brought back from his whaling days in the far South Pacific, Ben studied the northwestern arm of the ledge. There was no sign of the *Gideon*. Probably the high tide had lifted the hull and washed it off to the northeast. Depending upon how the day progressed, her crew might be able to scour the leeward coast of the island for any personal items that may have floated ashore. Later he would take the dory out at low tide to see what flotsam might be retrieved.

As he finished his survey of the light station, Ben was taken aback by the sight of the tower itself. Perched at the highest elevation on the rock, the structure had escaped the surging waters, yet the base was ringed around with a ghastly heap of birds, most dead but some struggling in the final throes of living. The horrific berm reached nearly two feet tall in places – hundreds of feathered bodies that had flown into the tower only to be killed or maimed by the impact. There were birds of every species Ben had ever seen, and a few that were entirely unknown to him. Surprisingly most were birds rarely seen so far from the mainland: crows, ravens, cardinals, grouse, hawks, owls, mallards and robins. There were other birds that Ben recognized from the adjacent waters: buffleheads, mergansers, Canada geese, gulls, and puffins. The terrible scene was all the more graphic because the carcasses were of so many diverse colors; their feathers were whites and grays, blacks and browns, oranges and yellow. Ben could not distinguish whether the splashes of red were simply the distinctive coloration on wings of blackbirds or, perhaps more likely, blood stains. Most heart-rending was to see those unfortunate survivors struggling against their injuries to free themselves from the entangling broken wings, necks, and legs of the deceased.

Ben turned to go back inside, struggling hard to fight back similar visions of the dead and dying that he had witnessed in places like Manassas Junction or the aftermath of Groveton Heights. Just when the 2nd Maine prepared to attack Jackson's entrenched troops on Stony Ridge, Longstreet's artillery began a withering crossfire of their left flank. Hardly a man in the regiment escaped unscathed that afternoon; some unlucky fellows received two, three or more wounds. Ben himself was hit twice; once in the shoulder by a Minie ball that must have expended its energy to reach him because it broke the skin but went no farther. He was also struck in the thigh by a bit of shrapnel courtesy of the Confederate cannons. For days after the fighting, the Union dead and wounded lay together on that battlefield. After prior skirmishes, Ben had watched in horror from a distance as Confederates wandered across the battlefield bayoneting the Northern wounded, but not at Manassas Junction. Why did the rebels now refuse to be so merciful?

In a laggard response, the War Department recruited stretcher-bearers from among the government offices in Washington and sent them by train to provide aid; most of these desk clerks arrived too intoxicated to be of any assistance to anyone at all. Ordered to fetch an ambulance for the Second's wounded, Ben encountered these drunkards at the railhead. When asked for their help, a group of them –

bottles and flasks in hand – waved him away. Their apparent leader suggested that a delay might make their work easier; bodies are easier to handle in rigor mortis, he crowed. The man's friends were so inebriated that not one reacted for several minutes after the toe of Ben's boot connected with the drunk's chin. With the butt of his musket, Ben gave the sots hard work until he was ordered to stand down by one of the surgeons. Surprisingly the discipline that Ben dreaded for weeks after the incident never materialized.

Back inside the kitchen, he set to filling the cook stove with firewood and stoking the Franklin stove for heat. Swett was rousing from his slumber in the parlor, and the Newfoundland was agitating for breakfast. The old skipper moved slowly into the kitchen and peered out a window alongside the wickie. "I suppose we'll know the fates by the dinner bell, but I wouldn't regret the chance to buy our luck for today," he observed.

"You believe in charms sold by harbor aunties?" Ben asked in surprise.

"You would, too, if you had sailed with Cap'n Smith out of New London. Twice a soothsayer named Moll Corey predicted the turns of his life."

"Stories proven out later by the facts?"

Swett eyed Ben solemnly. "Would you accept the British Navy as the witness? Back during the second war for our independence, the Brits kept up a blockade on our ports. Young Robert and two friends went out fishing and vanished like a whale's fluke after the harpoon strike. For months, his momma fretted day and night, but Moll assured her he was alive in another country in a room where he couldn't see the sun. She promised that he would return missing only his hat. Later, the lad turned up in the middle of the night. He'd been imprisoned during the war in Dartmoor Prison along with many other Yanks where they never saw daylight. As he walked home after being released by the British, his hat blew off in a storm."

Ben chuckled a bit. "Would it have been too much to guess that he'd been captured by the British for violating the blockade? My grandfather knew many men who did a turn in Dartmoor; damn the Brits for the hell hole."

Swett rattled the pump handle a few strokes to fill a bowl with cold water with which he swabbed his face and neck. "Then perhaps her prophecy I witnessed myself will be more convincing. I crewed under Smith on the *Caledonia* in '28. Before we left, the captain went with other skippers to visit Moll before they shipped out. Despite what Moll told his mother, the skipper didn't believe in such things. When it was Cap'n Smith's turn, she predicted that his demise would be brought about by what she called a damned long snake."

"A long snake on a whaling ship?" Ben smiled at the thought of a reptile slithering up a mooring line.

"Yes, as it turns out. The poor skipper spent most of the voyage abed from his rheumatism. One day our boats were bedeviled all through the dogwatch by a giant sperm whale. The first mate was in charge of the boats, but the skipper watched the events through the porthole. When the mate called the boats in toward twilight, the skipper got himself out of bed, then came on deck and ordered us back out. He swore he would spear that whale if it took a month to recover from his pains."

"The skipper took the stick? My father was a boatsteerer, and I think he'd have been a mutineer before surrendering the harpoon."

"I don't believe the first mate, a feller named Young, was none too happy with the skipper at all. But he stepped aside and allowed Cap'n Smith to hurl the harpoon as we come up on the beast. As soon as it was struck, that whale went deep, pulling us on a Nantucket sleigh ride but good. All a sudden the line slacked free, and the skipper stepped into a slack coil in the line. Young shouted a warning, but the skipper was too bent with his rheumatism to move. As soon as the whale surged ahead, the line went taut around his ankle, and the skipper went right over the gunwale. Sure, we axed the line as quick as we could, but to no avail. No one ever saw Captain Smith again. Every hand aboard the *Caledonia*'s boats watched as a damn long snake killed the skipper. And I'll tell you, Moll never lacked for customers for years once that tale made the rounds amongst the whaling fleet." Upon completing his sea story, Swett went to the stove and poured a fresh mug of coffee.

Bosun now prowled about anxiously. Already given two opportunities when Ben had opened the door, the dog now stubbornly refused to leave the quarters for its morning session on the north side of the island. Ben wondered whether the animal was concerned because it had not yet seen Rebecca that morning, but he dismissed the thought as crediting the animal with far too much compassion. In the storm and dark, Bosun had stayed with Rebecca even as the snow and ice accumulated on its pelt. Would the beast have stayed on watch over her to the point of death had Ben not arrived when he did? Ben remembered that no less an authority than Lord Byron had extolled the virtues of his own Newfoundland, similarly named Boatswain, for the breed's fierce loyalties toward its owner:

"Whose honest heart is still his Master's own,
Who labours, fights, lives, breathes for him alone."

Ben fully understood that Bosun's heart, if a canine truly possessed such a thing, belonged to Rebecca. She had been its constant companion while the puppy learned to live on this inhospitable rock. The Newfoundland had scrupulously watched over the girls throughout their childhoods, but it was to Rebecca that Bosun went for comfort when a lobster clung by its big pincher claw to the dog's ear. For the first time, Ben began to think that the dog possessed some *honest heart,* as Rebecca believed.

As he performed the routine chores of filling the kettle and gathering ingredients to make an oatmeal porridge, Ben kept a watch through the kitchen windows to the northwest where the boathouse lay. Despite his pronouncements of certitude the night before, Mister Green did not appear nearly as early as Ben had expected. Instead, the women passengers of the *Gideon* came down from the bedrooms upstairs on individual missions to pour a cup of coffee and report to Ben that Rebecca looked much healthier in the dawn light. Missus Skevold called her complexion "peach" before returning upstairs; she also filled a basin with water so that the women could complete their daily ablutions. Miss Elizabeth claimed that Rebecca's face was more "rosy." Missus Russell deemed it "pinkish." Ben did not concern himself with exactly which hue was the most accurate description; it was enough that all three women agreed that Rebecca no longer bore the same pallor as the night before. He weighed in his mind whether he could afford to steal upstairs to visit his wife for a few minutes, to see for himself the change in her face and reassure himself that she would recover from her sojourn onto the icy slopes. This desire conflicted in his mind with the need to be prepared for Green's return. He felt that being caught unawares might give the Irish gunman some dite advantage, which could prove of dangerous consequence to the women, including his own family.

Soon enough Ben saw through one of the north-facing windows the reason for Green's tardy appearance. Crew and passenger of the Gideon emerged in the dawn light rigged together like a team of horses. They trudged slowly in a single line; first Gerty, then Tommy, Russell, and Pendleton last. To maintain their balance on the ice, they shuffled their feet along, never raising a foot in a full stride. Pendleton had a hand twisted in the back of Russell's jacket to keep the professor upright. No doubt complicating their procession, the men were bound at the wrists and tethered at the ankles. Around each neck dangled an individual noose, linking every man together in a queue with a single rope. Ben thought that no bully boy could have more thoroughly restrained an impressed crew of sailors. This display of marlinspike seamanship had clearly taken some time to accomplish. Ben assumed Pendleton had been forced to bind up the others before being encumbered himself by Green.

The five were all dressed in the same manner as they had been the prior evening, but something seemed odd about the Irishman's appearance. He wore the same black suit, but his necktie was missing. He had not fastened the upper buttons of his shirt. As their procession neared the living quarters, Ben realized that Green was much more heavily armed than he appeared the previous night. In addition to the revolver that he kept trained on the four men, the young Irishman had a second pistol shoved into the waistline of his trousers, just below his navel. On Green's thigh was strapped a long-bladed knife. Probably these weapons had been secreted in the valise he had carried the previous evening.

Ben watched Green march his little troop toward the entrance of the kitchen. He warned Bosun to be quiet. Swett seemed to follow the same caution without any additional direction.

As the five men mounted the steps into the kitchen, Green hummed an odd tune that Ben didn't recognize.

"Good morning, Mister Grindle," Green said amiably as the procession of men came inside through the kitchen door.

"What's that air? It doesn't sound familiar to me."

"No, I don't imagine that you have heard it before. It's something of an Irish tune." Then Green began to sing the lyrics lustily:

"We are the Fenian Brotherhood, skilled in the arts of war,
And we're going to fight for Ireland, the land we adore,
Many battles we have won, along with the boys in blue,
And we'll go and capture Canada, for we've nothing else to do."

Ben managed to stifle a snigger but still thought to himself that these were among the most delusional words he had ever heard, which for a man who had spent his life among the sailors, fishermen, and lobstermen along the Maine coast, as well as two years in the army – well, that was a damning indictment indeed. The Fenian Brotherhood's most recent raid on Canada, already ten years past, was an attempted incursion into Manitoba. According to accounts Ben had read in the Boston newspaper, the Fenians succeeded in capturing a Hudson Bay Trading Company post located two miles south of the actual Canadian border. The U.S. Army had little trouble rounding up the Irish "marauders," whom the American court promptly released from custody as mere dupes in a greater conspiracy.

"I see you've followed our agreement so far," Green said.

"Yes, so far as I understood you," Ben said. "If you'll let these men sit to the table, I've got water boiling on the stove. My girls will be down presently, and we'll have some burgoo prepared in two bells or less."

"*Burgoo?* What do you people in this province eat?" Green asked. "No, I believe we shall forgo a hot breakfast today," he said abruptly.

"At least coffee, then," Ben insisted. "Three of these men are sailors; they'll be of no use to you at all without some coffee in them."

Green cackled. "By God, I suppose you're right. All right then, gentlemen, have a seat while the wickie boils up some coffee."

The four men shuffled around in confused circles, trying to see how best to settle themselves at the table given the constraints of their bondage. Green came into the kitchen and leaned against the sink, one hand holding a pistol, the other resting on the pump handle. The kettle was already full and building to a boil, so Green's actions didn't interfere with Ben's preparations.

"I hope your wife is feeling better this morning," Green said quietly to Ben.

"Yes, the ladies tell me her color is much improved, and her fever has broken."

"That's good news, good news indeed." Green sounded earnest. "Tell me; I'm puzzled by your water pump. How in God's name were you able to dig a well down to fresh water?"

"It isn't a well at all; it's a cistern. The barrels catch the rainwater. And sometimes the snowfall, too." Ben explained, hoping that conversation might divert some of the tension created by the presence of an angry young man holding a pistol. "We also receive barrels of fresh water with the other supplies for the light house. It wouldn't do to run out of fresh water, even though an ocean surrounds us."

Green nodded in understanding. "Thank you. That resolves a little mystery for me. I couldn't see how you could have a well on this rock, and I was certain that you aren't drinking sea water."

At that point, both the elder and younger Russell women came down the stairs into the kitchen. Their clothes looked only slightly rumpled from the night's rest, but they had taken the time to comb and arrange each other's hair. The ladies paused briefly when they saw the men at the table were bound hand and foot, but then they appeared to act as casually as possible under the circumstances. Missus Russell relieved Ben of his kitchen duties. Elizabeth went into the main room to perch on the bench near where her father sat at the table. Ben brought out a bin of sweet shortbread from the Ladies Relief Association cabinet and laid it open on the table. No one seemed in any hurry to help themselves, so Ben went scouting into the pantry for anything that Rebecca may have baked recently. He had tried a Ladies Relief cookie once, and he too was in no rush to taste another. At the time, Rebecca had reminded him that the critical element was in the word *Relief*; folks who are sufficiently cold, wet, hungry or near drowned don't quibble about the taste of the first morsel of food they receive after their ordeal. For Ben, the tinned biscuits were too like the army's worm castles to suit his tastes. *Oh, hard crackers, come again no more.*

The four bound men at the kitchen table did not engage in any conversation at all until Missus Russell began handing out the steaming mugs. Even then, there were muttered thanks only and little more. No one seemed eager to engage Mister Green in a conversation to learn what plans he had for the coming day. Even the Newfoundland appeared to eye Green warily. When they had all relaxed enough to enjoy their hot coffee, Green chose that moment to announce his intentions for leaving Sorrow Ledge.

"Grindle, I've looked over the boat you offered me. It appears that the optimal crew size is five men. I assume the arrangement is so that two can row at a time and you have two men fresh in reserve. One man at the rudder?"

Ben chuckled. "Well, I've never had that luxury. She'll seat five or six, but that shortens her freeboard. She's called a Quoddy boat, but in fact, she's little more than a common dory, so she's built for one man to row and steer with the oars. The rudder can be set on those occasions when you could jury rig the mast and flow enough sail to catch the wind." Ben saw that both Molly and Phoebe had come into the kitchen and begun gathering the foodstuffs and wares required to prepare breakfast for the largest gathering of guests they had ever witnessed on the ledge in their young lives.

"Are you saying she'll ship water if she carries five people?" Green asked. "Or more than five?"

"I can't say for certain because I've never carried that many people at a time," Ben answered. "But, as I said, she's affixed with long oars so one man can row, navigate and steer. If you want to get ashore quickly, you'll want a lighter cargo than five people. Perhaps Pendleton and I can run you ashore. Sounds like Pendleton knows these waters nearly as well as I do."

The Irishman did not answer. He shoved the pistol into the waist of his trousers so that he now wore one angled toward each hand. He looked like a caricature of a pirate from one of the girls' storybooks, except that he now also carried a mug of coffee that he had accepted

133

from Missus Russell. With his other hand, he then took one of the Relief biscuits from the tin on the table.

While Green pondered his choices, Ben did his own calculations and concluded that getting Green alone was his best strategy, and sooner would be better than waiting for the Irishman's play. Minus Seamus who was in the tower, there were thirteen souls in the quarters. One had three weapons and a disposition to use them. Six were women; two of those children. Of the six remaining, Ben adjudged harshly, one was an old man and another was a bit of a dandy. The three able-bodied seamen were roped together like pack animals. This left Ben alone to prevent Green from causing any more harm to the survivors of the *Gideon* or the inhabitants of Sorrow Ledge.

Finally, Green spoke again. "All right, Grindle. I'll take you and the first mate. But I swear on Danny O'Connell's grave that I'll kill the first one of you that crosses me." Then he continued more pleasantly, like an actor changing characters. "I see where you provisioned the boat already. Is that your normal preparation for a storm?"

"No, not normal," Ben replied. "But yesterday was not a normal storm, even for these parts. A blow like that is no trifling matter on this island. Two earlier light stations here were destroyed in similar surges."

"Nevertheless, it appears that you have loaded it with all we'll need. The boat is lacking only one thing." His jovial tone continued, and the next sentence he spoke carried no hint of its true menace. "There is no figurehead."

Ben was puzzled by this comment; however, judging by his physical reaction, Pendleton clearly understood the inference. He put down his mug on the table and rested his hands in his lap as he turned to watch the Irishman closely.

"No matter, however," Green said. "We'll just take a maiden with us. Since you've volunteered for the voyage, wickie, I'll let you decide. Shall we take Miss Elizabeth or Miss Molly?"

A bustle of activity broke out in the kitchen as Phoebe hugged Molly while Hortense Russell hurried toward Elizabeth. Mister Russell attempted to stand, frustrated in the effort by the rope that connected his neck to Pendleton on one side and Gerty across the table so that he listed awkwardly away from the man he was trying to face. At the sound of this commotion, Bosun roused itself and went into the kitchen to stand near Ben's daughters.

"Now wait, there's no need for that," Russell said to Green. "We've done nothing to you. And you'll be getting ashore. Please just leave us be now!"

Green chuckled in apparent good humor, but Ben astutely observed that one hand had drifted somewhat closer toward a pistol butt at the Irishman's waist. "You expect me to go off boating with only a bully boy and a burnt wickie? My gracious, whatever would I do for polite conversation such as I've enjoyed from you? Would you prefer that I take your missus instead? I suspicion she might."

In the face of Green's mockery, Mister Russell collapsed back onto his seat. "Please don't take my wife or daughter. I have money. In a wallet inside my shirt. Take it all." His voice quavered in fear.

Green moved around the table to where he could lean over Russell's shoulder and stare into his face. "You'll give me money? To buy your daughter's safety and send the wickie's little girl instead? You'd do that?" Green's tone was venomous. "I'll bet you've done it before, haven't you? Did you hire a substitute during Mister Lincoln's draft? Sure you did. You paid another man so that you could stay home while Grindle here was fighting and came home looking that way. Now that he's volunteered to take me ashore, you'll pay to spare your daughter and cast off his. You aren't a man; you're just a wallet." Green looked around the table with a sneer. Gerty and Pendleton glared back at him. Ben was watching to ensure that neither of them tried to attack the Irishman. Tommy seemed to be keenly watching Elizabeth; she, in turn, did not seem to notice him at all.

Russell's next words came nearly as a whisper. "I have thirty thousand dollars. It's inside the waist of my shirt."

Green whistled in astonishment. "I believe that would have purchased a hundred substitutes. I've got to assume that's the high bid. How about it, wickie? Can you do better?" He bent over Russell and fished one-handed around inside the waist of his jacket, the other hand resting on a pistol butt. In a moment, Green held up a thickly stuffed cotton safe with which he patted Russell on the head. "I believe you've won, then. Well, let's not waste any more daylight. Miss Molly, would you please get into your togs?"

Ben watched as Molly shivered, almost imperceptibly. Bosun seemed to notice her quiver of fear, too; a low rumble emanated from deep within the dog's thick chest.

Green looked toward the kitchen and spoke sharply. "Grindle, tell your dog to mind its manners."

Suddenly Pendleton threw off the noose and sprang to his feet, his hands somehow free. "Leave the child alone!" he shouted. With keen aim, he hurled a coffee mug directly at Green's head. His target saw it coming and dodged away so that it caught only his ear. The mug shattered against the wall. Elizabeth shrieked. Bosun sounded a fierce bark that trailed into a prolonged growl. Ben raced forward just as Green raised his pistol and shot Pendleton through the chest. The first mate tumbled back and collapsed directly into Ben's arms. They fell to the floor together. The single shot echoed loudly in the room. Elizabeth's scream turned to a wail, as her mother tried to turn her daughter away from the sight of the dying man. Gerty and Tommy jumped up, still roped and tethered, but Green aimed his second weapon at them and motioned with the barrel for them to sit back down. As Ben rolled Pendleton on to the rug, Swett dropped to his knees next to them.

Pendleton's body was already slack and mostly lifeless. His head hung loose, and his mouth gaped open. Ben could feel no breath against the palm of his hand; Pendleton's chest did not rise and fall from respiration. Only the fingers of the first mate's right hand, which had pitched the mug, still twitched. Ben had seen this same type of convulsions before, after a surgeon's saw removed the arm. When he looked up, Ben realized that Elizabeth was transfixed by the dead mate's quaking digits. Likely, she had never seen a body freshly killed before but only those corpses already attended by the undertaker. Green now had one pistol aimed at this knot of men on the floor, and another pointed toward the three still clustered around the table.

Abruptly Green hooted aloud. "It appears that chivalry is dead." Then he cackled again as he shoved a pistol back into his trousers, keeping the other weapon aimed most closely at Gerty.

Swett whispered into Ben's ear, "I'd like to cut that hyena's throat."

"Here now, let's not have the mate bleed out on the floor. The wickie's family must live here." With his long blade, Green cut the rope dangling from Russell's wrists and then removed the noose from his neck, leaving only Tommy and Gerty roped together. Waving a pistol, he indicated that the tethered crewmen should go help deal with the corpse. "Lay him outside. We'll drag him down to the water's edge later. A good sailor deserves a grave in Davy Jones' locker." As the two crewmen hoisted their mate, Green issued another threat. "Come back soon, or your skipper will join him." He turned toward the Russell women and pointed at the kitchen where Ben's daughters were huddled. Bosun now stood between Green and the girls, head erect and tail fanned out, seeming to appear much larger than he normally looked. Missus Skevold peered meekly from the stairwell, probably drawn downstairs by the sound of gunfire. "All of you women must go upstairs, now. Go on, now. Wait. Not you, Molly. You stay."

In shock, the women moved slowly to follow his direction. Supporting Elizabeth with an arm around her waist, Missus Russell led her trembling daughter away. Missus Skevold took Phoebe by the shoulders and pulled the hesitant girl along with her toward the stairs. Ben watched from across the room as Molly slowly relinquished her hold on her sister's hand. When their fingers parted, Molly seemed to shiver; then she stood motionless and alone in the kitchen. After a moment, she edged forward to where she could rest her hands in the fur on the big dog's neck.

The two crewmen lifted the first mate by his limbs and carried him outdoors, trailing behind a small rivulet of Pendleton's blood in their wake. Ben helped Swett get up from his knees. Mister Russell sat alone at the table, head drooped and chin resting on his chest. From his hair dripped the coffee dumped when Pendleton had hurled his mug. Russell made no effort to dry his hair or sop up the liquid from his shoulders or lapels.

"Come here, Molly," Green said as he edged toward the kitchen, careful to keep his back against the wall so that neither Ben nor Swett could catch him unaware. The gunman was equally wary of the dog as well. "No need to worry, lass. I don't intend to take you with us. Your father ransomed you with his cooperation. Come and take this." He held toward her the thick money belt that he'd recently removed from Professor Russell. "Go on; it's yours now. Consider this your dowry." Unsure and afraid, Molly remained as motionless as the icebound Newf the night before. With a slight nod of his head, Ben indicated she should take the packet; he did not wish to test Green's temper. Slowly Molly reached out and accepted the gift. "Now go upstairs and help take care of your mother," Green said. Molly quickly did as she was told. Bosun also retreated to the stairwell. Ben knew the dog would have happily followed her up the steps if he was able, but instead he used his massive body to block the passageway to all others.

Without warning, the Irishman turned his gun on Ben and Captain Swett. "Seems your boys have been gone a good long while, skipper. Perhaps you should go look after them, no?" Another change of tone. "I don't believe it would be healthy for them to attempt to steal away in my boat."

Instinctively Ben looked toward the boathouse and the northwest bay to see whether the dory had been run out on the station's ways. There was no human activity at all in that direction, only the usual wreck of seabirds fishing on the slack waters. Ben was quite relieved when Ed Swett opened the kitchen door, revealing Gerty and Tommy returning to the quarters but at a snail's pace. The younger seaman's clothes were disheveled, and his cheek bore a hideous bruise from chin to ear. Gerty supported him with an arm around his waist and a hand on his shoulder.

"By God, tha ice's awful out thar," Gerty announced when they reached the threshold. "I've walked decks cov'd with blood and blubber from a flensed whale that weren't not nearly so slick as all that."

"What's happened to Tommy?" his skipper asked.

"Took a tumble on the ice," Gerty said. "Went down kinda hard. A wee bit stunned still, I think."

Swett lifted Tommy's head and pried open the lids to examine his eyes. Then he listened for the sounds of breathing in his chest. "Ok, then, put him down wherever Grindle says."

For his part, Ben directed the mate toward the same rocking chair where both Green and Swett had sat the night before. Gerty walked

Tommy into the parlor, with the younger man's feet stumbling along without much effect. Though smaller, the elder sailor had no difficulty navigating the larger boy through the house. The extent of Tommy's injuries remained unclear, but Gerty placed him in the seat with minimal effort. Swett laid the same quilt over him and felt at Tommy's head and neck.

"I don't feel any odd bumps, and his head seems to turn normal enough," the captain said. "If we let him rest, he'll probably be all right after a while."

During all these ministrations, Green kept a reasonable distance, curious but not directly involved. "So now you're a ship's surgeon, too, are you, Captain?" he challenged the skipper. "And if he needed mending, could you do that as well?" He leaned against the window frame and peered out at the dismal weather.

"Probably as well as any doctor," Swett replied. "I've done my fair share of fixing injured crewmen, from smashed fingers to busted legs. I've cut out bullets and sewn up knife wounds. On most ships, the skipper's a surgeon, too, yes indeed."

"Then, pray tell, what is the prognosis for our young friend? With your mate now indisposed, I was thinking that the lad would be a good man to assist the wickie with the small boat." Both the Fenian's pistols were now secured back in the waistline of his pants. He acted as casually as any man might while waiting for the matron of a boarding house to serve breakfast.

No one reacted to the gunman, and a silence fell over the quarters, upstairs and down. For long minutes, the only sound heard throughout the quarters was the rumble of the tide against the graveled southwest shore of the ledge and the raspy pant of the Newfoundland. Ben positioned himself to stand between the Irishman and the skipper, hoping to deter the old man from making good on his threat. Through the open collar of Green's shirt, Ben could see on the Irishman's neck a long nasty scar left by a passing blade. He also noticed, with no small concern, that the gunman was not perspiring. Despite Green's recent acts of violence, he appeared calm and unaffected. At the same time, Ben sensed that Swett's anger was rising, and he did not want to witness another shooting.

"Why this sudden whist?" the Irishman asked, turning from the window. "We need to get on about business while the day's still young."

"There's no need for Tommy to come along. I'll have no trouble getting you ashore myself," Ben told Green. "I make the trip alone often. From what I observed this morning, we should have fair winds and following seas. We'll be at Rockland in less than four hours. If the wind holds, I'll rig the mast and set a sail. With the wind at our backs, we could make port in three hours or less."

Green showed a big smile. "You misunderstand me, wickie. I don't believe you need help rowing me ashore. I believe you may need an incentive to get me there." He moved back toward the kitchen, where Mister Russell still sat alone. "Tell me if I understand you correctly. We're both soldiers. These others don't think the way we do. But you figure that if you can get me alone, you might find a way to get an advantage, isn't that right?" Green rested one hand on a pistol butt and then casually laid the other palm down atop Russell's head. "Yes, just you and I alone in a boat. Wouldn't that be quite an opportunity, Grindle?" The Irishman stroked Russell's pate like soothing a child.

Ben thought for several long minutes about how best to respond because he had thought exactly as Green guessed. "Yes, I was a soldier. More than fifteen years ago. Do I look to you like a man who has another Fredericksburg still to fight?"

"I can't guess how much scrap you've got left inside, but I've no doubt that you'll be more cooperative if there are more than just the two of us in the boat. Before last night, you had no idea in the world who this Pendleton was, but now you're burning with the injustice that I killed him as easily as you'd crack a chicken egg." Green paused, drew the Colt from his waistline and checked the number of rounds in the cylinder. This incessant habit, Ben decided, was simply a show of power, a frequent reminder to all present that Green held casually in his hands the power to kill anyone for any or no reason at all. "But you won't risk harm to anyone else other than yourself. Very well, I said I wouldn't take your daughter, so I suppose the good skipper must join us on our voyage. Why don't you both go prepare the dory while I secure Mr. Gerty and the boy?"

Gerty stood up from his tending to Tommy's injuries. "Let me take you ashore instead. I'm an able man with a set of oars. Let Grindle stay here with his family."

Green loosed a mocking twitter at this suggestion. "And what would possess me to do anything so stupid? At least Grindle has an incentive to return to his family. What are you after but vengeance for your mate Pendleton?"

"Well, I don't give a tinker's damn about your politics. I'm a sailor and better fit than either the skipper or Grindle. Go on an' ask Cap'n Swett when he last manned the sweeps. I swear I'll get you to Rockland safe. If I was to ever come across you again, then that will be when I settle up with you over the mate."

The Irishman erupted in such a jeering cachinnation that Swett lurched away, and Bosun barked from his post by the stairwell. Green grinned fiendishly at the three men in the parlor. "By God, I love an honest man." Green turned to face Ben and Swett. "But you are all witnesses to Mister Gerty threatening to kill me." With no more concern than a man exhibits swatting a fly, Green drew one of the revolvers and shot Gerty in the face. The sailor collapsed where he stood. The noise startled Tommy from his trance. He sat forward in his seat and then dropped to the floor next to Gerty's corpse. Tommy and the quilt draped over him were painted with the splattering of Gerty's blood and brains. Ben put his arm across Swett's chest to restrain him from charging at Green directly.

"I apologize, Mr. Grindle, for the deeds done in your home this morning. It may take some time to clean the blood from your floors." Green again checked the cylinder of his pistol and returned it to his waistline. "Now the hour is getting late. I believe we should be underway soon. Even with the wind and surf at our backs as you said, four hours is a long row in this weather."

Ben removed his oilskins from the coat rack. As he pulled on a pair of wool gloves and a pair of leather mitts over them, he looked at Swett's hand. "Cap'n Ed, do you have any gloves?"

"No, I left them aboard last night. But I'll be fine. I've pulled an oar more than any man on this rock."

"I beg to differ." Three men turned abruptly at the sound of this unexpected voice. Professor Russell remained seated at the wood table, working at the knot of the hemp noose around his neck. "I was on Harvard's sculling team for three years. Every year we beat Yale in races up on Lake Winnipesaukee. I believe I can handle a set of oars as well as anyone in this room. I'll help the keeper take you ashore."

Green turned to peer closely at Russell and sniggered derisively. "You can't be serious. We're not talking about a little regatta among college boys. It's more than 10 miles into Rockland. Your hands will be bleeding before we've made half a league." He turned back toward Ben, shrugging off the professor's comments.

Just as Russell stood and prepared to rebut Green's latest litany of insults, the alarm bell from the light tower began to ring in the kitchen, clanging even more rapidly than it had the night before. Immediately dropping his oilskins to the floor, Ben dashed toward the tunnel into the light tower, forgetting that an Irishman with two guns was holding his shipwrecked visitors hostage. Green was not prepared to let Ben escape his surveillance so easily, and he quickly followed Ben through the passageway. Inside the tower door, Ben raised the boatswain's whistle to his lips and blew the standard low and high notes that meant, "Pass the word." In a moment, Seamus was atop the stairwell.

"Ben, I believe I heard a ship's fog bell. Twice. Bearing west-northwest."

Green clapped a hand on Ben's shoulder. "Well, there's good news for you. Save you a bit of exercise today. So, what do we do now? Fire that cannon? Ring a bell?"

The excitement in the Irishman's voice alarmed Ben, and he knew that to stop further bloodshed he must prevent any communications with the vessel. In answer to Green's suggestions, Ben shook his head. "No, if she's sounding her bell, she's feeling her way through the fog. If she hears our bell, she'll likely believe there's another ship nearby and set a new heading to steer away to avoid collision. If we fire the cannon, she'll know there's a light house in the vicinity and steer off as well to avoid running aground. If her master was beset in the storm and steering by dead reckoning, he may not know his actual location." He looked up to where his assistant awaited orders. "Seamus, I want you to walk the catwalk. Do your best to ignore the direction where you think she lies and focus just on where the bell sounds loudest. Go 'round again until you've got the best feeling."

"Come now, wickie; surely you're not going to let another vessel run aground on your infernal rock. We might get a wee bit crowded." Green chuckled devilishly. "How can you get the skipper's attention before he sails by us? That may be my best chance to reach Augusta."

As Green schemed to lure his next victims into his evil plot, already Ben was making his own preparations. He draped the brass chain of the boatswain's whistle around his neck and handed a large silver hailing trumpet to Green. From the cabinet, he took two Coston flares and shoved them into a hip pocket of his trousers. He also hoisted the line that Gerty had knotted into a towline and slung it over a shoulder. "We'll be creative. We'll speak her." He tapped the hailing trumpet. "We'll see if she's close enough to hear the bosun whistle. If not, we'll fire off a flare. And we can use the rope to string a line of signal flags. We'll do our best. Shall we climb up?"

"First, kindly ask Seamus to come here. I don't believe it would be overly healthy for me if the two of you were to fling me from the top of the tower."

Ben raised the whistle to his lips and sounded again. When he saw Seamus had returned to the watch room door, he called out to him. "Come down at once! I'll need you to run out the small boat in case we're able to speak this vessel."

"Ben, I've had no chance to reach the catwalk even." The confusion Seamus felt at these contradictory orders was evident.

"Understood. Circumstances changed." With his neck craned back, Ben watched as Seamus began to descend the spiraling stairway carefully at the same time as he pulled on his wool keeper's jacket.

"Shall I load the *Gideon*'s passengers into the boat or wait for you to make contact?" Seamus asked as he reached the last flight of stairs.

Green interrupted at that juncture. "Let's not get ahead of ourselves. It may not be possible to take everyone off right now. We don't even know what kind of a vessel you've been hearing." With that, the Fenian turned and started up the steps.

"For now, just open the boathouse doors and run the boat out," Ben said, recognizing that Green did not want his captives in a position to escape. "Seamus, be careful of the ice outside. One of the mates took a nasty fall."

Seamus went into the passageway, and Ben turned to follow Green up the winding stairway. He wondered how his assistant would react when he discovered the scene of violence in the quarters that had occurred while Seamus had been on watch high in the tower. Ben paused to scan the cabinets to see if there might be anything else of use in contacting the passing vessel. He saw only the kerosene for the light, a cask of mineral spirits for cleaning all the glass, the gunpowder for the cannon and the Green's case of coal torpedoes – a combination of explosives gathered inside the base of the tower of which Lieutenant Clough most certainly would not approve.

Green whistled spryly another tune that Ben assumed was Gaelic. At times, Seamus hummed or sang tunes he had learned from his mother, but Ben had never heard him warble hymns of revolution. As they reached the landing Ben thought of as Second Bull Run, the gunman abruptly said:

"Here's to the grey goose,

With the golden wing;

A free country,

And a Fenian King."

Now Ben realized that this particular Fenian had made a grievous miscalculation upon learning of the nearby ship. In the parlor, between the murders of Pendleton and Gerty, Green had identified precisely Ben's strategy, which was to get the gunman alone, away from the *Gideon*'s passengers and his own family. After sending Seamus away, here was Green voluntarily climbing into a place where he would be alone with Ben. Green had claimed they were both soldiers. This Ben knew was untrue. In two years with the 2nd Maine, Ben had no doubt killed several men in the heat of battle though he did not keep a tally. But not one in cold blood. Shooting unarmed men in tethers was not warfare; that was simple murder. This prompted a thought in Ben's mind. "Tell me, last night when I described Rockland, you asked about a papist church. Will you have an accomplice when you get there?"

"You've much too suspicious a mind. No, the Church and the Brotherhood aren't one and the same. Besides, I would guess that the pastor of a Catholic church so far north would be a Jesuit from Montreal, not an Irishman from Boston."

"So why the question, then?"

"I don't know what the coming days will bring, but I suspected that leaving this place would bring events for which I will need to find a confessor." Green paused briefly and turned toward Ben. "I've no fear of dying, but I'm in no great hurry to explore Hell." Then he continued climbing the iron stairs.

When they reached the watch room, Ben immediately began preparing to hail the nearby vessel Seamus had heard sounding its way through the hazy mist. He showed Green the semaphore -- or wigwag -- flags stored there. Ben had learned the code from the Signalman's Corps over the '62-'63 winter encampment outside Washington. Kept tidily in a wooden chest in one corner of the watch room was a complete set of marine signal flags, with which Ben could spell out words or abbreviated messages. Ben gave Green paper and a pencil. "Write out the message that you want to send. I'll figure out the best way to communicate it."

The Irishman smiled, "You wouldn't try to trick me, would you? Send a different message from what I write? Scare off any vessel that comes near us?"

"Why?" Ben asked in candor. "What could I possibly hope to gain by keeping you on Sorrow Ledge a single minute longer than necessary?" As he said this, Ben closed the door to the tower stairway. The latch was a crossbar on the outside of the door, operated on the inside by a short draw rope.

"Well, then, I guess we understand each other." With that, Green bent over the work table and began to scribble out a message.

Ben pulled the cord to its fullest length and then severed it with his pocket knife. Once the short end of the drawcord disappeared through the hole when the crossbar fell, the door would not open from inside the watch room. Next, he quickly scanned the watch room for anything else he thought might be useful. He collected a marlinspike, an awl, a chisel, and a mallet. Green was too busy composing a missive to his next intended victims to notice Ben's activities.

"I'm going topside. Maybe I'll hear whatever vessel Seamus

thought is out there," he told Green. Ben clambered up the ladder, weighted down with the tools, flares, hailing trumpet, and Gerty's rope. In the lantern room, he realized that he had only brief minutes before Green would become suspicious and then alarmed. "I'm closing the hatch so I can hear better," he called down to the watch room. After lowering the flat door, Ben wedged the chisel so that the sliding latch would not operate, then drove it home with a strike of his boot heel. As a further deterrent, Ben placed the marlinspike between the hatch and its frame, then hammered it into place by two quick blows with the mallet. Now Green was unable to open either the door down into the tower or the hatch up into the lantern room, though Ben imagined that he might eventually shoot his way through either door. For the moment, Green could neither ascend nor descend; he was trapped in the windowless watch room, though perhaps not for long.

The wickie left all the tools he had gathered from the watch room – those which Green could have used to escape his captivity – on the floor of the lantern room. Ben quickly proceeded onto the catwalk. There he stepped across another heap of bird carcasses to reach the railing where he wrapped the bitter end of Gerty's rope work around a stanchion of the rail then tied it securely to an iron eyebolt on the wall of the light cupola itself. After stepping into the noose of the bowline and pulling it up to his chest, Ben climbed over the rail. He gripped the rope near the railing and took a step backward.

Ben planned to descend the tower in much the same way he moved up and down on a boatswain's chair when it was time to caulk any cracks in the exterior grouting of the granite structure. With his initial step, he discovered his first mistake. The tower wore the same mantle of ice as the entire island. He lost his footing on the slick wall and fell, crashing a shoulder against the iron catwalk. Then the second error in judgment became painfully apparent; he had not paused long enough to collect his leather gloves. The thin manila cord began to slip through his grasp. The sharp fibers strafed his palms as it passed through his clenched hand. The pain caused him to let go. He plummeted toward the ground. *So this is what it looks like to tumble from the top of a light house.* He closed his eyes but could not shut out the memory of another man falling to just such a gruesome demise.

Ben's plunge ended about 15 feet above the ground when he abruptly reached the full length of the rope. Suddenly the line came up short. The loop of the bowline knot strangled his torso, the cord digging into his armpits and sawing over the tender scars across his spine. He struggled to catch his breath as his own weight put a greater strain on the line. Dangling from the catwalk on three-strand manila, he swung to and fro but was unable to see a window ledge where he might get enough footing to relieve the tension on the line.

Thus, he dangled for long minutes, as exposed a target as the 2nd Maine hunkered down on the barren slope before Fredericksburg. By now, surely Green was aware that he was snared in the wickie's trap. Ben knew he could not just hang around for long, while Green wrangled his escape from the watch room. He drew his pocketknife from a trouser pocket. He pulled his legs up as tightly as he could against his stomach so that his back was aimed downward. With a quick swipe of the blade, Ben was in free fall.

He landed with a grunt that was echoed by a weak chorus of squeals and squawks. The downy bed of bird carcasses that ringed the base of the tower broke his fall. The impact knocked the wind out of him, and he strained for a moment to breathe. He rolled onto his right side stiffly and struggled to get to his knees. He knew that he did not have much time left to prepare a particularly suitable surprise before Green managed to escape his imprisonment high in the tower. Ben pushed himself upright, leaning his weight against the ice-covered base of the light house for balance. He stumbled around the tower, one hand supporting himself against the granite wall. The entrance was open, and Ben dashed inside. From far overhead, he heard the thudding and hammering of Green trying to break free through the door of the watch room; his angry voice echoed off the stone walls of the tower. If the Irishman managed somehow to reach St. David's in Rockland, he would need to confess breaking the Second Commandment as well as the Fifth. During Sunday services with the 2nd Maine, Ben had often wondered why profanity came before murder in the Bible's holy list of sins, but he reckoned early on that both regimental chaplains – first Mines and then Bates – considered swearing to be a breach of army decorum while killing was the army's primary objective.

With a firm clarity of intent, he went first to Green's case and laid it open. Next, from the cabinet that held the gunpowder for the fog cannon, he withdrew the five one-shot pouches already weighed and sealed with the proper charge. These he packed amongst the coal torpedoes. On the lower shelf were two five-pound canisters of black powder. Ben dumped the entire contents of the powder reserves over Green's open bag. The container of mineral spirits he placed atop the gunpowder covering the Irishman's deadly dunnage. Next, he went to the shelves where the kerosene was stored. He lowered one keg onto the floor, opened its spigot and knocked it onto its side. As the fuel spilled out and engulfed Green's satchel, Ben delicately retreated to the doorway, careful to avoid stepping in the pooling kerosene. Reaching the threshold, he removed one of the Coston flares from the pocket of his jacket and closed the door until it was only slightly ajar. From the top of the stairway, he heard Green screaming Ben's name in a vulgar torrent. Ben aimed the rocket through the small distance between the door and frame. As soon as he triggered the flare, he dove for the safety of the granite wall.

The initial explosion seemed to rock the island itself, and the stone tower appeared to Ben as if it swayed unsteadily for a fleeting moment. The resulting blast blew the wood door open with a black cloud that smelled distinctively of cannon fire. The billowing smoke was so thick that he saw little except the bright flash through the tower's windows and a brief orange corona around the base of the cupola. A second large detonation followed, probably caused by the other keg of kerosene. Broken glass rained down on Ben from a shattered window on the third tier. Next came a long series of dwindling eruptions, likely as each coal torpedo ignited. The smaller ignitions sent up flames that lighted the tower's interior. Ben smelled both the burnt gunpowder and the burning kerosene. For the first time, Ben was glad to have the kerosene for fuel; he was not confident that whale oil would have the same explosive force when ignited. Soon a plume of black smoke escaped through the broken windows and emerged from the cupola itself. As the explosions continued, Green's hollering turned to screams, then shrieks and finally silence.

When Ben tried to stand, he found Seamus at his side doing his best to assist. "My God, Ben, what's happened?"

"I blew up the tower." The keeper decided there wasn't enough time to explain all the details of the morning's events. "Seamus, I need you to go to the fuel house as quickly as you can. Bring back my pistols and the Enfield. And pray to God that any ammunition you find is dry. Just be careful on the ice."

"Aye, aye." He turned to start away but stopped himself abruptly. "You set off a blast in the tower, and I'm to be careful? So I'm curious, Ben. Was this just more of what you consider to be your duty?"

Ben nodded in assent as he watched his assistant walk away. Seamus moved delicately across the ice with the precision of a circus performer on a tightrope. Ben turned to determine whether the explosions damaged the living quarters. A few of the windows in the connecting passageway had cracked, but otherwise, there was no damage evident from the exterior. Ben settled against the cushion of dead birds to ponder what he must do next, what actions to pursue and which to avoid. When he took a deep breath, pain coursed through his ribs, causing him to cough violently.

When Seamus returned with the weapons, Ben would climb up the tower to confirm Green's fate. Head resting against the granite blocks, Ben closed his eyes. Perhaps he would find Green's corpse, and there would be an end to it. That was his hope. Not of cowardice. Ben had faced many living and armed men in battle. Instead, he knew these circumstances might leave the Irishman past help but not yet beyond this mortal coil, a situation in which Ben did not wish to be the sole arbiter of this man's life or death. That was a decision best left to Green's own God. He harbored no animosity toward the Fenian Brotherhood or the Irish population; no more than the Virginians or North Carolinians or Alabamans he had faced in battle. As he lay there now, atop Sorrow Ledge, feeling the pulsations from struggling and dying birds against his back, Ben prayed for nothing more fervently than respite from all such hatred.

Seamus seemed to be gone a rather long time, for which Ben did not begrudge him. Traversing the island across a crust of ice would be both dangerous and slow. Ben was unsure whether he dozed, but he awoke abruptly to the alarmed barking of the Newfoundland. Then he heard the steady approach of bootsteps. The wickie opened his eyes to discover three uniformed sailors coming toward the light tower. One was an officer with a golden epaulet on his shoulder and two rows of gold buttons down the front of his tunic; the other two appeared to be ordinary seamen or perhaps petty officers, both wearing blue wool coats and carrying rifles. They all walked in a somewhat bowlegged manner common among seamen accustomed to challenging shipboard surfaces such as listing, wet or icy decks.

The officer bowed slightly toward Ben and spoke rather formally. "Good morning, sir, my name is Myrick, third lieutenant, Revenue Cutter *Dallas*. Captain Hodgson inquires whether you require assistance."

CHAPTER 12

Still resting on the pile of bird corpses, Ben said, "Sir, I am relieved to see you. Your timing is most fortunate, but please give me a moment to find my breath."

"Well, certainly you may take a moment. We were outbound from Rockland this morning when we saw flotsam west of here. As we searched for its source to see if we might render assistance, the forward lookout thought he heard a gunshot as we approached the island, then we heard a series of explosions," Myrick explained. "The lookout was certain the sounds were more than a mere fog cannon. When we sighted the tower, we saw that your signal had been altered. The captain thought it all merited investigation."

"I'm rather glad you did," Ben said. Aided by one of the Revenue Marine sailors, Ben rose to his feet so that he could properly address the officer. Although he didn't know Myrick, Ben was familiar with many other members of the cutter's crew. Ben quickly laid out for Myrick his bona fides as keeper of the light.

"Yes, Captain Hodgson thought you'd still be the officer in charge. He sends his regards to Missus Grindle. I've been given to understand that he has dismissed at least two stewards who could not create a match to your wife's lobster bisque."

"Thank you, sir, for solving a mystery for me. In the three years since Captain Hodgson took command, we've had more visits from the *Dallas* than any other cutter since I've been here, which goes back to well before the war." Ben led Myrick toward the quarters. "May I go check on her? She took a nasty fall in the storm last evening."

"Of course. You know, in the boat coming ashore just now, the bosun's mate told me that Sorrow Ledge might be the best defended light house on the Atlantic coast, for which credit may go to your wife's cooking." Myrick gave Ben a genial smile. "I'd be most grateful to know her recipe. My promotion to first lieutenant seems to be somewhat lagging. I understand that a happy captain can fix such an oversight."

"We can ask, but I'm sure you know that getting a prized recipe from a Maine woman can be like wresting a three-cent piece from a codfish aristocrat." By Myrick's New England accent, Ben assumed the officer would know about prosperous merchants whose wealth came from the cod fishery of Georges Bank.

As they walked, Ben set about recounting the events of the past 24 hours. A more incredulous man might have been suspicious of Ben's claims, but Myrick seemed ready to accept the wickie's word based on the physical evidence all around him. The pile of carcasses encircling the tower was clear evidence of the bird strike. The loss of the *Gideon* was proven by the wreckage that the *Dallas* had encountered floating off the northwest coast of the Ledge. The storm's savage assault on the island was evident in the damaged chicken coop. A dozen feet away, Pendleton's corpse lay cold on the ice, arms crossed reverently across his chest. From a waist pocket dangled the same ivory pipe the first mate had lighted the night before at the kitchen table. As Ben pointed upward, Myrick could observe a rope hanging from the catwalk of the light tower.

"I want to make clear that murdering Mister Green was solely my plan and my work," Ben said. "None of the others were involved. No one," he added emphatically.

"Let's not get ahead of ourselves now," Myrick said. "From what I glean from your story, you're not entirely certain that the Irishman is dead. I would caution you against confessing to a crime until the time comes. Moreover, I believe our surgeon can best determine whether there was any murder involved." The young officer ordered the taller crewman, a man named Collins, up the tower to ascertain the status of the Fenian. Myrick seemed utterly unconcerned with Green's apparent death but vitally consumed with the potential damage to federal property. He requested Ben's permission to send for the ship's carpenter and the doctor from the *Dallas*. Myrick stopped abruptly when he saw Seamus moving slowly toward them carrying a rifle. The lieutenant drew his own pistol.

Ben threw up his arm instinctively. "Wait, that's my assistant. I sent him to fetch my weapons from the fuel house. I didn't want to go up to find Mister Green unarmed. In case I had to dispatch the poor bastard myself."

Myrick lowered his weapon but did not immediately return it to his holster. They walked a short distance farther and found Gerty's corpse lying in the shadow of the passageway, his upper body wrapped in the quilt from the rocking chair. Ben recognized the same gnarled hands that had done the quick knotwork in the wake of the *Gideon* the night before. Blood had seeped through the colorful shroud, creating a red blossom across the area over his face. Myrick and Ben continued onward and met Seamus outside the kitchen door. After his assistant finished stacking his load of weapons on the stoop, Ben introduced him to the lieutenant.

The seaman from the *Dallas* emerged from the tower door and scampered cautiously on the ice toward them to report to Myrick. "Sir, I was able to reach the top of the stairs. I found a dead man in the watch room. His clothes and body were burned. But his face wasn't like anything I've ever seen before. He was all purple, with his tongue clenched between his teeth. Looked like his hair was all singed off."

"Did you happen to find any papers about his person?" the lieutenant asked. To Ben, Myrick's tone and expression seemed to be couched in a slight suspicion.

"Aye, sir. Papers and dollars, both," Collins answered as he reached deep into his coat pockets. "I found more than five hundred dollars, not counting the shinplasters and wildcat money." From his left-hand pocket, the seamen drew a wad of crumpled cash that he thrust toward

Myrick. "It's all there, I swear." From his other pocket, he drew several folded sheets that he proffered to his officer as well. "Looks like a couple of hand-drawn maps, sir." The seaman was red-faced and huffing from his climb up the tower and descent.

"Thank you for confirming the man's dead." Myrick glanced at the papers before handing them to Ben. Then he tried to help Collins put the wad of funds from Green's corpse into a semblance of order. "Look familiar?" Myrick asked Ben.

Ben studied the pencil drawing of lines and squares, a few of which had names crudely scrawled nearby, leading him to conclude this was intended as a city street map. At the center, a square was labelled "Weston." Another appeared to be an architectural diagram of a large building. Ben recognized neither image, but the third he guessed by the names carefully printed in pencil adjacent to a long arching line. On the far right of the page was the word Buffalo; on the opposite edge was Halifax. In between was a series of other names, including Sherbrooke,

"I know the Canadian border," Ben said as he tapped the paper. "I've no idea about the other two pages."

Myrick folded the sheets and shoved them into an inside pocket of his uniform tunic with the money. "I believe one shows the streets of Augusta. The last I'm not familiar with either, but perhaps the captain will recognize it."

"Do you wish me to go drag the body down here?" Collins asked.

"No, better to leave it where it is until the doctor has a chance to examine it. I'm sure he'll want to write a dozen reports about his find-ings. Go tell the bosun to fetch the doctor and the carpenter." Myrick turned to Ben. "May we go meet the others now?"

Ben opened the door into the kitchen of the quarters to find the way blocked by Bosun, standing tall and fierce with its head up stiffly and tail upright in a menacing stance. When the dog recognized its master, the change of posture was dramatic; the tail began waving, its entire body began to waggle back and forth, and the big head went down in a submissive gesture. The dog pressed against its owner's legs so firmly that they nearly toppled over together.

"I believe that's the largest dog I've ever seen in my life," the lieutenant observed from over Ben's shoulder. "Is he friendly?"

"Too much so, I fear," Ben cautioned. "Mind your uniform. The dog drools."

Bosun dutifully sniffed at Seamus and then approached the officer cautiously. Ben was relieved the dog did not extend its usual slobbery greeting to Myrick. The only actual damage was a smear of drool across the lieutenant's high-topped black boot, which Myrick removed with a handkerchief. Inside the quarters, the three men encountered a surprising bustle of activity. Captain Swett was at the stove, tending two skillets of eggs and bacon with a wooden spoon. Nearby Missus Skevold was pumping water into a blue ceramic pitcher. Mister Russell was stacking firewood between the fireplace and stove. In the parlor, Tommy was on his knees, working a holystone across the wood floor to scrub off the bloodstains. Ben winced at the site of the young seaman cleaning up the blood spilled by his shipmates.

"Would you excuse me, sir?" Ben asked. "I'd like to go topside to see how my wife fares this morning. Seamus, please introduce Mister Myrick to our guests and make him as comfortable as we can." Then he crossed the parlor and climbed the stairway to his bedroom, which he found surprisingly crowded. Standing around the bedstead and chatting amongst themselves were Missus Russell, Elizabeth, Phoebe and Molly. They were in the midst of a variety of chores, from wringing towels into a washbasin to folding a sheet. Elizabeth stood by the headboard, draping a compress across Rebecca's forehead. Missus Skevold arrived with the pitcher of water. Molly spotted Ben and squealed in surprise. Phoebe turned and launched herself toward Ben, wrapping her arms around him.

"She's awake! Mommy woke when we heard the terrible racket! Did something explode, Daddy?"

The gaggle of ladies parted so that Ben could see his wife. Her eyes were open, and her complexion was as rosy as Miss Russell had suggested earlier that morning. Rebecca smiled up at him when Ben leaned over to kiss her forehead. Her head rested against a mound of pillows. "Thank God, you're well," he whispered. As he pressed his lips against her temple, he could not detect any fever.

"You, too. Our guests have been telling me about all the events that I've missed over the past day." She placed a hand on his wrist. "Will everyone be safe now?"

To Ben's dismay, Missus Russell jumped into the conversation. "What's happened? We heard the explosions, and Molly saw smoke come from the light house. Captain Swett told us that we were to stay up here until we were certain Green wasn't coming back for my Elizabeth or one of your daughters."

"I can't believe that evil man killed Mate Pendleton and Gerty," Missus Skevold said.

"Are we safe now?" Missus Russell asked.

"Yes, quite safe. Green is dead, and there's a Revenue Cutter anchored just offshore." Ben turned back to Rebecca. "The ship's doctor is coming ashore, and I'll ask him to come check on you."

"Oh, I believe she's going to be quite all right," Missus Russell observed. "We've just finished washing her and getting her dressed again. She tolerated that ordeal rather well, I'd say."

Molly came to stand beside her father. She rested her hand on his wrist. "What happened to Mister Green?"

Ben turned so that he could sit on the bedside and drew the girl into his arms. "When he came off the *Gideon* last night, he was carrying a large case of explosives." Ben spoke loud enough so that the women could hear the details from him just once. "After he threatened to take you, and then he murdered two men who had done nothing to harm him, I couldn't let him take those explosives onto another boat or into Rockland. I knew that he intended to hurt quite a lot of people. While he was in the light tower, his own explosives killed him."

"And good riddance," Missus Skevold muttered.

Ben was grateful that not one of the women asked for details of the explosions they had heard.

"It's true, then? This man killed two people in our home? And he threatened to take Molly?" Rebecca's face flushed, and she reached to pull Molly down to her side. With her other hand, she reached toward Phoebe. "I'm so sorry I wasn't there with you."

Ben rested a hand on his wife's cheek. "Be still now. They're quite safe." He kissed her forehead again and then hugged both his daughters. "I must go speak with the lieutenant. It may be possible to have the *Dallas* carry our guests into their next port of call."

Gently Ben extricated himself from his family's embrace and trod downstairs. He found the men seated around the kitchen table, drinking coffee. At the center of the table was a pile of four plates that had recently held their breakfasts. He pulled a chair over from the wall and sat near Myrick and Swett. The two sat opposite each other, reflecting the near polar differences in their carriage and character. Young and officious, Myrick sat erect in his chair. Without his high uniform hat, his face appeared angular. His muttonchops and hair were both well clipped back; his uniform was clean and recently pressed. Swett was stooped and rounded by age, with unruly hair and beard. His garments had seen hard use for years. The sole similarity the two shared was the apparent pursuit of a life at sea. Professor Russell sat at the table with the two mariners, sharing virtually nothing in common with these two men. Seamus stood in the kitchen trying to scrape from the skillets and pans enough remnants to call a breakfast while Tommy remained hard at work scrubbing the wood floor.

"Well, skipper, have you made arrangements with the lieutenant to discharge your passengers?" Ben asked.

"We're still negotiating. Still working out the finer details. Listen, there's plenty of fat in the skillet yet if you'd like me to fry up some bacon for you. I'm afraid we've used up all the eggs that were in the pantry."

"No, thank you. Just a little coffee, if I might. My stomach hasn't quite settled yet." Suddenly Ben felt Bosun sidle up next to him and lay its large furry head entirely across his lap. Ben stroked the Newfoundland's thick neck to comfort the animal. Ben thought it odd that Swett had not yet asked for the details of Green's death, or even inquired whether Green was dead. He concluded that Myrick had already shared this information.

"When the doctor comes ashore, I may take the duty boat out to the *Dallas*," Myrick said. "I'll explain to the captain what has happened. I'll ask whether he wants me to take statements from each of you as to what transpired overnight. His decision may rest with what Nolan, the ship's carpenter, finds in the way of damage to the structures."

Russell spoke. "Lieutenant Myrick, I'd be willing to assist with that inspection. I'm a professor of civil engineering."

"Thank you. I'll pass your offer onto Nolan." The lieutenant shifted in his seat to face Russell more directly. "Please don't be offended if Nolan declines. He is what the lads in the foc'sle call an ornery cuss."

At this juncture, Collins knocked on the kitchen door to announce the arrival of the cutter's surgeon and carpenter. Much like Ben's impression of Swett and Myrick together, these two could not have been more different. The crewman called Nolan was a tall, burly man, thick of waist, neck and arm. The wool coat he wore gaped open, with the buttons nearly two hands apart. The cotton jersey exposed under the jacket was stretched taut by his heft. Almost his physical opposite, the cutter's surgeon was a small man, in stature and girth. Doctor Josiah Satterlee was also surprisingly young; it struck Ben that the doctor might not yet need to shave daily. Ben directed Seamus to escort the carpenter through the light tower to examine the structure for damage from the explosions. The lieutenant asked the doctor whether he preferred to begin with the three dead men or the female patient. The question struck Ben as almost ludicrous on its face until he realized the officer's tone of voice was more obsequious in nature. As a third lieutenant, Myrick had no authority to direct Satterlee's activities, and this offer of options reflected the officer's thinly veiled resentment of that fact.

"We always treat the living before we examine the dead." Satterlee's icy response seemed intentionally dismissive, which Ben thought may have contributed in turn to Myrick's disdain.

Ben tried hard not to betray his misgivings at the doctor's youth; he would have preferred to deal with an experienced veteran of those army field hospitals where at least he knew every diagnosis came from the surgeon's often-bloody experience. Missus Skevold, who was back at the kitchen pump for another basin of water, led the doctor upstairs but soon returned with Ben's daughters.

Perhaps sensing Ben's unease, Myrick sought to reassure him. "I believe you can trust Doctor Satterlee. I worried myself when I first came aboard and met such a young man in that office. But I've observed him amputate crushed limbs, revive drowned men and even treat the moonblind."

"Moonblindness? What balderdash!" Russell said suddenly in raw disgust. "You can't seriously believe such a thing exists."

Before Myrick could adequately respond, Swett raised both palms toward Russell. "I don't want to tangle with you again, but until you've shipped 'round the world, you shouldn't question sailin' men. I've lost as much as half a crew to moonblink when we cross't the equator. On hot nights, men slept on deck. Soon they were blind when the moon rose. At day, perfect sight. But the moon stole their vision each sunset. When I's younger, I'd put a man in irons for shirking duty when they claimed to be struck blind. But I saw it so often, even among good mates, that I finally become convinced it's real."

"I've only observed the malady once," Myrick said, nodding in agreement. "Twelve men, including two midshipmen. I thought the skipper would have the crewmen flogged and the middies given extra watches. But instead, he listened to the doctor and told them all to stay below deck for five straight nights, dusk to dawn. Soon they all were hard at work again, every last man jack of them." Myrick related this story with a firmness that made clear he was growing impatient with Professor Russell.

Ben thought this was an excellent time to direct the conversation elsewhere. "Mister Myrick, do you think you'll be able to carry Captain Swett and his passengers into Rockland?

"I'll discuss the matter with the captain," Myrick said. "As I told to Captain Swett and Mister Russell, we've just come from Rockland. I understand that our orders take us up to Boston."

"Even if I offered to pay passage for my family into Bangor?" Russell asked.

Myrick's tone betrayed his exasperation. "As I've said, Mister Russell, a revenue cutter is not a vessel for hire. I strongly encourage you not to mention that notion to Captain Hodgson, if you have an opportunity to speak with him. I may be able to persuade the captain to return to Rockland or perhaps set you at Portland. I assure you he will not proceed Downeast when orders take us 180 degrees in the opposite direction. If you persist, you may find yourself and your family stranded on Sorrow Ledge until Mister Grindle is able to hail a packet ship, which may be several weeks away."

Belatedly Ben realized that this had been the topic of conversation while he had been upstairs with Rebecca. In the wickie's absence, his guest had seemingly pushed the lieutenant beyond his patience. He was grateful when Nolan returned to request assistance.

"Mister Myrick, sir, I guess I may need some help. I've been a ship's carpenter for ten years, but I'm no mason." As he spoke to the officer, Nolan stood at attention. His body remained still and erect, but his eyes roamed across the kitchen and finally came to focus on the pots and skillets that sat on the stove. By the clock, Ben could see that in all likelihood lunch was being served aboard the *Dallas* at that hour, and Nolan did not appear to be a man who missed many meals.

"At ease, Nolan," Myrick said, crisply. "What have you found so far?"

Nolan's posture relaxed further. He placed his hands on his hips and stood akimbo. "There are several shattered or cracked windows in the tower and this here passageway. I can cover those with wood until a glazier can come with new glass. Then I went up topside. I'm no small cargo, but I felt no movement in the stairs. I saw some running cracks in the tower walls, but I don't know if they threaten the structure itself or even if they are new. As I said, sir, I know wood; hulls, decks, and masts. Granite and mortar is beyond my ken."

Myrick turned to Russell. "If your offer stands, professor, we would appreciate your expertise in examining the tower. If there's any danger that the structure might fail, we'll need to inform the captain as well as the Light House Board."

Russell nodded solemnly. "I'll climb the tower to examine the cracks Mister Nolan found, but I believe it will be more important to survey the exterior." The professor turned to the light house keeper. "Do you have any method by which you might raise and lower me so I may examine the granite?"

Seamus spoke up from the kitchen where he was eating a late breakfast of last night's stew. "Aye, we can rig a boatswain's chair for you. Each window has eyebolts so that we can move you about as needed. Ben, would that be all right with you?"

"When I attempted to descend earlier, the whole tower was encased in ice from the storm. Between the warmer temperature and the explosions, that may not be much of a problem any longer." To tell the bitter truth, the wickie was not eager to have Russell inspect the tower before Ben had that opportunity himself. Ben knew that the granite blocks were unlikely to have been severely damaged by the blasts. Instead, any cracks would likely emerge in the mortar. Ben hoped that Portland cement was durable as advertised. If the tower had suffered significant harm, Ben understood his career would be at an end. Further, his family's residence on Sorrow Ledge would terminate abruptly with an eviction notice from the Office of the Fifth Auditor.

"Mister Myrick, I'd like to assist the wickie," Nolan said. "I've never seen a boatswain's chair used on a light tower before."

The lieutenant nodded in assent, and the three men – the engineer, the carpenter, and the junior wickie – began to don their winter garments. Ben went into the passageway where his foul weather gear was stored and returned with a pair of old brogues. He offered these to the professor.

"I believe these will provide better footing than your dress shoes. The ice is still quite bad today."

As if by instinct, Russell seemed poised to protest, but he looked first at his own feet and then at the footwear of the other two men. "Thank you. You're quite kind." He then knelt and quickly changed out of his own shoes.

When the ad hoc inspection crew had departed, Swett addressed Ben. "Do you have any sail cloth that I may use? We'll need shrouds for Pendleton and Gerty. I want to bury them at sea, if your skipper would allow that," he said to Myrick.

"I'm certain he'd grant that request. I'm certain as well that he would allow you to read the service over them."

"There's a cabinet full of canvas in the loft of the boathouse," Ben said. "Much of it was flotsam that I found along the shoreline. Living on an island, I try not to let things that we find go to waste. You're free to use as much as you need. On the workbench, you'll find my needles, a sail palm, and waxed twine. Would you bring canvas enough for three men? I've no place to bury Green, so he'll need to go to the deep with the others."

"Tommy, do you recall where you slept last night?" Swett turned so that he faced the young lad, still crouched on the floor and scouring the bloodstains on the wood in the parlor. "The wickie says there's a locker of canvas up there. Would you go up and get us enough to commit our shipmates to the deep? Enough for Green's sorry corpse, too. Remember to bring needles and twine from Ben's workbench, as well."

The remaining mate of the *Gideon* rose stiffly from his knees. The bruise on his face had only darkened over the past hours, and he seemed slightly unsteady on his feet. Still, he did as ordered and shuffled off toward the kitchen door, pausing only to get his black woolen jacket and pull on a blue watch cap. Swett stood to look through a north-facing window as Tommy made his way back to the boathouse. Then he settled back into his place and faced Myrick.

"Any chance, sir, that the *Dallas* has need for an able-bodied seaman?" Swett asked. "Tommy was mighty fond of Gerty. I worry that if he isn't occupied, if he dwells on these events too much, that he'll have a hard go of it. You know, idle hands."

As this conversation proceeded, Ben noticed that Hortence had come down the stairs into the kitchen, carrying a pitcher. When she saw the three men talking around the table, she suddenly turned and went back upstairs. Shortly, she was back with Elizabeth in tow, whispering instructions into her daughter's ear.

Myrick smiled and nodded toward the old skipper. "As it happens, we had two men desert the cutter when we were last in Portland. I'll discuss the matter with my captain." The lieutenant paused and gave Swett a look of consternation. "I'm afraid, though, that the billet for our sailing master is currently filled. I don't believe we could offer you any commission that meets your experience."

Swett settled back in his chair. His hands rested flat on his thighs. "I understand, lieutenant. I'm not asking anything for myself. You may drop me at any port where you call. I can manage again. You know, if I remember correctly, your *Dallas* was built by Fessenden in Portland."

"Yes, indeed," Myrick agreed. "She was commissioned in '74."

"Oh, Gawd. You say '74?" The skipper leaned forward and rested his forehead in the palm of one hand for several minutes. When he raised his head, he gave Ben and Myrick a look of sorrow. "It's worse than I even figured. That means I've been at sea ten times longer than your keel, and no doubt I was born when your main mast was just a seedling in the North Woods. The damnedest thing about living, gentlemen, is when you find your usefulness runs out before your breath."

At that moment, Ben saw Hortence standing nearby with her hand on Elizabeth's sleeve, waiting for an opportunity to swoop in and introduce her lovely and charming daughter to the young and handsome officer. He wondered briefly if this social activity would be entirely appropriate, given that two men had died in the same room within the past few hours. Yet he also recalled officers from both sides of the Mason-Dixon hosting dinners, banquets or balls for the sweet flowers of local society while the troops they commanded were engaged in mortal combat. More urgently, Ben worried for Swett's discouragement.

As the Russell women rushed into this moment of silence at the table, Ben stood and motioned for Swett to join him outdoors. With Bosun leaning itself tightly against its master's leg, the three went outside and stood on the stone threshold.

"You know, I hadn't thought that you would be in a hurry to leave Sorrow Ledge," Ben said. "As you can see, I've got quite a bit of work to get done. Repairs to the tower, clearing out dead birds, building a chicken coop, well, that alone will take several days. I may not be able to pay you in anything more than puffin feathers and an occasional lobster bisque, but the quiet may do you some small good."

Swett stared off toward the northeast horizon for several minutes. The high lingering clouds that trailed after the storm seemed to be scurrying away to catch up with their heftier nimbostratus cousins. The increasing sunshine ushered in the tinkle and trickle of melting ice. "You'll never guess how I met Pendleton," Swett said finally. "I was running a cargo of dry goods from New York to San Francisco. My first cruise as her skipper, and I had a lot to prove. I drove the boys hard, but we were becalmed for four days coming north from the Horn. We started to run short of supplies, so we rationed what we had. I could-n'na have been less popular if I'd been Lucifer himself. I knew there was a cunning few of them talking mutiny, till one day they all came up on deck. The leaders marched right up to the helm and demanded I surrender. My Gawd, they were surprised when I snapped a leather bullwhip around the neck on the closest one and pulled him over to where I could get my pistol into his ear. Another one rushed at me, but I clubbed him with the barrel of the gun and down he went. They were no more happy with me than before, but by Gawd, they feared me after that."

"Just you against the entire crew?" Ben asked. A wind off the sea put a chill into him. He now wished that he had stopped to pull on a coat before coming outside.

"Aye. Until I won over those two men I whipped. Big Red was a Swede with a hell of a temper. Snaring him with that whip got his attention that was for dammed sure. The other fellow I had to sew up. I'll tell you, though, that seeing all the blood streaming down his face set all those bastards back on their heels. After that, I couldn't of bought a better first mate with Montezuma's gold."

"I don't believe Pendleton was Swedish," Ben ventured. He ran his fingers through Bosun's thick ruff for warmth.

"Oh, no, Pendleton hated Big Red," Swett said this with a certain exasperation that his story was unclear. "It was Pendleton's head that I cracked open and then sewed back up again. Oh, he'd complain now and again that I ruined his face for the ladies, but I never noticed that any of the fillies ran from him once he'd flashed around his wages from a cruise."

Remembering a scar at Pendleton's hairline, Ben nodded. "The strangest circumstances can make the best friends. Sometime remind me, and I'll share with you how I came to know Seamus as well as I ever knew my own brothers."

Swett scanned the sky for a last time and said, "I suppose we should go back in and see whether the lieutenant has become betrothed to Miss Russell yet."

"She's a fine young lady," Ben observed. "I'm sure her parents want to assure a good match."

Abruptly Swett roared with laughter. "You missed quite a scene while you were out saving Maine from the Fenians. Young Tommy dared to ask Miss Elizabeth if she was well after what Green had done. Her parents swooped down on Tommy like he had thrown her down on the table and stripped her naked. Her mother hauled the lass upstairs straight away, while the professor tore into the boy like he was the last of the Molly Maguires."

The wickie smirked at Swett and chuckled. "Why just a few hours ago, you were lecturing me about Miss Russell's dignity and how Pendleton intended to keelhaul the lecherous Mister Green."

"Yes, yes, that's all true," Swett agreed with an air of bemusement. "But now we're talking about Tommy, who couldn't offend a church mouse with a fart. No doubt Miss Elizabeth would have given him the mitten in good time. But they didn't need to treat him like no mick."

As the pair turned to go into the kitchen, the sounds of hollering somewhere overhead interrupted their conversation. "Now, let me down six feet again," Russell shouted. He was sitting in a boatswain's chair, dangling about 20 feet below the peak of the light tower. Nolan stood on the catwalk, leaning over the rail to monitor the engineer's progress. At this instruction, the ship's carpenter raised the hailing tube and shouted into the open door of the cupola. "On the line, now. Lower away a fathom. Steady. Steady. Avast." Ben assumed that Seamus was inside the tower, handling the ropes and pulleys that controlled the seat. Russell looked to be handling the situation well, ably fending himself off the tower with his feet during his descent to the next level. At that distance, Ben could detect no hesitance in Russell's movements around the tower, nearly 50 feet above the ground.

Swett appeared to experience a surprise like Ben's own. "You know, as long as I've been at sea, I hate going aloft. Full sail or bare poles, doesn't matter a whit," Swett said as he watched Russell adroitly move and swing around the tower. "For the past three days, I've thought that man a coward."

Ben knew of nothing to say so said nothing. The two men watched Russell on the light tower for several minutes. At last Swett spoke. "I'll go help Tommy prepare Pendleton and Gerty for the deep."

"Yes, and I must speak to the ship's surgeon about Rebecca."

Swett nodded in silence and walked toward where Tommy squatted on the frozen rock between the two cold corpses. Ben looked up and watched as Russell moved to and fro across the tower's face, knowing that the report the engineer provided to Captain Hodgson would go a long way in determining Ben's fate. Then he went inside to learn Rebecca's prognosis.

CHAPTER 13

*I*nside the living quarters, Ben was surprised to find Myrick sitting alone at the kitchen table. The Russell women had come to pay their social call on him and were gone already. Satterlee had not yet returned from his examination of Rebecca. By the sounds emanating from above, Molly and Phoebe were together in their room, though they seemed somewhat subdued compared to their usual exuberance, singing and role-playing.

Myrick greeted Ben by raising a mug. "I am curious, sir, whatever inspired you to load your light house like a cannon and touch it off with a flare?"

Ben brought the coffee pot from the stove. "Something that the army lieutenant who built this light station told me when he designed our fuel house." He described Clough's concerns over explosives and his solution. "Not something I quite understood until this morning."

"Fascinating. Quite ingenious." Myrick sipped from his mug and reflected quietly. "What would you have done if your assistant had not heard our bell sounding?"

"Captain Swett and I would have rowed him halfway to Rockland and then tried to find a way to subdue him," Ben explained. "Or perhaps more likely to kill him."

"What do you think he was after?"

"Green constantly spoke of reaching Augusta. There was something else afoot that drove him to want to reach the Capitol so fiercely. The Russell family mentioned that Green complained about Governor Chamberlain preferring Scandinavian immigrants to Maine over Irish."

"Perhaps he planned some strike while Chamberlain is dealing with these election issues."

Ben nodded. "That's the skipper's guess. I don't know how we'll ever be sure." Ben sat forward in his seat and spoke quietly. "I know you haven't spoken with Captain Hodgson yet, but I'm wondering what you think the prospects are that he will carry the *Gideon's* passengers into port. If I'm to host five souls for any great length of time, I'll need to look to the food we've laid in for the winter."

Myrick leaned toward Ben and lowered his voice as well. "As soon as I have the doctor's report, I'll ride out to speak with the captain. My guess, just my guess mind you, is that Captain Hodgson will choose to stay our course. He may agree to carry the lot into Portland, but as you say, five people can eat a lot of food. They aren't in any immediate distress now, so the skipper may decide to let them remain your problem."

"Thank you, sir. I appreciate your candor. I believe I should prepare to feed five extra mouths. Perhaps for several weeks, just as you told Russell and Swett." Ben rose and walked to the foot of the steps in the kitchen. In a raised voice, he called up the stairwell. "Molly, would you please bring your sister and our guests downstairs?"

Within the matter of a minute or less, he heard overhead the sounds of chairs scraping across the wooden floors and footfalls heading toward the stairwell. Soon the full contingent of women on the island, minus only Rebecca, mustered in the kitchen. Ben was relieved to see that they were mostly smiling, despite their state of flux and his urgent summons.

"Ladies, God sometimes leaves gifts upon this rock. Providence has now given us a blessing to help in the event we have extra mouths to feed for the next few days or weeks. Missus Russell, I would be grateful if you would be so kind as to continue looking after my wife.

The rest of you I'd like to ask you to please dress as warmly as you can and follow me. We're going to gather fowl."

While the women and girls tied and buttoned themselves into their winter gear, Doctor Satterlee came down from his examination of Rebecca and motioned for Ben to join him and Lieutenant Myrick in the parlor. When Molly started to follow him, Ben stopped to instruct both her and Phoebe to get the ashbins from outside and fill them from the furnaces and stoves in the kitchen. Then they should spread the ashes around the quarters and the light tower to help provide traction on the slick ice. Quickly the girls were off to do this chore as their father directed.

Satterlee rested on the settee opposite the rocking chair where Myrick waited. Ben settled next to the young doctor, who smiled when Ben sat down.

"How is my wife, sir?"

The ship's surgeon leaned forward and, with his eyes closed, began a clinical recitation of his examination. "I believe you have no reason to worry. As you doubtless know, there are many dangers associated with a fall in the winter. Broken limbs, disorientation, frostbite. I have examined your wife thoroughly and found no such symptoms." Satterlee looked up at Ben with opened eyes. "Missus Russell was present the entire time, I assure you. I understand that she was a nurse in the war." Eyes shut again; he continued, "I found bruising on the patient's hips and shoulders, suggesting she fell hard. I am most concerned about a minute amount of crusted blood that I found in her hair just behind her left ear. However, I was unable to find any corresponding wound on her scalp. Because she is both awake and alert, I don't believe it merits shaving her head to find the source of so little blood."

Ben smiled at this suggestion. "That alone would give her apoplexy. And could end rather badly for you as well, I fear."

Satterlee opened his eyes and nodded, smiling at Ben. "Yes, your wife is a lovely woman, and I would not wish to be responsible for either disfiguring her or causing her any more consternation."

"Did she break any bones when she fell?"

The doctor's eyes closed again as he began speaking. "No, I didn't observe any sign of that. Her limbs are straight and responsive. Other than the bruises I mentioned, I don't see any sign of injury to her body. She complained more of my examination than any pain. I believe she'll be up walking before long." When he finished, Satterlee opened his eyes and looked between Ben and Myrick. "I have asked Missus Russell to give your wife some soup to bolster her strength. I think it best that she doesn't get up and about for a few hours yet. Any questions, gentlemen?"

Ben stood and extended his hand toward the doctor. "Thank you for your kind attentions to Rebecca. I know she can be somewhat difficult if she feels her privacy breached. I'm certain you'll find your remaining examinations on the island much less adversarial." After shaking hands with Satterlee, Ben put his cap back on his head. "If you'll excuse me, gentlemen, I need to put the ladies to work."

By this time, the women were dressed in their outer garments, though Missus Russell fussed with the ribbons of Elizabeth's velvet bonnet. His oilskin jacket being closest at hand, Ben pulled that on though he knew it would not be as warm as his wool coat. He didn't plan to remain outside for long before he went up the tower to talk with Mister Russell about the tower's condition. He walked into the kitchen, where he raised his voice to get the attention of the ladies. "I have a crucial task to ask of the lot of you. In the event the Revenue Cutter is unable to transport all of you off the island, we'll need to have extra food to carry us through to when we can hail another vessel. As I said, God has provided for us. I need all of you to work together to sort through the dead birds that struck at the light tower last night. They are mostly in a heap that rings the base of the tower. From what I saw, I believe we may eat rather well over the next few days. Any questions?"

Elizabeth spoke up first, her tone betraying an obvious disgust with the assignment. "You expect us to pick through the dead birds for our dinner?"

Missus Skevold interrupted before Ben could begin to respond. "Mmm, I don't know but what we'll find something marvelous out there. Back in the Old World, many birds make quite a fabulous dish, ja? When he was a boy, my father traveled through France with his own father. One night dinner was a small plucked bird seasoned in brandy and served piping hot; the whole ortolana but the head just popped into the mouth. He'd always said it was the most wondrous thing he'd ever tasted."

Ben quickly saw that the imagery of this unusual delicacy did not sit well with either of the Russell women. Both stared at Missus Skevold in wide-eyed horror, and Elizabeth was growing rather pale. He decided to take back charge of the conversation. "Well, I'm sure we won't gather any birds here that a French chef would find of interest. I saw mallards, mergansers, ducks and grouse, along with gulls and puffins," Ben recalled. "You'd need an enormous mouth to chew a whole duck at one time." He hoped this jesting would alleviate the ladies' obvious disgust.

"Puffin, now there's a tasty bird," Missus Skevold continued as if Ben had not spoken at all and equally unaware of the blanched faces of the ladies from New York City. "I've eaten their breast meat raw. Also, I've heard of some who eat the heart while it's still warm."

"Missus Skevold! If you please!" Ben said, nodding his head forcefully in the direction of the other survivors. "Like counting chicks before they hatch, perhaps we should not eat the birds before we know what bounty we have." He turned toward his daughters. "Girls, fetch the bushel baskets that your mother uses for the wash and gather up whatever the women select. Miss Elizabeth, would you help Missus Skevold sort through the pile? Look for woodland birds. Ducks, pheasant, and grouse have the most breast meat. I believe there could be more than two hundred birds in the pile. We'll take the most edible and offer the rest to the cook on the *Dallas* for broths and soups."

As the women filed out the kitchen door toward the light tower, Ben saw on the face of Miss Elizabeth a look of apparent dread. At that moment, Myrick came into the kitchen where Ben was pouring a final indulgence of coffee before following the ladies outside. "Are circumstances really so dire that you may not eat unless they harvest enough carrion?" Myrick asked. "Should I ask the captain for some victuals out of the stores? We just loaded supplies to last several weeks."

"No need for that, but thank you kindly for the offer. We might as well eat the birds. It isn't as though I could dig a pit and shovel the carcasses into it."

"You haven't a single spade on the whole island?" Myrick asked in astonishment.

"The problem isn't lack of a shovel; it's the lack of dirt. Sorrow Ledge is just a rock thrust up out of the ocean. Well, that is, apart from the few barrels of soil I hauled out from Rockland so that my wife may cultivate a little garden. However, it appears all that washed away in the high tide last night." Ben stepped closer to Myrick and dropped his voice to a conspiratorial whisper. "Besides, as an officer, I'm certain you know the danger of idle hands. My Rebecca says it's doubly true of women. They start to gossip, and soon there'll be hell to pay." Ben started for the door that Molly had closed only moments before. "However, if you could convince your skipper to part with a barrel or two of fresh water that would be something that may come in handy."

Myrick appeared puzzled by the request. "Even after yesterday's snowfall, you fear your cistern will run short of water?" He sat back at the dining room table.

Ben nodded in affirmation. "I've learned from times when my wife's sister Anna comes to visit that just one extra woman can double the amount of water used each day. They always find something to clean or cook that needs extra water. Now it may be that Anna is simply auditioning her housekeeping skills for the benefit of Seamus, on whom I think she is sweet. But I fear that rationing will do no good. On your return visit, you'll likely find six immaculately clean women, the quarters all spick-and-span, but four men died of thirst."

"Come, sir, you exaggerate," Myrick chided.

"I was infantry for two years," Ben explained to the officer. "And you're accustomed to life aboard a ship full of men. In all your time at sea, have you ever encountered a sailor you thought was overly fastidious? Unless you were putting into port for a liberty call?"

"You mean day-to-day, on a routine patrol? No, I'd say the men are often more forgetful of their daily routines while underway than normal manners would suggest."

"Now tell me, sir, have you ever encountered a frowzy widow?"

The question appeared to present Myrick a puzzle. "When you put it that way, then, no, not that I recall, no." The officer pondered this for a moment or two. "Perhaps I should ask the captain if we can spare three barrels. We've just replenished, and you have no idea how long you'll have the extra company."

Ben smiled at the officer. "Let me see if I understand our bargain correctly then. You'll inquire with the captain on behalf of delivering the *Gideon's* passengers into Rockland or Portland. You'll also ask whether he'd be willing to take young Tommy aboard as an able-bodied seaman. Lastly, you'll see if he'll part with several barrels of fresh water. In return, I will do my best to convince Rebecca to share her bisque recipe. However, no promises on that score. Does that about summarize all that we've discussed?"

"You said you were infantry, but are you sure you weren't a commissary officer at some time? I've no doubt you'd press the devil himself to serve lemonade." Myrick clapped his hat on his head, settled it in place with a solid tug and then gathered his notebook and pencil. "I'll go out to the *Dallas* now. I should be back ashore before Doctor Satterlee finishes with his post mortems of the dead men."

Just as Ben began to thank Myrick for interceding with the captain, a chorus of shrill cries arose outside. The two men rushed out together to see what had alarmed the women in their harvest duties.

CHAPTER 14

"*A* rat!" Phoebe screamed. "Daddy, I nearly touched a huge rat!" She raced toward him and flung herself at his trunk.

He hugged the girl to comfort her. "Where was it?" Ben asked.

"It was burrowed under the carcasses," Molly said. "I think we woke it."

"Did anyone see where it went?" Ben asked the ladies.

All the women pointed in unison at the crumpled chicken coop. Looking around, Ben saw that the remaining men had also come out to see what caused the commotion. Captain Swett and Tommy stood near the corner of the quarters where they had been sewing up the funeral shrouds. The carpenter and engineer were high up on the catwalk of the light house. The young doctor had just emerged from the tower's door and appeared to be getting his bearings.

"Are rats particularly uncommon on your island?" Myrick asked in confusion.

"Fortunately, yes." Ben walked in the direction where the rat had gone. "May I borrow your pistol, lieutenant?"

"Well, actually, no," Myrick whispered. "If the captain ever heard that I'd surrendered my weapon to a civilian, he'd bring me up on charges."

"You think Nolan would report you?" Ben asked.

Myrick responded with a quiet murmur. "With Doctor Satterlee standing not far off my starboard stern, I'm certain the captain would know of it almost as soon as you pulled the trigger. However, I assure you that I'm a reasonably good marksman."

"Then stand back and keep a clear view. I'll try to drive it out for you to get a good shot."

The lieutenant drew his weapon from its holster. He cocked the trigger quietly while Ben moved slowly to the left. With the thrust of a leg, Ben pushed the remains of the wooden chicken coop onto its side. The shed tumbled over slowly, gaining little momentum as it fell, as though the muck and feathers had greater tenacity than the nails themselves. When it finally crashed to the ground, a solitary brown rat jumped free and fled, loping awkwardly on the icy rocks. The lieutenant tracked the creature with the sight on his barrel. When the rodent paused on its rear haunches about three rods away, Myrick fired. The rat collapsed under a small cloud of blood, and another shriek of surprise arose from the chorus of women.

Ben walked over to the lieutenant. "A very handsome shot, sir." He extended his hand and lowered his voice so no one observing them could hear their conversation. "I think the young doctor may now have cause to think twice before he challenges you."

The lieutenant scoffed at this suggestion. "I believe you're thinking of the Navy back in Decatur's times. A Revenue Marine officer who fights a duel today won't be an officer much longer, no matter how much of a cretin the foe was."

"Perhaps. However, in my experience, a man with such good aim generally garners a rather wide berth." Ben waved at Satterlee, who stood near the base of the light tower. The doctor began to walk toward where Ben stood.

"I don't believe you know the doctor well at all," Myrick observed quietly. "I'll wager he'll offer some pithy comment about this scene. He's not a man given to holding his tongue."

Satterlee soon validated the officer's prediction.

As the doctor approached, he clapped his hands together at a slow, mocking pace. "Mister Myrick, I am quite astonished by your marksmanship in this war on rodents," the young doctor exclaimed. "You could well be the subject of Ned Buntline's next dime novel."

The wickie watched the officer's face redden, but he could not discern whether it was embarrassment or anger. Ben recognized the need to defuse the mounting tension, but he also understood the urgency to get the women done with their task before more rats emerged to frighten them or compete for the bird carcasses.

"Lieutenant, would you allow your men to help the women gather the birds they have sorted and get them into the kitchen?" Ben asked as he walked toward the tower. "Doctor, once the women are inside, can we remove Green's corpse from the tower so Captain Swett can prepare him for his voyage to the deep?"

Myrick did not reply directly to Ben but instead called out instructions for Nolan to muster the landing party. As the men approached, the women seemed only too eager to abandon their unsavory task. Molly and Phoebe stood, and both jumped over the pile of birds that surrounded them. Elizabeth helped Missus Skevold get to her feet.

Ben began to bark orders like a boatswain's mate preparing to get a ship underway. "Phoebe, please go to the boathouse and fetch a dozen burlap sacks. Molly, let's get those birds into the baskets and into the kitchen. Be sure to keep Bosun away from the carcasses. Missus Skevold, would you kindly supervise the plucking of these birds? Stuff all the feathers into the sacks; they'll make the best feather tick Rebecca could imagine." Ben then raised his voice so that the men in their various situations could hear him. "Gentlemen! I'll need your help. We must get the three corpses onto to the *Dallas*. And if the ship's cook has any interest, we'll wrap up the remaining birds for his stews and stocks. Then I'll need your assistance with a bit of a hunting expedition."

With the men and women working as teams, little time passed before the pick of the litter selected by the women was stacked bushel by bushel in the kitchen. Bosun watched this operation with great fascination. Missus Skevold assumed command of the actual plucking and dissection, carefully explaining to Molly and Phoebe the delicacy of gamebird preparation, much to the girls' mutual chagrin. Both Phoebe and Molly had been cooking at their mother's side for years, gamebirds or not. Their experience was mostly with various species of fish and shellfish Ben and Seamus harvested from the waters around the Ledge. While the women were busy inside the quarters with the dead birds, Nolan and Seamus carried the carcass of Green out of the tower and laid him alongside his murdered victims. Their skipper and mate were loath to prepare the man who murdered their shipmates for the deep, so Ben knelt to the task. Behind Ben stood a choir of seven mariners, from Lieutenant Myrick down to Tommy, the deck-hand. All damned Green's murderous ways in an impious chorus. As he sewed closed the shroud with sail needle, the wickie felt his rheumatic joints stiffen. The longer Ben hunched over sewing closed the canvas tomb around the Irishman, the more painful his struggles became apparent to the others. First Tommy came to his assistance, shoving at the base of the needle threaded with a long, waxed thread against the sail palm wrapped around his hand. As Ben continued to struggle, Swett also knelt on his other side and helped to draw the needle through the canvas. Nolan carried over a pair of rocks that once weighted down the covering of Rebecca's garden to now anchor the dead man to his place in his watery grave. Before long, Ben stood back to let the others finish the work. Then with the respect due, the three corpses were loaded onto the small boat for transportation to the cutter.

"Mister Myrick, I understand you planned to visit with the captain, but I wonder if I might have your assistance a little longer before you return to the cutter." Ben turned to the ship's surgeon and asked, "And I wonder, sir, if you have any skill with a weapon? Either rifle or sidearm?"

"I'm no Myrick, but I have a good eye and a steady hand," Satterlee quipped and chuckled. The doctor laughed alone. His wisecrack did not seem to sit at all well with the other *Dallas* crewmen who served under Myrick. They knew better than to make merry at the lieutenant's expense. Satterlee's mirth was short-lived, and his face grew red. He coughed. "I suppose a pistol would be best."

Ben chose to ignore Satterlee's gaffe. Instead, he knew that time was critical for what he yet needed to accomplish before sunset. "Mister Myrick, would you allow Collins and your men to take the dead back to the *Dallas*? If we are fortunate, I believe we'll finish by the second bell of the dog watch."

"What matter requires our urgent assistance, and also the use of weapons?" Satterlee asked, with a bemused smile on his lips.

Ben felt rather pleased with this turn of events. "As you suggested just a short while ago, we must now wage war on rodents."

CHAPTER 15

*O*nce the small boat and its solemn cargo had departed Sorrow Ledge en route to the *Dallas*, Ben turned to Captain Swett. "Skipper, did you know that the *Gideon* carried rats?"

Suddenly the old sailor roared with laughter. "Of course. My Gawd, man, what did you expect? We moored at Boston's North End for more than a week. I ain't seen a hull yet come away from that pier without some new conscripts."

"Have you a guess as to how many?" Ben asked.

Swett chuckled again as he stepped closer to where Ben and the officers from the *Dallas* stood on the rocky coastline. "I didn't list any rat's name on the ship's manifest, if that's what you're asking."

Ben took a deep breath to compose himself. He did not necessarily expect any sailors to understand what concerned him. Men who lived on ships too long became accustomed to a wide range of vermin in an assortment of sizes, from lice to wharf rats. "I don't want to make too much of this problem, but a breeding pair of rats could be a disaster on this island. They have no predators here. No cats, no raccoons, no weasels. Trust me that our dog isn't suddenly going to acquire a taste for rat meat."

The skipper continued in his humorous vein. "What harm could a couple of rats do to a granite tower?"

"During all your whaling cruises to the Bering Sea, did you ever stop at Rat Island?" Ben asked.

"Well, no, there's nothing on that island but ..." Swett stopped and looked at Ben in surprise.

"Excuse me, gentlemen, I'm not familiar with an island by that name," Myrick said. "Could it have another name on the charts that the Revenue Marine uses?"

"No, lieutenant, there's no reason you'd be familiar with it. Rat Island is in the Bering, west of Dutch Harbor." As he explained this to Myrick, Ben kept his eyes steadily on Swett. "My father knew it from his whaling trips to Point Barrow. He'd heard that a Japanese ship ran aground there in about the 1780s. The ship's complement of rats got onto the island. When the Russians arrived 40 years later, the rats had taken over. They ate all the bird eggs; they killed the young of every other living thing. My father's ship would anchor off, and the crew went ashore in small boats to kill rats to improve their gunning skills."

Swett was visibly irritated. "Ben, I don't understand all this yip about rats. My *Gideon*'s not the first keel broken on Sorrow Ledge."

"There's been no wreck here in 20 years. Before that my father killed any rats. He was an old whaling man, so he managed to get a ratting dog. He set it free on the island at nights." He thought about his siblings confined to the quarters all night to keep them safe from the snarling beast.

Myrick seemed inclined to agree with Swett. "Let the rats kill a few birds. From what I see, fewer birds around this island may not be such a bad harbinger. So much less chance of birds striking the light beacon."

"Those birds aren't from Sorrow Ledge; most of those carcasses are woodland birds. We have some puffin nests on the north end of the island, but there aren't many. Birds in a blind flight come from miles off. Now, I'm more worried about us."

"I believe I'm beginning to see Mister Grindle's concern," Doctor Satterlee said. "Rats procreate every other month, as much as a dozen at a time. In a year, he'll likely have hundreds of rats on the ledge. Such a population could…"

Ben interrupted sharply. "I'll tell you what they could do. They'll eat the eggs and then our chickens. We won't be able to grow a garden. Then when they get hungry, they'll hunt out our food. They can chew through wood and metal. Nothing on the island will be safe."

"I'm sorry, Ben," Swett said this, but his voice did not sound apologetic in any way that Ben could discern. "I'm sorry I wrecked my ship on this damned ledge and infected it with this plague. I'm sorry I agreed to bring Green down east. I'm sorry two good men got shot to death for nothing but a mick's senseless hate. And I'm sorry for the damned rats." The skipper turned to stride away in anger, but as the five men on the strand looked after him, they were shocked to see the defiance in his squared shoulders slump into sobs.

Ben took Swett's surviving crewman by the arm. "Tommy, take your captain up to my quarters. Ask Molly to show you the shelf in the pantry where I have a wee bit of John Barleycorn stowed away. Pour a mug halfway and put a little color in the mug with coffee. Maybe he'll sleep then." Ben turned to the remaining men; his assistant keeper, the Revenue Marine officer, and a ship's surgeon. "Please forgive Captain Swett. I'm sure we've all been in a place where we didn't know how we might ever get home again."

In surprising harmony, all three said, "Amen."

CHAPTER 16

*T*hen began the most curious spectacle on Sorrow Ledge that Ben, as its longest surviving inhabitant, could recall. Carrying cooking pots from the kitchen and hammers from the boathouse, the two wickies began at the southeasternmost extremity of the island and progressed in a northwesterly direction. As the western horizon rose toward the sun, this approach would put the intended targets in silhouette against the sunset. Whooping and whistling as they walked, they beat a steady rattle, creating a terrifying ruckus. The two officers from the Revenue Cutter *Dallas* walked behind them. Myrick strode with his pistol at the ready about five feet behind Seamus. Doctor Satterlee carried one of Ben's 1861 Navy pistols raised at his shoulder, so the barrel pointed safely skyward. In addition to making a terrible ruckus, Ben and Seamus served as the official spotters when the din scared up an enemy.

"Off the port bow! On the flat ledge!" Ben yelled.

On a massive tide-washed rock with a flat surface as large as Rebecca's kitchen table, a bulky rat was crouched over the broken shells dropped by seabirds. The doctor stepped past his hunting guide and leveled the barrel of the Colt pistol. Both wickies paused their cacophonous racket. Satterlee pulled the trigger, and the four men cheered to see the vermin caught full on and hurled against a boulder. The animal appeared to struggle to move. For good measure, the doctor added a second round into the wretched corpse.

"Nice shot, doctor," Ben said.

"Very well done. Looks about 30 feet distance. A rather small target for that range." Myrick's tone was not ironic, which surprised Ben, given the doctor's earlier mockery.

Satterlee glanced at the officer. "Why, thank you, lieutenant. You're most kind."

Ben struck his steel pot with the hammer and moved out with Seamus only a step or two behind. They proceeded only a few paces when Myrick observed a gray rodent passing between the assistant's quarters and the granite blast berm around the fuel house. The men stood nearly 15 yards from this target. Myrick raised his weapon, then paused and knelt to brace his arm on his knee. The wickies stopped their hammering. Myrick fired. The impact sent the rodent tumbling snout over tail nearly a fathom.

"Lieutenant, I believe you've fully doubled my distance," Satterlee observed. "Well done, indeed."

Not waiting for this round of congratulations to end, Ben immediately set off again, and Seamus remained apace, as they continued up the slope that led toward the light tower, along the same path that Ben had carried Rebecca on the previous evening. Their noisemaking brought faces to the windows of the keeper's quarters. The hunting party was also watched closely by the five-man crew of the small boat returning from *Dallas*, who gazed in obvious puzzlement at the source of such clangor and gunfire. The boatswain steered the boat into the cove on the northwest side of the island and moored at the small pier where the island's supplies came ashore.

Seamus spotted the next critter scurrying away from the wrecked chicken coop, its long tail glinting in the sunlight. Myrick's shot struck the rat near to the same location as his first victim earlier in the afternoon. Beyond the coop, Myrick killed another along the stone wall at the rear of the boathouse.

"This hardly seems fair, Grindle," the young doctor said with a chuckle. "You've arranged to have all the targets on Lieutenant Myrick's side of the island."

No sooner had he said this than a furry target appeared along the west wall of the keeper's house and then another chance under the sluiceway that carried wastewater and sewage away from the living quarters. The surgeon proved himself quite capable with his pistol. Again, Myrick was effusive in his congratulations to Satterlee. The two men shook hands before they headed off behind the keeper's quarters toward the northwest side of the ledge. The shootists claimed one more kill apiece before this team reached the high tide mark. The harvest of nine vermin pleased Ben, though there was no way to be sure whether the *Gideon* carried a complement of a dozen or a hundred.

The lieutenant and the doctor were in high spirits when Ben released them from the hunt. They strolled together back toward the quarters, recalling each other's exploits as though they had been shooting bison on the Western Plains. Seamus watched them go, shaking his head in confusion at the sight.

"Two hours ago, I worried they might come to blows," he observed.

"As did I," Ben replied. "Nothing quite brings men together like a little hunt. Even the worst squabbles amongst the men back in the 2nd were settled and forgotten if we got the opportunity to kill a few rebels." For all the truth of it, he never fully understood why that was so.

CHAPTER 17

$\mathcal{A}$s Ben and Seamus arrived at the doorstep to the quarters, they found Myrick and Satterlee engaged in a covert conversation with the boatswain. The wickies passed by quickly to go indoors, careful to give the Revenue Marine men their privacy. Suddenly Myrick called to Ben.

"Just a moment, if you please," the lieutenant said. "As I mentioned to you earlier, I will be visiting the *Dallas* now, to discuss those subjects that we talked about earlier."

"I appreciate anything that your captain can do on our behalf," Ben said. "I haven't yet been able to ask Rebecca about that recipe, but I will soon."

"Thank you. I'll report as soon as I return from the cutter. May not be until the morning."

Inside the quarters, the two wickies discovered a hive of bustling activity. Missus Skevold was in the kitchen, skinning a duck with a long-bladed scaling knife. Beside her were piled four other carcasses that she had already denuded. All the while she shouted instructions to Elizabeth and Hortense who were at the kitchen table preparing to hang a dozen dead pheasants in the pantry. Some birds cooked better with the skin intact, and Ben knew that plucking was easier after aging the birds a few days. Molly and Phoebe was dashing here and there on errands for the ladies; fetching twine, filling water buckets, tending the stove and furnace, shooing the dog away from the puddle of bird blood accumulating around Missus Skevold's boots. Ben was glad to see the girls being so helpful with preparing and cooking the woodland birds, a rare sight on Sorrow Ledge because of the distance to the nearest forest. Rebecca had taught their daughters how to cook coot to be edible, despite the terrible reputation the birds had acquired as being tougher to prepare than an ax head. A common Maine recipe suggested boiling a coot in a pot alongside a brick; the coot was done when the cook could stick a fork into the brick.

In the entrance to the parlor, Tommy knelt once again, hard at work holystoning the bloodstained puncheon wood floor by hand. Nearby Captain Swett rested in the rocker, his chin firmly planted on his chest. Earlier the old man had swallowed a liberal dose of Balm O'Gilead, a conventional treatment in the State of Maine for nearly any ailment including cuts, coughs, colds, and catarrh. At a small table in the back corner, Professor Russell was writing a document, with Nolan nearby, leaning forward to offer comments. Ben harbored no doubt that this was their report to Captain Hodgson on the state of the light tower. He watched the two men draft their statement until a subtle motion overhead caught his eye. From the top of the stairs, Rebecca descended slowly, one hand on the banister and the other prodding at her unruly hair. Ben went to meet her.

"Look there, an angel descending from above," he whispered when she reached the bottom step.

Rebecca shoved at his shoulder playfully. "Well, move and let me get out of her way then." She wore a gray wool dress with a tall collar around her throat and wide cuffs at her wrists. The hem of her skirt brushed the floor. Her auburn hair hung loosely down over her shoulders, which was a rare style for her. She almost always wore her hair in a long braid or coiled on the back of her head. "I hope this old drape doesn't look too hideous. I can't seem to get warm."

Just as Ben reached to embrace her, he was abruptly knocked aside. Bosun shoved its way between them and stepped up with its front paws on the bottom stair, straining to get to Rebecca. Its attentions left swaths of white slobber up to the waistline of her dress. From snout to tail, the dog's entire body wiggled with joy.

"There's my Bosun," Rebecca squealed in an exaggerated tone of delight. "You're my furry hero, aren't you? Just my best dog ever."

"Biggest dog ever," Ben quipped. The Newfoundland's thick tail whacked Ben hard across his thigh as if in reprimand. "It's not as though *it* carried you home," Ben said, a clear pique in his voice. "It proved to be quite an obstacle."

"Don't be jealous of the dog. You know I prefer you, but the dog works for scraps," she said with a slight twitter.

"I'm relieved to see your memory is preserved. Aren't I just a wee bit heroic?"

"Why certainly!" She leaned across the dog and gave Ben a quick peck on his unscarred cheek. "Perhaps I'll make a fuss over you some-time," she whispered into his good ear.

Their dalliance ended when the girls arrived on the quick step to greet their mother. Ben stepped away, and even Bosun fell back at the crush of Molly and Phoebe wrapping themselves around Rebecca. The dog was thwarted in its efforts to insert itself into their embrace. Instead, it settled its haunches heavily on Ben's feet and leaned back firmly against its master's thighs. Ben ran a hand through the tangled mess behind the dog's long earflap.

"Sorry, Bosun, that's just the natural pecking order in a woman's affection. Daughters, then dog. However, at least you still outrank a mere groom."

With nary a glance in her groom's direction, Rebecca went off as the girls took her in tow to meet the *Gideon* passengers and the crews of both ships and see the work underway in the kitchen. Apart from Doctor Satterlee, she had not yet met any of the menfolk. Although Ben knew she would be polite to the sailors, he also had lived with his wife long enough to understand that her primary concern was what these strange women were doing in her kitchen. As protective of her galley as any lobsterman of his pots, Rebecca was wary when even her own sister Anna brewed a pot of coffee to carry up to the watchstander in the tower during her visits to Sorrow Ledge. As Ben eventually came to realize that these servings of coffee never reached the tower cupola while he was on duty, he began to wonder whether Rebecca's concern was for the sanctity of her kitchen or rather the chastity of her only sibling. That was a conversation Ben chose never to pursue with either sister or Seamus.

Russell and Nolan stood to greet Rebecca and introduce themselves. Even Tommy got to his feet and stepped around the dark stain on the floor to meet her. Swett continued to snore gently, even when Bosun nuzzled his cheek. The ladies of the *Gideon* nodded salutations but did not pause in their tasks to make any further fuss at Rebecca's arrival in the kitchen. Their industriousness appeared to impress her because she watched without comment or criticism. Ben knew this silence was a struggle for his wife, and he admired the fortitude displayed in her restraint. While the girls returned to bestead the women, Bosun settled near the hearth and yawned expansively. As she helped to string the partridges, Elizabeth hummed a song that Ben did not recognize.

"Is that tune popular back in New York?" Rebecca asked.

"Quite so," Elizabeth replied. "It has such a charming sentiment."

"Elizabeth, let her hear the words," Hortense said. "She has such a lovely voice. I don't hear it hardly ever often enough."

The daughter blushed at her mother's remarks but did not balk long at the suggestion. Ben soon agreed that Elizabeth's voice was one of the loveliest he had ever heard. She sang loudly enough to rouse Swett where he sat in the parlor.

"Are you tired of me my darling?
Did you mean those words you said
That has made me yours forever
Since the day that we were wed?"

Ben slipped his right arm around Rebecca's waist and turned her toward him. He caught her left hand in his own and began to sway her body gently. She smiled as she lifted her skirt with her free hand.

"Tell me could you live life over
Would you make it otherwise
Are you tired of me my darling?
Answer only with your eyes."

With a little pressure of his hand on the small of her back, he swung her slowly around. She released the gray skirt and pressed the delicate fingers of her right hand against her forehead above her closed eye. "Ben," she whispered.

"Do you ever rue the springtime?
Since we first each other met
How we spoke in warm affection
Words my heart can ne'er forget."

"Oh, figglestits." Rebecca stumbled against him unsteadily. "Ben, dy wed jurts so." With his arm still around her waist, he waltzed her one final turn toward the bench by the hearth then lowered her gently. As she settled in repose, her eyes closed.

PART II

Pennsylvania
July 1863

Here in this little Bay,
Full of tumultuous life and great repose,
Where, twice a day,
The purposeless, glad ocean comes and goes,
Under high cliffs, and far from the huge town,
I sit me down.
For want of me the world's course will not fail;
When all its work is done, the lie shall rot;
The truth is great, and shall prevail,
When none cares whether it prevail or not.

— *Coventry Patmore*

CHAPTER 1

<img_1> en was an early arrival at the field hospital that sweltering July afternoon.

When the 20th was pressed to defend a Pennsylvania hillock, Ben was given one of their newer .57 caliber Enfield rifles for which the prior owner abruptly had no further use. Ben had fired not more than two dozen shots before the breech of his newly acquired weapon exploded in his face at point blank range. When the weapon misfired, the left side of his face took a greater impact from the burning powder and shrapnel. For long moments on that hillside, Ben could not hear the distinctive hollering of the advancing rebels or even the gunfire of the Union men around him. He guessed that he had been both blinded and deafened by the explosion. A violent shake of his shoulders soon taught him otherwise.

"Quit your caterwauling!" screamed a voice he recognized as a sergeant in the 20th. "The colonel's about to order a charge. Half the regiment can't hear a damned thing cause of your squealing."

Blinded by the burst of gunpowder so close to his eyes, Ben was led by one of the regiment's pioneers to a field hospital. There he waited on a bench in the hot sun; his blue uniform tunic folded neatly across his lap. As the various skirmishes progressed during the day, he heard orderlies call to the surgeons a description of the wounded soldiers they carried in on stretchers.

"Gunshot!"

"Cannonball smashed his arm."

"No wounds, sir, just bleeding from all over. Oh, God."

Although Ben could not see these new arrivals, he could easily picture them in his mind. He had witnessed each wound a dozen times or more in his two-year pilgrimage through the battlefields of Virginia and Maryland. A man gutshot with a Minie` ball was bound to die or live only to regret surviving for the havoc the bullet caused. Cannonballs sometimes bounced through a formation, shattering the limbs of a half dozen men or more. The common result was amputation. Soldiers with blood seeping from their ears, eyes, or nostrils were likely cornered in a building, house, trench, or amongst rocks when artillery, such as a mortar, exploded within. Whenever he heard of men so afflicted, Ben remembered Lieutenant Clough's concern for the structures of Sorrow Ledge. If the force of an explosion more than 100 yards off could knock down a granite light house, what damage could occur inside a man standing only feet away?

During a brief lull in the flow of seriously wounded arriving in the hospital tent, the regiment's surgeon examined Ben's head wounds. After offering a dose of laudanum to ease the pain, the doctor cleaned Ben's face, plucked out a few of the larger pieces of steel, stitched closed several gaping wounds and removed a dangling portion of his severed ear lobe. Finally, Ben's head was wrapped with cotton bandages from his nostrils up to the hairline.

"I'm sorry, son, but I know of no way to remove the gunpowder from your skin," the doctor explained in a tone that sounded to Ben genuinely apologetic. "If you're lucky, the burns will scab over, and the powder will come off when the scabs do."

"And my eyes, sir? Will I be able to see once the bandages come off?"

"That I cannot say, and you may not learn for weeks yet to come. Perhaps months even. I saw only a few grains of powder in your eyes, so this blindness may be temporary."

"How long should I wear these bandages, sir?" Ben touched tentatively at his face, his fingertips feeling the extent of the linen wraps.

"I suggest for as long as you can stand the discomfort. Eyes are delicate. If you expose your pupils to sunlight too soon, you might make any damage permanent. Beyond that, I can't offer much advice. I have no expertise in the area."

"Thank you kindly for your care," Ben said, as he turned to feel about for his clothes.

"Good Lord! What's happened to you?" the doctor exclaimed. Ben felt the surgeon's finger poke tentatively at the scars that traversed the bony ridge of his spine. "These look like lash marks. Were you a guest down at Libby Prison?"

"No, sir. I was imprisoned on an island Down East before the war."

"Really? I wasn't aware of such a place."

"Few people were."

"These scars seem well healed. Some time has passed, then? Do they continue to hurt?" the surgeon asked.

"Yes, sir, at times"

"The back of your hands look burned. I'm going to ask a nurse to rinse your hands in vinegar and linseed oil. Then let's get you settled so you can rest. Try to keep your head up and do your best to sleep while sitting. If you lay down, you may lose more blood than you have lost already."

To make room inside the hospital tent for soldiers more seriously injured as the battles and skirmishes progressed throughout the afternoon, a surgeon's mate walked Ben a dozen steps outside and settled him against the trunk of a nearby tree. Separated only by a few paces and the canvas wall, he was close enough to hear the conversations between the doctors and the wounded. For long hours, Ben listened to the sad bargaining as each new patient tried to negotiate with the surgeons between amputation or death, a discussion that most often ended in crying, then sawing.

Sitting shirtless in the swelter of the Pennsylvania afternoon, Ben felt small rivulets of moisture roll down his neck and shoulders. Wondering whether this might be blood from his wounds or merely sweat, Ben dipped a finger into the small puddle amassed in the hollow of his sternum. He raised the liquid to his lips. The taste was most prominently salty, which did not fully resolve the principal question in his mind. Still, he felt more at ease; there was no evidence that his life's blood was gushing from his head wounds. He folded his uniform jacket and adjusted it so that it padded the scars along his spine from the rough tree bark.

Several times, the pounding of horse hooves stopped abruptly not far from where Ben sat, and he heard the rank and name of an officer announced. "Colonel O'Rourke." "General Weed." "Lieutenant Hazlett." After the announcement of each name, a respectful silence settled across the hospital. When a polite interval had passed after the banns of an officer's death were pronounced, the routine sounds of cursing, cutting, and dying within the hospital tent resumed.

In the shade of the tree and unable to see the sun, Ben had no way to measure time. The thunder of battle continued to come from several directions, approaching and retreating without clear resolution. During a lull in the hostilities, a woman's voice offered him water and hard biscuits. He accepted the drink but declined the food. Perhaps others within the tent were in far greater need than his own hunger. Ben was happy to pass on the proffered breadstuff if only so the less fortunate patients would not die on an empty stomach. For those soldiers, Ben thought, hard crackers might indeed come again no more.

"Where are you from, soldier?" a male voice asked, followed by a heavy grunt. Ben felt the man's weight against his shoulder as the stranger settled next to him under the tree.

"Maine, sir."

"Sure, always Maine boys around when there's trouble, it seems."

"Begging your pardon, sir, I don't know what you mean by that remark," Ben said, uncertain if this was a challenge or merely an insult.

"Oh, easy, easy now. Can't you see I'm no officer?" A long pause. "No, I guess you really can't. Can't see at all, then?"

"No. Breech blew out."

The man commiserated in language that Ben would never use himself, but he felt reassured that someone else would exercise on his behalf. "My Nancy wouldn't like me to talk that way," he said. "But sure been a hell of a day. I think the rebs have thrown about half their arsenal at us this fine afternoon. But I'm gladder to be here than anywhere else. Can't let the bastards stay in Pennsylvania."

"Your home here?"

"Hell, yes. Wouldn't wanna be from any place else. Prettiest land. Finest soil. Best rain. No copperheads at all, hardly."

Ben pondered briefly whether the man referred to the snakes or to the Northerners who espoused Southern sympathies, thereby conveniently disqualifying themselves from military service. Unless they emigrated to the Confederacy, which so many failed to do. He decided on balance that it made little difference which copperhead was the topic, though Ben felt less animosity toward the reptile. "What's your regiment?"

"The 83rd Pennsylvania. My farm is near Edinboro. That little college in town there reminds me some of our normal school back home." The man paused, and Ben heard him guzzling a drink. His companion suddenly spat urgently and violently. "Ugh. The boys must have drawn the water from a hog wallow this morning. Need a drink?"

Ben felt the weight of a canteen rest on his thigh. "No, thank you kindly. Just a little while ago, a woman came around ladling out water. Must have come from a deep well because it was still cold."

"Did she now? One of Miss Barton's gals, maybe? Seems I'm never in the right place at the right time. I could do with some good water, not this muddy swill."

Ben heard a canteen clatter on the rocky ground. "I'm sure she'll be back soon."

"Maine, you said? What's your regiment?"

Out of habit, Ben nearly answered by naming the 2nd Maine, but he'd learned in a few short weeks to refer instead to the 20th. Since the departure for Bangor of the bulk of the 2nd Maine regiment, the reputation of the remaining "three-year men" had fallen to that of malingerers, mutineers or worse.

"By God, the 20th Maine!" the Pennsylvanian exclaimed. "Let me congratulate you, soldier." The man reached into Ben's lap and lifted a hand, which he grasped firmly. "That was a hell of a trick you boys pulled. All the shot boxes are empty, so the colonel says, 'Fix bayonets,' as cool as asking for more lemonade at a Sunday church social. I didn't see it myself, but the boys on our left flank said that charge was the prettiest thing they could ever hope to see. What did you boys capture? A thousand rebels?"

Ben smirked, thinking that he should regret missing those final moments of the battle but at the same time feeling that he had already seen enough killing and dying as just a "two-year" man. "I don't know. I've been here most of the day."

Ben felt the man lean heavily against him and then pat Ben's knee with a broad, meaty hand. "Don't worry. I'll wager you'll get your chance at 'em again before this is over. We ain't got 'em licked yet. But my major says Bobby Lee'll try to run for Virginny tomorrow or the day after, and Meade'll hit the rebs while their army is spread from here to the Potomac." With his neighbor resting so close against him, Ben could not avoid smelling once again the curious stench created when sweat mingled with gunpowder.

Hoping it was not for want of patriotism or courage, Ben admitted to himself that he harbored no great longing to chase the rebel army south yet again. Just a few days earlier, his regiment had dogged Lee's shadow north since Maryland, marching from Frederick into Pennsylvania on the double quick. On the first day of July, they had tramped 25 miles before stopping to bivouac. Then came word that a rebel sniper had killed General Reynolds and Lee's boys had driven the federal First and Eleventh Corps into a small town called Gettysburg. Soon the Maine men were on their feet again and trudging north once more until well past midnight, completing a forced march of 40 miles or greater in little more than 24 hours.

"The major said we might even finish it up within a week and be home in time for first wheat harvest." The man's body shifted away from Ben. "I'd like to get home to my Nancy. End of the month will be two years I've been away." Ben felt the farmer's hot breath on his neck. "You think that sweet lady with the water will be back soon? I'm as parched as a coon pelt curing on a barn door."

"You should call for one of the pioneers or an orderly. I haven't heard a woman's voice in a long time."

"Yes, I'm supposing so."

The farmer fell silent, but Ben continued to feel the man's shoulders rise and fall against his own. Perhaps he'd dozed off from exhaustion after a day spent in heated battle. Eventually, the man roused in a most talkative mood.

"You heard the bastards shot Colonel Vincent? Best officer I ever saw. Maybe they're taking care of him and ain't got time to bring fresh water round to the rest of us. Say, you've seen the elephant, right? I hope we get home for harvest this year. God, I miss my Nancy. Prettiest girl you ever saw. Maine, you said? A New Yorker from the 44th told me the best dinner he'd ever had was boiled lobster and sweet corn up in Boston. You've got lobster in Maine, right? Just pull 'em right out of the ocean? Tell you what. I'll bring all the corn you can eat, and my little Nancy will shuck it. We'll get a huge pot boiling and put in a couple of those big lobsters you catch. Do you net 'em out of deep water? Well, makes no difference how you land 'em, I guess. You think they'll bring the water around soon? Lots of butter. My Nancy churns the best butter in the county, wins a blue ribbon every county fair each year. Prettiest blonde hair you ever saw. Cold for July, don't you think? I'll tell you, Colonel Vincent is just about the prettiest man I ever saw, and a Harvard man to boot. Fresh butter, sweet corn, and lobster? Can you imagine anything better? I've got a dozen Jerseys. Always good milk. You hear O'Rourke was killed? Nancy makes the best butter you ever tasted. You ever been to Boston? A New Yorker told me it was the prettiest place he ever saw. From the 44th, I think. What do they say about a cold day in July? Can't wait to see my Nancy. Prettiest hair you ever saw. You ain't got no water, have you? My canteen's full of mud. You hear that the rebs shot Vincent and killed O'Rourke? Just today. I'm thinking we've gotta give 'em something to remember O'Vincent, you know. When the hell did it get so cold? If you see the paymaster, tell him I want all my money paid in water, for Christ's sake. Nancy wouldn't like me to talk that way, no. But, God. You seen the elephant, right?"

Ben felt the Pennsylvanian's weight lean heavily against his shoulder and then slump slowly into his lap. Ben rested a hand on the man's back to feel for his breath but felt no movement at all. Blind to the man's injuries, Ben wondered whether he had bled out from a wound or just died from the heat and the exertion of his bout of logor-rhea. In the course of two years spent marching and fighting, Ben had seen other men collapse and perish from unknown ailments. He wondered how this terrible news would be delivered to Nancy and how she would receive it. His death would not be announced amongst the surgeries and field hospitals. Perhaps the widow Nancy would find the money necessary and arrange to have his remains embalmed and carried home. Though probably not. Ben found nothing around the Pennsylvania farmer's neck. Soldiers from wealthy families routinely wore a metal tag on a leather cord that identified an undertaker back home to be contacted upon the bearer's demise. If the burial detail found such identification on a corpse, the body would be set aside to be shipped home. Too often, Ben knew, there was little time or effort in the wake of battle for such sentimentality. Often times, the gravedig-gers expressed their resentment at this final inequity that those poor killed in action were dumped into a deep pit while the remains of the well-off were shipped home for interment in a proper grave.

Thinking about the dead man's Nancy brought to Ben's mind a girl he intended to court back home in Rockland. Rebecca worked in her father's general store on Main Street. Over the years, she had blos-somed into a young woman whose beauty was the envy of the ladies of Rockland. Yet she remained sweet and kind to Ben, who felt he was a poor match even before this most recent wound. Now he began to surrender all hope.

As the din in the hospital tent continued unabated, Ben made no fuss. There was no reason to raise an alarm over a dead man when the surgeons might better serve the army by attending the wounded first. Thus, he remained seated with his back to the tree, holding the corpse of the dead farmer and husband of pretty Nancy across his legs well after the sounds of battle had ceased echoing across the fields. Eventu-ally, a pioneer passed by and stopped to inquire about the farmer's health. Soon two surgeon's mates came to examine the casualty and carry the corpse away.

After a while longer, another surgeon's mate returned to examine Ben's bandages, and he determined that a fresh dressing was in order. He helped Ben to his feet and escorted him slowly back into the medical tent. By now, the arrivals of new patients had slowed, and Ben waited only an hour for a surgeon to survey his wounds. The same doctor as before concluded it was indeed time to replace the bloodied wraps but was reluctant to expose Ben's injured eyes to light so soon after the injury. With new linens in place, Ben settled on a cot just inside the tent door where he might enjoy the shade against the harsh sun, and the surgeon's mates could monitor how much blood seeped into his bandages.

"Pardon me, lad. Are you with the 20th Maine?" a voice asked.

Ben instantly recognized a familiar Maine accent. "Currently, sir. Previously I was with the 2nd Maine for two years."

"Ah, yes, one of the three-year men, then?" the Mainer asked.

"Yes, sir, in a manner. You know of our situation then?"

"Fully. My name is John Chamberlain. Lieutenant Colonel Chamberlain is my brother, as is his adjutant, Captain Tom. I serve with the Sanitary Commission."

"The colonel seems like a good man. We understood that he received permission to shoot us, but he fed us instead."

Ben felt the cot shift as a weight settled next to him. "I heard about the three-year papers that some of you 2nd men were asked to sign. My brother says it was a very clumsy business, indeed. Is there something that I could do for you?"

"Your brother, the colonel, said he'd speak to the governor about us. I'll be most grateful if he would." Ben lowered his voice and added, "I'm no mutineer, sir. I've never refused to serve, to fight in any battle, to do anything that I was ordered to do."

Ben felt a thick palm rest on his knee. "Yes, Joshua, uh, Colonel Chamberlain, has told me that he sent a letter to Governor Coburn asking for a clarification of your regiment's predicament."

"Mister Chamberlain, I don't mean any disrespect, but my situation isn't what you may think. I'm not one of those who signed up for three years. There's been a mistake. My term expired with the two-year men, and I need to go home as soon as I can."

Ben's cot moved yet again as the visitor stood. Ben had the sense that Mister Chamberlain did not believe him or else simply wanted to avoid becoming drawn into this controversy.

"If my brother ... Well, uh, if the colonel has plans to come by the surgery this evening, I will ask him to visit with you about your situation. How does that sound?"

"The best I could hope for," Ben said in earnest. "Thank you kindly."

For long hours afterward, Ben sat in his darkness, pondering how he had come to carry the Enfield. When Ben first enlisted in '61, the 2nd Maine was issued smoothbore 1840 Springfields. These were just old .69 caliber flintlock muskets that had been modified to percussion recently. Along the banks of the Chickahominy River in '62, the regiment exchanged their surviving 1840s for new 1861 Springfields, a .58 caliber. That rifle Ben carried until the soldiers of the 2nd Maine turned in their weapons in anticipation of being discharged and sent home. However, Ben was held back with more than a hundred other men who had signed three-year enlistment papers and who were instead bound over to the 20th Maine to finish out another year of service or be shot for mutiny. After the first fusillade of the morning, a sergeant handed Ben an Enfield taken from an early casualty.

From what he heard about him, he concluded that twilight had settled over the armies surrounding Gettysburg. The shrill screams from men emerging from the anesthesia after amputations and other surgeries had relented over time; now the most common sounds were the curses from the wounded and the groans of the dying. The rattle of distant gunfire on various battlefronts had also declined gradually to be replaced by the chirping of crickets, that in turn, fell silent when interrupted by the occasional gunshots from sentries, skirmishers, and snipers.

As he listened to the sounds of suffering within the surgery, Ben recalled Lieutenant William Clough and his war wound. Clough walked with a pronounced limp from his injury during the war with Mexico. At the end of each evening, Ben observed that once his father was asleep, the lieutenant retrieved a flask from which he quietly sipped for nearly an hour. The secret elixir appeared to help ease the lieutenant's discomfort so that he could eventually sleep for a few hours.

Lieutenant Clough did not see his labors on Sorrow Ledge through to completion. Begun in the summer of 1852, construction was suspended in October for the winter months. When warmer weather returned to Maine with the spring of 1853, the quarrymen and masons came back to Sorrow Ledge. But not Clough. His absence slowed progress on the tower considerably. Ben missed talking with the young officer about his exploits in Mexico and his experiences building light houses in an exotic locale where it did not snow. Ben's father asked the skipper of a visiting Revenue Marine cutter to inquire with the Light House Board about the engineer. The reply came instead from the War Department. *"It is with regret,"* the letter stated, *"that the Secretary of the Department of War informs you that Lieutenant William Clough died tragically in May 1853 while returning to his assigned duties in Maine when the New York & New Haven train on which he was traveling failed to navigate a swing bridge in Norwalk, Connecticut, that was at the time open to allow the passage of the steamship* Pacific.*"* For years young Ben resented this tragedy befalling a young officer with a promising career.

Now Ben felt no such depth of sorrow for the infantryman from Edinboro who died on his shoulder. After the havoc of each battle over the prior two years, Ben felt within him a gradual wilting of his capacity to mourn. He prayed this loss of sympathy came not from any defect of soul. He merely wanted to go home to Sorrow Ledge, as was his due; he hoped only to board a train or sail on a packet boat as close to Rockland as he could reach with the money in his pockets.

Ben was contemplating how best he might travel when he heard other voices in the tent. He was worried that lying down on his cot might increase the pain he felt in his head or cause more blood to flow out of his wounds. He also did not want to be caught unawares if the Confederates suddenly overran the hospital tent in the early dawn. As he sat hunched on the edge of the hospital cot, he overheard a discussion from across the tent.

"Good evening, doctor."

"Good evening, Colonel. Congratulations on your brilliant success this afternoon. I believe you are the talk of the entire army tonight."

"Thank you, though the boys deserve all the credit. They behaved more courageously than I had any right to expect of them. I've come to inquire about how the men fared today."

"To be quite honest, sir, I have come to think of the day as a mixed blessing. Some I was unable to save; some I did manage to save, and I fear that a certain number of that latter may come to envy the other lot."

"Were there many amputations?" Ben heard the colonel ask in his distinctive Maine accent.

"Less than usual; no more than necessary. I understand you were holding a hilltop. Hard for the rebels to bring their artillery against a high position. Seems like cannonballs always take more limbs. And troops charging uphill tend to have little accuracy with their muskets."

"From what I've seen of battle, I'd agree," Chamberlain said. "But I wouldn't scoff at the damage a Minie ball can do to a man when fired from any angle."

"You're absolutely right, Colonel. What a musket round can do to a man's insides is truly unholy. Many of your men came in with bayonet wounds."

"Doctor, have you met my brother, John Chamberlain with the Sanitary Commission?"

"Yes, sir, he was here a few hours ago, checking on some of your boys, I believe."

"He asked that I visit with one of the men who transferred to us from the 2nd Maine. John said the man's head was completely bandaged over."

Ben sat up straight when he realized that the two men were discussing him.

"He's just over there, Colonel. From what I could ascertain, the breech of his rifle exploded. I removed all the shrapnel I could see and sewed his ear up, but he's now blind and has a face full of gunpowder. I've seen men blinded by a misfire who recovered their sight in a few weeks. May take some months. Perhaps never at all. I cannot say so soon after the injury."

"Thank you for taking care of my men today. I don't wish to think what our casualties would be if you had not been here to take on whatever General Lee sent our way."

"Thank you for that, sir. I'm going off duty now if you please. Good night, Colonel."

A few moments later, Ben felt a warm hand settle on his bare shoulder. His body shuddered at the surprise he could not see coming.

"Good evening, soldier. I'm Chamberlain. Colonel Chamberlain. I believe you were one of the men who came to us from the 2nd. Is that correct?"

Ben immediately recognized the voice he had heard first when he and the remaining men of the 2nd Maine were given over as prisoners to the possession of the 20th. Colonel Chamberlain had informed the remainder of the regiment that he had received permission to shoot any one of them who failed to fulfill their obligations. Surprisingly Chamberlain had gone on to assure them that execution was not his preferred method to address their situation and then fed them their first meal after several days. Because of the civil way in which Chamberlain had treated the so-called mutineers, the remaining men of the 2nd had grateful, if grudging, respect for their new colonel. Ben struggled to stand at attention in the presence of his commanding officer, but Chamberlain gently held him down with a hand firmly in place on Ben's shoulder.

"Relax, Private. I understand you asked my brother if I might speak with you."

"Yes, sir, that was me. I did not intend to ask for you to make time for me tonight. I heard that you and the boys had been sent to clear the rebs off Round Top."

Chamberlain's laugh sounded hearty. "Ordered and done. Through a nice little ruse, we captured quite a few Texans up there."

"A great day for the 20th all around then, sir."

"Indeed. Though we lost many good men today. It appears you were quite fortunate that you were not among them. What's your name, soldier?"

"Grindle, sir. I'm Ben Grindle." Ben now felt relaxed by Chamberlain's gentle style.

"Where are you from?" Chamberlain lifted his hand.

"I enlisted in Castine with Company B. I grew up on Sorrow Ledge, southeast of Rockland."

"I wasn't aware there were homes on Sorrow Ledge," the colonel said, with a tone of surprise in his voice.

Ben felt the cot shift as the officer sat next to him. The colonel's uniform reeked of gunpowder long after the battle. He also detected the scent of a recent cigar, perhaps from a celebratory repast with his fellow officers after the day's victories.

"Only the light house."

"Of course," Chamberlain said. "I've sailed past it a few times. The surgeon told me he believes your rifle exploded in your face."

"Yes, Colonel. I've been thinking about it all afternoon, and it was my own damned fault, begging your pardon, sir." Ben sighed heavily at this admission. "When we went into battle this morning, one of the sergeants gave me an Enfield off one of the early dead. But I didn't take the dead man's cartridge box. I used the old Springfield rounds out of my own box. The rounds fit a little snug, but I just kept firing until the thing blew up in my hands. Weren't nobody's fault but my own."

"Don't be harsh on yourself. Every commander knows that danger. We all hate when the army switches out weapons because there are always problems with munitions. But my brother mentioned that you were concerned about a special situation regarding your enlistment." Ben felt the cot under him move as the colonel shifted.

Ben took a deep breath as he prepared to convince the colonel that he wasn't merely another mutineer or deserter. "Colonel, I know you don't know me, but my family has kept Sorrow Ledge since '53. My father died a few years later. My mother was appointed in his stead, but she can't run the light alone. Before the war, I stood most watches. Since I enlisted, my younger brothers are helping her."

"I imagine that must be a hard life for a young man to live on a remote island, working by day and night."

"I make no complaint, sir. It's the duty I inherited when my father died. The problem is that when I enlisted, I signed two-year papers and expected to go home with the regiment. I believe there was an error in the regimental rolls because there were so many men with the same last name in our unit. Now both my brothers have gone and enlisted. If they don't appear in Bangor, Captain Low will have a pretty good idea where to send the sheriff to arrest them for bounty jumping or perhaps desertion. When they leave, my mother and young sister will be alone on the island to man the light tower without help. I don't believe that together they could carry the kerosene up the tower. Sara hasn't yet turned 12 years."

"Your mother has no other males in the family to assist her, then?"

"I've got an aunt in Portland and another in Bangor. For men, we've got a slew of cousins, but most of them just went home with the 2nd or are here now with the 20th. My mother sent me to enlist in Castine so that I'd be among relations. Seven other Grindles were enlisted in Company B beside myself. They've all gone home except my cousins Ben, Joe, and Frank."

"When were you expected home?"

"Back in May, sir."

"And when are your brothers required to report?"

"Later this month. I believe on the Friday two weeks from yesterday."

Ben felt the cot move again as Chamberlain stood.

"Let me look into the matter. I can make no promises tonight, not after this day. However, I'll not let your situation go without some manner of resolution."

"Thank you kindly, sir." Ben then said in earnest, "Congratulations on your victories today. Good night."

Ben heard the colonel's footfalls as he walked away, then felt a cool breeze as the tent's canvas rustled. The night air brought in the smell of campfires. Ben listened to the clamor of the army around him bedding down to sleep: a bugle calling out tattoo; the barking of dogs and sergeants; the whinnying of tethered horses. Gradually, this evening clangor of the camp was replaced by the symphony of crickets and hoot owls. Much closer, from within the hospital tent itself, came the drone of buzzing flies and mosquitoes tormenting the already suffering patients. From somewhere at a distance, the bellowing of a distressed cow came to Ben's ears. After a time, he heard the high-pitched yelping of coyotes as they staked out their territory among the meaty bodies of the dead sprawled across the day's battlefields. These carnivores were unconcerned with the color of uniform worn by the corpses.

The lucky dead no longer suffered in the same way as the inmates of the surgery tent. In the darkness that enveloped Ben arose a chorus of gasping and rasping as so many men clutched after the breath of life. As the long, sweltering hours passed, Ben heard too the whispers of women. A few nurses and local residents had come to render aid. They covertly shared news of the deteriorating conditions of the hospital's inhabitants. As needed, individual ladies were assigned to sit with a patient, to soothe and ease the dying man through his passage. Sailors referred to the struggle as crossing the bar – fighting current and tide to reach a safe harbor across the breaking surf. Ben had performed this comforting role many times on battlefields, gripping a comrade's hand or hugging the man on his lap. No duty was harder. Yet it came to everyone who saw the elephant often enough; a random shot strikes a soldier in the ranks and the man marching alongside him kneels to offer a canteen, a bandage or a prayer. If they were messmates, the Samaritan might stay a few moments longer. If the enemy hard pressed the regiment, the dying man was left behind until after the stakes of battle were settled. Later the battle-weary survivors returned to search the fields for the wounded, driven by guilt shared among those fortunate enough to emerge unscathed or only lightly injured. A surgeon once told Ben that the walking maimed made the best surgery attendants. They felt no more worthy than the wounded they gathered for the hospital trade or the dead they helped heap into the mass graves.

Trying to ignore the agonies of comrades he could not see nor help, Ben lifted his feet in turn and slowly untied each boot. If he were to drop one, he knew he would be blindly scrabbling about the hard ground on his knees to find it again. He tied the laces together and with a bowline knot secured his shoes to his suspenders. He folded his shirt and jacket, then laid them neatly on the cot before he sat on them. From First Bull Run onward, he had heard the stories of soldiers who awoke in the hospital to find that they had lost a limb or more to a surgeon's saw, as well as all their possessions to a hospital rat. As he dozed off, he wondered, too, about Nancy in Edinboro. Who shall tell her? What will she do then? Get on with the churning? What would become of her and their little farm? Would anyone on either side of tomorrow's battlefield give a tinker's damn about Nancy?

Thoughts of Nancy led him back to reflections on Rebecca. How would she respond if she heard the details of his wounds? Would she recoil at the sight of him? Were the scars of his childhood and war now too repulsive for a woman's sensitivities? He felt in his heart that he already knew the answer.

CHAPTER 2

A hard shove woke Ben from his slumber just as the roosters on the farms surrounding Gettysburg began to raise their dawn alarm.

"Come on. You gotta get back to your unit now," a sharply nasal male voice said. Ben thought the accent sounded like the voices of men from the 44th New York that the 20th Maine had followed up Little Round Top just the day before. "The doctors think our beds will see plenty of trade if Bobby Lee takes another run at us today."

Ben untied his knotted boot laces and pulled them on as quickly as he could. Given the tone of the man's voice, he assumed the hospital attendant had no interest in waiting around long for a blind man to dress. Ben held out a hand for assistance in rising from the canvas cot. When no help came, he struggled to push himself off the cot. Upon standing, he felt suddenly dizzy and staggered slightly. The orderly caught Ben's biceps and held him upright.

"The 2nd Maine, right? Where's your unit camped?" the orderly demanded harshly.

"Bangor, I suppose," Ben said. "But if you'll take me to the 20th Maine, I'll be grateful."

"You was with the 20th? When they's whipped all them rebels

yesterday?" the orderly asked with surprising respect in his voice that sounded sharply at odds with his tone just one breath earlier. "I'z heard that was somethun!" They emerged from under the cool shade of the hospital tent into the muggy air of morning.

"Yes, I suppose it was," Ben agreed. "Unfortunately, I didn't see it all for myself."

The orderly's change of attitude was startling. "Tell you what. I's gonna have one of the boys take you down to where your regiment camped, but I'll walk you down there meself. I's heard all da Maine boys are all over six foot. I's like to see dat. Friend of mine was on the Mud March and said a bunch of youz Maine boys whipped two other regiments with your bare hands. Wish I'd saw dat, by Gawd."

With this sudden rush of words, the hospital rat's breath hit Ben full in the face. Evidently, the man's breakfast that morning had included at least one stout shot of whiskey. Ben didn't fault the man. Personally, he could not think of an assignment worse than hospital duty. Killing and wounding at a distance was one thing; picking up the limbs and bodies of the wounded or the dying was more ghoulish than anything Ben could imagine. Yet if the orderly required a nip of John Barleycorn for the courage to face the coming day, Ben wondered, what would be necessary for the evening to put that past day's events to rest?

In his excitement to see actual Maine men, the Yorker hustled Ben down the road at a breakneck pace for a man newly blind. Ben stumbled on the uneven ground more than once and even fell to his knees several times. His escort impatiently helped him back to his feet after each tumble and hurried Ben along to regain lost time. When the orderly's grip on his elbow relaxed some, Ben halted abruptly.

"Why don't you go on without me?" the blind man asked. "That would be quicker for you and easier on me."

For a long moment, Ben stood in silence waiting for a response. He felt the sunlight on his back, and a breeze chilled the sweat on his neck. His shirt and uniform tunic hung loosely over his arm. He no longer carried any bedroll or other gear. He hoped that one of his comrades or a pioneer in the 20th had thought to retrieve his tack after he had been taken off to the hospital.

"Fine then, and to hell with you," the New Yorker said emphatically. "Wanna find your own way? Dat's jus' fine with me. Take your own damn time about it. Ain't no war around here nowhere. Why don't you rest on your precious arse?"

Without warning, Ben smelled the strong odor of liquor up close and suddenly felt the New Yorker shove him with both hands against Ben's chest. Ben staggered backward, then tripped over some rocks in his path. He landed on his back with a painful thud and yelped in surprise. The strong odor of horse dung greeted his landing, and Ben hoped he had not fallen directly atop a fresh dropping.

"Ain't so tough now," the orderly sneered. "You Mainers ain't dat big and mean after all, is you?"

"No, we ain't all big, but we're mean enough to whip your sorry ass," a voice called out. Ben recognized both the Downeast accent and the speaker's unique cadence.

"Who the hell are you?" The New Yorker's voice sounded defiant, but Ben also sensed there was a measure of fear in the tone of the question. "What's your regiment?"

"I'm Frank Grindle. This here is my cousin, Joe. We were 2nd Maine until recent, and now we're 20th Maine. Perhaps you've heard of those units. We're the fellows fighting the actual war. Ain't a battle worth mention that we didn't smell the smoke." Frank let free a sardonic hoot. "Well, we were just on our way to the hospital to see our cousin. Maybe you saved us a little walking, perhaps. Ben Grindle, is that you under all that wrapping? We heard you had a rifle explode in your hands."

"Hello, Frank," Ben said from where he sat on the ground. "Good morning, Joe. It's good to see, er, well, to hear you. Glad you both survived yesterday. Heard it was quite the romp."

"Morning, Ben," Frank said. "Looks like the hospital done wrapped you up Jesus to Jesus and eight hands around. Can you see anything at all?"

"Not yet, but the surgeon thought I might get my sight back in a few days or so, maybe." Immersed again by the familiar morning smells of wood smoke and burning fat, Ben wondered where they were situated amidst the Northern army's large camp. Recalling the

Mud March, Ben hoped his cousins might refrain from starting a new brawl between the various regiments surrounding them. If there were New Yorkers or Pennsylvanians around, this might not be the best time or place for a squabble. With Bobby Lee's boys likely poised to strike Meade's position, another such melee that distracted any Union troops from their vigilance might end with the Grindle cousins being court-martialed. In such an event, Ben planned to disclaim these other Grindles as woodpile cousins, distant relatives for whom he could not account.

"Well maybe a little blindness is a good thing then," Frank said. "You won't have to witness what we're going to do to this here *soldier*." Ben thought his cousin's added emphasis sounded so contemptuous that it did not bode well for the hospital orderly. "I mean I think it would be wrong for him to go through the entire war without experiencing any real fighting."

"Wait, now, boys," the orderly objected. "I's just bringin' 'im back to camp. He stumbled and fell. I was getting fixed to help…"

"Stumbled and fell, then?" Joe asked, as though this explanation defied all credulity.

"That's what the man said," Frank observed in a sarcastic tone. "Stumbled and fell. Another blind man just one more sad victim of gravity, I suppose." Frank cackled heartily in a manner Ben now thought reminiscent of his father just before he reached for a baleen rod. "I always knew Ben was a little clumsy."

"That's true enough, I suppose," Joe concurred. "Every time we went out fishing in the bay and stopped by the ledge to cousin, I wondered how he might ever walk all normal if he came ashore. Thinking, you know, about the way a landlubber has to get his sea legs on a ship."

Frank chuckled again. "So Ben's got it all backward. When he stumbles, I guess, he don't pitch forward like most folks do; instead, he flips backward and lands on his ass. Is that what happened here, Yorkie?" The sharp change in Frank's tone could be mistaken for nothing but a clear accusation.

Where he sat on the ground, Ben heard the whisper of a knife blade leaving a sheath.

"Stop!" Ben yelled. "Frank, let this go. Even a blind man can see this isn't worth killing and a court-martial."

"Ben, I'm not the one what pulled a knife," Frank said with surprising calm in his voice.

"Oh, dear." Ben tried hard to picture the scene playing out directly in front of his face; two of his cousins staring down a stranger with a knife. "Listen, the surgeons will be needing all hands today if Bobby Lee unleashes all his pills our way. Can't you find a way not to kill him and send him away with a lesson learned?"

Ben felt a kick of a boot against his thigh. "You moron, I've got the knife," the orderly said defiantly.

In the silence that followed, Ben heard another blade drawn from its scabbard. By the longer duration of its metallic passage, he knew this was a bayonet. Then he heard the tell-tale click of a Colt revolver being cocked.

"Yes, I know you do. And I'm trying to make sure you remain more alive than dead," Ben said. "Now hold on, Frank. Out of respect for Colonel O'Rourke, just let this hospital rat scurry away."

Another kick to Ben's thigh followed. "Shut up, you pine-head bastard!"

This second kick confirmed Ben's calculation of the New Yorker's bearing and range. He rocked backward and thrust upward with his left foot. When he felt an impact, he straightened his knee with all the strength in his leg. Ben heard the orderly land heavily a short distance away with a loud thud and then explode in a torrent of obscenity. Instantly, he perceived more scrambling footsteps and what sounded like a brief kerfuffle.

"Here now, why don't you let me take this little knife before you hurt yourself?" Frank asked in a most solicitous manner. "Come on, now. We're going to send you back home all safe and sound. Just git out of those lousy clothes you're wearing. Just leave your pantaloons on. I wouldn't want you to embarrass the Union Army in front of the enemy."

Ben felt a warm hand on his shoulder. "Nice aim, cousin," Joe Grindle said. "But a couple of inches higher and he would provide a soprano to Sunday services for a few weeks to come."

Ben heard still more wrestling and yet more cursing, which he assumed was caused by Frank relieving the New Yorker of his weapon and attire, all in preparation for a humiliating walk back to the surgery.

"Please, Frank, don't go too hard on him," Ben called out. "He was coming to see what us Maine boys look like, on a count of all the stories about us being giants and such. I'm betting the tales he'll tell now will make the Mud March sound like a church social."

"Sure, he'll be telling quite a tale," Frank replied. "He'll be claiming he was jumped by 20 of us big, brute Mainers instead of being laid out by a kick from a blind man. So, we're going to stand here and watch him walk all the way back to his hospital. Well, at least Joe and me will watch him. That way everyone in the Union Army will know there was just the three of us, not some invisible regiment that ambushed him." He stopped abruptly and sniffed at the air loudly. "Hell, Yorkie, you smell like boozefuddle awfully early in the morning. You been stealing alcohol out of the surgery? That's just one more reason for me to whip you hard. You'd better get moving along before I change my mind and filet you like a flounder."

Ben heard the clear sound of someone scrambling in the dirt to get away. Then a calloused finger tapped his shoulder. When he raised his arm, someone gripped his wrist and helped Ben off the ground. Ben felt the thick wrap of a bandage wrapped around the palm of the hand helping him.

"Joe, were you hurt yesterday?"

His cousin snorted dismissively. "Don't worry. Not nearly so bad as what you came away with."

"What happened to you?" Ben insisted.

"When we charged down that hill, the rebs were coming up a third or fourth time. A reb captain tried to take my head off with his saber." Joe's voice trailed off as if he lost interest in telling his tale.

"And then?"

"I put my hand up. I guess the reb was winded and didn't have much strength left. Cut down to the bone and stopped."

Ben felt a relief. "Joe, you might have lost your fingers."

"Nearly, I guess."

"Did he surrender to you?"

"No, I thought it best not to give him a second chance at my neck," Joe said, dismissive as usual of the dangers he had faced on the battlefield. "Ben, you've got some blood running down your neck here," Joe observed as he wiped it away with a kerchief as Ben felt a cottony whisk across his skin. "Did that little bastard open up a wound when he knocked you down?"

"I don't know. Kind of caught me by total surprise," Ben said. "I've no idea what came over him. I hadn't said a word."

Ben heard Frank return. "Can't be he objected to your looks none, cause nobody can see your ugly face now. Maybe he just didn't like your accent." Frank was starting to vent, which Ben knew was not a particularly rare occasion. "Now, you ask me, I've got no use for Yorkers, at all. All mouth and spleeny. Tell me just one place where we were hunkered down under rebel fire that we ever looked about and said, 'Thank God, the New York troops are arrived.' Not one time. Just a bunch of parlor soldiers."

"Except for the Fighting 69th, of course," Joe said quietly.

"There you go, quibbling again," Frank replied angrily. "No, not the 69th, but hell there were hardly any of them from New York at all. They was all Irish. And an Irishman will fight a stone if he thought it had a penny or a potato."

Ben heard a low groan from Joe. "So now the men in the 69th New York can't be from New York at all because they're Irish. I'm afraid our cousin Frank has gone daft."

"Seems mighty quiet down the lane there," Frank observed, sounding desperate to alter the course of their conversation. "Let's see if we can't stir up some attention for Ben's little Yorkie friend."

Without warning, Ben heard a single gunshot ring out, echoing painfully in his left ear. He lurched away to shelter his hearing from a second discharge. Soon enough the morning din of the army camp all around the three Maine men fell abruptly silent. This moment of quietude ended in a rising tide of uproarious laughter that seemed to ripple slowly away across the Pennsylvania hillside from the Grindle men.

"What did you do, Frank?" Ben asked.

"Cousin, I don't know whatever you mean by that," he answered in the voice of a contrite boy. "I just sent your friend back to work. I'm guessing he won't have so much interest in Maine men after today. I'd say he'll keep quite a safe distance till the war ends, and then maybe he'll head onto California or some other place out west. No, I don't suppose he'll want to go too close to Maine men ever again."

"Joe, what did Frank do to that man what's got the whole camp in an uproar all the sudden?"

"Well, it's a damn shame you can't see this for yourself," Joe said. "In some ways, it don't make much sense the ways they're all snickering so. Like army soldiers ain't never seen a naked man before. At least Frank let the man keep his boots. Hold on, Ben, you got a little more blood running down there."

Ben felt a dry cloth swab the left side of his neck. He decided he might feel more comfortable dressed in at least a shirt. He also hoped that the humiliated hospital rat would not return with friends to hunt down his cousins. "Come on, boys, why don't you take me to the 20th?"

"In a moment," Frank said. "Don't be so impatient. I'd say that scamp has another dozen rods to go before he can hide from the daylight." Indeed, the tide of mirth continued to recede from Ben's hearing. "I'd hardly ever admit Joe's right, but you wonder why an army would find a naked man funny. You'd expect they'd all get naked at least once every year to get washed, whether they needed it or no."

"I'm glad you boys were on hand to gibbet the fellow," Ben said. "I still can't figure what I could have possibly said that got him all of a biver."

"Don't worry none over it," Joe said. "Maybe the bastard's just dyspeptic. I calculate that's Frank's problem about half the time. The rest I chalk up to just his normal yip."

"Careful, now. Cousin or no, those could be fighting words," Frank said.

Joe cackled in his usual sardonic manner. "*Could be* is right, if you understood what the words meant. I'd guess dyspeptic is just about six letters beyond your ken."

"Well, aren't you just the regular Yankee Jonathan?" Frank retorted. "Talking like a book and all."

Ben felt Joe's hand on his arm. "Let it be, Ben. Our cousin likes to play the fool. But he mailed a letter to Governor Coburn about our situation when the rest of the 2nd went home that made the Governor weep from the horror. Yet now Frank calls me the Jonathan." Joe's snicker showed he was no angrier with Frank than he would be upset if General McClellan himself were to ride over the hill and resume command of the federals.

By that moment, Ben was hardly following his cousins' banter. Instead, he was struggling to get into his shirt. As he flailed about trying to find his second sleeve, he felt a calloused hand come to rest on his shoulder. "Avast there. I'll help you." Ben felt a second hand lead his wrist into the errant sleeve. As he drew the shirt around Ben's back, Joe observed, "I swan, that bastard did a terrible thing to you." Joe abruptly changed his tone and the subject of discussion. "Well, I don't guess they fed you any breakfast before they sent you away from the hospital."

"Well, no, other than the steak and potatoes they served all the convalescents last night, I haven't had a bite to eat since we bivouacked two days ago." In the long silence that followed, Ben wished that he could see the reactions on the faces of his cousins as they considered his claim. Ben let the two Mainers stew in their hunger for another long minute. "Come on now, you know I'm just joshing you boys. All I had from the hospital was hard biscuits and water. Right about now, I'm near hungry enough that I could maybe eat a boiled owl and not even wait for it to boil."

The cousins' hesitant laughter suggested a lingering suspicion. However, Ben knew that both men had been wards of the surgeons often enough during the prior two years of marching into every lead storm the rebels could concoct, so they were fully aware of the standard bill 'o fare served in every army hospital tent. Perhaps a convalescing officer might be served a meal of a well-cooked ribeye and a spud. However, most enlisted men enjoyed a steady diet of embalmed beef and desiccated vegetables to the point that many soldiers would develop an affinity for hard biscuits, even those flat iron cakes that had gone to worm castles.

Joe's grip shifted to Ben's elbow as they sauntered down the hill. Although he did not know the exact time, Ben assumed it was still early in the day because he smelled campfires, which in turn meant burning bacon and boiling coffee. Two other telltale signs were the sound of men chopping firewood and the absence of roaring artillery. If the rebels were planning to come at the Federal forces again that day, the prelude would be the usual mid-morning barrage of cannon fire intended to weaken the Union defenses. The silence of the rebel cannon seemed to Ben more disquieting than actual explosions.

"Tell me how you both fared yesterday?" Ben inquired. "I didn't see much of the battle, though I think I heard it echo over the whole countryside." He assumed they were heading still north because the sunshine warmed the back of his neck.

"Oh, hell, it weren't no Malvern Hill or even Fredericksburg," Frank said with a dramatic inhalation as if stifling a massive yawn. "I'd say it's embarrassing to the whole State of Maine that these 20th boys go on about it so much."

"Gosh, Frank, did you cuddle a porcupine all night?" Joe asked. "You're darn prickly this morning, considering you weren't even the one blinded in battle."

"Now, dammit, you know I wasn't talking about Ben, but there you go twisting my words. People that don't know better might think I'm a copperhead if they listened to you."

"Say, Ben, you remember that fellow named Tozier who was with Company F? I think he was from across the bay toward Pittsfield," Joe said.

After a long pause as he searched through his memory of the names and faces of the 2nd, Ben was forced to admit he didn't know the man. "No, I can't place the name. I'm sorry."

"Don't fret none. Heck, we started out from Bangor with more than a thousand men. You couldn't know every last one of them," Joe commiserated. "But this Tozier fellow, I'd say people will likely remember him now. See when we came into the 20th, the colonel put Tozier in the color guard.

There come a time yesterday when the rebs had charged us two or three times, and the smoke was so thick nobody could hardly see who was killing who. Well, all sudden like, the air cleared at the center of the line, and there was Tozier standing all alone. The entire color guard was dead or busy dying on the ground around him. But there stands Tozier, holding the staff of the flag upright in his left arm and just firing away with the rifle in his right hand. It was a sight I'll never forget. God, if only Brady had been there. I'd buy a picture of that to put up on a wall in my house."

Ben heard an impatient scuffling in the dirt. "Tarnation, next you'll want to give the man a medal for shooting a gun while holding a flag," Frank roared. "I don't recall hearing anybody named Tozier saving the day at Groveton Heights."

Joe leaned so close that Ben could feel his cousin's warm breath against his neck. "Try ignoring Frank. I swan he's woken on the wrong side of the bedroll for going onto two years now."

"You saying I've got no right to air my grievances?" Frank demanded loudly.

"No, cousin, I'm saying that all you've got is grievances, day in and week out." Joe had no more chance to hide the exasperation in his voice than a bull moose behind a birch tree could avoid a hunter's aim. "Some days I think it would help the Union cause for the rebels to capture you. If you were quartered down in Libby Prison, they'd most likely need more than half the Confederate Army to satisfy all your demands."

Curiously, Joe's denunciation elicited only a guffaw from Frank, who – as Ben could only guess by what he heard – abruptly stalked away. This left Ben and Joe alone. Around them, Ben heard just the mundane hubbub of an army's morning routine. Officers called out to their regiments, which sergeants repeated with emphatic clarification and profanity freely added. Men shuffled their feet in the dirt as they marched. Horses whinnied in protest. From not far off, Ben heard the familiar sounds of artillerymen rolling their carillons into position.

"Don't worry none," Joe said. "Colonel Chamberlain said we're in about the safest place in the Union Army. Just south of the center of the line. Not even an idiot reb would try to attack us here. I wish you could see this site because whoever picked this high ground darn well knew his business. It's the prettiest place to defend that I ever saw. If the rebels want to attack us here, they'll need to cross more than a mile of open ground. The reb general that orders that charge will find a court martial and then a noose waiting for him on the morrow."

Suddenly the entire camp around them erupted in cheers. As the hurrahs continued, Ben felt himself swept up in a crowd of men. They smelled of sweat, smoke, lard, gunpowder, dried blood and rarely soap. Their shouts were a confused chorus.

"Meade! Meade! Meade!"

"On to Richmond! On to glory!"

"Hang Bobby Lee!"

Even as he was jostled about among his comrades, Ben did not join this raucous celebration. He recalled the jocularity of the recruiting advertisements printed in the newspapers back home: *"Grand Excursion to Richmond, by Steamboat and Rail! Ticket entitles the bearer to passage to Richmond. Fare, food, and clothes, gratis, and $160.00 given each one. Tickets free."* He remembered the exuberance of his fellow recruits as they awaited in Bangor for the arrival of the buttons that would complete their uniforms and the muskets that would become their constant companions every step of a war that stretched a million leagues into the future. How they sang as the steamer *State of Maine* carried the regiment toward New York City. He thought about the high spirits with which the 2nd had marched into First Bull Run, followed in short order by panicked retreat.

"Grindle!" a loud voice shouted over the clamor. "Grindle! Colonel Chamberlain is asking for Ben Grindle from the 2nd Maine."

Ben felt Joe's grip on his shoulder tighten. "Damn, what have you done, man?" Cousin Joe asked. "It won't be easy hiding you with that white turban on your head. Let's hope they're looking for Cousin Ben from Stockton."

"It'll be ok, Joe," Ben said. "I spoke with the colonel last night at the hospital. I don't believe I've gotten into any mischief since then, except getting knocked on my ass."

Joe's grasp slipped from Ben's shoulder to his wrist. "I'd better come with you. If it's about that hospital rat, I'll swear it was all Frank's doing." Ben felt himself pushed along with a strong grip.

"Come on; the colonel's a busy man. Won't help your case to keep him waiting none."

After they had pushed their way about two dozen rods through the cheering throng, Joe stopped. "Pardon me, sir, were you the one looking for a Grindle?"

"Which one of you is Grindle?" asked a voice that sounded to Ben more Portland than Bangor.

"Both, sir. I'm Ben Grindle; this is my cousin Joe." Ben explained.

Joe quickly added: "There's two more Grindles in camp, another Ben and a Frank, but the colonel would be better off to avoid Frank as best he can."

"All right, at ease. I'll take this Ben to see the colonel. Wait here." Ben felt another hand catch his opposite wrist and pull him forward.

"Sir, wouldn't it be better if I came along to explain what's happened to him?" Joe asked.

"No, Private, I don't believe that will be necessary. I can see your cousin is blind, but so far I see no evidence that he is also deaf or mute."

"Well, sir, it's just that he's suffered a serious head wound. With respect, sir, I don't believe he's making much sense today."

Ben felt the officer stop abruptly. "At ease, Private Grindle. Colonel Chamberlain simply wants to speak to the man. I'm sure the colonel doesn't plan to hang your friend without the courtesy of a court-martial."

"Cousin, sir, he's my cousin," Joe said.

"Then I'm sure the colonel will treat your cousin with all courtesies," the officer said as he tugged Ben forward. "A buttonhole relation is he, or just an arsehole relative?" the officer asked Ben.

"Those would be my cousin Frank," Ben said.

Within a dozen steps that the officer led him, Ben felt that he was entering under a cool shade. Ben guessed they were now beneath one of the large canvas pavilions where the officers loitered between the grand events of killing and maiming.

"General Meade, this is the young man from the 2nd Maine whom I told you about." Ben immediately recognized the Downeast accent as Colonel Chamberlain's voice from the prior night.

"Yes, you indicated that he's one of your mutineers?" Meade's voice sounded thick and flat, without the usual accent that Ben detected among the many New Englanders he knew from other regiments in the brigade. His accent matched most closely the late Pennsylvania farmer from Edinboro. "You said there might have been some error regarding his enlistment papers. I thought Sherman gave you a hundred men all claiming the same thing."

"Yes, sir. About one hundred twenty all told. However, I believe there may have been a genuine error in this man's case," Chamberlain explained. "Grindle, I have asked General Meade to review your situation. Please tell the general what you told me last night about your brothers."

Ben felt stunned to be summoned so abruptly before the newly appointed Commanding General of the Union Army. He was unprepared for such an audience, but he immediately recognized that this might be his only chance to win an immediate discharge. Suddenly he was grateful that Joe had helped him get back into his shirt, though his blue tunic hung loosely over his shoulder. He quickly explained his family's plans for his brothers to enlist at the end of his own term of service and the family's commitment to maintaining a light house. Ben explained how this plan had gone awry due to mistaken identity as the 2nd Maine had mustered out according to erroneous rosters.

Ben heard Meade's somber voice echo in the tent. "Colonel, have you met my son, George? I have recruited Captain Meade to be my adjutant. Captain, would you see if you can find the paymaster's records for the 2nd and 20th Maine?" A long pause followed, and Ben sensed that the general was pacing the tent around him. "I'm curious, Grindle, what lens does Sorrow Ledge show?"

"A second order, sir, one of the first Fresnel lenses on the Maine coast, as I understand."

"You know, I've got some knowledge of light houses myself. I built them in Florida and the Great Lakes after the war in Mexico."

"Yes, sir, I know. I know quite a lot about that. The officer in charge of constructing the third tower at Sorrow Ledge was Lieutenant William Clough. He told me a great deal about the light houses that he built with you, as well as your service together in the war in Mexico. He always spoke quite highly of you, sir."

"Yes, Lieutenant Clough was a damn good man. One of the finest officers I had the privilege to know," Meade said. "Terrible tragedy to lose such an excellent man to a stupid railroad accident. You know, Grindle, ten years ago I displayed a Fresnel lens at the Crystal Palace during the Industrial Exposition in New York City." Abruptly the tone of Meade's voice changed. "God, ten years. It's hard to believe all that has happened since then."

"Yes, General, the crews finished construction of Sorrow Ledge ten years ago. I've been there since, up until I enlisted."

"I'm not particularly familiar with the Maine coast," Meade said. "Is Sorrow Ledge off Portland or farther north?"

Chamberlain spoke up at this juncture. "Sorrow Ledge is located in Penobscot Bay, the waters that lead into Augusta and Bangor."

"An offshore light, then?" Meade asked.

"Yes, sir, just one of many islands in the bay. Owls Head and Matinicus are the closest lights," Ben explained. "Sorrow Ledge is intended to steer mariners away from the ledge, while the others are intended to navigate ships into the bay."

"Fixed or occulting?" Meade asked.

Ben found this challenge rather childish but dared not betray any irritation. "Occulting, sir."

"Captain, have you found a Grindle in the pay lists?" the general demanded gruffly.

"Yes, sir, a whole passel of them. Let's see, we've got an Augustus, Ben, Hiram, and John whom all went home. Now we've got a Ben, Joseph, an Ed and a Frank that transferred to the 20th."

"Begging your pardon, General," Ben said. "There were originally three of us named Ben in Company B. My cousin Bentley mustered out with the 2nd in June. Cousin Benjamin is in camp here somewhere about. Also, then me, of course."

"What's your Christian name, soldier?" the voice of Captain Meade asked.

"Bennington, sir."

Ben's response evoked a chorus of laughter to which Ben had become increasingly accustomed during his tenure with the army.

"Bennington, you say?" General Meade's deep voice asked. "Like the city in Vermont?"

"Yes, General," Ben said. "My great grandfather marched to Quebec in 1775 with Arnold. He served with the Northern Army until the battle of Saratoga. He named his children for battles of the Northern campaign, and that became a family custom. My uncle and aunt are named Kennebec and Quebec. I am named for Stark's defeat of the Hessians. In some ways, I was the lucky one. Ben's not so terribly uncommon."

General Meade seemed to stifle a chuckle. "If you were the lucky one, what were your siblings named?"

Ben was becoming increasingly anxious as the interrogation progressed. "I have two younger brothers, sir, twins. The one that came first was named Valcour Island, but we call him simply Val. The next brother was named for Fort Stanwix, so we dubbed him Stan."

Ben heard Chamberlain snicker in his distinctive Downeast accent. "Any other children in your family?"

"Yes, Colonel, a sister. We call her Sara. Short for Saratoga, which she despises fiercely. I've no doubt that when she is emancipated that she'll change her name to Mary or Patience."

"General Meade, I think I see here what happened," said the voice of Captain Meade. "In the roster of men discharged with the 2nd, there is a line for Bentley Grindle and on the line below that is a name that spells Grindle correctly but ends the name Ben with two consonants. They may have been trying to abbreviate the word Bennington to fit the margin. But then someone crossed out that line completely."

Chamberlain interrupted: "Yes, I see where you mean. I wonder if someone thought the second entry was just a mistake, not realizing how many Ben Grindles were in the regiment. And each with a different given name. Little wonder things may have gone askew."

When General Meade began to speak, the others fell silent. "Your regimental book tells me that you enlisted in the 2nd Maine's in '61. An imposing list of engagements. I believe it would be beneficial to have an experienced soldier such as yourself back on Maine's coast to fight the rebels up there."

Colonel Chamberlain spoke. "I don't understand your inference, General."

The general emitted an abrupt sigh of exasperation. "Well, you've been marching the past few weeks, Colonel, so you may not have heard about the Confederate raids on the Maine coast last month."

"No, sir, that news hasn't yet reached us," the colonel said. "Tom, were you aware of these events?"

"No, Colonel, not word one. What was the damage?"

"A ship, by God, we lost a ship! The dispatches say that the rebel pirate Read went into Portland and stole away with a Revenue Marine Cutter," the general explained. "The good folks of Maine pursued him, but the devil blew up the ship. The *Cushing* was fresh out of the Navy Yard in Boston and carried more than a ton of munitions. An audacious crime, to be sure."

"And the Home Guard, sir, did they perform well during the incident?" Chamberlain asked.

Meade's laugh sounded to Ben rather like a horse snorting; he chose not to share this opinion aloud. "On that subject, the dispatches were silent. I assume that means there was scarcely a one of them to be found on the streets when this war arrived in Maine," Meade said harshly. "So, Colonel, I'll have the captain write you out an order to send this man home. I've no doubt that even blind that this man would be more effective than a squad of the Home Guard."

Although he had not once observed the Home Guard drill, Ben had read accounts of their activities in the newspapers from home that the men of the 2nd Maine shared amongst themselves when the mail caught up with the unit. The Bangor broadsheet reported that the local Home Guard unit had purchased a target with which to practice their artillery maneuvers. One clever editor took the occasion to assure the gentle people of Maine that the target was in no danger of harm from the Home Guard's efforts.

"I hesitate to agree because I know men in the Home Guard personally, but I accept your verdict. As for Private Grindle, I do have one caution. After yesterday's casualties, I don't believe I can spare anyone to escort him back to Maine safely. The regiment is well below strength."

"I have yet to hear of a regiment at strength, so Colonel, I will leave those arrangements to your capable hands." Abruptly Ben felt the general's rough hand rest on his shoulder. "Bennington Grindle, I am approving your discharge effective today. I happen to believe that a wickie's duty is just as important to the country as a soldier's. Keeping a light is quite a responsibility. As is so often the case, few people truly appreciate the real value of our lighthouses. Having built them myself, I think I'm one of those few."

"Thank you kindly," Ben said simply. As suddenly as it came, the warm feel of the hand on his shoulder withdrew.

"And Colonel Chamberlain, please send a telegram to your governor. I'd like to know that Valcour Island and Fort Stanwix Grindle will be under your command and care. Captain, two fresh cigars, if you please."

Ben wondered how he might graciously accept a cigar from the Commanding General to celebrate his mustering out of the army. He caught a whiff of sulfur and moments later a gust of tobacco smoke.

"Here, Colonel, please join me in a good stogie," Meade said.

Ben felt great relief that he was not required to make a grand gesture of appreciation for a cigar not proffered. As the smolder of cigars engulfed him, Ben remained in place for several minutes more, waiting quietly to be dismissed by one of the officers.

"Thank you for your time, General," Chamberlain said. "I suppose you have many other commitments today."

"Let me give you a little piece of advice, Colonel." Ben heard an audible inhale and then General Meade's voice continued at a quieter pitch, "Once you reach brigade command, stop. Beyond that, you spend your days protecting the army and defending yourself from the General Dan Sickles of the world."

"Thank you for the warning, General, but I'm certain I run no danger of attaining such rank."

"Colonel, many men are forced to eat their own words during wartime." Meade lowered his voice, yet Ben stood close enough that he could still hear his deep intonations. "So, let me tell you this much. I have been in command of this army for six days, and in that time, I have lost four generals in battle. Such a terrible rate of attrition must make room for promotion. I've read yesterday's reports. I know what you were able to do on the Round Tops. If you don't get yourself killed before then, I'll wager the end of this war finds you with at least one star on your shoulder."

"I'm honored by your faith, sir," Chamberlain said. "Thank you kindly."

Ben smelled another burst of cigar fumes and then heard shuffling in the dirt as several men marched away. After a brief rustle of leather, the beat of horse hooves nearby seemed to proceed away from him. He wondered where the general and his son were needed to adjudicate the army's next crisis of the day.

For a long moment, Ben stood in awkward silence.

"Oh, yes, Grindle, I haven't forgotten you. We've got to find a way to get you on your journey home." Ben felt a flat moist palm pat his bicep. "I've no idea how, just at this moment, but I'm sure we'll think of something."

"Thank you, Colonel," Ben said.

"Tom, come here," Chamberlain called out. "I've got a challenge for you."

Ben heard a brisk set of footfalls, followed by the slap of boot heels.

"Yes, sir, you know I always enjoy whatever challenge the army presents us." This voice had a similar accent to Chamberlain's own. Ben had spoken with enough lobstermen over the years that he could place its origin somewhere between Kittery and Portland.

"Tom, General Meade is sending this man home to Maine, but I can't spare another soldier to escort him. Any suggestion of how we might accomplish that? He may not see again for weeks, but without some type of guide by that time he could be in Kentucky or Illinois."

"Or we maybe we point him in the direction of Richmond," Tom mused. "When he arrives there, he takes off the bandages and shoots Jeff Davis dead so we all go home to Maine."

"Stop joking now. This is a serious matter."

"Then in all seriousness, I offer my services to escort him home myself."

"Tom!"

At this juncture in their banter, Ben began to suspect that the brother officers were conversing as though they considered him struck deaf as well as blind. He raised his hollow fist in front of his mouth and coughed for effect.

Colonel Chamberlain, too, coughed abruptly. "No, Tom, I can't spare you. We don't yet know the butcher's bill from yesterday's losses. Moreover, I can hardly send off a cook or camp steward on such a mission. We'd likely never see one of our pioneers again."

Tom suddenly spoke in excitement. "Colonel, over there. See that red-haired boy up the lane there a ways? Why not recruit a colporteur to take him home? They're all keen on helping their fellow man."

"A boy?"

"And why not? We were all a boy once, excepting perhaps yourself. Could be a trip that will change the lad's life forever, going from battle-fields to beautiful Maine for a few days. He may not want to come back to save the army's soul. And I see few other choices before you, Colonel."

"All right Tom, I'll talk to the lad. While I do that, please see if you can find Grindle's cousins and ask whether they have his haversack and bedroll. We can't send a man off without a blanket or mess kit even."

"Excuse me, Colonel. And Captain, sir," Ben said, at last, addressing both officers to be respectful. "I doubt my cousins will know the whereabouts of my tack. When we came to the 20th, sir, we divided among the different companies of the regiment. We weren't in the same mess. Not meaning to be more of a problem, sir, but I lost track of our baggage yesterday when we went up the Little Round Top on the quick step."

Captain Chamberlain spoke first. "Shall I equip him with all neces-saries, then?"

"Yes, I suppose so. Find the paymaster, too. Let's settle that account. Grindle won't be on army rations for his travels, so ask the officers of the regiment to donate a small token to the cause. Tell them their colonel will be appreciative."

"Begging your pardon, Colonel, I don't wish anyone to ask charity on my behalf," Ben said firmly. "I've never asked others for help. Ever."

"I appreciate your streak of independence. It speaks well of your Maine upbringing. However, I've got to assure General Meade that you will reach Sorrow Ledge safely, and that includes feeding your hunger," the colonel said. "For the past two years, all your food and transportation has been provided courtesy of the army. Starting today, you'll be on your own for both. Suppose you exhaust what pay you receive today before you reach New York City, well then, you'd be stranded wherever you are. The army will be of no use to you in that event. If I load you with enough army rations to reach Maine, you'll likely not get to Philadelphia before you're dead of exhaustion or a thief's knife. No, Private, you'll need to have some pocket money to see you home. And someone to guide you there, if I can help it. Tom, go see what you can scare up for this man."

After some brief hesitation in his own mind, Ben spoke up, "I appreciate that, sir. Thank you kindly."

"I understand your feelings," Colonel Chamberlain said. "I would look none too kindly on charity for myself either. However, you said something last night about duty that has stayed with me. Now General Meade has assigned to me the duty of ensuring you reach home safely so that your brothers can come along in your stead. If the general were to ask me to go request the surrender of all rebel forces, I'd believe it was my duty, no matter the danger." Ben felt a hand clasp his wrist. "Well, I feel the same about this duty I have been given toward you. Now I want you to wait here while I try to find someone who can escort you home."

"Colonel, anything else I should scare up for Private Grindle?" the younger Chamberlain officer asked.

"Well, yes, I suppose that there could be another concern." The colonel spoke with a hesitancy that surprised Ben. "With all the ruffians and scalawags on the roads, I don't wonder that we shouldn't give him some weapon to protect himself. It would help if you didn't say anything, Tom. Yes, I know he's blind. As do you. I'm certain he does as well. Short of sending him off to Maine with a platoon to escort him, I don't know how else to keep him safe but to arm him. At least he might bluff his way through a bad situation. If you've got a better idea, I'd like to hear it now."

Ben heard Captain Chamberlain whisper a response. "No, sir, I've no better plan. No ideas at all really. I've never given much thought to how blind travelers get around or how they respond when confronted by highwaymen. I'll see whatever I can find."

"Thank you, Tom, I do appreciate your efforts. Your resourcefulness." The colonel paused. After a moment, Ben heard a groan of frustration. "All right, Tom, send that boy over to see me. Let's see whether he's up to the task."

Standing in the shade of what he had assumed was the officers' marquee tent, Ben felt the heat of the day increasing. After the colonel had invited the General of the Army to review Ben's personal situation, he now felt uncomfortable asking for something so mundane as a drink of water. He was certain there would be a bucket and dipper available for the officers' comfort, but he could not blindly feel about clumsily with both hands. So he remained standing – hot, sweaty, thirsty and blind. After a few minutes, Ben heard Chamberlain strike up a new conversation with a young boy.

"What's your name, lad?"

"Seamus, Colonel." The answer came in one of the thickest Gaelic accents that Ben had ever heard. "I'm Seamus Dinneen."

"Where are you from, lad?"

"Ballyvourney, in County Cork."

"I see, and do you have a home in America?"

"Well sir, New York, I guess."

"You're not certain?" the colonel asked with some skepticism in his voice.

"No more now, sir. My mum died two years ago. Dad was killed last summer."

"I see. So, you're alone in the world?" the colonel's voice softened.

"Gosh, no, sir. Back in County Cork, I've got cousins thick as flies on a mincemeat tart."

"So why are you here then? You look much too young to enlist soon."

"Working, sir, for the American Bible Society, giving these religious pamphlets to the soldiers to comfort them in their distress. After I give away another 15,000 tracts, when I go back to Philly, they'll pay me ten dollars."

"Ten dollars? What an extraordinary sum," the colonel observed. "How many have you handed out so far?"

"Almost 10 thousand. It's really easy; much easier than hawking newspapers back on Wall Street. The troops like the pamphlets, but it's the free Bibles they want more of. I can't carry as many of those in this bag."

Ben stood nearby, trying to keep from itching along the edge of gauze across his cheeks. He knew the boy's story was true because inside his own kit was a collection of religious tracts. He also knew that many soldiers who accepted these pamphlets and Bibles held no interest in divinical studies. Any source of free paper was welcome among the troops when it came time for starting campfires or toileting. Ben kept this thought to himself. He also chose not to comment on a curiously unpleasant odor that reached his nostrils soon after the Irish boy came near.

"So, you know your way back to Philadelphia?" Chamberlain asked. "Do you think you could lead this man to a train station? Take him to Lancaster or Philadelphia and help him get on a train bound for Boston or Maine?"

"What's wrong with him?" the young Irish voice asked in a hushed tone. "Does he have the great pox?"

"Goodness, no. What a terrible thought. His rifle exploded in the battle yesterday, and the gunpowder blinded him. It may be only temporary. By the time you reach Philadelphia, he may be able to find his way on to the train himself."

"Sorry, Colonel, I've still got all these papers left to give out. If the armies decide to fight it out to the end today or tomorrow, I imagine there'll be quite a lot of tormented souls here, all searching for the holy path to eternal redemption."

This last sounded to Ben's ear to be rather well rehearsed.

"Yes, I see what you mean. You said just now that the Society will give you ten dollars if you distribute everything in your bag. Suppose I was to give you that ten right now and add another five dollars. I'll give the literature to my men, and you'll assist this man on his way home, which is a Christian thing to do. What do you say to that deal?" Judging by the tone of Chamberlain's voice, Ben could tell the colonel seemed delighted that he had found a possible resolution.

"You mean Union money, sir? No Confederate dollars, right?"

The boy's insolence shocked Ben. Having grown up under the strict supervision of his own father, he could not imagine himself haggling in such a manner with someone either his elder or a superior officer. Equally surprising to Ben was Chamberlain's willingness to spend such a princely sum to procure this boy's services as guide and guard.

The colonel did not seem to react to the boy's tone. "I'll go you one better. I'll pay you in silver dollars, not paper. Five dollars hard money now. When you reach a train station, either in Philadelphia or New York, Mr. Grindle will pay you the balance. However, you must swear not to abandon this poor man along the way, that you'll get him to a train station or a port of call. Agreed?"

The lad began to respond, but his voice was quickly subsumed in a terrible din. Without warning, a distant artillery barrage began, a chorus of cannons from the rebel position sounding off in quick succession, spitting fire and shot toward the Union Army. The awful noise echoed for miles across the open fields. Newly blinded, Ben found this surprisingly unsettling given the many prior occasions he had served through a nearly identical cannonade. The shrieks of the mortars seemed to fly in all directions. He knew that most of the Federal Army had begun making sudden preparations for Bobby Lee's attack and wondered for just a moment whether there was a duty that he might yet serve that day. His ability to fire a rifle with any accuracy was limited. He knew that equipped with a bayonet at the end of a musket he was a threat to friend and foe.

The Irish lad spoke again. "Deal, Colonel. Here's my satchel. May I keep a few pamphlets? They got other uses on the road."

Ben realized that he might have underestimated young Seamus Dinneen.

CHAPTER 3

"We've no time to spare," Captain Tom Chamberlain's voice said close to Ben's ear in surprising urgency. "I asked your cousin to find your mess kit if he can. Meanwhile, I have an Enfield for you, along with a full cartridge box." Ben felt a new belt being snaked around his waist and fastened at the front. "If your cousin finds your kit with your old cartridge box, be certain you don't confuse the ammunition you carried for your Springfield with the cartridges for the Enfield."

Ben nearly took offense at the captain's remark – given the cause of his blindness – but he knew that most officers held the intelligence of enlisted men in a contempt beyond patronizing. However, he just never could speak rudely to a superior officer, not even as Seamus had responded to the colonel. The captain's other gift was a wide-brimmed straw hat taken from rebel baggage left behind by Oakes' Alabama men between the two Round Tops. The hat was nearly large enough to fit Ben's head around his thick bandages.

"Thank you, sir. I appreciate all that you and the colonel have done for me."

"I've given this boy here, Seamus, a sack to carry for you. You'll find some biscuits and victuals, an extra canteen, a rubber sheet, and some other useful items." The captain took Ben's hand and pressed some paper and coins into it. "Here's the remaining ten dollars my brother promised to pay the boy when he gets you to a train station in Philadelphia or New York. Added to that, the officers of the 20th voted to fund your excursion with ten dollars. I hope it will be enough."

"Thank you kindly." Ben placed the money in the pocket of his shirt. "Please let the sirs know that I am extremely grateful."

"You're most welcome. Now we need your cousins to arrive."

"With respect, Captain, do you have a suggestion on the route we should follow to avoid the rebels?"

"Well, no, I... Didn't the colonel talk with you?" The captain stopped talking to Ben and shouted, "Sergeant, where did the colonel go?"

Ben heard a distant voice reply. "Sir, he went to brigade headquarters, I believe."

"He'll be there hours," Captain Chamberlain muttered, though it sounded more of a verdict than a criticism. Then he called out again. "Sergeant, see if you can find a spare map of Gettysburg." A pause followed in which Ben began to wonder how he might read a map. The captain hollered one more time, "Belay my last, Sergeant. Please go to my tent and ask the orderly to give you the compass from my baggage."

Standing uncomfortably in his personal darkness while surrounded by the thunder of rebel artillery and the ominous response of Union cannon, Ben didn't see how the captain's second idea was a better solution than the first. Nor did it get at Ben's real concern. Finding a cardinal direction was hardly an issue for a young wickie who had grown up with a sextant in his hand, calculating an azimuth daily just for practice. From the sun's position, Ben could tell both the time and the direction he faced. Ben was as accurate nearly as any sundial or compass, even blind. What he needed to know was the name of a street or turnpike that would take him to a train station from where he could travel to Philadelphia. Once there, he hoped to be able to relax in the comfort of a Pullman car all the way to Augusta.

"This will sound more confused than it needs to be, Grindle. I'll give the boy some basic directions to get you as far as Philadelphia.

From there, you'll take a train as far as your funds allow. Pardon me while I find out about your pay. And I'll need to get your orders."

The barrage of cannon fire in the distance seemed to redouble. A whiff of smoke from the big guns filled Ben's nostrils. All around he heard the noise of an army preparing to engage an enemy. Ben hoped that he and young Seamus would be away from the Union encampment soon, before the commencement of actual hostilities. He understood he could be no better than a liability and perhaps worse than a curse when combat began.

Ben heard a Maine accent calling from a distance. "Ben! Ben! That's my cousin there. I've brought his gear. I've got to talk to him." Suddenly Ben felt someone grab his arm. "Ben! Thank God, you're still here."

"Joe, I'm glad you found me." He was genuinely pleased to have a chance to say goodbye to one of his cousins remaining behind. He did not feel as keenly about Frank's absence.

"I have your gear," Joe said. "I knew it was your haversack because I found those French books wrapped in your rubber sheet." He chuckled and added quietly, "And a damn fine set of Colt pistols."

Ben was greatly relieved to hear that his two volumes of the Alexandre Dumas novel had survived. In the back of his mind had lurked a fear that other infantrymen might have scavenged the books for their paper. He thought briefly about the time spent with Clough building the light station. This, in turn, reminded Ben of his father's wrath. *"Wait and hope,"* he thought.

"I'll tell you, it created quite a stir when folks learned you were going home. I never saw so many men get to writing on the spur of the moment. I think half the regiment gave me a note for you to carry home."

"Joe, how am I going to deliver the mail if I can't see where I'm going?"

"Well, listen to you now. I'm not as stupid as all that. All their missives have a stamp, or it's marked 'Due 3 cents,' just like regular mail. When you get on your way, just drop this ditty bag at the first postal office you come across. Here, let the boy carry the bag for you."

The purpose of this ruse eluded Ben. "So why then am I pretending to be a mail carrier?"

"You know the only way to get a penny from a soldier is to steal one from his dead eyes. So I spread the word that you were carrying messages home, and the boys opened their pockets like buying an ice cream for their sweetheart. I collected twenty-seven dollars and some coins. Now before you go thinking you're Jakob Astor, let me say that more than half is postal money. They'll still buy your basics in most places, but don't think you'll be strolling down Fifth Avenue in New York to pick out your new manse cheek and jowl with Commodore Vanderbilt. I just thought you could use a little pin money for your travels."

"How did you possibly find enough men from the 2nd to raise twenty-seven dollars, even with the postage? It wasn't more than an hour ago that the General released me."

"You understand the 20th is all men from Maine, too, don't you?"

"Well, it isn't as though we know them well. How long have we been marching with the 20th? Has it been even two months yet? I couldn't tell you the names of more than a few dozen, other than the officers and sergeants."

Ben felt Joe's hand on his shoulder. "My dear cousin, I assure you every enlisted man in any Maine regiment knows your name. I suppose you're just as famous among the Pennsylvania troops. Did you notice that the whole time we were under guard by the 118th until they delivered us to Chamberlain that a certain Pennsylvania captain never came near us? Because he once set out to stop a whiskey riot and ended up face down in the mud, courtesy of one Private Bennington Grindle."

Ben recalled quite well that moment in the Mud March when a captain of the Pennsylvania 118th brought two pistols into what had been to that point merely a fistfight between three, maybe four, regiments as they wallowed in the bottomless Virginia mud. Indeed Ben did, as Joe described, send the Pennsylvania officer sprawling. Even this breach of decorum was insufficient to end the mud feud, which lasted until most of the men simply collapsed from exhaustion. Rumor had it that the officer was never able to recover those Colt pistols from the mud.

The acrid smoke from the artillery barrage filled Ben's nostrils. He knew the Confederate attack would commence soon. He was impatient to be away, feeling extremely vulnerable as a blind man during a battle between two armies intent upon killing as many of their fellow man as they could. "Do you see Captain Chamberlain anywhere about?"

"I believe he's coming just now," Joe observed. "Coming fast, too."

"All right, Grindle, I believe I have gathered everything you'll need now. Here's your discharge, signed by the General's aide de camp, Captain Meade. I'm sure it's all legal. Also, here's a pass signed by Colonel Chamberlain. That should get you past Gettysburg and onto any train hired by the army, if you encounter one. I visited the paymaster, and here's what he claims is your due. I'm sorry, but it appears your pay was suspended in May when you were declared a deserter."

Before Ben could respond, Joe Grindle spoke up vehemently. "With respect, sir, does a paymaster have the authority to make that decision? For the past two years, we marched everywhere the army told us to go. Two days ago, we marched some 40 miles without any real rest. We went into the battle yesterday just like the rest of the 20th. Now Ben may never see again. Still, after all that, some weasel of a paymaster decides Ben ain't fit to be paid for his troubles? God damn it, Captain, have you seen this man?" Ben felt hands roughly pulling at his waist, lifting his shirttails over his chest to his shoulders. "Forget what happened over yonder yesterday. He's gotten shot and stabbed. At Fredericksburg alone, he was hit twice. Now some fool pay clerk decided he hasn't earned his pay? So all the men from the 2nd Maine who fought yesterday for Colonel Chamberlain won't get paid? Is that what you're saying? First, the army says we must fight another year, and now they say we won't see a red cent for it. Is that fair somehow?"

Ben reached out, searching with both hands to find Joe's arm. "Stop it now."

"No! Dammit, they can't do it to us. This isn't just about you. All the three-year men will get swindled for two months of pay, maybe more. Hell, maybe the whole year we have left. It isn't right, sir, begging your pardon. Two month's pay is twenty-six dollars. That's a lot of money to us, Captain. If this scheme isn't bunco, there ain't another word for it."

At last, Ben found his cousin's arm and pulled him up close against his side. "Thank you, Joe. I believe you've ably shown the captain why the army calls us mutineers." During Joe's whee-up about the paymaster, Ben noticed that the volume of the artillery barrage had declined by half. The Union batteries had fallen silent. During a winter encampment, the artillerists had told him that it was sometimes necessary to allow the cannons to cool so they did not foul with unburnt gunpowder from the constant firing. The Confederate bombardment continued unabated.

"It's all right, Private. I happen to agree with your cousin," the captain said. "It seems rather unfair to me as well, and I'll raise the topic with the colonel when he has the time. But for now, I think you should move out. I would expect that the rebels will be coming at us soon."

"What route shall we travel, Captain?"

"Yes, yes, I was just getting to that," To the blind man's ear, the captain's tone sounded closer to aggravation than mere impatience. "Seamus, come here boy, you'll need to hear this as well. You're name's Joe, correct?"

Joe's arm escaped Ben's grasp. "Yes, sir, Private Joseph Grindle, late of Company B, Castine Light Infantry, 2nd Maine." Ben supposed Joe was formally saluting the captain.

"All right, Private Grindle, I'd like you to guide your cousin until he gets out of camp. Take him south along this main road over there, Taneytown Road. Just south of where Doubleday's men are encamped, you'll turn them left and set them on a heading due east. Then you are to return to the 20th's camp as quickly as you can. Understood?"

"Aye, sir, I can manage that."

"All right, then. Seamus, do you know how to use a compass?" Ben didn't hear a verbal response from the Irish lad, but the captain continued speaking directly to the boy. "Good. After Mr. Grindle turns back, you'll walk east until you come to where the road divides into two. Turn left to the northeast. In two miles or so, you'll reach the Baltimore Pike. Turn right and follow it southeast toward Two Taverns. Can you remember all that?" Again silence, and Chamberlain continued. "Keep this compass with you to check your course; whenever you have a choice take the road that goes most easterly. When you get to New York, you may pawn it. It should fetch you at least a dollar."

"Much obliged, sir," Seamus said.

Ben assumed this meant the Irish lad responded primarily to bribery. He felt a strong hand grip his right bicep. "I think your safest course will be to travel east as best you can. The rebels block Chambersburg and Harrisburg to the north. Lee has Longstreet and Hill to the west; Ewell and Johnson are north of Gettysburg. A week ago, the local militia burned the bridge on the Susquehanna at Wrightsville to prevent Jubal Early's horde from reaching Lancaster. I believe you'll be able to find a ferry to cross the river. Depending upon the outcome of today's battle, Lee may head toward Baltimore or Washington. That's why I'm sending you by way of Philadelphia."

From a distance away, Ben heard the sergeant's voice again. "Captain Chamberlain, sir, I think you'll want to see this. It looks like the whole of Bobby Lee's army is coming out of the trees over that way. Christ, that's about the prettiest thing I think I ever saw in this whole dammed war."

Ben heard faint drumming that sounded far off, probably setting a cadence for the march of rebel infantry.

The same grip that held his bicep raised his arm gently, and a second hand grasped Ben's right hand. "It's time for you to move out. Good luck, Ben. I hope you recover your sight soon. Private Grindle, be sure you remember to come back to the 20th before you reach Kittery."

When the captain stopped shaking his hand, Ben touched the bandage across his forehead in an awkward salute. "Thank you, sir. You and the colonel have been most kind to me. I hope someday I will have an opportunity to repay your generosity."

"By your leave, Captain," Joe said. "Come on, Ben. There's a reb army coming this way. There could be trouble for the both of us if any of them were there at Hanover Court House."

Ben felt a hand take hold on his right bicep and then another grasp his left wrist. On both sides, his guides began to move forward, tugging him along between them. Ben shuffled his feet, uncertain of what lay in his path. As they moved out, Ben heard the clamor of an army coming to life. From each direction arose a choir of bass and tenor voices shouting out commands. More ominously, the distant drumbeats sounded closer. A wagon rumbled past them, the horses' hooves thumping apace. In their wake, Ben inhaled a taste of dust. At nearly the same moment, Joe began to cough.

"Nothing like a good snort of Pennsylvania smutter," Joe gasped.

When Joe had recovered his breath, they continued walking out through the thronging army. Ben felt jerked and pulled to and fro as Seamus and Joe dodged and yielded to moving troops, mounted officers, supply wagons and more. Reacting in surprise when a nearby cannon fired suddenly, Ben stumbled and went down on one knee. His left ear throbbed in pain for several minutes. This sudden detonation seemed to signal the renewal of the Union bombardment toward the oncoming rebel ranks, prompting Joe to push Ben to move more quickly.

"Well, there's a sound to wake the echoes." In a hushed, almost conspiratorial tone, Joe whispered, "My God, what does that look like to you?"

"I don't see what you're talking about," Ben said.

"Down there." Joe sounded exasperated. "Doesn't that remind you exactly of the Chickahominy?"

"I wouldn't know."

"Don't you see … Dammit. I'm sorry. Ok, here's what I'm seeing. It looks like Lee's sending out his infantry. All of it. Nothing else worked, so he's throwing Longstreet's entire division at us. Just like on the Chickahominy. Gawd, I hope our line holds."

Surrounded by the burgeoning sounds of imminent combat, the trio trudged on without speaking for several minutes. Ben felt they were heading south, as the sunshine fell evenly across both cheeks and his chin. The bandages were beginning to irritate the skin on his forehead. Inside he felt a growing headache that throbbed in harmony with the chorus of artillery all around them.

Out of the blue, Joe began to speak. "Tell me, Ben, do you suppose they give the officers a better quality of soap than the sutlers have for just us enlisted folk?"

"I can't say that I've ever given it much thought. Though I am rather curious about why it's a topic of concern for you all sudden like?"

"No reason, really, but did it seem to you that the captain smelled better than most men we've been marching with these past two years?"

"Have you considered that it isn't the soap, but how often he uses it?" Ben asked mildly.

Seamus, who so far had been silent for the duration of their march, erupted abruptly in laughter that reminded Ben of a quarreling raft of ducks on the leeward waters north of Sorrow Ledge. "He sure walloped you with a sockdolager, didn't he?

"Be quiet, boy," Joe hissed. "You ain't a party to this conversation."

"You be quiet, too, Joe," Ben said. "You're walking me about a mile, but I need Seamus to help me find my route all the way to Philadelphia."

Joe shoved Ben hard to the left just as the blind man heard a horse thunder past. "Careful there, Nancyboy!" Joe shouted after the rider. "The enemy wears gray!"

As the three weaved their way through this stream of horses, troops, and wagons, Ben realized that they struggled like Atlantic salmon running upstream against the current of the Penobscot River. He stopped abruptly, pulling his guides up short. They both were walking with such determination that neither failed to notice until they had nearly jerked Ben off his feet.

"What's wrong?" Joe asked earnestly. "Need to rest?"

"Oh, hell!" the Irish lad swore loudly. "We won't get to Philly before snowfall. Can't we get out of rifle shot before your nap time?"

"Scared of a little gunfire, are you?" Joe's ridicule sounded to Ben to be a little too harsh for addressing a young boy. He thought he might intervene.

"Listen, boyo, I'se followed this army for a year on my own, scrounging every meal. All that time your sergeant nursemaided you every day. I wager I spent more time in surgeries than you, sittin' with the lame and dying." The boy paused a moment, and his voice sounded deeper when he resumed. "I've cut many a man bigger than you."

At this remark, Ben concluded that Seamus could handle himself well enough. He waved his arms to get the attention of his escorts. "Stop this din! We'll move along in just a minute. I think we'll be safer if we go in single file. We'll make less of a target in this stampede if we aren't spread out like a kite."

A long silence followed.

"Well, sure, I guess that makes sense," Joe said, almost sheepishly.

"Sure. I'm just following his lead," Seamus added in a tone not quite accusatory.

Ben decided that he should take charge of the situation to stop the quarreling between these two. "Joe, why don't you go first? I'll wager you can convince people to make a path for us. Would you please carry my musket? I'll hold onto your suspenders. Seamus, please follow me to be certain I don't drop anything in the road."

They set off walking again, now in a line much like a string of army pack mules. Ben thought they covered more distance in less time, but more importantly, there was much less pushing and pulling at his arms as they dodged the onslaught of a mobilizing army. Joe was unafraid to holler out, "Gangway! Make a hole there. Can't you see I've got an injured soldier here, you cretin? Coming through!" The main impediment to their pace was now Ben's unsteady footing on the road that was deeply rutted by the narrow wheels of artillery caissons and supply wagons.

When Joe stopped again, Ben realized he had lost all track of time. The din of the main battle seemed to come from directly behind them; however, he heard the rifle and small arms fire of a smaller, distant skirmish off on his left, somewhere toward the northeast. He also smelled the distinctive odor of burnt gunpowder on the wind.

"Damn, Ben, it looks like you're bleeding again." Ben felt another sweep of Joe's handkerchief across his cheek and along his chin. "Perhaps I'd better stay with you a little while longer to be certain you won't swoon from the blood loss. I don't think the lad can carry you back to the hospital from any great distance."

"Have we reached Doubleday's encampment?"

"Yes, I believe so. And this here road seems to head due east, just as the captain described. He said I should take my leave of you here, but I don't think he'd want you to bleed to death on the road." Joe paused a moment before adding sarcastically, "Not given all that the officers have invested in your travels."

"Now listen, Joe, they owed me nothing. No more than any of the men in the 20th did." Ben paused a moment, then lowered his voice. "It's rather likely I've more money in my pocket now than I've ever had at any one time in my life. I'm sure I'll make out fine. If you stray from Captain Chamberlain's instructions, you may well hang."

"I think I'd prefer to be shot.

"How about we vote?" Seamus asked.

"You little brat," Joe snarled. "I'll lash your backside like…"

"Like my father would?" Ben asked quietly.

"Now Ben, you know I didn't mean anything…"

"Sure. But I'd prefer you didn't talk about whipping the boy, even if you didn't plan to follow through." Ben did his best to seem casual about this topic, but he was not certain how convincing that sounded. He could not see Joe's face, so he decided to lighten the tone and added, "It's still something of a sore subject with me."

"Surely. I'm sorry, Ben. I'm sorry. You're right. I probably need to get heading along back to camp."

"Before you go, I need a favor from you. General Meade instructed Colonel Chamberlain to telegraph the governor to have Stan and Val assigned to the 20th so that the colonel can look after them. I'd be grateful if you'd show 'em the ropes when they report."

"Of course, I will. I can't say that I'd recognize them today after so much time. Just let 'em know to search me out when they arrive. I'll look out for them; I promise you." Ben felt two calloused hands clamp onto his shoulders. "I wish I could take you into the city and get you on to the train myself. I hate to leave you in the charge of this young turk."

"We'll be fine," Ben assured his cousin. "We're walking away from the fighting. You'll be heading straight back into it. I think you'll need to look after yourself and Frank rather than worry about me. Good luck, Joe."

"It's a long way back home." Both hands lifted from Ben's shoulders and settled around his right hand. "Be careful."

"Would you say goodbye to Frank for me? I'll expect you to come by Sorrow Ledge whenever you get home. In the meanwhile, don't let Frank do anything to get you both shot."

Joe suddenly pulled Ben close and hugged him around the shoulders with one arm. "I guess we'll see about that. A year in a war. Who knows what will happen in all that time?" Just as abruptly, his cousin's embrace ended, and Ben heard footfalls trailing away on the gravel.

In the July swelter, Ben felt a curious chill. He wondered how Joe and Frank would fare in this day's action, or in the battles to come during the remaining enlistments of the "three-year men." Would either man be alive to cousin at Sorrow Ledge after they returned home? He thought for a moment about whom he would and would not see when he arrived back in Maine, or whether he would be physically able to see anyone or anything at all by that time. Would the two-year men of the 2nd Maine welcome or shun him? Who would greet him at Sorrow Ledge? In the last letter he received from Maine, Valcour reported that their mother already had left for Portland, taking Saratoga with her. She paid for their travels with Ben's enlistment bonus. Valcour and Stanwix would leave to join the army as soon as he arrived home. He hoped Colonel Chamberlain would make good on General Meade's instruction to ensure that the brothers were assigned to the 20th. Ben knew he might well be destined for his own Chateau d'*If*. There was also a letter he would need to pen in the next day or two after he had more time to ponder the words appropriate for such a task as breaking a betrothal that existed only in his mind.

"Bennington is your Christian name? Don't know what I've ever met anyone named for a town," Seamus said. "You born there? In Vermont, right? Before your family went to Maine?" While the boy's Irish brogue was distinct, Ben heard also a nasal quality that reminded him of the New Yorker from that morning's little incident.

"No, I've never been there," Ben explained. "My father named me for a battle in the war for independence from Britain." Judging by how the heat of the sun fell on his right flank, Ben guessed that they were walking now due east from the Union Army's position.

"Sadly, there's no such a way forward for Irish freedom."

"You mean a war against Great Britain?" Ben asked in astonishment. He knew only a little of the situation in Ireland, but he felt that the Catholics there had even less chance of emancipation from the Queen's rule than the Confederacy did in its efforts to secede from the Union.

"God, that would be bloody suicide."

"I'm sorry, lad, I don't follow what you're saying."

"Well, tarnation, why won't England allow all true Irishmen to come to America?"

Ben wondered if the boy's tendency toward profanity in each breath was an effrontery intended to make him sound more mature than his years or size. Another curiosity was the odd aroma about the boy that seemed to Ben's nose to grow stronger as they emerged from the smoke of campfires and cannon fire. In his experiences living on the sea coast and marching with the army, Ben rarely encountered quite its equal. Yet he did not know how to raise the delicate matter with the lad.

"Ben, we gotta move. Here comes a whole regiment of cavalry right at us."

Seamus pulled Ben's arm, leading him off to the right side of the track. Ben stumbled on the thick berm of weeds and grass. He landed on his knees just as he heard the first rider approach. Dust filled his nostrils.

"What have we got here?" the rider demanded loudly. "Shouldn't you be back with your regiment? Sounds like a hell of a battle going on over there. What are you, a deserter? Or just a coward?"

"Gawd, I hate cavalry," Seamus whispered behind Ben's back. "Act like stallions; stink like dung."

"On your feet, soldier!"

Ben struggled to his feet, hugging the barrel of his Enfield against his chest for leverage as he pulled himself upward. He heard more horses approaching, coming on fast. When he came upright, he felt a massive shape butt up against his chest. Then a horse snorted directly into his face. The animal's breath was hot and wet on Ben's chin and neck. He raised his hand and stroked the animal's snout.

"Take your hand off my mount before I shoot you dead where you stand," the cavalryman shouted.

The sound of other hoof beats ceased, and Ben heard what he assumed were now other horses huddled close about him. He felt the warmth of their breath on his exposed skin. He heard their anxious pawing at the ground.

"What's going on here, scout?" a new voice demanded. The accent sounded flat except for a curious pronunciation of the *r* in 'here,' which sounded nothing like the distinctive range of New England inflections.

"I captured this man while he was running away from the battle, sir."

Now the second voice assumed the role of inquisitor. "Don't you know to come to attention and salute when a general officer approaches? What, are you blind?"

"Yes, sir." Ben removed the straw hat, exposing his bandaged head to the daylight. "At least for the moment. The surgeon said it might be only temporary."

Ben heard another horse draw closer; its horseshoes scratched at the dust. "Who is this man?" yet a third voice asked.

"Show some respect, soldier," said the voice of the first horseman to arrive. "Can't you see this is General Custer?"

Seamus interrupted with a contemptuous tone. "He just tol' you he's can't see nuthin'."

Ben felt the boy duck behind him as another horse pushed forward against him. "Be quiet, Seamus," he hissed. As the horse pushed it snout over Ben's shoulder, it abruptly grunted and reared back. Perhaps the steed had gotten close enough to smell the lad's unusual odor and smartly retreated.

"Would someone tell me why we've stopped?" the third rider asked. "Who is this man?" Repeating the same questions revealed in this man's tone an evident and likely long-standing exasperation.

The second man tried to clarify the situation. "General Custer, Sergeant Ingram found these two. The man appears to be a deserter or a spy. He claims to be blind. However, only temporary blind – whoever heard of such a thing?"

"And there's no chance he could be blind?" asked the voice now identified as General Custer. "Even *temporarily* blind? No chance, *whatsoever*, Captain?"

"Well, General, I suppose so. I'm no medical man myself." To Ben's ear, the junior officer sounded like a man who was often corrected by his superior. The captain clearly resented this.

"What's your regiment, soldier?" General Custer asked.

"When I enlisted, I was with...," Ben began to explain.

"He's a spy, General," the sergeant protested. "A man should know his regiment."

"I enlisted with the 2nd Maine," Ben said.

Now the captain interrupted. "Well, there you go all right, General. He's no spy; he's just a mutineer. The 2nd Maine went home two months ago. He must be one of them that signed for three years and then refused to serve. I believe General Sherman wanted them all shot."

"We should do the army a favor and carry out Sherman's orders," the sergeant said in a tone of excitement that alarmed Ben.

"*General* Sherman, if you please, Sergeant," General Custer said firmly.

At this juncture, Ben realized that this conversation was not progressing in his favor. "Those that signed the three-year papers were transferred to the 20th Maine. Colonel Chamberlain said he had permission to shoot us, and he might have, but the 20th's roster was a notch below fighting strength." Ben started to feel uncomfortably warm in the afternoon sun. One of the horses still pressed against his chest, and the boy hugged him around the waist from behind.

"General, sir, the man admits he was one of the mutineers," the captain said. "And I don't see Colonel Chamberlain or his Maine boys around here. So he must be a deserter as well. Let's just shoot them both and move onto camp." Now the captain sounded rather tetchy.

"If you would be so kind as to allow me to interrogate this man without the constant disputation, I would be most grateful, *Captain*." The general accented the officer's rank more keenly than a harsh rebuke. "How did you come to be wounded, soldier?"

"Powder burns, sir," Ben said simply. "My weapon's breech shattered." By the sounds of their hooves and constant whinnying, he guessed the horses were equally impatient as the cavalrymen to get on down the road. Ben, too, felt edgy, though he attributed that to the threat of imminent execution.

"When was this?" Custer asked. His voice sounded a pitch higher than the tone of his fellow riders. Rather unpleasantly so.

"Yesterday, General, on a hill west of town."

The captain scoffed. "Now you're claiming you were with Colonel Chamberlain on the Round Tops, when the 20th defeated Oates and his Alabama boys?"

Ben now tired of the captain's challenges. "I claim nothing, sir. I am stating a fact."

"I'll caution you to watch your tone of voice, soldier," the captain said.

Abruptly Ben heard a shuffle in the dirt he took to be a horse moving about, but then a man landed on the ground heavily. Ben felt a hand on his right wrist, and another hand sought out his hand. "I've heard a lot about the 2nd Maine," Custer said. "I believe that we fought in the same battles at a few places." Custer's handshake was firm but also sweaty, no doubt from his earlier exertions in combat.

"Yes, General. I've heard your name in a few places, too."

"So where are you going now?"

"I'm going home, sir, back to Maine. General Meade's orders. He said there's been trouble on the coast with rebel pirates. I am the keeper of a light house outside Penobscot Bay. Colonel Chamberlain hired this boy to lead me to a train station to get me on my way. I'm hoping I'll have my sight before I arrive home. If I'm not completely restored, at least my right eye wasn't burnt so badly as the other."

"I'm sure you have orders, then, from Colonel Chamberlain? Or General Meade himself, perhaps?" The general's voice was now quiet and sounded almost sympathetic. "Do you have a woman back home in Maine to take care of you? Mother or a wife?"

"Here are my papers, sir." Ben fished the documents from his trouser pocket. "Discharge papers signed by Captain Meade on General Meade's staff and a pass signed by Lieutenant Colonel Chamberlain, 20th Maine." He thought there was no exact answer to the general's second question, so he felt no need to respond.

The general took the paperwork for a perfunctory review and

quickly pushed them back into Ben's hand before abruptly turning away. "You see, Captain Foster, there's nothing wrong with this soldier's story. You were right to doubt the bloodied bandage as proof of his claims; but this fresh blood running down his neck would be hard to fake. And I don't believe you'd find a Southern spy or Northern deserter anywhere who would admit connection to the 2nd Maine mutineers. No, I believe Private Grindle is exactly who he says he is. Let him pass." The blind man sensed this display of logic was just another routine performance intended to bolster the newly appointed general's air of superiority. Ben suspected that if the captain had first taken the position that the blind man was an innocent bound for home, then Custer might have summarily executed Ben on the spot. Just to be contrary.

As Ben heard the horse closest to him wheel about and canter off, Custer bellowed, "Wolverines, forward!" Soon the mass of the 7th Michigan cavalry thundered past, headed in the direction from which Ben and Seamus recently had come. A cloud of dust raised by their passage filled Ben's nostrils. The Irish boy stood behind Ben still, muttering a crude torrent of vulgarity as the horsemen passed. He accused them of drinking, gambling, whoring and other profligate activities, some quite unspeakable. Finally, Ben objected.

"Perhaps you've been marching with a different army," Ben said.

"Really? How long you been blind?" the boy asked with a mock incredulity. "The colonel let on it was recent. Or was you marching the whole time with the blessed St. Patrick's boys' choir?"

Ben adjusted the straps of his gear across his shoulders and began to amble down the road of his own volition. "Come on," he called. "There's still a war going on, and a big part of it's just back there a piece. Perhaps we could discuss the injustice of it all at some greater distance." He did not know how far they had come from the army camp, but for the first time, the banter of shrieking crows somewhat obscured the sounds of battle. In the same distance they had walked, he had grown more accustomed to moving in complete darkness. He eased his way forward with his feet in a shuffling motion like how he'd seen a gang of rebel prisoners toddling along, hobbled in single file. The smell of burnt gunpowder from artillery and shoulder arms from the Gettysburg battlefield still followed them even after so long a distance.

After tramping alone for a rod or two, Ben felt a hand clasp his wrist as the boy began again to guide him. "Sorry, Ben. Just what all I've seen this year; I wish to God I might unsee again."

For at least two miles more according to his blind reckoning, Ben trudged on silently as Seamus tugged him along by his sleeve. All the while the boy kept up a profane diatribe about every dodgy behavior, crime or atrocity the boy had observed since becoming a camp follower. No doubt the Irish lad had listened to a great deal of such testimony on the subject. Without a family in New York, he had chosen to remain with the army. When he was forbidden to overwinter with the Federal troops outside Washington, the boy instead quartered inside the city as best he could amidst the abettors, accomplices, collaborators, victims and villains. After this distance of listening intently, Ben thought Seamus might hire himself out to the many Confederate newspapers as a correspondent on Northern transgressions. Sadly, Ben knew that the boy wasn't telling tall tales of fictitious debauchery. He preferred not to think of his fellow soldiers in such worst of terms. Surely, they deserved no small credit for their feats in battle, or in the very least their willingness to serve. They had come for the fighting, and in return, many were now wounded and dead. He had heard of the eligible men back home in Maine – home of Abe's vice president Hannibal Hamlin, no less – who had knocked out their own front teeth with a hammer, believing that if infantrymen tore open their gunpowder cartridges with their teeth that this self-inflicted injury would disqualify them from service. The chief recruiter for the State of Maine, Captain Low, was only too happy to disappoint the practitioners of this curious dentistry by announcing that inductees so deformed were still welcomed into the cavalry, who used pistols, pikes or sabers primarily and therefore would not need their teeth to rip apart a rifle cartridge.

CHAPTER 4

*A*fter the hoof beats of Custer's Michigan Brigade faded behind them, Ben sensed other traffic returning to the turnpike. If he was a ship's lookout, the Irish boy could do no better at identifying approaching travelers: dispatch riders; sutler wagons; army scouts; and a carriage with lost newspapermen arriving late from the railway station in York. Farmers scurried east to hide their prized heifers or west with old steers for the consideration of the commissary officers in either army.

"I'm a bit peckish," Seamus said. "Wanna see what the captain put in this knapsack?"

At this question, Ben realized he had not eaten a single bite during the entire day. Breakfast was forgotten in the hospital rat's rush to get the blind patient back to his regiment. Dinner, too, was neglected in Captain Chamberlain's hurry to get the blind soldier away from the corps before the rebels again tested the Union Army's tenacity. Curiously Ben did not feel hunger pangs in his gut; instead, a rush of fatigue overcame his entire body. Suddenly feeling dizzy, he turned abruptly toward his right without a word and in a few steps felt the dirt beneath his feet turn to grass. After a few more strides, he collapsed to his knees.

"I'm so hungry I could eat a hard cracker," Ben said.

"That's a yes, then?" the boy asked.

Ben drank a long swig from his canteen then poured some water onto his kerchief, with which he wiped the back of his neck, his throat and the lower portion of his face. He listened as Seamus pulled out each victual from the haversack and commented upon its insufficiency. "Two pounds of flour? What are you to do with that? Make bread as we walk along? Look here, then, half a pound of salt? A pound of coffee beans. A tin of peaches? Gawd, lots and lots of hard tack!" The boy's exasperation seemed to increase as he burrowed deeper into the knapsack. "Tarnation. Why not jerked beef or pemmican? A summer sausage, even?" The boy sniffed once or twice. "Well, look here, dried sassafras, sticks of peppermint and horehound candy. Looks like enough horehound to last a full life."

"Sounds like quite a hodgepodge," Ben observed. "But nothing particularly edible. Why don't you open the peaches with my bayonet?"

"Peaches it is, then," Seamus said. "I'll come right back."

The blind man assumed the boy was answering the call of nature in the woods nearby. Although he knew the lad was close, he felt somewhat vulnerable sitting alone on the berm of the road, unable to see who might be coming or going along the turnpike. Ben had long observed in the course of his guard duties around various encampments during two years of army service that war attracted people of many loyalties, mixed emotions and unpredictable motives. Men visited most often to provide their goods and wares; sometimes they offered information. Blacksmiths and tinkers came into camp to sharpen knives, hatchets, and bayonets. Women came proffering fresh fruits, vegetables, and meats that the army commissaries seldom provided; sometimes they too tendered information about the enemy or services of another sort. Also, among them, were the petty thieves and highwaymen looking to steal whatever they could from whomever they might meet.

After a few moments, Seamus returned and pressed a small, fuzzy orb into Ben's waiting hands. "These were just hanging on a tree not 20 feet off," the boy said.

Ben took a bite of the peach. The fruit was ripe and juicy, drenching his chin and neck with its sweet nectar. He fished out his handkerchief to dab around his mouth and jowls. "By God, that's good. I can't recall ever tasting better. Thank you kindly."

"I bet the hospital hardly fed you much at all, then."

"I don't recall that the ladies served any other than a hard biscuit and a few cups of water. Listening to the mortal passing of the badly wounded tends to remind the living that they haven't so much to complain of," Ben said. He did not often reflect upon the random quality that brought death to the few among the many in battle. "A fellow from the 83rd Pennsylvania passed away while waiting outside the surgery. Before he died, all he could talk about was water and food. Lobster and corn, both slathered in his Nancy's best butter. I ain't hardly thought about food none since."

"You'll want a filling supper, then, I guess? I could soften up these hard biscuits in water or boiled coffee," Seamus said. "I did see smoke from a chimney up the road a little way. Want that I fetch some eggs or even a chicken? I'll bet I can get us some tasty dinner unseen."

Ben reflected upon these choices a few minutes. "I think you may find the Maryland Catholics more generous to an Irish boy than these local Mennonites. Not that I favor any begging, but I think there'll be increased resistance as we travel north."

The lad seemed to listen attentively and reflect upon all this silently for several minutes. "I can be quiet enough, so they won't know what we've borrowed then," Seamus observed in a conspiratorial tone.

Ben nearly objected to that line of thinking but stopped himself. There could be a time in the coming days when their meals might well depend upon the lad's wily ways. Much of their traveling kitty included postal money, which Ben could not predict how well it would barter among the local populations. With no notice or reason, Ben suddenly hoped that in Philadelphia they would encounter a fish-monger peddling wares from the Atlantic. The panfish and puny crabs from Virginia's rivers and estuaries never satisfied the hunger of Ben or his comrades from Maine. By Ben's reckoning, merely the claw of a Maine lobster yielded more meat than a dozen Chesapeake blue crabs taken in their entirety. After his father's death, Ben put to sea in a dory at slack tide each morning to draw up from the deep the wooden traps set around the ledge that yielded lobster. On some days, he would also cast a net to haul cod from their schools or the salmon running into the Penobscot River. Army rations rarely included fish, for which Ben was grateful despite the disappointment to his palate. Given what commissary officers and sutlers managed to pass off as edible, Ben felt good cause to be fearful of what might be served as seafood.

"Camp here tonight or walk farther?" Seamus asked.

"What do you suppose we have remaining of daylight?" the blind man asked.

"Enough to walk five miles or so, I guess."

"Let's go on. Perhaps we'll come across some supper farther along down the road." Ben scrambled about a bit on the ground as he tried to stand erect while maintaining balance in his darkness. So far as he could discern, the boy did not react to his curious movements. "Be sure to pack all our foodstuffs. Poor as they are, we may come to rely upon what the captain gave us. And may I have a bit of peppermint?"

"We got enough flour to make carrion pie when we're desperate," Seamus said. The boy chuckled, but Ben did not doubt that between the two armies there had been many occasions when men ate rotted fowl flesh and were glad to have it. He had heard it said that the rebels in charge at Libby Prison provided little else for the Northern inmates to eat. Even rats were rumored to be regular entrees on Libby's notorious menu. The time had long passed in Ben's war when he came to hate the Confederates more for their treatment of the wounded and captured than even their rebellion against the Union. *"Wait and hope,"* Ben whispered to himself.

They had traveled far enough that the sounds of the two armies at war had receded entirely from Ben's right ear. In the quiet, a curious bell began sounding in Ben's left ear that did not desist no matter how he held his head. Afternoon became evening, which Ben knew turned to twilight when the air against his skin cooled. Travelers along the road were sparse now. Instead, he heard the woodland creatures resuming their own business. Crickets and crows sounded foremost, but he also listened to the distant yip of coyotes. In response, farm dogs howled their resentment of the varmints. Having grown up on a barren island off Maine, there were some sounds in the Pennsylvania night that Ben did not immediately recognize. He dismissed this other din because it could not be the elephant stalking him still. Whatever damage Bobby Lee's boys and Meade's men inflicted upon each other no longer mattered a whit to Ben. He was going home.

For the first time, home was a word he feared. His mother and Saratoga were already gone; his brothers would leave for the army once Ben arrived home. He no longer harbored any hope that Rebecca would accept his overtures; she had far too many better opportunities among the young men of Rockland. He would be alone on a rock far at sea, with only a wickie's duties to occupy his days.

CHAPTER 5

*B*en woke to the smell of bacon frying in a skillet.

"Thank God, you're awake," Seamus said. "Feared I'd need eat a pound of bacon myself."

Ben propped himself on his right elbow. He struggled against the natural desire to open his eyes and see the world upon waking. "How did you find bacon? I don't recall you listed it among our rations last night."

"A little farm over there a ways. Nice folks. Loyal to Lincoln, too. Your rifle was on my shoulder. Might be loyal to Jeff Davis, too, if Bobby Lee was on their porch."

"You didn't threaten them, did you?" Ben asked. The Union Army had strict, if largely unenforced, regulations about pillaging civilian homes, especially on the north side of the Mason-Dixon line.

"I threatened to pay them hard money. A silver dollar for bacon, fresh biscuits and a half gallon of milk. Better than Longstreet's men would give them. Eat up. We gotta move along. The farmer said the rebs got whipped pretty good. Thinks they'll be moving south. If they head for Baltimore, we'll be smack dab in their path."

Ben accepted the tin plate thrust into his hands. He felt about a bit with his fingers to identify the thick strips of bacon, a biscuit dripping with fresh butter and an apple. "I like eggs, too," he said.

"Well, now, there's a wee bit of a story there," Seamus said, followed by an amused chuckle. "Past year I've worn away two pairs of shoes walking throughout Virginia and Maryland. Of all places I've been, that was one of the most curious farms I've seen."

"How so?"

"Well, they had a chicken coop but no chickens, and a barn but no cows, and a corral with no horses. Yet they had piles of stinking dung everywhere you looked."

Ben chuckled at the description Seamus gave. Even blind, Ben could imagine perfectly well the scene described for him, as the farmer had likely moved his livestock away from potential confiscation by either of the warring forces, especially a harried army that might pay the man for his goods in worthless Confederate script. Worse, perhaps, the livestock might simply be slaughtered in the fields to prevent a pursuing army from eating fresh meat. Likely all the farms within a day's ride of Gettysburg were in a similar condition that day.

"By chance, are we heading into any hills?" Ben asked.

"Yes, the farmer said we'd cross several high ridges if we go on walking east."

Ben reflected upon this information a moment. "I think you'll see a surprising amount of livestock up there. You and I can hike over a mountain easily enough, but an army of thousands of men would be most likely to stay in the valley. They'll take the least challenging route, which means marching up a hill or mountain as little as necessary. So, if you want to hide something from an army, where would you put it?"

Seamus giggled. "I suppose there'll be lots of dung on the road ahead, then."

The rain began to fall soon after Ben finished eating and Seamus had packed their tack into the haversack. First came a light mist that cooled Ben's chin and neck. As the morning wore on, the showers grew in intensity so that the humidity increased as well. They marched with rubber blankets draped over their shoulders. Ben's straw hat proved poor cover against the downpour, and he felt the cotton bandages around his head grow soggy with rainwater. This change of weather seemed to bring out a flight of mosquitoes that pestered them both as they walked.

By his reckoning, the veteran of many marches thought they had hiked at least five miles in silence before Seamus spoke up next. "I see a town ahead. Couldn't we find shelter till the rain slackens?"

Ben pondered this option a few minutes as they continued to trudge down the road. The wind blew steadily out of the northwest, and the temperature had not changed. To Ben, who grew up observing and recording the weather daily, this did not indicate an imminent change. "We've no idea how long this rain may last. We might be sitting for a day or even three. If you don't mind, I would prefer to push on."

"If you say."

Ben stopped in his tracks. "Seamus, I don't mean that as a command. I'm just saying that if we stop for the rain, we may be holed up for a few days. I prefer to be as far away from here as possible when Bobby Lee tries to slip away from Meade because Lee has poor options. He's got to try for Baltimore where he'll find sympathetic copperheads, or he'll have to turn tail and run back toward Virginia. In either event, I don't believe we'll fare well. I've no interest in spending any time in Libby Prison."

"I guess I'd be hung or shot," Seamus said quietly.

"Why would you think that?" Ben asked. "That's what they'd do to spies." Then he laughed. "What's in these religious tracts you give away?"

"No, Ben, but I need you to understand that I told them rebs some things that didn't turn out so well for their cause."

Ben stopped abruptly at mid-stride. His mouth hung agape as he considered what this could mean for them. "You gave information to the Confederates?"

"Wait. Not how you think," the boy protested.

Ben tried hard to think of a way in which providing intelligence to the enemy could be a good thing. He fell to his knees, staggered by the weight of this revelation as when his father heaved a sack of Portland cement onto his young back. "Do you understand what this means? If the rebels think you're a spy, we'll both go to prison or the gallows?"

Abruptly Ben had a new thought. "You said just a minute ago that what you shared didn't help the Confederate cause. Is that what you were trying to do? Please tell me what the hell has been going on."

Long moments passed in which Ben's anxiety continued to grow while he waited for Seamus to respond. "I swear I'm no spy, no copperhead and not a lousy sympathizer," the boy said finally. "I go between lines without question. Even more so when I have Holy Bibles. You know how soldiers need paper. Some backwoods bumpkins use tree leaves to toilet. So I am welcome in any camp. A Union officer asked me to pass information on to the rebs. If a butternut asked how many Union infantry or artillery were across the way, I had a ready answer. When the Union number was small, I was told to say it was bigger. Whenever their number was large, I was told to let on that there were fewer troops and cannons."

Ben still knelt on the wet ground. A puddle soaked his trousers from knee to ankle.

"I did no spying," Seamus continued in earnest. "I took no papers or counted troops. I gave out bad information. It's the rebs' own fault; they had no business in trusting me. I'm from New York, not New Orleans."

"You said a Union officer asked you to do this?" Ben was incredulous at both the officer's audacity and the lad's pluck.

The boy's voice lowered. "I owed the major for a good turn he did me. He's a fellow New Yorker. I had planned to winter over with his regiment. Some of his men got into the spirits and thought to do me some mischief. First time that happened to me. Few people try to get close to me because I got this asafetida bag. Not many folks can stomach the odor. Somedays I hate the odor myself. Being how drunk they'd gotten, they wouldn't have noticed the stench of a dead body. The major had to beat them men with the flat of his sword to divert their attentions."

With this anecdote, Seamus resolved two mysteries lingering in Ben's mind. First was the source of the peculiar aroma he had detected upon meeting the lad in Chamberlain's marquee tent. Some Maine folks wore asafetida bags as preventive medicine to ward off vapors and vampires. Ben's mother wore one, a small linen sachet filled with a mix of herbs from the Middle East, when he was young. Her bag was not nearly so odiferous as the one Seamus wore. From what Ben remembered, his mother's talisman was most effective at repelling his father's affections. She stopped wearing it after her husband's death. This story Seamus told also explained the lad's aversion to the various proclivities of the army when it was not about the business of fighting a war. Ben now understood the cause of the boy's harangue as Custer's Michigan cavalry passed. There was another sin that went unspoken in that prior rant: pederasty. Ben felt embarrassed that he didn't know how to comfort the boy; he couldn't imagine the fear Seamus experienced even though he bore the scars of a different style of cruelty on his own back.

Ben held out his hand for assistance in getting up from the ground. "I suppose we should move along in case the rebs are coming this way."

The boy took the extended wrist and gave a powerful tug. "Won't do you no good to be soaked through any more than you already are."

As they walked through the small village of Abbottstown, Seamus resumed his narration as lookout. There was a dry goods store, of course, along with a livery, black smithy, pub, and meetinghouse. Ben did not hear the hubbub of many residents along the street; although as they passed the tavern, he heard what sounded to be a good trade for late morning.

"If you see a bench near the mercantile, sit me there."

"Want that I go buy foodstuffs for our travels?"

"Yes, I believe we'll be more economical and less obvious if we cook our own meals along the way rather than go into an inn or pub. Or shop among the farmers."

After another hundred paces, the boy settled the blind man on a wooden bench. He relieved Ben of the tack he wore: rifle, bedroll, haversack, and canteen. "I'm sorry to leave you sitting out in the rain, but I don't see anywhere there's a bench covered at all."

"I don't mind," Ben said. "Seemed like Southern skies opened up every time a Northern army set out to march somewhere. Except when it got so hot and dry that even the vultures wouldn't bother with us."

"What do you want me to buy, then?"

Ben fished his money from the pocket of his trousers and handed the entire bankroll of paper currency to Seamus. He thought it point-less to try to dole out a few bills because a blind man had no way to determine their denominations. Ultimately, he knew he must choose to trust the boy, who could, if he desired, simply murder Ben and take all the cash and kit they carried for himself. Captain Chamberlain's compass would pawn for a pittance compared to the dueling pistols in Ben's kit and the musket with which Ben was armed.

"Any food you want me to look for?"

This question puzzled Ben more than he expected. His tastes were limited by experience. After his mother excluded him from family meals, he ate mostly fish from his daily catch that he fried in a skillet over the warming stove in the barren assistant lighthouse keeper's quarters. These meals were supplemented by the hardtack and oatmeal he purchased while in Rockland and the occasional biscuits or cookies that young Saratoga sneaked out of the kitchen and left on his bedroll. Each morning, he left at the kitchen door of the keeper's quar-ters the bushel basket containing the catch of his dawn haul from lobster pots and fishing nets. Each week he would set there the food-stuffs he had purchased from the store in Rockland. Ben might go without seeing the shadow of the island's four other inhabitants for days at a time. Soon after enlisting, he discovered that the meals served under a variety of names by the U.S. Army all tasted curiously similar.

"I don't believe we can carry too much more weight than we have now."

"I'll look around for a place to leave this mailbag," Seamus suggested. "That alone will free us of more weight than we need to bear."

"You mean a post office, right? We can't just leave all those letters lying about. They may contain some information that shouldn't go into enemy hands."

"No, I hadn't thought that exactly but I wasn't planning just to leave it to feed the goats."

Hickory-scented smoke reached Ben's nostrils, and his thoughts returned to the problem at hand. "We should get mostly what we can eat without stopping to cook. Some jerky, biscuits, cookies, summer sausage, hard candy, like that."

"Don't forget that we have horehound already."

"I had in mind something edible," Ben said. "You know, I wouldn't mind some apples and pears because they should carry well. I think we'd only bruise plums and peaches in the satchel. Can you think of anything that you'd like?"

"If I get just half your list, we'll add ten stones to our load."

"Use your judgment and get what looks good. Just don't forget I'm waiting out here in the rain."

After hearing the lad splash away across the muddy street, Ben sat alone in the rain except for a passing wagon pulled slowly along by a team of oxen that snorted their distress in unison. As he listened to the drizzle falling on the rubber sheet, his thoughts settled on a letter he would need to write back to Rockland. His previous letters from the battlefields always began with "My darling Rebecca." That salutation now seemed in the present circumstance – given his current physical condition – as outdated as a gentleman's powdered wig. Addressing her as formally as "My dear young lady" or even "Dear Miss Rebecca" would likely serve only to puzzle and then infuriate her once the riddle was revealed. Ben sensed the challenge in settling on these first few words did not bode well for completing the remainder of the letter. He secretly hoped – against his desire – that Rebecca had already met another man and was herself struggling with how she would tender the news of their nuptials in a forlorn missive to Ben. Were that the case, it would be fitting, he thought, if she, too, now struggled with the appropriate greeting to him.

Not long after the showers slackened, Seamus returned from the general store. He was whistling a lively reel that Ben had heard the New York troops humming, and though he'd been told its title more than a dozen times, he still could never remember the name correctly. When the boy sat on the bench, he smelled sweetly of peanuts.

"How did your foraging mission go?"

"Well, I think. At least I hope you're pleased," Seamus said. "I did what you said as best I could. Here, I found peanut brittle." The boy pressed a flat, sticky cake into Ben's hand. "I bought some apples. The pears seemed wormy, but the cheddar felt firm enough, so I bought a small round. We've got beef dodgers; cornbread and apple butter; a summer sausage; jerked beef and a pound of hard candy. I thought we might suck on that during hot days so we could keep walking. Oh, and the store keep said he'd be sure to pass that sack of mail along to the postmistress."

"I'd say you did quite well, indeed." Ben hesitated for a moment. "How much did all this cost us?"

"All we have," the boy said calmly. "Shall we stay over to morning and rob from the bank over there?"

A brief panic struck the frugal Mainer. Beyond the paper cash, they had left only coins, which Ben had not bothered to count. By its weight alone, he guessed there was not enough money to buy train fare for two passengers to New York or book ship's passage to Portland or Bangor. Abruptly Seamus chortled.

"To be honest, I believe we received a red-haired discount," the lad said as he pushed a thick wad of cash into Ben's hand. "I didn't steal. Promise. When I first went in, I was careful so the keeper saw the wad of cash I was carrying, just so he'd want to have our business. After I had some things up on the counter, I took off my cap. Then I roamed around a little bit, looking here and there. All sudden like, he seemed kinda anxious to see me out the door. I guess he didn't want to earn a reputation for selling to Irish."

His miserly New England caution relieved, Ben chuckled at the boy's account. "Sounds like you've developed a keen sense of horse trading. Unfortunately, I need to send you back into the store. I forgot to ask you to fetch some writing paper and a few pencils."

"Then let me have back some of the money."

"Why don't you just hold onto all of it until we reach Philadelphia?" Ben held out the bankroll, but an odd thought struck him. "Can you read and write?"

"I've read the Bible all the way through a few times this past year. And my scratch is tolerable good, I suppose."

"You could write a letter for me?" Ben asked. "To a young lady back home?"

The boy seemed to ponder this challenge for a while. "I never had the benefit of school, but I can draw the letters if you can spell the words to me."

"Fair enough. Get several sheets as I expect we'll probably work through a few tries before we get it done right."

The afternoon's drizzle had ceased, and Ben pushed the rubber sheet off his head. His thoughts returned to the question of addressing a letter to a woman whom he might never see again – literally. He tried to recall her face but was able to envision only dark, rough shapes. The few colors in his mind seemed to burst and fade away like artillery shells in an aerial bombardment. Then he concentrated on the letters of her name. For a few months after his mother stopped schooling him, Ben continued to practice writing in script but finally abandoned the effort and instead printed with block letters all the journal entries, correspondence, reports and requisition forms required of a light keeper.

"Three pencils, 15 sheets of paper and two envelopes," the Irish lad announced upon his return, surprising Ben who was distrait. "I put the paper in one of the books in your haversack and wrapped them in your jacket. That should keep it flat and dry."

"Thank you kindly."

Seamus helped the blind soldier to his feet and burdened him with a share of the gear they carried. Ben had become accustomed to balancing his haversack over his left shoulder while carrying the Enfield with the stock resting in the crook of his right arm. His fore-finger remained in the trigger guard, creating the appearance – at least from a distance, Ben hoped – of a man armed and able to defend the pair. He settled the broad-brimmed straw hat over his bandages. They each drank from the canteen that hung by a strap around the boy's neck and then set off walking east. Unable to feel the sun under the overcast sky of the afternoon, Ben had little choice but to trust the lad's reading of Captain Chamberlain's compass to ensure they remained on an easterly course.

The pair walked on for what Ben guessed was nearly five miles in quiet as they both sucked on hard candy. The boy held the man's sleeve gently, tugging only when Ben needed to be directed to avoid a deep puddle, a rut or the many piles of fresh dung on the road. Ben had decided to set aside for the moment the question of the proper salutation with which to address Rebecca and focus instead on the content of the missive. To be too vague as to the physical condition in which he would return from the War of the Rebellion would likely raise only more questions in Rebecca's mind; however, to be too explicit might sound more like a plea for her sympathy. He remembered times when the men of his mess would sit around a campfire after dinner – some whittling; some engaged in draw poker; some smoking or spitting tobacco – while they discussed a common theme of warfare. Few men among the 2nd Maine had escaped their many battles unscathed. As the evening conversations wore on, talk frequently turned to the men's thinking on wounds. They debated the best or worst ways to be wounded; the type of injuries that most often led to the surgeon's saw; and the relative value of bragging rights that accrued to each manner of hurt. Shallow scars left by bullet or bayonet were among the most favored because they left visible signs of combat but were not likely to impede a man from returning to his field of labor once back home. Losing a hand, a wrist, or the length of an arm was considered preferable to the amputation of any part of a leg, for rather practical reasons. Curiously, those that Ben considered among the most horrific mutilations, such as gut shot or punctured lungs, were not among the most dreaded. The soldiers generally feared instead those freakish disfigurements that surgeons could not fix: the missing ear or nose; the deformed jaw; the twisted spine. At Hanover Court House, a rebel bullet had pierced the cheek of Sergeant Major Ellis, breaking his jawbone, carrying away most of his teeth and shredding his tongue. Almost to a man, the men of the 2nd Maine preferred to be crippled or even paralyzed rather than be sent back as what many at home might consider a freak. Upon reflection, Ben couldn't recall a single time when the topic of blindness – temporary or not – was ever discussed by the war-weary veterans.

These thoughts did not help Ben as he tried to frame his letter to Rebecca. When he finally reached Sorrow Ledge, he would be alone. Sorrow Ledge would become Ben's Chateau d'If, his island of despair. *Wait and hope*, he reminded himself. *Wait and hope*.

Abruptly Ben stopped walking. He stood in his darkness amidst the corn and wheat fields of the Amish farmers, smelling the manure they spread over their croplands. He heard the squabbling of crows and the distant bellowing of a cow. An easterly wind cooled his sweat.

"Are you okay?" Seamus asked. "Do you need to rest?"

"No, nothing is okay, but let's go on," Ben said no more to the boy. No explanation. They still had miles to walk. At that moment, as he stood on the road heading east toward some unknown train station, Ben realized he now possessed neither hope nor any desire for which he might pray. His unease continued into the evening as they proceeded down the road until Seamus identified what he felt was a suitable camping spot. By now, the noise of travelers, carts and draft animals on the highway had ceased. Ben heard a gurgling stream nearby, along with the yipping and chuckling of squirrels at play. These sounds lulled him to sleep as he rested against a stout tree with his blanket wrapped around his shoulders. He draped a handkerchief over his face to deter the pestering mosquitoes.

A terrible din of explosions woke them both. To Ben, the sounds seemed to come at them from all directions. He scrabbled about on the ground, feeling with both hands for his rifle. Had Bobby Lee doubled back into Pennsylvania to evade Meade's troops? The roar of explosions and subsequent echoes suggested he and Seamus were in the center of the conflagration, yet the opposing sides sounded far apart. Perhaps both armies were feeling out the other's location in the darkening night. Was the elephant chasing after Ben still?

"Are you awake, Seamus?" Ben demanded. "What do you see?"

"Bright bursts high in the air, like mortars or flares all around us." The boy spoke in a whisper, even though Ben felt they were in no immediate danger. "Some seem closer than others. But I can't see any muzzle flashes from the cannons making all this noise."

Squatting low next to a thick tree, Ben was already digging into his haversack to retrieve the Pennsylvania officer's handsome Colt pistols when he stopped abruptly. "Zounds! Am I losing my mind as well as my eyes?"

"Ben? What's wrong?"

Ben chuckled quietly as he gathered his thoughts before he answered. "Two days ago, I went up a hill with the 20th Maine. That was July second. Yesterday General Meade and Colonel Chamberlain sent us on our way. On July third. We've walked all day today. That makes this July Fourth."

Then Seamus cackled. "Look at us," he said. "Afraid of Independence Day." After a few moments, the boy spoke again. "Don't it make you angry, knowing we're surrounded by people all whooping and hollering and setting off fireworks to show their patriotism, but here they are at home. Surely there are men among them not in the army. Now you're going home looking like, uh, well, looking like you do, I guess. And I'll bet hardly one of them ever raised a hand to help out the war or even a wounded soldier."

Ben reflected on this idea a few moments. Sure, the question had been raised in the regiment as they marched through towns and past farms, seeing plenty of young men who looked able-bodied enough but stood by idly. A sergeant, previously himself a farmer from Skowhegan, opined rather loudly as they passed a wagon being loaded with hay by a clique of farmhands that a man who could plow a straight furrow behind a team of oxen should be able to handle a musket well enough to serve in the army. Ben remembered, too, the grand send-off the 2nd Maine received in front of the First Parish Church as they prepared to depart Bangor. A band played patriotic songs, and the important men of the city gave inspiring speeches. All the while their own dandy sons stood aloof from the regiment's ranks, yet they watched closely the crowd of wives and sweethearts dressed in their finery to see their beaux off to Boston and then onto war. Vice President Hamlin, a Maine native himself, spoke to the troops about 'throwing off this mortal coil," which utterly confused Ben at the time. Once aboard the train, he asked Captain Tilden of his company what it meant. "Don't worry about it, lad" the captain said. "It's just a fancy way of saying that some of us won't be coming home again."

As the noise of the raucous celebrations faded in the chilly air, a choir of crickets in the surrounding woods took up their own festivities.

"Ben? Did you hear me?" Seamus asked.

"Yes, I did. I've been thinking about your question. I can't bring myself to resent another man who was smarter than I was. You know, when I signed the paperwork to enlist, the state of Maine paid me a bounty of twenty-two dollars. Those of us who reported to camp were given more funds raised by local businesses, amounting to more than one hundred fifty, which I sent home. Then Uncle Sam paid me the princely sum of thirteen dollars every month that I was able and willing to kill other men." Ben paused and took a long swig of luke-warm water from his canteen. "I've been hacked or shot more than a dozen times. Now I'm going home, as you said, looking like this. This damn war took my sight and lost me the girl I'd hoped to marry. I can't say anyone forced me to enlist. No, it was all about my own choices; and so I own all my own costs."

CHAPTER 6

*a*s they walked in the cool morning, Seamus doled out a few rations for breakfast so they could eat without taking time to stop and build a fire to cook. After both had eaten an apple, the boy carved a few bits of summer sausage for each of them. Next Ben sucked on a bit of peppermint while Seamus ate slivers of peanut brittle.

"Seamus, I'm sorry that I spoke badly to you yesterday. I've no reason to doubt your loyalty to the Union. I didn't understand what you said about passing word to the rebels."

"I know how it must sound," the lad said. "You're the only person I've ever told about that incident. So I'd be grateful to never speak of the whole thing ever again."

"I believe I can understand."

Seamus spoke in a hushed voice. "I thought that you might. I saw the marks on your back. Did you crew on a ship?"

"No. However, my father was a mate on a whaler. And I'd also rather not speak of that again."

"Have you found not talking of it makes it any easier, then?"

The soldier thought about this question as they walked. He realized that Seamus was now about the same age as Ben when he had endured the worst of his father's wrath. Then came the terrible accident. Now Ben had spent two years fighting through eleven battles as friends and comrades around him were shattered by Minie ball or cannon shot. He had always been fortunate that his wounds were the kind that other soldiers envied – scars that wouldn't prevent him from working at a wickie's trade when he reached home. Until that Pennsylvania hillside.

At last, Ben answered the question Seamus had posed. "I can't say that talking or not has made any difference at all. I suppose I've simply become accustomed to not telling anyone for fear they'd wonder what I had done to deserve what I'd gotten. I am no shirker."

"I understand that. I believe that I was among evil men at a bad time. I'm lucky that an officer came along as he did."

When they began to ascend a steep incline, both fell silent. Before long, they began to breathe more heavily. Ben felt a tug in his calf muscles. This added strain continued for what seemed to him to be about 200 rods. He was startled when Seamus began to laugh abruptly.

"I'd say you were sure right yesterday," the boy said. "I don't think I've ever seen so many cows in one place. I wonder how they ever got driven so far up this hillside. Hell, I'm a little winded myself. Now they're all just running loose. There's a big corral full of sheep, but the cows are free to roam."

"I suppose they'll be safe here. I can't fathom Bobby Lee's boys scouting this far up the mountainside." They continued climbing for a few more rods before Ben stopped abruptly, pulling the boy up short when he did so. "Seamus, do you see where the cows are getting their water?"

Several moments passed as Seamus left Ben's side to scout the hillside. "Looks like somebody built a stone dam on a little stream here," he hollered back. "So now there's a pond. Lots of water. They even put rocks around the bank so the cows and horses didn't get stuck in the mire."

"Can you see the spring that's feeding the pond?"

Ben heard the clattering of rocks as Seamus scrambled up a slope. "Yes! Here it is," Seamus called. "It bubbles clear and cold right out of the rock."

"Please go ahead and fill our canteens," Ben responded. "That should keep us till we reach the next stream."

When the lad was done with the canteens, they resumed their walk eastward. They paused at the summit to catch their breath and sip the fresh, cold water. From the vantage of the mountain's height, Seamus did his best to describe the countryside he saw below them to the blind man. The picture he created was of a patchwork quilt of pasture and crops painted in hues of browns, greens, and yellows. These fields, in bloom or fallow, were woven together by the tan threads of roads. On either side of the ridge where they stood, rivers coursed down the broad valleys. Suddenly Seamus became excited.

"Black smoke, Ben!" he shouted. "Off on the horizon ahead of us yonder is a column of black smoke."

"Is it moving? Can you see if the base of the column is moving?" Ben knew that farms generally burn wood for all their needs, so their chimneys typically emit white smoke. A black plume so far from a city most likely indicated a coal-burning train engine rather than a factory.

"Yes! Yes, it's moving! It must be the railroad. It looks like it's heading south. We're almost there."

Ben was not ready to share the boy's enthusiasm. Ben knew that distances could be deceptive. He didn't know the height of this ridge where they stood, but the horizon in Seamus' sight could be as far as 50 miles away. On clear days, he could see from Sorrow Ledge as far away as the peak of Mount Washington in New Hampshire. With his father's telescope, Ben was able to identify the mountain's summit by the structures that rose from the usual snowfield.

"We could be riding on the train day after tomorrow, rather than walking out in this swelter," Seamus said wistfully.

Ben grunted, not wishing to disappoint the boy outright. As they went down the slope before them, he knew, the black smoke would recede from them, like a departing ship slipping over the horizon. When they reached the bottom of this ridge, the plume would be no more visible to the boy than to the blind man. For Ben, restless walking in the interminable hours and days ahead would have only the same relentless dark of a moonless night in Maine's bitter winter.

CHAPTER 7

*O*n Monday afternoon, Seamus read aloud the railway schedule scratched on the blackboard at the York station. After several minutes, he returned to where Ben sat comfortably on a bench in the shade. "This makes no sense. There's a list of stations in both directions up and down the line but the times are all chalked out. There's no trains coming or going for today or tomorrow."

With the fingertips of both hands spread to fullest reach, Ben scratched his bandages against his scalp. Pennsylvania's July swelter left Ben sweaty and miserable. With the boy's help, he poured some water from the canteen onto his handkerchief then wiped his neck and cheeks. He wondered how he looked after three days on the road, with blood likely seeping through his bandages and streaming down his throat onto his clothes. No doubt that the good folks of Pennsylvania were shocked to see the war pass directly by their doorsteps.

"Let's talk to the station master," Ben said. "I suppose Bobby Lee could disrupt train service anywhere he goes, even if it's just a rumor."

"You think we'll have to walk to Philadelphia, then?"

"I hope not. These army boots won't last a million miles, but I've marched nearly that distance already."

When the stationmaster finally came to the ticket window, his tone of voice suggested he was annoyed by the distraction even though it was clear to a blind man no trains were passing through the station and no other passengers on the platform awaited assistance. Ben smelled the strong odor of cigar smoke coming at him through the open window. Seamus coughed loudly and released his grip on Ben's sleeve.

"How can I help you, soldier?" the stationmaster asked gruffly. Then he seemed to realize the extent of Ben's condition abruptly. "You be one of the wounded from over near Gettysburg? Would it help you to come inside and sit yourself down for a spell?"

Ben wondered how thick the tobacco smoke might be inside the station proper. He decided to stay outdoors in the fresher air. "Thank you kindly for the offer, but I'm fine out here. I expect we'll need only a moment or two of your time. I'm curious about the schedule posted over here. My young friend says there are no trains whatsoever coming through either today or tomorrow."

"Yep, all true. Any other question yet?"

At that moment, Ben wished to have his sight back so he could shove the point of his bayonet – or possibly the muzzle of his Enfield – into the hollow of the man's neck between the chin and Adam's apple. "Can you tell me why there are no trains?"

"Don't you know what for?" the man scoffed. "There's a war going on all around us."

"So I've heard," Ben said, followed by a well-intentioned chuckle.

"Dare I guess there may be no trains again till next week," the stationmaster added.

"How could that be?" Now Ben was worried he might be stranded in Pennsylvania while his brothers were arrested for desertion and taken to jail in Bangor.

"It wonders me. We were told the War Department telegraphed to the railroad that it needs to be that way. They don't wish the rebels to commandeer any of our trains, but they want the trains available near Baltimore in case our boys need to move south to protect the Capitol. If you plan to grex on it, you should most likely write to Mister Lincoln."

"I suppose he might be a trifle busy these days. Thank you kindly."

Ben turned to walk away, but the stationmaster called after him, "Does that boy with the struwwely hair belong with you?"

The question puzzled the blind man, who was not sure what kind of hair that would be or whether there were other children around the station platform. The answer came quickly enough.

"Why don't you leaven him go? He has the Irish. Folks here will help a soldier but not an Irish."

"Well, thank you again." Ben thought he might spit on the platform to show his opinion of the stationmaster's remark, but found his mouth was too dry. "Come, Seamus. We can't stay here any longer. We've been here too long as it is." Quietly Ben whispered to Seamus, "Leave your cap off until we get down the street a ways."

The Irish lad with the struwwely hair snickered in a way that suggested he did just as he was told while he carefully helped the blind man get down the steps from the station platform. They walked onto the cobbled street and paused while Seamus took a compass reading, then they began walking once again in an easterly direction, as Ben knew by the sun warming the right side of his face.

"True, then? No trains?"

"He said no, and I suppose he has no reason lie to me. Though he might if it were you asking."

"Yup I heard. I has the Irish. Glad he told us," Seamus said. "Guessing by his face, I think he had the pox as a boy. Maybe twice." Then he chortled again.

Ben smiled at the lad's poke. "I suppose it won't make much difference to us in the end. The train here would have taken us only as far as the Susquehanna. We'll need to find our own way across the river since the bridge was destroyed."

"Train would've spared us another day walking," the boy said sullenly.

Now came Ben's turn to chuckle. "Only if a train came along. I don't know but what we could have sat here for ten days without any train passing one direction or the other."

"I suppose that's right." Seamus released his hold on Ben's sleeve, and they stopped. "I'm ahungry. Have an apple?"

"Yes, thanks." The apple felt solid and firm in his hand. Ben took a large juicy bite. He started talking as he chewed. "Were you able to find out how far to Wrightsville?"

"I asked around a bit while you were at the ticket window. The porter said about 15 miles by road, less walking the rails. Which do you prefer?"

Ben mulled this choice as he finished eating the fruit. When he finished, he handed the core to Seamus. "Please pitch this into the weeds." After another moment, Ben heard two mild thumps as the apple remains hit the ground. "I think I'll do better on the road. If I can move fast enough, maybe we can camp along the river tonight."

"I wouldn't mind me no swim," the boy said. "This asafetida bag reeks terrible on my skin after a wee bit without a bath."

Now keenly attuned to the odors around him, the blind man could reflect on the peculiar odor he first whiffed when Colonel Chamberlain had brought the Irish lad into the officers' marquee tent. The stink had surpassed even the smell of damp, mildewed canvas that emanated from the army from when they set up camp until the tents were struck. Ben reflected upon this for a long moment. Soon he realized that after Custer's men had galloped away, he had sensed only the strongest of smells, such as the dung that farmers used to fertilize their crops. He could recall only the aroma of the stationmaster's cigar smoke, though they had walked through the entire town of York. Was there no stockyard or livery in town? No smithy or bakery? For two days, Ben had detected few scents other than the boy at his side. Could there be another benefit then to the asafetida user? To avoid the daily potpourri of stink and stench?

"Suppose no ferryman will carry us over the river because I've got the Irish. What will you do? Trawl me after the boat, then?"

Ben chuckled at the suggestion and said, "Just moments ago you said yourself that you wouldn't mind a swim."

CHAPTER 8

*J*ust as the York stationmaster predicted, Ben did not hear nor smell a train all through the long afternoon. The pair trudged along the muddy, rutted road in silence for some time before Seamus spoke in an almost conspiratorial whisper, "Look at that. There's an eddy in this creek along the road that seems about waist deep. I wonder if you would wait a few minutes while I wash this grime away?"

"I don't suppose I'll wander far without you," Ben said. He then reflected upon the events of the past few weeks: the forced marches; his short role in the battle; the stench of the hospital and their hiking through the Pennsylvania swelter. "Might do us both some good to be reacquainted with water."

The boy laughed at this comment as he led the way down the embankment. Within a few minutes, Ben heard splashing in the water. He thought at first that he might just go into the water in his uniform to cool off but decided against it when he remembered how much the wool outfit weighed when wet, a lesson he had learned on the 2nd Maine's many marches through torrential rain. So he set about getting undressed, which he discovered somewhat more challenging without his sight than he expected. Shirt buttons were more numerous than he recalled, and the knots on his boots that he hurriedly tied back in the hospital did not come slack readily when he tugged at the bitter ends. As best he could manage in his darkness, he folded his tunic, trousers, shirt, and undershirt. He carefully placed his uniform atop his brogans. He wore only his underdrawers, a thin cotton trouser held up by a cord at his waist that fell almost to his ankles.

Ben waded in no deeper than his knees when the sounds of the boy splashing in the stream stopped. A long whistle followed. "Holy mackerel!" Seamus exclaimed. "I saw your back before, but this is my first good look at your front. Has every surgeon in the Union Army put a stitch in you?"

"Yes, but only after every damned rebel put a hole in my hide," Ben said while feeling his way into the stream as deep as his waist. After the initial shock of the cold creek, he cupped his hands to splash water across his chest and abdomen, careful to avoid wetting the bandages around his head. He shivered from a chill as the sun was blocked briefly by a cloud. He decided that was a good time to retreat to shore; however, when he came up the bank, he was unable to find his clothes.

"Stop where you are," the boy shouted. "There's a raspberry thicket to your right. You tangle with that; you'll have a whole new set of scars. Come three paces to your left and then two more steps uphill."

Carefully following the boy's directions, Ben located his clothes without tripping over them. He dressed quickly to avoid being observed by anyone chancing along on the road. As he did, he heard Seamus climb out of the stream and shake off. "That was a great idea," Ben said. "Now I've got a dozen more miles in me for today."

"Are you planning to reach Philadelphia tomorrow?" Seamus asked. He chuckled.

"No, but we have no idea as to where the armies are moving. Even the stationmaster didn't know. I want to get as far afield from their routes as possible, so we don't tangle with any more scouts. If General Custer hadn't come along when he did, I'd have been hung for desertion, and you likely shot for spying. His men didn't seem inclined to ask too many questions before killing someone."

As they started down the road again, with Seamus tugging the sleeve of Ben's tunic to guide the way, the boy spoke up. "Speaking of dying, do you believe there is one true path to eternal redemption?"

By an odd happenstance, Ben recognized this as the title of a religious tract he had read somewhere in the course of the prior two years. "I suppose that's true enough," Ben said. Then he stumbled on a large stone. "But I hope God keeps the one true path in better shape than this stretch of road."

"See, here's what staggers me," the lad said, seeming to ignore Ben's sarcastic comment. "I walked between the lines and gave the same pamphlet to men in the hospitals of both armies. I gave away the same Bibles. Those who couldn't read themselves then I read for them all the same passages, not worrying about North or South. Weren't ever a one of them about to walk down the valley of the shadow of death ever stopped me to ask whether there were a reb or a yank already there, waiting to ambush him. Not one asked if whether there was one heaven for the yanks and another for the butternut. Every preacher or chaplain I ever heard in either camp swore their cause was righteous and God was on their side."

Now Ben was himself perplexed. In three days of traveling together, he could not recall hearing the boy utter so many words in a spell. Equally confounding to the soldier was the boy's abrupt religious inquiry. He felt some obligation to answer the boy's question as best he could. He knew he couldn't offer much wisdom from the Bible itself given how much time Seamus himself had spent reading the holy texts aloud in the surgeries of the two armies.

"Do you think you have strayed from the one true way to heaven?" Ben asked, wishing to himself that they were once again breathless from climbing a steep hill, too winded at least for this conversation.

"The Bible commands us to honor thy father, don't it? So if your father was harmed, wouldn't you need to avenge that? Deuteronomy says, 'And thine eye shall not pity; life take for life, eye for eye, tooth for tooth, hand for hand, foot for foot.'"

The pair walked along in silence for another mile. Ben enjoyed the quiet because he found the boy's questions to be suddenly much more challenging. Rarely did conversations among the marching army wax so philosophical. Those discussions typically waited for night and whiskey. Ben knew the passage Seamus quoted well; the most worn pages in the Bible at the living quarters on Sorrow Ledge were in the books of Leviticus, Numbers, and Deuteronomy. Though hardly a devout man, his father readily quoted the Scriptures to justify whatever cruelty or wickedness he intended.

"Ben, do you think it's wrong that I don't want revenge on those what killed my dad? Isn't that my duty?"

Ben was stunned by the boy's revelation. "I'm sorry. I didn't know your father was murdered. How did that …?" His voice trailed off as he wondered whether he should inquire any further. "I do apologize. I don't mean to ask what would make you sorry to answer."

"Hell, he probably bought it himself, given the bastards who bet his dogs."

"Your father ran dogs?"

"No, he fought them."

Ben wasn't sure he had heard the boy's words exactly right. "Your father fought dogs?"

"Well, trained them for fighting."

In Ben's experience of the dogs in Rockland, they were mostly docile if not catatonic, rarely emerging from the haven afforded by a porch or the shade of a tree. Even a large Maine coon cat could stroll down any street in town unmolested. Generally, only little boys throwing firecrackers or the fire squad could rouse Rockland's dogs from their stupor. The one dogfight that Ben ever witnessed was precipitated by a barrel of salted pork knocked from the stern of a freight wagon. The canine quarrel lasted only until each of the dogs stalked away with a ham hock in its maw. The one vicious dog Ben ever saw was kept caged on Sorrow Ledge and only loosed at night to kill vermin. When its job was done, so was the dog. Another victim of his father's brutality.

The boy's pace seemed to increase as they discussed this topic, as though his father's death were a physical location on the road from which he wanted to distance himself. "He did well at it. As though born to the work. Took pups just weaned, but then starved and beat them 'til no one else could go near them. Trained them to fight by shoving a stray animal off the streets into their cages. That was their supper. God, he was a terrible bastard."

Ben wished he was more shocked by this revelation, but his father had recited many stories of men gambling as their chief diversion at sea. Sailors groomed roosters for cockfighting or kept terriers for "ratting" the vessel's rodent population. When these entertainments were unavailable, they might challenge each other to top the mainmast, engage in knife-throwing contests or just fight with their fists – at least when they could be constrained by such civility. These contests often resulted in hard feelings that accounted for many whaling ships finishing a voyage with fewer men in the ship's complement than what was aboard when it had left port. Ben frequently wondered just exactly how many men his father had murdered at sea under whatever excuse came to hand. The old bucko mate told so many grim sea stories as they polished the brass and glass of the big Fresnel lens that Ben could only guess which confession might bear some resemblance to the truth.

Seamus continued telling his story. "Lord, he was splendid good at his job. He sure could teach a creature to hate. At her end, my mother loathed him. After she passed, I stayed away from him what I could. Just one mean son of a bitch."

"I'm sorry, Seamus, I didn't mean to raise any of this." Ben stopped and felt the pull on his sleeve slacken. "Could I have a sip of water?"

After removing the stopper, Seamus placed the canteen in Ben's outreached hands. "Aren't your fault none. I think of it a bit often. Don't honor needs me to go kill the men what killed him?"

"You know who murdered your father?" Ben asked in astonishment. "You're certain?" With a swig of the lukewarm water, he rinsed the dust from his mouth and spat away from where he thought Seamus stood. He took a second sip to moisten his dry throat then handed the canteen back to the boy. They started walking east again.

"Sure I do — the gang what hired him to train the dogs. And I know just why they did it, too. He were no honest man, but he survived until the roughs in the Bowery caught onto his fix. See, when he trained the dogs, he also taught them to stop on a certain whistle." Seamus blew out a low note that Ben might have ignored if he did not have the warning to listen for it. "Every few weeks, the old man would have a friend lay a big bet against one of his own dogs. Once the dogs were in the rat pit and going at it, the bastard would lean over the pit like he was watching the fight. With all the cheering and yelling, no one could hear him whistling but his dog to halt. That's all the other dog needed to get their fangs deep into the neck of the bastard's poor dog. Once or twice he even whistled his dog when it was in the pit with a woodchuck."

With Seamus tugging at Ben's sleeve, they trudged on together in silence for several minutes. They were moving faster than Ben liked, but he did not want to intrude on the boy's thoughts. Again, this ugly story Seamus told reminded Ben of his father, who relished Saratoga's horror at his tales of killing seals in the hundreds by clubbing the creatures on the snout with a gaff. "How did someone find out about his scam?" Ben asked.

"Those fellers from the Bowery aren't no common dupes. They hear talk of a whore who lifts a couple of centuries from a mick in a bagnio; they wonder how a son of Ireland came into such wealth. They ask about; people talk, the mick dies. The boys bound him up, put a gag in his mouth and dropped him into the rat pit with his dogs. Maybe dogs remember good as people. The roughs hung what bones was left when the dogs were done up in the rafters over the pit as a warning. I heard that his head went in a bag full of rocks and pitched into the East River so the coppers could never identify the carcass."

As Seamus related this horrifying story, Ben was struck by the dullness in the boy's voice, as if the events held no greater consequence in his life than butchering a lamb for Christmas dinner. The blind man could not see whether there were tears on the boy's face. The only change in Seamus that Ben could detect was that the lad's pace quickened yet again as if he were trying to flee from the terrible scenes he described. Although he could see nothing about Seamus, he pictured in his mind a boy about the same age as Rebecca's younger sister, Anna, who had certainly never encountered anything so horrific during her life in Rockland. For his part, Ben bore the scars of cruelty down his back, and he too knew precisely where his own father's bones rested. Rather than cite another Biblical verse, Ben turned to the story he knew best.

"Have you ever heard of a book called *The Count of Monte Cristo*?" Ben didn't hear any indication either way from Seamus. The only sound was their dogged footfalls in the dirt. "It isn't a text from the Bible, but I've read it over and over since I was just about your age. The story tells about a man who is falsely imprisoned. While he is locked away, his father starves to death, and his betrothed marries another man. When he escapes from prison, he devotes his life to revenge. He even thinks that he is a weapon of God."

"Did he get revenge, then?"

"Yes, he does. But many more people get hurt than he planned. Then he realizes that he can't know God's plans. No one can. Remember what Paul told the Romans, 'Vengeance is mine,' sayeth the Lord, 'I will repay.'"

The boy's pull on Ben's sleeve stopped abruptly. "That don't seem hardly right, to leave everything up to God. What is it then that a body does while waiting for God to act?"

"In the book, the Count of Monte Cristo found that all we can do is wait and hope for God to spare the good and damn the bad. Just wait and hope."

"Wait and hope," the boy said quietly. "Are we waiting and hoping for justice or for vengeance?"

Reflecting upon the boy's quandary, Ben thought about his own father's death and whether God was now extracting His own revenge for it.

CHAPTER 9

*a*bruptly Ben heard a dog bark and a man's voice shouting. "Make way there! Make way!" He felt a hand on his shoulder as Seamus pushed him to the side of the road. Ben made a show of lowering his rifle from his shoulder. He hoped the stranger could not see his bandaged face.

"Easy, Ben, it's just a freight wagon and a team of six. I guess I didn't hear them coming up behind us for the mud."

"Hello there," Ben called. "Good day, sir. Are you heading into town?"

"Who's asking?" There was just a subtle hint of the local Germanic accent in the teamster's voice.

"He's got a pistol aimed at us," Seamus whispered.

Hearing the boy's observation, Ben now aimed the weapon so its muzzle pointed into the ground. "My name's Ben Grindle. I was with the 20th Maine until the events of this week at Gettysburg." Ben doffed his straw hat, revealing his linen-wrapped head. "The boy's walking me to the next railroad station. This war's over for me." Ben heard the metallic click he recognized as the hammer of a Colt pistol being cocked. He stepped forward a pace and pulled Seamus behind him. "Just tell me what you want."

"How long were you in the army?" the man asked.

"Two years."

"What money do you have?"

"Some paper, a few coins, and some stamps," Ben said. "I was just a private in Mr. Lincoln's army."

"What's in the bag the boy carries?"

Ben felt Seamus step firmly against him before the lad spoke up in response. "Foodstuffs. Mostly hard biscuits. A few apples. Lots of horehound. You can take all the horehound you'd like. We've no use for it."

"Keep your candy, son. You keep everything you have. I'm no thief."

"Why do your horses have Confederate brands, then?" Seamus asked, sounding innocent enough. Still Ben jabbed his elbow back at the boy to hush him. Would do neither of them any good, Ben knew, for the stranger to shoot a few holes in them.

The teamster guffawed harshly at the boy's question. "Keen eyes, son, very good. Well, they're branded CSA because they were indeed property of the Confederate Army until recently. The wagon and all the supplies in it all belonged to the rebels as well. I *requisitioned* them from a line of wagons in Maryland while the rebels were preparing to ford the Potomac back into Virginia. Took me two days to get around the east flank of the Union Army to come back home."

Ben shifted his rifle again, now resting the butt on the ground and leaning against the barrel for support. The distinct sound of flatulence reached his ears just before the smell of fresh horse dung assaulted his nose. "Whereabouts do you call home?" he asked.

"Over in Wrightsville. I run the general store there, or I did until June when Early's rebs came to town and *requisitioned* my entire inventory – lock, stock, and barrel. When I heard you boys whipped them over to Gettysburg and sent Bobby Lee running for home like a scalded dog, I decided to tag along behind to see what I might recover. Somehow, I managed to get myself between the two armies. So when the rebels stopped at Williamsport to cross the Potomac, I grabbed this wagon and six, then set out as fast as I could down the National Road toward Hagerstown, before I turned north. I knew I'd find my way home eventually."

"The rebel army just let you take a wagon and go?" Seamus asked, incredulously. "Nary a cross word said?"

Again, the Pennsylvanian laughed heartily as if he had never heard anything more ridiculous. "Oh, there were curse words enough. Also, a few bullets in the grain sacks piled back there. I suppose if they kept their noses to the ground, the reb cavalry could likely trail me by the smell of molasses dripping from a hole they shot in that barrel. I stoppered the hole with a cloth, but there's still a leak."

Ben made a show of coming upright and raising his right hand to his forehead. "I salute you, sir. Must take a courageous man to steal rations from a hungry army."

The stranger chuckled at this compliment. "Thank you, but it was no more than survival. My missus was hopping mad that I did no more to keep the rebels from riding off with our store goods, as well as the little bit of cash we had on hand. Those rebels came in June. Well, see our customers are mostly farmers who keep a tab with us until July when they start to see a little profit from summer harvests. By the time Early's boys left town, we had no money in the till and no merchandise to let on credit. I've gotta say that I'd rather face a swarm of reb horsemen than my wife when she's got her dander up."

"So what were you able to steal back from the rebels?" Seamus asked.

"Not nearly as much what they took. Foodstuffs mostly, I guess. I haven't stopped long enough to do any inventory. I've been focused on staying clear of either army."

"Ben, what do you think of asking this good fellow if he'd consider a little bartering with us?" the boy asked quietly.

"What did you have in mind? We aren't carrying much to start with."

Seamus responded by speaking directly to the storekeeper. "Sir, the army burdened us with foodstuffs we aren't likely to use in our travels. Would you consider giving us a ride as far as you're traveling if we give you what rations we have?"

During the brief pause of discussion that followed the bargain Seamus proposed, Ben detected another metallic sound that he assumed – or at least hoped – was the hammer of a pistol being relaxed from its cocked position. The longer the stolen team of six stood at bay, the more sounds of their unrest Ben heard as they whinnied, pawed anxiously at the ground and farted noisily.

"I'll go you lads one better. I'll carry you into town if you help me offload this cargo into my store. As for your army rations, I'll provision you with vittles more suitable for travelers in exchange for whatever you carry. Except for the horehound. That ain't no use to nobody."

Ben smiled at this comment, even though at that moment he had a small pebble of the dreadful candy wedged between his cheek and gums. He'd been sucking on it for hours without noticing any appreciable change in its heft. Ben had always assumed that the army bought horehound in such large quantities exactly because it was economical in the sense that one piece could sustain a man for a day or longer. "You're most kind, sir. We'll do what we can to help you, given that I'm blind and he's just a boy."

Seamus started to object, but the man spoke first, "Well, the lad looks sturdy enough. Three sets of hands will be better than one."

"You seem like a decent man," Ben said. "May I ask why you inquired about how much money we carry?"

"There are a lot of deserters and ruffians about. I figure that a man who is honest about his money isn't likely to steal mine. Come along and climb aboard the back."

The boy wasted little time in pulling Ben over to the wagon and relieving him of the musket, haversack, and canteen. The blind man felt his way along the wagon's sidewall until his hand fell upon the rear wheel. Using the spokes as the rungs of a ladder, he climbed up and settled on the burlap sacks piled in the wagon bed. The dray lurched forward suddenly, and Ben felt the boy topple onto him.

"Hold on back there, lads! Let's see if we can get to Wrightsville while it's still daylight."

When Seamus had moved away, the blind man felt another creature climb into his lap. The storekeeper's dog had come to investigate the strangers, focusing its attentions almost immediately on Ben's bandages. The dog barked sharply when he tried to push its muzzle away.

"Get off, Ruby!" the German shouted. "I'm sorry, mister. The bitch came with the shop when we bought it from an old butcher. She still has a nose for blood. She gets on you again, give her hard with the back of your hand."

CHAPTER 10

To Ben's great delight, they arrived at the Columbia station before the first scheduled train on Tuesday morning despite not waking with the first light of dawn. Neither the blind man nor the boy could recall the last day either woke under a shelter more substantial than canvas. The storekeeper had permitted them to spread their bedrolls in the newly filled stock room aft of his shop. Perhaps giving the travelers more credit for their role in the return of the store's inventory than rightly due, his wife graciously brought them a breakfast of coffee and hot oatmeal mixed with the molasses only recently liberated from the rebel army. The proprietor furnished their haversack with food for their trip and sent his son to arrange a boatman to carry the pair across the wide Susquehanna.

"Suppose no trains through here are hired by the army. How much will it cost to get us to New York?" Seamus asked.

"I have no idea," Ben replied. "Not taking into account any loose coins, I reckon we have some forty dollars remaining, not including the colonel's money I have for you. I'm sure we'll have no problem."

To his great dismay, Ben was entirely wrong.

Although he could not see the crowd, Ben sensed a considerable number of people milling about on the station platform around him.

They smelled variously of cigars, lavender and alcohol, namely whiskey. He perceived the low rumbling of a cart, probably burdened with luggage; a squeaking wheel warned the crowd of its transit. At times the porter shouted out, "Watch yourself there. Coming through." Ben could not see whether the crowd heeded this warning, but he sensed they did not, given the frequency with which it was repeated. Weaving their way through the throng, Seamus led Ben to the ticket window.

"Pardon. We're traveling to New York City." Ben called out, removing his straw hat. He didn't expect or desire sympathy for his wounds in this situation but felt it would not hamper their cause.

The response came quickly enough in a masculine voice with the now familiar Germanic accent. "Good Heavens, man, what in the sacred name of the Lord has happened to you? You look like you've been cudgeled." The smell of tobacco smoke that emanated from the window was equally familiar, and Ben wondered if there might be a familial connection to the stationmaster back in York.

"I was in a little skirmish over in Gettysburg you may have heard about, but my musket misfired," he explained, not entirely convinced that the Columbia stationmaster cared a whit. "General Meade is sending me home. I hoped you might have a train coming through that would get us to Philadelphia."

"General Meade himself? Really, now?" The skepticism in the ticket man's voice was as plain as a boatswain's whistle in a church choir recital.

"Here are my papers, since you asked." Ben laid on his best imperious New England tone as he fished his discharge and travel orders from the pocket of his blue uniform tunic. Seamus had returned to sidle up against Ben, quietly urging him to transact their business without making any further fuss. "You'll see there's the signature of Captain Meade, the general's son and adjutant."

Within a moment, Ben felt the papers pressed roughly back into his hands. "I meant no offense. Thank the Lord that General Meade chased Bobby Lee and his hellions back to Virginia. Was the combat there very terrible?"

"What I saw before I was blinded was terrible enough." This ticket man's comment struck Ben as absurd. When was combat ever any less than terrible? In the violent history of humanity, what battle ever ended in tickles and giggles? "I know we lost many officers while I sat by the surgery, and a good man died in my lap."

Seamus leaned closer to Ben and whispered, "People are looking at you."

"Any chance we might see a passenger train come through today?" Ben asked.

"A chance, I suppose, though I wouldn't consider it a good one," the railroad man said. "We were informed that General Haupt has directed the railroads to prioritize the movement of fresh horses for the pursuit of Lee's rebel hooligans and the transport of injured from Gettysburg."

Ben heard another puff and then nearly choked when the cigar smoke hit him full in the face. He fought down a strong urge to vomit but could not help but cough loudly. "So, were we to wait, does this line go into Philadelphia?" he asked once he'd recovered his breath.

"Well, sure. This here is the Main Line that runs right into the station at Vine and Broad streets."

Ben was puzzled by the ticket man's story. If there was so little chance of a train, why was the station platform crowded with passengers? A lot of other people seemed optimistic about their chances of reaching Philadelphia, and Ben decided to try his luck with them. "How much for two tickets; myself and the boy?

The stationmaster lowered his voice so that Ben had to lean close toward the window to hear what he said next. "You mean the boy there with the struwwely hair?"

"Yes, that boy. The army hired him to escort me back to Maine."

"Though I may be glad to hear the army thought about getting you home in your condition, there presents a problem. I can't sell him a ticket."

Ben sighed, then nodded. "I'll purchase both tickets myself. Will that be ok, then?" He had not seen the lad's mane personally and did not know even what the word *struwwely* meant, but he could only guess why it was so objectionable to so many people.

"Dare I say he has the Irish?" the ticket master asked in a low tone, almost conspiratorial.

"Yes, but at the moment he's in the employ of the commanding officer of the 20th Maine Infantry." Of course, this was not technically the truth, but that statement came closer than what Ben said next. "And I can vouch for him personally."

"I'm sure he's a perfectly fine lad, if you say so, vouching his character or no. It wonders me how I could send him down the line after what happened at Duffy's Cut, with the curse yet."

"Begging your pardon? What was it happened at Duffy's Cut to prevent the boy from riding into the city?" Ben was beginning to suspect that railroad men – with this talk of hair – were nearly as superstitious as sailors and soldiers. "What's all this about a curse?"

The stationmaster's voice lowered again as if revealing a dreadful secret. "Back in '32, the Philadelphia and Columbia Railroad was building this here line from Philadelphia westward. A contractor named Duffy hired some Irishmen to work a section of rail near Malvern. Just two months in, every one of the men were dead all the sudden – more than fifty all told. My father worked this line and met the blacksmith that buried them all together. No one knows just what killed them, but some said there was an ancient Gaelic curse those micks carried on them from Ulster. This line won't carry no Irish since."

"*Aufhören, dummkopf!* What a great load of malarkey!" Seamus bellowed when he heard this last remark and gripped the soldier's arm tightly. "Come on, Ben. No point wasting more time here."

The soldier barely had time to snatch up his musket as the boy dragged him away from the ticket window. Seamus was in such haste that the sightless man nearly toppled down the plank stairs. Ben was saved only by his fortune of blindly grasping the handrail just as he stumbled upon the top step. He heard a thunderclap of laughter behind them as they walked away from the train station. This din reminded Ben of the hullabaloo as the hospital rat walked naked through the Union Army at Gettysburg. Seamus continued tugging at Ben's sleeve for about 200 paces before they spoke. When he could no longer stand the pace, Ben jerked his arm from the boy's grasp. "Could we stop before I end up with a broken leg?"

Seamus stopped but did not speak.

"Have you heard about Duffy's Cut before?" Ben asked. "Is that how you know it's a rotten canard?"

"No. This is the first I've heard of it, but what a bogus story. *Wonder* that any such thing ever happened at all." The lad's mimic of the railroad man was quite keen.

"You think what he said was just a sham?"

"Did you hear what he said?" Seamus snorted but then began to choke. "An ancient Gaelic curse? Ulstermen were likely Protestants." Seamus chuckled again. "Ever hear of an ancient Protestant curse?"

The two resumed their march toward the east, with Seamus again taking the lead. Ben was grateful that the boy had slowed their pace to a steady march, rather than the quick time as they left the station. Only three days into his darkness, Ben was prone still to stumbling.

"What do you guess happened to those fifty men, then?"

The boy was quiet for a long while as they hiked eastward. Only when the hubbub of town receded behind the pair did Seamus share his suspicions. "I wouldn't know what happened for sure, but let me ask you a question. Somebody hires men in the city and takes them out to the woods. After two months of work, all those men happen to die at the same time. So, what would you suppose happened to all their pay for the proceeding months of hard labor?"

"You know this has happened?" Ben asked, incredulously. "Elsewhere, perhaps?"

"No, not for sure, but from what I've heard railroads always have one scheme or another to part working men from their rightful pay, be they Irish, Chinamen or darkies. I know for sure that the other thing he said about the Irish was just a lie."

"About what?"

"Remember what he said, that the Pennsylvania Railroad won't allow Irish on their trains? That's balderdash. Who in all creation does he think swayed these rails for miles? I know plenty of boggers who worked the tracks. Each morning the railroad carries them out to where the work needs doing and then back home again every evening. Now sometimes the rail company deducts the fare from the workers' pay. But no railroad ever said no to any man with a strong back and a weak mind."

Ben now stopped in the middle of the road. "So why do you think he refused to sell us tickets? That's his job."

Seamus snickered. "You likely have no idea what you look like now, but it probably ain't how you turned out when you first marched off to Bull Run. Certainly not what the great Pennsylvania Railroad wants their genteel customers to see on the Main Line. So sure an Irish lad with *struwwely* hair might raise a concern among the gentry. They'd be all afraid that their wallets and purses might disappear in a puff of leprechaun magic. Wouldn't surprise me to learn that the feller at the York station didn't telegraph ahead to announce that we were coming this way."

Ben was surprised to hear that Seamus harbored the same suspicions about communication between the two stationmasters he felt. Then he touched the bandages on his face and felt the growth of beard on his chin. "Is it as bad as all that?" the blind man asked.

"Yes, I'm sorry to say this to you, but my mother would say you were no better than a streel," Seamus said in earnest. "But at least you don't have *struwwely* hair, then."

"That's true enough, I suppose. I don't speak German, either."

At that, Seamus laughed until he began to sputter and gasp for breath. He released his grip on Ben's wrist. "Well, just so you know I speak a grand German vocabulary of two words. *Aufhören, dummkopf!* I should know them well enough. Heard them so often from the butcher who chased me with a cleaver for stealing a few links of his sausage. *Aufhören, dummkopf!* Means just, '*Stop idiot.*'" Ben heard a soft chuckle like a man reminiscing about a humorous incident from his past. Then the boy's tenor changed. "I took only what we needed. Promise. That was just about all we had to eat after Mother took sick. The priest brought bread and rice pudding each week, but it were hardly enough. Oh, I could snatch some fruit now and again, but not much. She weren't no more than bones under her skin when she passed."

Ben knew not the words to comfort this boy made an orphan by disease and murder then left to fend for himself in the harsh times of hate and war.

"We're lucky, then, don't you know?" Seamus said. "We stayed on that platform any longer, that *dummkopf* would next be calling us lepers. And then where would we be?"

CHAPTER 11

*J*ust after noon, the blind soldier with the blood-soaked bandages wound around his head sat cross-legged in the grass, chewing at an apple so juicy that he nibbled it down to its seedy core. At his crotch rested a canteen that he felt no need to touch. His thirst disappeared along with the fruit he devoured. Unusually for Ben, he could not decide where the sun stood in the sky, likely because of passing clouds as the day wore away. The afternoon felt unpleasantly warm to Ben. His comfort was not improved by the dressings, which had been parched by the several days of rain and sun to the rough consistency of dry burlap.

"Another apple?" Seamus asked.

"How many are left?"

"Just two. We also have the pears."

For a question that seemed simple enough, Ben struggled as though debating a Hobson's choice. He was not sure how much food remained in their shared knapsack, nor how much money they would need to fund their travels to Maine, nor even how many miles remained in their increasingly confounding trek. He did not know how best they might reach New York City or points East. At that moment, Ben realized that he had no greater knowledge of the territory that lay ahead of them than his father's ken of the southern oceans when he first ventured out on the whaling ships in pursuit of the giant mammals of the deep oceans that he sought to slaughter.

"Ben, do you think we'll get any better reception at Lancaster? Might we need walk all the way to the Philadelphia station before we get seated on a train?" Seamus sounded nearly as tired as Ben felt.

Ben remained seated and silent, stumped by this continuing rejection he and the boy encountered. Could the entire railway be awaiting orders from the War Department for transport? Was it instead his own unfortunate appearance in disheveled uniform and bloodied bandages? Perhaps the smells emanating from his garb of soil, sweat, and smoke, whether from campfire or gunfire? Were locals resentful of Union soldiers because the rebels had invaded the North? Ben had heard just such a sentiment from locals as the 2nd Maine marched toward Sharpsburg in western Maryland in September of '62. Perhaps it was just some simple misunderstanding. The mere coincidence of the next eastbound train having no more seats available?

"I'm sorry, Ben," Seamus said. "I feel this has all been my fault. I can't really hide my Irish, and this crucifix from the Sisters of Charity on my neck probably don't help none. You couldn't have a worse companion unless I wore a priest's frock."

"I don't think you can take all the blame. I know places don't allow Irish or hire Irish. But what would possess that fool to tell us some fantastical tale about Duffy's Cut?"

"I suppose it doesn't matter to us. We're stuck here, together. I can't set you loose to wander around the mountains. And you can't go far without me; wouldn't be long before you were mired in dung."

"I don't know what choice we have but to go onto Lancaster," Ben said. "Without a map, we couldn't find our way to New York, even with the compass. At least we know which direction this railroad line goes – straight into Philadelphia."

"Ben, I think we should move on now. Since we've been sitting here, there's been seven vultures gather in the top of that dead tree over there. I don't mean to offend you, but they might smell your bandages a bit. You're in a bad way now, so I don't think tangling with them will help you overmuch."

CHAPTER 12

*A*s man and boy trudged on toward the train station in Lancaster, Ben heard the din of the twilight routines at each farm they passed. Heifers coming in from pasture bellowed their response to their farmer's distinctive yodel. Dinner bells summoned families in to cleanse in time to sup, and mothers cried out the names of those youngsters who failed to heed the dinner bell. Crows shrieked their displeasure at the disruptions that all these activities caused. Ben heard the thunderous clap of wings as flocks of birds rose from the croplands in unison.

More powerful than even the asafetida bag that Seamus wore was the stench of the cow manure that the farmers spread as fertilizer on their fields. When Ben first encountered this malodorous agricultural practice, he could not imagine living inside a house that must surely smell like excrement for several months out of the year. Among regiments in the Union Army, Maine men seemed to Ben to be especially sensitive of this redolence, perhaps because coastal breezes blew most odors away, except for the enchanting bouquet of the ocean. The only smell Down East that approached acres of cow dung was the decomposing corpse of a right whale that was occasionally stranded ashore. Ordinarily, the air was so fresh back in Ben's home state that many residents claimed they could smell on the breeze when a change in weather was imminent. Ben's forecasting skills relied more heavily on observing the weather vane, barometer, and clouds just as his father had taught him.

Seamus tugged at the blind man's sleeve. "There's a cart with two horses coming toward us," the boy whispered.

"Is that a secret somehow?"

"I don't know just what to make of it," Seamus said quietly. "The teamster's a darkie, but I don't see anyone else abouts."

Ben did not share the boy's apprehension. "Unless I've erred terribly in navigation, I believe we are still well north of the Confederacy. Perhaps he's simply a freeman."

"Sure, I suppose he might be." Seamus snorted in derision. "Though I think we've more chance in these parts to meet a leprechaun."

"No chance at all he's a freeman?" Ben asked, doing his best to imitate General Custer's interrogation. "So, you've seen other actual leprechauns hereabouts, then?"

Seamus responded with sarcasm. "If I had such a chance as that, don't you think I'd have stolen me a pot of gold? I sure wouldn't be peddling Bibles and tracts between warring armies." He tugged Ben's sleeve to move him onto the berm of the road.

The cart was close enough that Ben could hear the metallic grinding emanating from its wheels and the labored breathing of the horses. "Hello! How are you this day?" he called out. Abruptly he sensed a swarm of flies buzzing about his head. He waved his hand wildly to drive them off.

"Pull up there, girls," the teamster called to his mares. "Good day, gentlemen. Beg your pardon for forcing you from the road." Ben knew the deep resonance of the man's voice would be the envy of any sergeant in either army.

"No need to apologize," Ben said. "Can't expect you to pull aside for us."

"Coming back from the war, are you?"

"Yes, we left the army at Gettysburg on the third," Ben replied.

"That was a grand day for the Union," the teamster observed in a booming voice. "And Mister Lincoln, too. So tell me, where are you gentlemen heading now?"

Seamus spoke up, "We're on our way to Lancaster. Where are you heading off to, then?"

"I am on my way to Allentown. I work for Reverend Dickey at the Ashmun Institute. A friend of the reverend is a minister at Muhlenberg College there and has offered the reverend 250 volumes that the library there considers obsolete."

"The Ashmun Institute is a school, then?" the boy asked.

"Yes, the good Reverend Dickey created a school for Negro men down near Oxford. I learned well enough that the reverend kept me on as a kind of sexton of sorts. The reverend and Missus Sarah treat me so well that I cannot imagine ever leaving."

The conversation between Seamus and the wagoner proceeded without Ben's participation, like the passage of a stream in which he was not angling for a salmon to strike his line. He was distracted by other sounds – the pawing of the horses at the ground, the buzzing of flies, the distant bellowing of cows, the barking of farm dogs – that filled his ears in the same manner that the din of battle prevented him from hearing the man standing shoulder to shoulder with him in the ranks. Was he more acutely aware of noise now that he lacked sight? Perhaps the same was true of his other senses as well, he mused. Marching hither and yon for two years, he had only rarely cast much thought upon the noises or odors about him.

"Ben, did you hear him?" Seamus asked loudly. "Moses says we should avoid going near Philadelphia. He thinks there may be trouble in the coming days."

"Yes, indeed, all true. Reverend Dickey was recommended by authorities that Ashmun men not go into the city and to avoid other towns around there for a few weeks," the teamster said. "They expect unrest among the Irish, as well as among others."

"Unrest among the Irish?" Seamus asked. "Hear that, Ben? I wonder if that explains our troubles with the railway."

"What's upset the Irish?" Ben asked when he had recovered from his reverie. "I know Democrats and copperheads don't want to be fighting a war for abolition. Why are the Irish angry?"

"I believe conscriptions are set to begin in a few days," Moses said quietly. "I've heard the Irish believe that others can pay someone to go for the army in their stead if they have 300 dollars, but there aren't many among the sons of Ireland who can readily put their hands upon so much money. I understand that the Irish believe it will fall to their lot to fill the Army's ranks."

"Sure then, I can understand their fret. Many of my cousins feel they came to America looking to get out from under the thumb of the monarchy and the aristocracy," Seamus said. "Now they may find themselves forced to fight for someone else's freedom."

"I suppose I can understand the feeling that way some," Ben said. "No offense to you, stranger, but I'd heard the same thought from many of the New York men that marched north with us to Gettysburg."

"No offense taken, sir, none at all," Moses said. "For myself, I would want to be indebted to no man for my freedom. I am grateful to Reverend Dickey for his teachings, but I don't feel I owe him more than that. How will there ever be anything but hate if everyone feels they're owed something while at the same time they all resent each other?"

"Sounds a great deal like Ireland," Seamus said.

Ben stifled a laugh into a cough. Even a blind man could see that this curious assemblage of an educated black man, a young mick and a bloodied Yank soldier would arouse hatred of one kind or another across the nation, on either side of the Mason-Dixon Line. They were shy only Benedict Arnold and Aaron Burr to boast a royal flush.

"If we should avoid Philadelphia as you say, do you have any suggestion as to how we might travel on to New York or Boston?" Ben asked. "I need to reach the State of Maine as quickly as workable."

A long silence followed. To Ben, the noise of swarming horse flies became more fierce, so loud it sounded that the horses pawed at the ground as if encouraging the teamster to move forward. He hoped the solution would be quite simple because he knew so little about Pennsylvania that the names of towns and cities meant about the same to him as the hamlets and villages around the boy's home across the ocean in County Cork. The longer that Moses took to suggest a route, the more anxious Ben became.

"Damn it all. If I knew it were going to be so difficult, I would have held onto my tracts and let that colonel keep his silver dollars," Seamus exclaimed. "Among an Army on a forced march, paper can be worth good money."

Ben remembered that from their first meeting the lad's proselytizing seemed to be more mercenary than missionary. Given the state's enlistment bounty and monthly pay that Ben had accepted, he felt he could not reproach Seamus in the least. Compared to the misdemeanors he had learned about among the Army's commissary officers, contractors, jobbers, sutlers and bounty jumpers, the boy's sins were merely venial. If he had learned nothing else, Ben knew that in war some men died, some were wounded, some escaped unscathed, some turned coward, some supported the war effort with words, some turned a handsome profit and the lucky few – most far from combat – became wealthy. The "Great Pecking Order," as Ben's father had called it, was as valid in war as on a whaling ship. The crew of the whaleboat who were at greatest risk stood to take but the least portion, what the men called a lay, while the lion's share of profits went to the shipowner who stayed clean and coiffed in his office ashore.

Finally, Moses spoke up. "I should like to propose a plan that may yet get you to New York City without venturing into Philadelphia. If you would consent to ride in my wagon, I would happily carry you with me to Allentown. From there I believe you could easily travel by rail or stage into New York."

Ben heard Seamus clap his hands. "Sounds just fine to me! Sure beats us hoofing all the way to Hell's Kitchen and beyond."

"Seamus! Curb your tongue, if you please," Ben barked.

"I'm sorry, Ben," the boy said, sounding contrite. "With my folks both gone, I've got no call to go back to Five Points now. But I've still got an uncle and a few cousins in the Kitchen that I could stay with until I go back to the war – if'n there's a war to go to at month's end."

"Are you saying there's a place called the Kitchen, or, Hell's Kitchen? In the middle of New York?" Ben asked. He felt rather sheepish after snapping at the boy. He recalled that for many years a few blocks of Bangor was known as the Devil's Half Acre.

"Oh, I see. No, I weren't swearing none, Ben. Honest. The neighborhood's been called that because no one less a personage than Davy Crockett himself said the Irish he met there weren't decent enough to swab the floor of hell's kitchen. Well, it weren't any stretch for my Irish relations there to turn an insult into a badge of honor. Myself, I wondered at what old Davy would have said had he gone on to Five Corners. Now that's a place to make Satan jealous."

"You're sure we won't be a burden?" Ben asked the wagoner.

"To the contrary, it could help to have a white man on my rig," Moses said. "Especially a soldier. I'll be safer than travelling alone."

"Are you worried about us Irish way out here?" the boy asked as he tugged Ben closer toward the wagon.

"No. Unless they are slave traders. There are men who come north to kidnap Freemen to take back south and sell them into slavery. I am cautious whenever I travel away from the Institute."

"What would you do if you were approached?" Seamus asked.

Moses laughed. "I don't suppose Reverend Dickey would approve, but my father gave me a Derringer a few years ago. I carry it in my boot whenever I leave the Institute, even to fetch honey from a nearby farm. Climb aboard back there. I think the girls are eager to go."

"Allentown will get us closer to New York?" Seamus asked.

"A sight closer than here, for sure," Moses said.

Ben thought about the destination that awaited him at the end of this long travail. A granite fortress on a stone island at sea. His Chateau d'*If*.

CHAPTER 13

Seamus contrived to arrange a sort of bed in the wagon upon which Ben reclined. His hat rested on his lap so that any passerby could easily see the bloodied bandage wrapped around his head. Seamus sat nearby, asking many questions about Maine and light houses while also offering occasional narration of their trip. Moses hummed to himself tunes that Ben knew from many Sunday services when the armies on both sides sang to pass the time between bouts of mundane and murder.

They made only three stops that afternoon after Seamus suggested they try to purchase a ham or mutton at a farm along their route. The men waited in the wagon along the road; Moses watched as the boy went to each farmhouse. He described to Ben how the boy motioned toward them as he recited a speech the three together had scripted and rehearsed in advance. Seamus was to apologize for the intrusion, explain Ben's condition and ask whether the farmer had foodstuffs for sale. At the first two farmsteads, the Irish boy was run off before he even finished his introductions. On the second visit, the white-bearded codger sicced a snarly gray dog after the lad. As the barking grew near, Ben heard a pistol being cocked. Fortunately, Seamus climbed in next to him before it became necessary for Moses to kill the cur.

After watching Seamus chased by the snarling mongrel, Moses favored abandoning the effort. He proposed instead combining their rations to make what supper they could. He carried dried beans and sweet corn in a basket, along with peaches and cherries. Seamus complained that their steady diet of fruits and candy was causing him great personal discomfort. Without soliciting any more detailed information, Ben consented to allow Seamus a final attempt to purchase new vittles.

According to the boy's account of his third venture, Seamus met a farmer's wife, a youngish woman engulfed in a crush of small children. He described how the woman carried a toddler straddling one hip while cradling an infant in her other arm. When she heard what Seamus sought, she placed the tot in the charge of an older girl and lay the baby in a crib. Once she had the silver coin in her hand, she led him out to the family's root cellar. In just a few minutes, she emerged with a smoked ham hock, two sealed ceramic canisters and a glass jar containing cucumbers.

"The soldier on the wagon? He has other injuries, yet?" Ben heard the woman ask as they walked toward the wagon. "What for a man is he?"

Ben wondered how Seamus would reply after their short acquaintance.

"He is a good man, ma'am. In two years I've been giving Bibles to the armies, I have not met a soldier more wounded," Seamus said. "I have seen his scars. Now he is blind from a gunpowder blast. I was asked to get him on a railroad to his home in Maine."

"Here, you give this dollar back to the soldier," Ben heard the woman say to Seamus. "I wonder but that he may have greater need of it. We have the Lord's bounty from our lands. I could not face the Judgement knowing that I had accepted this silver piece if it caused you or the soldier there any greater hardship in your travels."

In other circumstances, Ben would have objected strongly to accepting this charity – this pity, really – from the farmer's wife, but he stopped short. He could not now identify a good argument within himself to challenge the woman's good intent. Was he not a severely wounded soldier? Was he not going home? Was he not blind to the world, with little reassurance that he would see again? Was he not then helpless, in need of assistance to complete the simplest tasks such as walking and eating? At last, Ben chose to remain silent.

After Seamus had loaded his purchases beside Ben, the wagon rolled on for another three hours. Ben wished that the horses would keep a quicker pace, but he dared not question Moses for fear that it might sound ungrateful. In some ways, the slow progress suited the needs of Seamus, who would occasionally absent himself to visit the countryside, but caught up again quickly. Moses observed to Ben that Seamus was doubtless still performing his missionary duties because each time he jumped off the moving wagon, the boy carried with him a handful of religious tracts which he did not have in hand when he returned. Ben decided not to explain to Moses the other purposes the tracts served among the armies. When he was aboard the wagon, the boy gave fine voice to the lyrics of the spiritual songs that Moses hummed. At other times, the teamster simply increased his own volume. "I hope you are not disturbed by these hymns," Moses said to Ben at one time. "I find that a show of faith allays the fears of others toward me, whether they are faithful themselves or no."

"I have never been offended by another man's display of his faith," Ben said. "I only wish that I were so certain in my own."

"Yet, surely you believe?" Moses asked. "In God and the miracle of our creation?"

Ben thought for a few moments about how to respond to the man's question. In his years of attending Sunday services with the regiment and fighting battles throughout the week to ensure that His Truth was marching on, Ben had never felt the certainty that the chaplains preached. "Please forgive me, Moses. What I have seen among men is more hate than help; more cruelty than kindness. If man is made in God's image, what does that say about God? Preachers ask me to believe in our Father in Heaven, but it was my own father on Earth who whipped me like a mule."

For a long while, Ben heard nothing but the creaking of the wagon and the complaints of the horses. Apparently, Seamus was off on one of his personal missions. Overhead a hawk shrieked.

"You probably know that many times in the Bible, God tested the faith of men," Moses said to Ben at last. "Look at the story of Job in the Old Testament or Judas in the Gospels. God asked Abraham to sacrifice his own son."

In the quiet that followed, Ben knew that Moses expected a response yet he remained silent. Most of his early education had come from the Bible, courtesy of his mother. Even then, when he heard these tales of faith in the face of adversity, the question he most wanted to ask was, "What for?" Even as a young boy, he wondered what benefit either God or any man derived from such arduous tests. He also knew better than to ever speak this notion aloud. One of the regiment's chaplains had explained to the men of the 2nd Maine on a Sunday morning the danger of such thoughts; doubt begets doubts, and doubt spoken aloud is heresy. Were 'His fiery gospel writ in rows of burnished steel,' doubt might even be considered treason. Ben carried his doubt deep inside and never spoke of it to anyone.

After a long silence, Moses finally raised another topic. "Do you believe that you and the boy are ready to stop for the night? I wouldn't mind seeing what that woman provided us for dinner, and I see a field where I could hobble the horses so they could graze."

"Yes, it's been a long day for us, as well," Ben said. "We walked ourselves a good distance today before we met you. How long until sundown?"

"I suppose we have another hour at least. Here comes Seamus now. May I ask him to scout up some wood from that stand of oak trees there?"

"Yes, I am sure he will." Ben thought it odd that Moses asked permission to solicit the boy's assistance. "He's been a great help these past few days. I can do little for myself other than walk and sleep."

"I cannot imagine living that way nor traveling such a long distance that you have. I do admire you. I think I would feel bewildered."

"That's a good word for it. Were it not for Seamus, I would likely be lost in the woods or shackled and heading for a Confederate prison."

When the lad returned to the wagon, Seamus and Moses began making camp. Before long, Ben smelled the smoke of a fire. This was soon followed by the whistle of a steam kettle and the odor of burning grease. Faster than Ben thought possible, Seamus pressed a pewter plate and a trio of utensils into his hands.

"That lady sure knew what to give traveling men, then," Seamus said. "Here's a slab of ham, along with potato salad and sauerkraut. If you still need a dessert when you finish, she gave us a jar of pickles."

"And this potato salad is delicious," Moses said. "I would never admit this around the Institute, but it's better even than what Mrs. Dickey makes, bless her soul."

"Kindly pardon my lack of manners," Ben said. "It's hard to handle a knife and fork in this cursed bandage." He did his best to scoop the potato salad into a spoon with his thumb. He agreed it did taste wonderful. Next, he piled the sauerkraut onto a wedge of the ham and took bites almost like eating a slice of pie. He asked for a second helping of the potato salad and finally ate a pickle. Given that the 2nd Maine's "three-year men" had been denied rations from the time their "two-year" comrades had departed until they were assigned to the 20th, Ben couldn't remember when he had last eaten such a full and satisfying meal. Soon after finishing the pickle, he rested his head on his knapsack and drifted to sleep while listening to Moses identify for Seamus the constellations visible overhead, replete with the mythology of each. Nearby a chickadee whistled his lonely love song into the night.

CHAPTER 14

$\mathcal{T}$he sharp report of a gunshot woke Ben the following morning. He felt about on the nearby ground for his musket but could not feel where he had left it. Instinctively he reached to retrieve a Navy Colt pistol from his baggage. Only when he had the weapon in hand did he stop to question what he might do next. Fire a warning shot? Because there were only two directions in which he could discharge the gun safely; into the ground or into the air.

"Don't worry, Ben," Seamus said quietly. "The rebs ain't here. That's just Moses. He took your rifle into the field across the way there. He told me that he saw a drove of rabbits. He thought we might do well to take a few. I've been honing your jackknife on the whetstone so we can flense one." A second gunshot echoed through the valley. Seamus giggled. "Or possibly two. He bragged he was a keen shot."

"You are recovered then from your malady yesterday?" Ben asked.

"Sure now, and thank the Holy Mother. I've never felt any worst in my stomach during this life, except for a few occasions when Mother and I went a week or so without any food whatsoever."

Nearly every member of the 2nd Maine had endured the discomfort of dysentery at some time during the past two years. Ben had once heard about a man named Jones from the Bangor Light Infantry who was much afflicted when the regiment was engaged in the siege of Yorktown. The 2nd Maine remained entrenched in pits half filled with water from the April rains while McClellan moved men and artillery inch by inch closer to the rebel stronghold. Rather than relieve himself in the trench, Jones crawled out and rested behind a large tree while Confederate snipers fired upon him. After watching Jones take this risk a dozen times throughout the afternoon, one of his messmates declared Jones to be the bravest man in the Union Army. Like much of the effort of the Union forces, the courage Jones displayed all came to naught. After McClellan's 30-day siege, the Confederate Army slipped away in the night, taking with them their whole kit and caboodle before the main Union assault.

"I'm supposin' that it's been some time since you ate fresh meat," Seamus said.

Ben nodded. "Long enough that I don't recall the when or where of it. Before Antietam, or perchance longer."

"Don't get too eager, then. We'll need to cook the bunnies a wee bit before we sup."

A new thought struck Ben. "Seamus, keep an eye out, would you? I suppose this land belongs to someone. They may not be keen to the idea of us poaching their game."

Just at that moment, Ben heard footsteps. Their pace was steady, not hurried or panicked.

"Any luck?" Seamus asked.

"Two shots, two hares," Moses said. "My father claimed that the devout hunter is never lucky, but only gathering the bounty of God."

"Did you and your father hunt a great deal?" Ben asked.

"We had little enough choice," Moses explained in his husky voice. "I grew up on a small farm down in Maryland, toward Mechanicsville. My father owned a parcel on the north side of Catoctin Mountain, but the soil was too poor to grow much. Even tobacco failed. My mother managed a small plot of herbs and a few chickens. For all else, we hunted. Goodness, we hunted deer, cottontail, squirrels, fox, you name it. We trapped along Owens Creek for muskrats, mink, and raccoon. When I was old enough to handle a birding gun, I went out with him for turkey, pheasant, grouse, duck, geese. No one who came to our little cabin ever left hungry or empty-handed."

"How did you come to go to school here in Pennsylvania, then?" Seamus asked.

"Just a lucky happenstance, I suppose," Moses said. "Every year the congregants of Weller's Methodist Church in Mechanicsville hosted a Christmas feast for the town. Each year, my father sold them a goose that I delivered. While I was about that chore one year, I met Reverend Dickey. He asked if I had any interest in books and science. Then the reverend went out to our farm and spoke with my parents. My mother thought I was too young to be away from home, but father said I had learned all there was to learn outdoors and it was time I went to an actual school building."

"Must have felt strange to go off to school where you didn't know anyone," the boy said. "Least that's how it was for me at the orphanage, and the reason I could not stay."

"Yes, it seemed queer when I arrived. I missed my folks terribly during the first weeks. Then I looked about and saw that the whole student body were boys just like me, and a few members of the faculty were Freemen. I felt at home there. So, I have now stayed there for nine years."

As they spoke, Ben finished breakfast, a curious rehash of foods left over from the night before. Seamus had brewed coffee and seared the remaining ham in a greasy skillet. The potato salad went down smoothly, but a bite of the last pickle did not sit well with his palate so early in the day. He rinsed his mouth with a nip of water and spat it out fiercely. More coffee also helped, followed by a chunk of horehound. When he finished, Ben did what little he could manage to help break camp. Soon he was again perched in the back of the wagon, moving toward a destination he could not see.

"Ben, our young friend mentioned to me that you need to write a letter home to a young lady," Moses said. "I don't mean to intrude on your affairs, but perhaps I can help. I have assisted some young men who were new to the Institute to write letters to their folks back home. Also, sometimes to the sweethearts they left behind them."

"I would be most grateful for your suggestions," Ben said. "I've been at a loss on how to begin. What is the proper way to address her, and then how does a man tell a woman who expected to become betrothed that he is now a blind invalid?"

"Seamus said your colonel thought it might be only temporary. Was he wrong?"

"That is what the regimental surgeon said. But 'might not be blind forever' isn't what any young woman hopes for in a husband."

"Perhaps not." Moses agreed. "Anything you might think proper to tell me about her?"

"I have known her since we were young. She's so clever that she runs her father's store when he is away."

"Goodness. How would you describe her?"

"Men come to the store just to see her. I heard a woman in Rockland complain that if she had a half of Rebecca's beauty that she wouldn't need a license to steal."

"Get along there, girls," Moses called with a shake of the reins. "Well, Ben, I think I understand your challenge."

CHAPTER 15

 llentown, Penns.
1863

DEAR REBECCA;

"As I write this, I am coming home to Maine. Val and Stan have both enlisted, so I must arrive to maintain the light house before they go off to the Army. You will be relieved to hear that they will serve under Lt. Colonel J. L. Chamberlain, commanding officer of the 20th Maine. He is from Bowdoin and taught at the college there before the war. You may have heard that the 20th Maine won the second day at Gettysburg; but less known is that about a 100 of us men from the 2nd Maine were caught up in the battle as well. This included my cousins Frank, Joe, and Ben, as well as myself.

"General Geo. Meade is now commanding the Union Army. When he learned that my brothers were enlisted and coming to join the Army, he discharged me to go care for Sorrow Ledge. I am to keep watch against any *rebel pirates like Read, who stole a revenue cutter from Portland harbor and destroyed it with a load of munitions aboard. Probably that story has been in all the newspapers at home by now.*

"I am fortunate to leave when I do because the Union Army is now following the rebels under R. Lee into Virginia. I hope you will not think ill of me that I do not wish to go with the Army south once again. Many of the 2nd Maine went home in June, and I now wish that I had been with them.

"I am sure you can see this letter is not written in my own poor script. I was injured at Gettysburg and have asked someone to pen this letter on my behalf. So I must refrain from the expressions of affection that I previously shared with you, sentiments that no doubt would have inflamed your father had he read them.

"This war has left marks on me to which my father's baleen rod cannot compare. Some may heal while others will not. The regiment's surgeon could predict neither which nor when. So while I asked if I might call upon you as a suitor when I return, now I ask instead for your tolerance and continued friendship. Of all the folks in Rockland, I feel I know you best and hope to enjoy your amity whenever I patronize your father's business.

"With warmest regards,

"Bennington Grindle"

CHAPTER 16

$\mathcal{T}$he capful of wind off the Hudson River was a balm for a man who had spent his childhood within 200 yards of the Gulf of Maine. The cool air rising from the water kept the New Jersey swelter at bay.

Standing on a Weehawken pier, Ben had not felt such a level of calmness since when he had traveled up to Bangor in '61. Seamus was off purchasing tickets for the ferry that would carry them over to Manhattan. The boy had already laid out a course they would walk through the city to get Ben on a train heading north. Once in the care of railway porters, Ben expected to have no further difficulties until he reached the Maine coastline where he would need to hire a boat to carry him out to Sorrow Ledge. No other complications awaited him. Even the dreaded letter had gone to post in Allentown. Sealing the missive and placing the stamp seemed to break a dam of apprehension for Ben.

When Moses had arrived at Muhlenberg College to accept the books for the Ashmun Institute, Reverend Fletcher invited the three travelers to stay in his carriage house near campus. He even asked a neighbor, Doctor Williams, to come to the main house to examine Ben's wounds. The doctor changed most of the bandages on Ben's head, leaving those patches covering his eyes in place and encouraged Ben to allow them to remain for as long as he could tolerate. On Saturday, Moses said good-bye and started on his journey southward back to the Ashmun Institute. Later that day, Seamus and Ben both accepted the singular luxury of baths, during which one of the kind minister's servants had washed their clothing. Finally, at the end of Sunday worship services, Reverend Fletcher had asked on their behalf whether any of the congregants planned any travel to New York City in the coming days. After church, a merchant in the dry goods trade offered to take the two vagabonds with him on Monday morning, though he planned to leave as early as false dawn. He planned to get into the city and return to Allentown in a single day because a cousin in the city had wired of trouble brewing due to the pending Army conscriptions. For Ben, the more significant conflict was now about 400 miles south-west and moving farther south with each hour. He thought that without any further troubles he might be standing on a pier in Rockland within two days, just waiting on a boat to take him home.

Home. He smiled wanly at a word that meant so much to soldiers. Home for Ben was an island he shared with puffins and seagulls, where his only companionship would be two corpses interred under a stone monument. Ben inhaled the sea breeze. He heard the cries of gulls and a buoy bell ring in the distance, and he felt the rhythmic rise and fall of the boat dock. On Sorrow Ledge, he would be alone and likely still blind, at least at first if not forever. Again, he thought of Edmund Dantes imprisoned at Chateau d'*If* without Abbé Faria. Ben knew that for him there would be no hope of escape.

CHAPTER 17

 he ferry voyage across the river was too brief for Ben, who stood forward on the ship's foc'sle feeling the sun and breeze on his chin. Again, and for perhaps one of the last times, Seamus stood at his side narrating their voyage as they approached the middle of Manhattan Island. Soon the boy would be returning to his own family. Ben heard the shrieks of seagulls, a noise he had not heard for the months since the Maine 2nd marched away from Chesapeake Bay. The fleet in the Hudson River that the boy described included hulls as diverse as steamboats, paddle wheelers, brigantines, and simple fishing boats. On the water once again, suddenly Ben felt a keen desire to taste freshly cooked lobster dipped in warm butter.

The ferry delivered them to a pier on the western end of 42nd Street in the early afternoon. Seamus said the most straightforward route for them was to walk east on 42nd and then follow Fourth Avenue north to a station on the New York and Harlem Railroad line. This was a bit of a guess on his part because he rarely ventured farther north than 35th Street. Once Ben was safely seated on the train, the Irish boy said he would seek out his distant family members in Hell's Kitchen or Five Points. Along their walk through Manhattan, Seamus suggested a few taverns where they might stop to eat, but Ben was too eager to get to the railway for any such distraction as hunger.

"Slow down a bit," Seamus said. "People are noticing us, especially you with a musket."

"People don't carry weapons in New York?"

"When they go hunting over in New Jersey or plan to murder the wife's lover," the boy said. "Although sometimes it's the other way around, and the wife arranges to have the husband murdered. Or kills him herself. It's in the penny press all the time."

"Seamus, what smells so bad around here? It stinks like a latrine or the putrid offal in a sutler's wagon."

Seamus did not answer because he was quite busy dodging obstacles. They stumbled along together with the boy venting his frustration at the trash in their way or maneuvering Ben around more substantial items. The streets of New York were far more challenging to a blind man than the backroads of Pennsylvania. As Seamus explained to Ben, they were navigating amongst animals, wagons, vendor carts, pedestrians, and carriages. As they progressed along the streets, they heard a cacophony of noises, including both dogs barking and barkers hawking their wares. Ben heard male and female voices arguing loudly. He wished he could see this human drama unfolding all around him, but once they were away from the river the day's humidity began to settle on them like the swelter of a Virginia swamp. His impatience grew to be on a moving train with fresh air coming through the open windows. As they continued east, the din of the city grew louder and harsher.

"Ben, there's people running through the streets," Seamus said lowly. "Sounds to me they're calling out and chanting about the draft."

Ben heard the hollering echo in the streets and smelled smoke. "Do you think the Irish men are protesting here like Moses thought they might in Philadelphia?"

Seamus pulled Ben to a stop. "I don't like this, Ben," the boy said. "There are crowds rushing about everywhere. Some are carrying torches. Let's get off the street." The boy pushed the blind man against a building. "I don't know how we get out of here. Ben, take off your jacket. Your uniform might attract bad intentions."

Ben did as he was told and stuffed his tunic into his haversack. "How far to the railroad still?"

"I guess we're four, maybe five blocks away. I wonder if we're better off to go back to the ferry. We could walk north on the Jersey side to the next ferry, or go on up to Tappan Zee or West Point. Ben, this is looking to me like a mob starting. There could be a riot." The boy jostled against Ben as if he was shoved from behind. "Hey, watch yourself there, bucko!" Seamus yelled.

"No. Take me to the train. We're running out of money, aren't we? If we go north on foot, how many days will it add? So then what money will remain to you for your troubles?" Despite what he could smell or hear, Ben was unable to see the turmoil growing about them.

"I don't care about the damned money. I see mobs up and down the streets. Not just the one, but a half dozen gangs maybe, or even more, all told. I don't know that I can talk us out of harm if they set upon us. Looks like there's houses and stores afire south toward the Kitchen."

Ben started walking forward, in the direction he assumed would take him to the rail line. "If I go on this way, I'll find the train, right? I'll keep to a straight line. There's no need for you to come with me. I'll make it fine from here." He used the butt of his rifle to feel along the building fronts. He had not gone more than 20 feet when Seamus pulled at his shirt sleeve.

"Damn it, Ben, you don't seem to understand. Men are rioting in the streets because they don't want to come back from the war looking like you! If the mobs see you, it won't go well. You're not able to fight back or even run away."

The soldier reached out and felt for the pack the boy carried over his shoulder, which he lowered to the ground. "Here, take the money that Colonel Chamberlain promised you. I thank you for all that you've done for me this past week. If I don't get on that train today, I likely won't make Sorrow Ledge in time." Ben assumed, as a soldier is trained to do, that he could overcome whatever obstacle or enemy presented itself. "Be sure to take the captain's compass, too."

"You are the most stubborn son of a bitch I've ever met," the boy said harshly. "You can't see your own hands, but you think you'll go find a train station in the middle of New York City on your own?

Christ Almighty, does the Union Army reward stupid?" Still, Seamus took Ben's arm to lead him further east toward the New York and Harlem Railroad. The boy narrated their trip just as he had in the past, pointing out each danger they dodged. Abruptly he stopped. "God, I don't like the looks of that crowd. A lot of people are carrying off beds, chairs, and linens back toward Five Points. There must be looting somewhere, but I don't see any coppers anywhere."

The stink of decay that Ben detected earlier gave way to an unmistakable smell of burning wood and trash. "Do you see something afire?" Ben asked.

"Yes, I hope it's just a bonfire, but there sure looks to be a huge mob outside the Negro Orphanage up on Fifth Avenue," Seamus said. "There could be real trouble."

"Take me up there," Ben said simply. "We need to know someone is there to protect the children."

"And if not, what are you proposing to do about it?" The lad's voice betrayed fear and apprehension. "I don't understand what you're thinking. One minute you're all hell-fire to get to a train, and next you want to stop for a riot. I wish to God you could see just what the hell we've gotten ourselves into."

"You said an orphanage, didn't you? Somebody needs to help them. No one ever raised a hand to help me, not one damn time, on a Rockland street or in my own home. We need to see if someone's on the lookout for those children."

"And if there ain't?" Seamus asked.

"We'll cross that bridge then."

At Ben's insistence, they walked a block up Fifth Avenue and came to the corner of 43rd Street. Seamus described to Ben the angry crowd that filled the intersection and covered the lawn of the asylum. The boy left Ben's side long enough to climb the front stairs of a house across the street for a better view of what was happening at the building's entrance. Soon he returned to the soldier's elbow. "It's ugly all right. Looks to me there's an officer from the fire squad near the front entrance trying to keep the mob from setting the place ablaze, but my guess is that he's outnumbered thousands to one. I don't see any coppers about. The mob is throwing bundles of burning tinder at the building, trying to set it afire. Ben, it looks to me like that one man is all that stands between the mob and their plan to burn that building to the ground, orphans or no."

Judging by the vicious noise of the crowd all around them, Ben nodded in agreement with that assessment. He turned and felt with his hands along the handrail of the stoop. Soon he settled on a lower step with his baggage in front of him. He fished around in the bottom of his haversack for the Colt pistols.

"Seamus, load these please," Ben said. "Fill both cylinders, and put a round in the rifle."

"What in tarnation are you thinking, Ben? You can't take on an angry Irish mob when they've got their minds set to cause mischief. Hell, they intend a lot worse than that. Mischief is just an average night in the Kitchen."

The boy's last words were drowned in the chants of a hideous choir screaming, "Down with the naggurs!"

Ben said nothing more but began to unwrap the bandages swathed around his head.

"My God, what in the name of hell are you doing?" Seamus asked. Real anger sounded in his voice. "The doctor told you to keep these bandages on as long as you ever can."

"Sure, he did. And now I can't wait any longer.

Seamus snorted loudly. "And what are you going to do?"

"First, find out if I can see. Then we'll figure what we can do to help."

When the bandages were in a pile before him, he peeled back the cotton patch covering his right eye. He felt a stab of agony as daylight touched upon his pupil for the first time in more than a week, reminding him sharply of coming into the lighthouse cupola and seeing the intense light of the Fresnel lens after climbing up from the dark tower below. At first, he saw only large dark shapes with a fiery glow around the edges, but gradually they turned into distinct figures before finally becoming buildings, houses, and people. As this change occurred, the raucous rioting around them continued to intensify. After a few minutes longer, he removed the dressing over his left eye. He was alarmed that the same improvement to his vision on the first side did not occur as quickly on the second. Objects retained a shimmery light at their edges, like the blue halo that encircles a full moon on a crisp night. Ben assumed this was because the exploding rifle breech fell more keenly along the left side of his face. The clamor of the riot sounded more muted to his left ear as well.

"I can see a bit," Ben reported. "What's happened with the man by the asylum?"

"Well, nothing's gotten better if that's what you're asking. The crowd's not as large because it looks like the looting is better a few streets east of here. But there's still one man standing up to a few thousand. I wouldn't put money on him."

"Okay, bet on me, then," Ben said as he stood. He blinked repeatedly and wiped tears from his cheeks as his sight adjusted. He affixed the bayonet to the muzzle of his Enfield; he had done exactly that so often he could have done it while still blind. "You're going to march me straight through the crowd with the rifle aimed at my back, just like I'm your prisoner. When we reach the porch, I'll relieve you of the Enfield and give him one of the Colts. You'll disappear into the crowd. A mob won't go after an unarmed boy, but they won't be as brave against two men armed with guns."

"After you kill the first ten, what are you going to do about the next hundred? Then the hundred after that?"

Ben surveyed the streets and marveled at the size of the mob as he did. The burning torches created curious luminous auras before his eyes. The angry horde danced as they shrieked their hatred toward nearly everyone. "Don't worry about that. First shot will scatter the hundreds. Then we'll have just the ten to reckon with. Men aren't as brave as you might think when it comes to dying for themselves. Besides, a lot of this crowd are women and girls. They came here to carry away whatever clothes or linens they might find. They'll scatter at the gunfire." Still, he had to admit to himself that Seamus was correct about how the odds lay for what he proposed. Throughout the throng, Ben could see burning rags wrapped about sticks and an assortment of blazing flags. The weapons carried by the throng were everyday household items: knives, hammers, and axes, but there were table legs and other bits of furniture pressed into service as cudgels.

Ben also saw a few military items, such as sabers and pikes, hoisted over the heads of the rabble.

"You've gone insane," the boy said. "Why are you doing this?"

"Would you have me leave that fireman to fend for himself. What if the orphans are still inside?" Ben tucked the pistols into his waistband and donned his uniform tunic to cover them. "I'll need your help to carry off this ruse, to distract the mob. Please, Seamus, just get me down to the front and then get yourself out of there. Go find your relatives. Keep them safe. I don't think this day will end well ..." His voice trailed off, and he reached out to rest his hand on the boy's shoulder, seeing the lad for the first time if still somewhat hazily – struwwely red hair and all. The boy's cheeks were dappled with freckles from ear to ear. Seamus was taller and perhaps older than Ben expected. Ben hoisted the baggage onto his own shoulders. "Thank you for everything. You've done far more for me than the colonel ever expected." He lurched a step forward under the added burden that Seamus had previously carried. Then he took the silver dollars from his trouser pockets and put them in the lad's hand. From another pocket, he drew the remaining paper currency and peeled off several bills that he extended toward the boy. "Thank you, Seamus."

"Are you sure about this plan, Ben?" the lad asked, still focused on the scheme to rescue the fireman and any orphans they could find. "I've never seen a mob wanting so badly to kill just one man as they do that fire chief. I hope the orphans themselves are all gone and rescued, or this day will put a stain on my people forever."

"Don't worry about that now. We'll try to save the Irish from themselves." Ben extended his hand toward Seamus. "We'll do the best we can. But first, you must promise that you'll get away as soon as you can. You're to give me the rifle and go on the double quick. Swear it on your mother's grave."

"I do. Swear. God, I see this going wrong in so many damned ways. How can I help you if the orphans are still inside? What if the fire officer refuses to leave?" The boy looked at the enraged horde. Their noise grew more fierce by the moment.

"You can't, and you won't. You'll be running by then. You just swore it. When I take the rifle from you, I want you to run as far and as fast as you can. Don't stop until you are with your uncle. Understood?"

"Yes, sir."

Ben was still adjusting to his fresh sight as they crossed Fifth Avenue. The bright sunlight burned his eyes, creating dazzling colored orbs that burst and reshaped to blur his vision. He was relieved somewhat when a plume of black smoke drifted up the avenue from somewhere to the south and cloaked the sun in a black shroud, but a gray tint still clouded his sight. His eyes watered more in the acrid fumes created by the burning piles. He searched for a place where the seething mass surrounding the orphanage was sparse so they might encounter less trouble, but he didn't see such a path. He instructed Seamus to call out with his loudest voice; then Ben began to shove the rabble aside as he drove toward the front of the building. Once again he carried the burden of a forlorn hope.

Seamus began to shout. "Make way there! Here's what the bloody politicians want for us sons of Ireland! Look at this poor damned bastard, straight from Gettysburg. Gangway, I said! Want to come home to the missus or a sweetheart looking like this ogre? Hell, your own ma won't know your face once Mister Lincoln is done with you!" he called. "Make a hole for the beast! Daughters of Erin, is this what you want for your man or boy? Don't touch it, who knows the kinds of disease it brought back? He's gone to the South. Probably he carries smallpox, French pox and maybe even plague! Watch yourself there! All morning he's been showing signs of ague and consumption. Look what the bastard politicians want to happen to all of us next. Go on, ask those recruiting bastards how much a man in the ranks earns and think whether it's enough to become an ogre such as this one. Every Irish man or lad who can't find three hundred dollars will be left to walk the Earth looking like this poor disgusting fiend."

The ruse worked well, and the angry crowd they encountered fell quiet and separated to make a path for them, much like infantry falling away before a cavalry charge. Ben saw many among the dirt-streaked faces of women who comprised the multitude turn away at the indelicate sight of him. He thought that Seamus was perhaps a little too persuasive. So far, at least, not one of the screaming ruffians had proposed to hang or burn Ben. That was a small comfort as they walked farther into the rampage and came closer to the center of the crush of hate and fury.

All went well until about 20 paces from the front porch of the asylum. A barrel-chested lout with a soot-streaked face reached to grab Ben's neck. With his other hand, he waved a small black club overhead. Ben began to unbutton his uniform tunic to retrieve a Colt when a bright flash of steel flickered in the corner of his eye just as Seamus cried out.

"Which of you bastards tripped me, damn it?" the boy screamed. "I might'a killed my prisoner. And looker what happen to this man! All right, where's the sot what done it? I'm sorry, mister. Looks that you got a mighty bad scratch there, all right. "

Ben watched the rioter step away to stare at the bloody red gash across his forearm. The thug seemed at a loss to explain how it happened, even as he tried to stanch the bleeding. Ben wondered where along his travels amongst the armies that Seamus had learned to wield a bayonet as smoothly as some officers brandish their sabers. At first, the hooligans nearest to them seemed willing to accept that the stabbing was an accident. The pair walked on another 15 feet before the mood of the crowd toward them began to turn uglier. Ben and Seamus now hurried to where the fire chief stood alone.

"Where are the orphans?" Ben asked. "How do we get them out of here?"

"All gone, I hope. I've been out here while they were smuggled out the back. With God's will, they're already holed up in a police station until this madness ends."

Ben jerked open his blue tunic, buttons flying in all directions. These same buttons had delayed the 2nd Maine from leaving Bangor two years prior. They were a hindrance yet again. Ben handed one of the Colts to the fireman. "Use it if you must. Aim over their heads. We've got a chance to escape if we threaten, don't kill." The soldier looked back to where Seamus stood behind him. The boy aimed the rifle level toward the crowd, but at the muzzle end was a burly man trying to snatch the weapon away from Seamus. Hand over hand, the man pulled the barrel stock toward himself, tugging the boy along with it. With a firm grip, he tried to yank the musket from the lad's hand, but Seamus had a finger hooked around the trigger. The rifle exploded in a deafening noise that brought an unsettling silence to the asylum yard for a moment. The man staggered backward, a crimson flower blossoming across the waist of his filthy work shirt. Behind the first victim, a red-haired woman shrieked as she collapsed to her knees on the ground. Her hands could not contain the blood flowing from her thick belly to stain the lap of her skirt.

Ben immediately fired off a pistol shot into the air as he pulled Seamus behind him. He took the Enfield from the boy, hoping that the mob would think Ben had pulled the trigger. He looked toward the fire officer, who seemed shocked. Black soot from the day's fires covered the man's skin and clothes. Sweat trickled down his face, white streaks revealing the only mark of his race. "We've got a minute, no more than two until they get over the shock and come at us," Ben said.

"I'm hoping for my squad to come back, but there's bedlam all over the island now. We must go through," the man said, nodding his head toward the asylum's front door.

Ben looked at the motley crowd gathered around the two fallen victims on the lawn. The fiery globes created by their burning torches caused Ben to feel a little dizzy. "Take the Colt and bring the boy with you," he told the fire chief. "I'll cover your retreat. Don't stop for me. Understood?" The two men began to retreat toward the doorway; however, Seamus remained motionless, his eyes affixed on the bodies of these two people killed by the one shot from the Enfield he had carried. The fire chief grabbed the boy's collar and jerked him into the dark, smoky building. The soldier waited outside to give the other two a chance to escape. He looked down at the dying woman on the lawn one more time, before turning toward the dark orphanage. Once inside, Ben paused to reload the rifle before he followed along behind them. As the clamor of the mob increased again, he fired off a second warning shot through the doorway, aiming the Colt high to scare away anyone who intended to pursue them through the dark building. Much like a forlorn hope, a rearguard action was no new thing for Ben.

Despite his instructions to proceed without him, Ben found Seamus and the fireman waiting at the southwest corner on the backside of the asylum. Although they had ignored his instructions, he was frankly relieved. Without them, he would have no idea where he might find safety in the city with so many people riled against the draft, the army, the war, the President, and all else. He might be, as Seamus had said, one among the likely targets for the mob's ire that day in New York. Though he would not have chosen the same terms, Ben knew he embodied the fears that many men newly eligible for the draft harbored – though gratefully without either a pox or the plague. When Ben arrived, the three immediately began running down the back alleys of Manhattan, away from the abandoned orphanage.

When they were two city blocks away from the gutted asylum, the fire officer stopped running and introduced himself as Chief Scott Perkins. His accent sounded to Ben identical to the New Yorker who had led him away from the hospital back to the 20th Maine on the morning after the skirmish at Little Round Top. Perkins was a muscular man, nearly as tall as Ben, with straw-colored hair. As he wiped the soot from his face with a handkerchief, a reddish complexion emerged. His immediate concern was whether the mob had followed them. Ben listened patiently to the debate between Seamus and Perkins who sounded equally familiar with the various routes through the city. Neither agreed to a course of action. Ben used the delay to remove his blue tunic and shove it back into his knapsack. He plucked at his sweat-soaked shirt where it clung to his chest.

"Please, gentlemen, like the infantry says, 'Anywhere but here, Lord, anywhere but here.'" Ben said.

"I say we're closest to the coppers on 35th," Perkins said. "I know a few of the boys in the station. If we go around to the alley, we'll avoid the mob and the front desk sergeant. Now there's a Scottish cur you don't want to contend with. But at the alley door, there'll be fewer questions if one of them recalls me."

Perkins led the way, and Ben remained the rear guard. Seamus walked between them, with Ben's straw hat pulled down over his hair and face. They halted at each corner as the fire chief surveyed the street for dangers before they scurried on to the next safe backstreet. From the vantage of a concrete stoop, they watched a gang drag the corpse of a Union officer down the street, a kepi cap carried aloft by one of the protestors on the point of the captain's sword. The procession often stopped so bystanders could spit or urinate on the corpse. Each new desecration caused the rabble to shriek like a squad of charging rebels. Ben recalled the warning given to Moses and the men of the Ashmun Institute regarding the dangers in Philadelphia. He wondered if these same horrors were occurring across the nation. What would happen to Lincoln's army then?

At another juncture, they saw a mob chasing a young Union soldier up an alley toward where the trio stood. His uniform cap and belt were missing, as well as the left sleeve of his blue tunic. The man's nose was bloody, and a nasty brown bruise was blossoming on his cheek. A noose hung limply from his neck, and a fathom of rope trailed behind him. Apparently, the man had escaped being lynched by a hair's breadth. Ben ushered the boy and the fireman back around the corner of a building then fired a round from the Enfield into the air. The echo resounded against the brick walls of the tenements as loudly as any cannon fire Ben had heard. The Irish throng seemed to pause at once as if staggered by a single stunning blow. The soldier continued running until he reached the corner, where Perkins grabbed his arm and pulled him to safety. By then, Ben had reloaded the musket, which he handed back to Seamus. The fire chief removed the escapee's hemp necktie. "We may be able to give you a two-minute head start," Perkins said. "Be careful. Trust no one today, not even a mick you've known for years. Understand?"

The soldier took a swig from the canteen that Seamus offered. Ben was struck by how young the boy looked. He wondered if he had ever looked or felt that young. Ben extended his hand and said, "Grindle, 20th Maine. Good luck, Private."

"Thank you, sir," the boy said breathlessly before turning away to make good on his escape.

"Here they come again," Ben observed as the mob surged forward. "Two shots over their heads, then we'll each have four in reserve for the persistent ones. Cover us, Seamus, so no one gets behind us. Ready?"

Perkins nodded, and they stepped into the alley together. They fired their warning shots individually over the heads of the Irish throng. As Ben predicted, the first rounds discouraged most in the crowd, who stopped to mill about rather aimlessly as if they were merely out strolling the boulevard. Two ruffians continued stalking toward the corner where Ben and Perkins stood.

"Come on, lads," the older one bellowed. "There ain't but two of them. To hell with conscription!"

"Allow me," Ben whispered. He lowered his pistol and fired a single round at the cobblestones where the bellicose forerunner stood. The bullet raised a spray of rocky chunks that hit many in the first row somewhere about the ankle. Their leader seemed especially vulnerable, as he dropped to one knee and clutched at the other. He belted out a scream of pain as blood appeared between his fingers. The remainder of the angry horde seemed to lose interest and walked away sheepishly, except for the few who helped their injured comrades. The instigator stayed no longer than any of the others, apparently now content with the mischief already done.

As the multitude drifted away, Perkins held his hand toward Ben. "Nicely done, soldier." After they shook hands, each added rounds into the cylinder of the Colt they carried. "You've got mettle enough for ten of those lousy bastards. They get all the courage they can muster from a mob or a bottle."

Carrying all their gear, Seamus walked over to Ben and offered their canteen. "I suppose this incident won't help our standing with Irish society," he said grimly.

"True enough," Perkins said. "We should go quickly now before they get the notion to come back."

The trio went on the double quick south down Manhattan Island until they reached a darkened alley where brown rats scurried in droves amidst crates of rotting vegetables. A pile of tomatoes there had turned to black. The stench of the trash behind the grocer reminded Ben of those deliveries provided by the army's sutlers. Perhaps due to the rats and the fetid odor, the alley was empty. Perkins led the way about one hundred feet down the lane before he knocked at a steel door. He wiped his face with a handkerchief to remove more of the soot. A watch hole opened in the door.

"State your name and business," a gruff voice barked.

The fireman leaned up to the opening and whispered. "Perkins, chief on the fire squad. Come from the orphan asylum over on Fifth."

"Hold on." The sentry hole slid closed. From inside the building, Ben heard the same voice call out: "Anyone know a Perkins, says he's from the fire squad?" A long pause followed. "Then come on and have a look. Well, how the hell would I know if he attends John Street Methodist? Why don't you get off your ass and come have a look for yourself?"

A few moments later, the small sentry door opened again. "All right, then. Put your face up where I can see you." Perkins leaned forward again. "Scott, what the hell happened to you? You look like a chimney sweep. Here, get this door open and let the man in. Don't you know what's happening on the streets to good people today? Come on, get the sergeant's key then. Sorry, Scott. All hell's a' breaking loose all over the damned city. Can't recall anything like this since the Dead Rabbits melee."

The soldier worried that in the alley they were vulnerable to being discovered by one of the roaming gangs. After an interminable time, the thick door swung open, and they were admitted inside. When the door clanged shut behind them, a copper set three deadbolts and lowered a heavy timber across the door frame. Once Ben's eyes adjusted to the darkness, he saw that they were standing in the station's cell block lined with iron bars. As they walked down the narrow passageway, he further observed in the gloom that dozens of dark-skinned children crowded the jail cells, likely the orphans escaped from the mob at the asylum earlier that afternoon. They lay on the cots or sat close together in small knots on the brick floor. Their big eyes stared at these newest visitors with fear and apprehension.

"So what brings you here, Scott?" a tall policeman asked, placing a hand on Perkins' shoulder. "We're a little busy today to help you find your station's lost runners." He chuckled as he looked around to see that his fellow coppers appreciated his stab at mirth.

Perkins stopped abruptly. "I know just where my men are. They've been out in the streets all day putting out fires and saving lives, just the way they should be. Since I've not seen a copper on the streets all after-noon, I suppose you're all too scared to be away from the station where you have the doors all locked tight." Perkins placed his hands on his hips in a defiant stance. Ben watched as a gang of four or five policemen in blue uniforms gathered around to face off against the fire chief. Ben quietly wrapped his hand around the barrel of his Colt so he could wield the gun butt as a weapon.

Abruptly a thick-waisted sergeant shoved his way into the knot of coppers. "What the hell's this all about, then? Today isn't the day for petty rivalries," the big man said in a thick Scottish accent. "And I'll bust up the first manjack of you that acts otherwise. Come on now, the captain wants every man to arm for the evening with something more than a nightstick." He then stepped close to Perkins and thrust his florid face within an inch of the fireman's nose. "And I'll remind you that you're a guest in my house. If you can't behave yourselves, then you and your ilk are welcome to find shelter from the day's troubles elsewhere." He turned to look over Ben and Seamus from boot to scalp. "Friends of yours, are they?"

"My apologies, MacDonald, for the disturbance," Perkins said. "These lads helped me out of a bad mess at the Negro orphanage. I would introduce them, but I've barely had that pleasure myself. I thought of nowhere else where we'd be safe but here." The fireman related a brief explanation of the troubles at the orphanage. "I see you have some of the children here already."

MacDonald shook hands with both Ben and Seamus. "I'm not certain but what we ain't got the whole passel of them because there weren't no other place close where they might be safe from the riffraff. Puts us in a wee bit of a spot because now we got no place to incarcerate any of the lousy micks that we might have need to arrest. I guess we're all playing by different rules today. Come on, then. Let's find a place where you can sit," the sergeant said. "So tell me, just when did the fire squads start carrying pistols?"

Perkins chuckled at the sergeant's question. "Right about an hour ago. If these two hadn't come along when they did, I might have been strung up." He handed the Colt back to Ben. "Thank you. My wife would thank you, too. She tells me she won't look good wearing widow's black for a year."

"Come sit over here where we'll be out of the way," MacDonald said. He unbuttoned his uniform jacket that seemed to fit uncomfortably tight. "And out of earshot, too. Would you like coffee? It's not good, but it's wet." He waved over one of his officers then made a circular motion with his thick index finger, indicating he wanted enough cups of coffee to go around. "And bring a bucket of water and a few washrags," he called. "So then, I guess my first question should be, why are the two of you in my precinct?"

The three men settled on wooden benches tucked in the far corner of the jail cells. Seamus sat cross-legged on the floor opposite them. Ben answered the sergeant's question as succinctly as he could manage. "I was with Maine infantry at Gettysburg, where I received this hurt." He motioned vaguely in the direction of his face. "I was discharged, and the boy is guiding me home. His job is to get me on a train so I can go back to Maine." Ben heard shouting and screaming from the mob outside. They maintained a profane litany of the real and imagined sufferings they had endured from which they wanted immediate relief. Ben was thankful that he did not hear any words to indicate that their anger targeted Seamus in particular. Neither McDonald or Perkins seemed much disturbed by the outcry.

"I've got family in Hell's Kitchen and Five Points," Seamus said as he accepted a steaming mug.

Ben realized that the police needed to be aware of the terrible incident, but he wished he didn't have to point the finger at the boy. "You'll need to know about an accident at the asylum. The boy was carrying my rifle. One of the rioters tried to take it from him. In the scuffle, the weapon fired. I think it may have killed the man, as well as a woman standing behind him. It looked to me like the woman may be with child." He dipped a cloth into a bucket of cool water and began to gently wipe his face clean from the filth of a burning city.

The sergeant looked at Seamus for a long moment. "You mean that this lad killed two people this afternoon? One of them a woman in the family way? Good Lord." He settled back on the bench to rest against the brick wall and looked toward the children sitting in the crowded jail cells. Ben followed MacDonald's gaze. Clearly, most of the children understood the intent of the shrieking from outside if not the literal meaning.

"It was an accident," Perkins said. "The man tried to pull the gun away from the boy." He, too, was scrubbing at his skin to remove the soot from his neck and hands.

"But the boy's finger was on the trigger when the rifle discharged, isn't that what was said?" MacDonald asked Ben, even though his eyes were watching Seamus intently.

The soldier looked about the dark jail to see exactly who was present to hear what he said next, then lowered his voice. "Here's the thing. Please tell me what you need me to say so no charges are laid against the boy. He carried my weapon for me. I never showed him how to use it properly. I put him in a situation. What else do you need me to declare? I'll make a statement for the magistrate. Whatever you need," Ben said quietly.

MacDonald nodded solemnly as he considered this, then smiled. "That's just about the nicest confession I think I've ever heard. Not to mention that you're asking my advice on how to commit perjury. So let's forget all that twaddle and get down to brass tacks. The captain won't hear of pressing charges against someone during this rioting other than the heinous mob. Why, hell, where would we start and where would it end? I don't have enough jail space to hold a thousand or more micks, especially now that we've taken on a few hundred or so of these orphans. I'm not at all certain that we'd have the support of the prosecutors, the mayor or even the governor. I just learned that the mayor has decided not to ask for federal help but leave it all to the men I have. Hell, half my men went off to the army after Bull Run." The sergeant paused as if to gather his thoughts. "Now to the matter of the boy. I understood that the mob in front of the asylum were hundreds strong. Or more even. If he were to go home to the Kitchen, it wouldn't be long before someone recognized him. Sure, we could get a theater artist to paint his hair and cover those freckles. However, those eyes sure won't be so easy to disguise at all."

For the first time in their hectic adventure that afternoon, Ben turned to look Seamus full in the face. True enough, the lad's eyes were uniquely striking. The irises in the boy's eyes were of different shapes and colors; one a neat green circle centered around a circular black pupil while the other was a misshapen turquoise oval surrounded by reddish streaks through the white of his eye. Ben had never seen before such a curious combination, even when the circus had brought its collection of human oddities to Rockland.

"Won't neither of them be safe in New York after today," the fire chief said. "Along the way here, we also helped a soldier get away from a lynch mob. No one got hurt badly, but I'm certain they'll remember this man's face. Not for nothing, you should know that this man knows how to handle himself around weapons."

McDonald laughed hard and slapped his thigh. "So, the two of you lads arrive in the city and thought that you'd set out to fix all the injustices in my district on just one day? On this of all days, no less?"

The boy seemed pre-occupied with the danger he had created for his only remaining family. "So, any of my kin what was to take me in would be in danger, won't they?" Seamus asked.

"Yes, but that might not be the worst of it," Perkins said. "One of your own family might be the Judas goat, to spare themselves from suspicion. Turn you over to the mob and anyone giving you shelter to boot."

"I'll second Perkins on that," MacDonald said directly to Ben. "If one of that mob had a good look at the boy's face, he won't be safe anywhere in the city. Neither of you really. With or without that burn on your face. The mob has been attacking soldiers and police all day. And the blacks have been hurt or killed, too, even by folks that been their neighbors in the past. Or maybe it's because they've been neighbors." The sergeant drank from the coffee mug held tightly between his massive hands.

As the conversation between the men waned, Ben heard the soft weeping of some of the black children in the cells.

"Would I be permitted to go back to the army?" Seamus asked. "The American Bible Society pays me to give away Bibles and religious reading tracts. Shouldn't be too hard to catch up with Meade's army moving through Virginia."

A gun blast outside quieted the melee on the street. The sergeant jumped up and raced upstairs. From above, Ben heard the shouts of policemen all asking at once to know what had happened on the street in front of the station. Several coppers shouted their explanations, but the common theme was that an Irishman brandishing a weapon had burst through the cordon protecting the front entrance, all the while screaming obscenities targeted at police and nearly all other institutions in the city, sparing only brothels and pubs. When the man refused to lower his pistol, a copper aimed carefully and put a well-placed bullet into the shoulder of the Irishman's gun hand. Before long, the ruckus in the street resumed as if nothing untoward had happened.

Perkins sat his mug beside himself on the bench and leaned forward to speak to Seamus. "I don't believe going to the army would be a safe avenue for you. This mayhem today is for the conscriptions. Some of them out there are likely to get conscripted. Even if they aren't drafted themselves, they may end up taking the money to be a substitute. So you'll have a lot more chance to meet someone who was here today. I advise you to steer clear of the Union Army for at least a year."

"Well, ain't this a holy muddle? Can't stay here or go back to the army." The boy's head drooped.

After several minutes of silence as they thought about how to spare Seamus from mob justice, Ben spoke up. "Why don't you come on to Maine with me? When my brothers leave, I'll have no help to keep the light house going. I may be able to have you named assistant keeper, which would have a little pay and some rations. The light is on an island offshore, so there wouldn't be a happenstance when an Irish assassin could sneak up upon us. Wouldn't anyone be able to cut your throat in the dark while you sleep. You'd be as safe as the puffins nesting there."

Seamus appeared to mull this offer for several moments. "How long do you suppose I'd have to stay there? Before I could come back home, you know?"

This question stumped Ben. "I don't know exactly. Tell me this: If something similar had happened to a family member back in Ireland, how long would you expect the suspected culprit to stay away from County Cork?"

The boy sat quietly for several minutes. His chin hung sullenly against his chest. When he finally looked up at Perkins and Ben, it was clear that tears had coursed down his cheeks. "I don't have much family here, but I had hoped to see them again. I see now that can't ever happen. We can go whenever you're ready, Ben."

"I think you've got a good plan. Disappear for a few years." Perkins reached over to put his hand on the lad's knee. "For now, relax. You can't go out while the hellions are bringing perdition down on the streets of the city. Let's see if the coppers can feed you first, and if you're lucky maybe we can arrange to get you off Manhattan without any great fanfare."

CHAPTER 18

A rough shove against his shoulder woke Ben in the darkness. To his dismay, he discovered that he had fallen asleep somehow on the brick floor in front of the benches where he had spoken with Perkins and MacDonald. Pain wracked his body from neck to heels. Seamus was leaning over him, looking directly into his face. "Wake up, Ben," the boy whispered. "Sergeant MacDonald believes he has found someone to help us get out of the city tonight. I guess it's near onto midnight. At least the mob hasn't been screaming for about an hour now. Probably because of the rain. We should be going then, I suppose."

Ben sat up and tied his boots. He thought about how he and Seamus would flee New York and how they could possibly reach Sorrow Ledge in time before his brothers departed for Bangor. On the floor near him, he found a mug filled with coffee, both cold and gritty. He drank it just the same. Not far away, he heard the snores and soft whimpers of the children who had been rescued from the Black Orphan Asylum. He wondered about their next journey to where they might be safe. Did such a place even exist? If not, would it ever again?

Once again Ben and Seamus shared the load of baggage between them. Seamus carried the Enfield, newly loaded. Ben reloaded both Navy Colt pistols and shoved them into the waistband of his trousers at his back. They were as yet unsure of what they would encounter on the streets of New York. Given the events of the past hours, there was little reason to believe their exodus from the city would be any safe passage. They went upstairs to where they found MacDonald in the lighted main gallery of the station. The brightly burning lanterns caused Ben to shield his eyes while his vision adjusted. MacDonald no longer wore his jacket, and the sleeves of his shirt were rolled above his elbows. He seemed to be dealing with a dozen crises at once.

As they waited, Seamus turned toward Ben and asked quietly, "I mean no disrespect, but I cannot see how we will make an escape from Manhattan with the hooligans all watching for us. So I wonder why you felt it necessary that we should put our necks out for a man we didn't know and likely won't never see again."

In silence, Ben thought about this question as he watched the big sergeant pace to and fro. He was not sure what this Irish boy would accept as a reasonable answer, but he finally offered up what he had long considered his own guiding principle. "Seamus, when I was about your age, I knew an army officer who was the engineer who built the lighthouse where I live. During the Mexican war, he was part of a scouting party that encountered the Mexican Army north of the Rio Grande. Seventy American cavalry against two thousand Mexicans."

"Really? That's a hell of a thing."

"Yes, I suppose it was hell, all right. They held out as best they could for hours."

"Sure they knew they couldn't defeat two thousand Mexicans. Why take on that fight?" Seamus asked.

"You know, Seamus, I asked the lieutenant that same question. And what he told me is what you might think about. He said, 'When all else is lost, just do your duty.' That's all. That's what I saw this afternoon, a man doing what he saw as his duty. I suppose no one can ask a man to do more than that. As long as I wear an army uniform, isn't it my duty to help a man doing as Perkins was?"

"Weren't my duty none," the boy said sharply. "My duty was to see you to a train station. By my recollection, I've done that twice already. No one hired me to become a pariah among kith and kin."

"I'm sorry. I had hoped to keep you out of the fight."

"I'm damned by the Bible," Seamus said plainly. "By Exodus, if two men fighting injure a woman with child, and the child suffers an injury, then the verdict is a life for a life."

Ben took a deep breath as he considered the lad's accusation. How could he answer the boy's grievance, especially knowing it was true? The boy did not want to engage the angry mob, yet Ben had insisted for his own reasons. Now the boy was burdened with the guilt of his tragic actions. The soldier felt curiously distant from these events, just as he had when the Pennsylvania farmer died in his lap at Gettysburg. As when other Maine men succumbed to wounds or exhaustion along the Potomac for two years. How could a man, Ben wondered, have such a void in his heart?

Ben was relieved that MacDonald chose that moment to signal for the travelers to come over to his big desk. "Good evening, lads. I hope you had yourselves a good rest. Perkins needed to go back to his fire hall to ensure his men were all reported safe. I swear that this has been a night to beat the band in our precinct. Worse even than the Dead Rabbits."

"Pardon, that's the second time I've heard of dead rabbits today," Ben said. "Why were those rabbits so special and what was it that killed them all?"

"I'm sure the boy can tell you all about it once you get out of the city," MacDonald said. "For now, you've got more important things to worry about."

"Tell me, sergeant, how do you think we'll be safe to travel out of the city if we are such obvious targets?" Ben asked.

MacDonald chuckled a bit. "I believe we've had a bit of good luck there. The mobs have mostly gone home because of the rains. Perhaps God has brought an end to this hate and madness with this torrential storm this evening. As far as traveling, I know someone who has spent the better part of 20 years getting people safely out of the city. Sometimes they go into New England and sometimes onto Canada. She knows the best routes and where to get shelter or help. I expect her to come at any moment."

"Can she be trusted?" Ben asked. "We have to assume that if those two people at the asylum this afternoon are indeed dead that there will likely be a good number of folks looking to do the boy harm."

"Yes, I believe you're correct," MacDonald said. "But my friend is experienced at helping people who are pursued. Beyond that, I can't say much."

When another copper approached, MacDonald waved Ben and Seamus away. Ben removed his pistols from the waistband of his trousers to his haversack so that he could comfortably recline on a wooden bench in the gallery. He and the boy sat watching the trickle of people who came and went to Sergeant MacDonald's desk. Many were inquiring as to the whereabouts of family or friends, which was to be expected given the long day's events. Seamus sat perched at the edge of his seat with his shoulder resting against the muzzle of the Enfield, as if ready to flee at the slightest notice.

"So, tell me about the dead rabbits," Ben said.

"Oh, God, the bane of New York," Seamus said in exasperation. "Every neighborhood down home in Five Points and the Bowery has a social club. Hell's Kitchen, too. Maybe even more than one. Each has a cute name, like Dead Rabbits or the Bowery Boys. They run all the crime in their little places. You know, gambling, whores, dogfights, anything for a couple of bucks. But sometimes they get into fights over territory. A few years ago, the Rabbits and the Boys went at each other and the police for a couple days. Killed maybe a dozen people, and the coppers put a lot of boys in irons."

Ben shook his head in astonishment. The conflicts he knew from Maine's history were mostly economic in origin, like the Aroostook War over timber rights or the Malta War over land rights in 1809. Then Ben remembered the Know Nothing Party bombed a Catholic church in Ellsworth in 1853, then tarred, feathered and rode the priest out of town literally on a rail.

"One thing I won't miss about New York," Seamus said. "Doesn't take much to start a riot or a gang war. Hell, the year I was born there was a riot over which actor played Shakespeare best. Two dozen people died. And who the hell really cared about who was the better Hamlet?

No one appeared much interested in the combat veteran or the boy accompanying him, at least until a small, trim woman walked directly up to Seamus. She was dressed all in black, from her well-worn boots to the bonnet secured on her head by a leather cord. She did not speak at first, and Ben began to worry that she recognized the boy from the lawn of the Asylum.

"Seamus?" she asked, holding out her arms to embrace him. "Seamus Dinneen?"

"Sister Jane, I can't believe you're here." The boy jumped from his chair and hugged her tightly. "I planned to come to the Sisters of Charity in the next few days, when I get down to the Kitchen to see my family that's left. Now I'm in trouble and can't ever go back to the neighborhood again."

Sister Jane settled onto the bench and took the boy by his biceps. "Tell me what's happened, Seamus." she said.

Before Seamus could speak, Ben moved into the seat next to her and whispered to her in a quiet tone. "He was with me at the Black Orphanage today. Two people were killed when I tried to help a fire chief protecting the orphans."

"Who are you?" Sister Jane's stare went back and forth between Ben and Seamus. "And how is Seamus involved in any of that?"

Boy and man began to talk at the same time, but Ben stopped short, thinking that Sister Jane would trust the story Seamus told her. He simply hoped the lad wouldn't take the credit or the blame for the deaths on the lawn. Ben didn't know if they could trust the nun to keep silent until MacDonald arranged their passage out of Manhattan. Seamus told an admirable tale of their week together but stopped short when MacDonald came away from his desk to meet the nun. "Good evening, Sister Jane. These are the ones who need your help. According to Perkins from the fire station, they saved his life at the Black Orphan Asylum and later stopped the lynching of a soldier. They can't stay in the city looking the way that they do. It won't be hard for the mobs to flush them out."

"So I've been hearing," the nun said. "Happens that I've known Seamus all his life. I tried to help he and his mother, but the father moved them constantly." She raised a hand to the boy's cheek. "Seamus, I was sorry when I learned she passed, but less so when I heard what happened to him."

Seamus took Sister Jane's hands. "I don't know when I'll have the opportunity, but will it matter if I confess to murdering that woman and her baby? I know Exodus 21. Can a priest absolve anything so heinous?"

She looked between MacDonald and Ben in confusion. "Is there something I haven't heard yet?"

MacDonald leaned toward Sister Jane and spoke quietly. "At the orphanage. A man was killed, as well as the woman who stood behind him. She was with child."

Sister Jane hugged Seamus and whispered, "Not to worry, lad, you've committed no mortal sin against her." She released the boy's hands and settled back on the bench before turning on MacDonald. "Whichever of your coppers needlessly scared this boy should turn in his tin shield. I just came from visiting your corpse. Kathleen Corrigan had the last of her eleven children a dozen years ago. If she is pregnant again at her age, that would be a blessed miracle."

"She's not dead?" Seamus asked slowly.

Sister Jane shook her head. "No, she's just cantankerous because the doctor told her she can have no whiskey for a week."

MacDonald gave Ben a sharp look. "I'd expect a soldier to know a dead body when he sees one."

Sister Jane laid her hand on the sergeant's wrist. "Now, Danny, I don't know that this changes the situation much for the better. Seamus and the soldier killed an Irishman and wounded a mother from a large Irish family. Whether he was a drunken lout and she a drunken sot aren't of much consequence at this juncture. Might be even worse if she's alive to give witness to what she saw. I reckon she can play a right good victim."

"So you, too, think I must leave the city for a very long time?" Seamus asked.

Ben thought Sister Jane took a rather long time to answer the boy's question. "Yes, Seamus, I think that's best. At least for a while until all this conscription nonsense is settled." She held his face in her chapped hands. "Seamus, you have a safe place to go?"

"Yes, Sister Jane, Ben has asked me to come help on his lighthouse in Maine."

She nodded her head. "Sounds like a good plan. And a safe distance. Is that why you asked me here, Danny?"

MacDonald leaned closer. "You see their faces as clear as I do. Won't be much challenge for the gangs to find them come daylight. I need help to get them out of Manhattan tonight and onto a train heading toward New England before dawn."

She touched the boy's cheek before she spoke to MacDonald again. "I need to give this some thought. It's no simple thing with the rioters amok in the city. I cannot risk the venture we have created, even for a boy I love like a nephew. Are you sure there's no ship sailing to Boston or Maine who could take them?"

MacDonald grunted as he moved from the bench to kneel on the floor in to keep the conversation private among the four. "I had a man go down to the East River. Lots of empty piers. Even the ferries have stopped. Skippers don't want the mobs coming aboard. I'm guessing Long Island Sound is crowded with every hull that doesn't want to be here and all the skippers that don't want to try to outrun the Confederate pirates. There was a rumor just last week that the *Shenandoah* was standing off Sandy Hook."

Abruptly MacDonald stood and stalked off in silence to his large wooden desk at the center of the big room. He pushed papers around a bit and spoke sharply to several constables about trifles. He jotted a few notes in a ledger and then sat with his arms folded for more minutes. Finally, he rose and came back over to the bench. He walked back and forth, like an officer preparing to reprimand his squad.

"Sister Jane, I believe that over these many years I have assisted you on some 50 occasions perhaps. Maybe even more. There's a knock on our back door, and I welcome in your people. Not just slaves, either.

How many servants or maids in wretched conditions have I helped pass through here? I ask no questions of them or you, do I? Despite the danger if anyone were ever to have known about our arrangement, don't you agree? Wouldn't take but a word from one of my men to Superintendent Bostwick for me to be working as a longshoreman."

The nun nodded in silent assent. Ben sensed that the sergeant's last comment was an admission of complicity in grave violations of the law, perhaps some act as dire as helping a young woman avoid motherhood. Ben knew such accusations would not end well for either Sister Jane or Sergeant MacDonald. At this, the nun stood up from the bench and went to stand directly in front of MacDonald. The top of her head did not reach as high as the sergeant's broad shoulders. She craned her neck to stare up into his face. "The two things are not the same. Do you know what is happening on your own streets? Your precinct is a battlefield. Freemen are being attacked as well as you coppers and the fire runners. When these rains stop, no one will be safe. And you want my friends and I to help now? I've no magical spell to calm these riots."

Ben watched this conversation in fascination. Despite what it meant for him and Seamus, he understood the nun's arguments. Their presence could put her or anyone trying to help them in danger from a host of threats: Irish gangs, copperheads, Democrats, and common thieves. Ben also knew that soon enough they would encounter many in New England who hated the boy's religion. Ironic, that Seamus was in danger in New York from Irish Catholics and across the river he would be in danger for being Irish and Catholic.

MacDonald rested his hands on the frail woman's shoulders and smiled at her as if she was a child. "I ain't asked you to put anyone to risk, have I? Or to make anyone discomforted? If you tell me now that the danger for your friends is too great, then I'll find another way if I have to carry them out of the city on my back."

"MacDonald, you do not hear my words. My friends have arranged to move hundreds of people north. I fear that you now ask for them to move in secret a pair of elephants."

"Say we cover the soldier's wounds in bandages. That disguises him. But what do we do for the lad? You weren't in the station a full minute before you recognized him. You think he could walk a hundred yards into the Kitchen or the Points before there's a knife in his ribs?"

From her purse, she withdrew a dog-eared Bible, which she held over her breast with the title in golden lettering fully visible. Her eyes were closed. For all appearances, she might be on a mission of mercy for a parishioner who needed her prayers. Ben wondered whether she had secreted an actual weapon somewhere about her person in addition to the Holy Scripture she carried.

Abruptly MacDonald spoke out. "Sister Jane, please! From what I hear, we're to expect no help from the governor. There's a rumor that Lincoln is sending troops from Gettysburg, but who knows when they'll arrive. These two won't be safe if the gangs find out I've got them in here. I'm not certain I've got the men nor weapons to fight back the mob that will be on my doorstep in the morning. It'll be even worse were the micks to learn I've hidden all those orphans in my jail cells downstairs. Surely you do not want to endanger those poor children. I've got a little window of time during the rainstorm. But you haven't even asked what route I planned to get them out of the city." The police sergeant shrugged his massive shoulders and turned away as if abruptly resigned to the impasse. "Well, then. Thank you for coming here tonight at my bidding."

Sister Jane glared at him moments in bitter silence. "All right then, just what is your plan?"

"Ben, could you join Sister Jane and me for a moment? It's ok to bring the lad with you."

As they approached the sergeant's desk, Ben thought MacDonald looked especially tired. His eyes were bloodshot. He had long since removed his uniform jacket in the evening's swelter, revealing dark sweat stains across his stomach and under both arms. The sergeant unrolled a black-ink map across his broad desk and anchored the corners with rocks that he appeared to keep in a pile on his desk for exactly that purpose. Taking a pencil from behind his ear, the sergeant pointed to the lower center of the island. "I have been given to understand that yesterday's troubles started down toward the Bowery and came north, primarily along Fifth Avenue. There was more trouble over in Hell's Kitchen. My thought is to take them north on Seventh

Avenue, then through Central Park. Beyond there, I would expect little trouble all the way up to 137th Street. The old Dutch and the few Jews who might be awake there so late tonight won't look twice. Then it's an easy stroll east over to the New York and Harlem line. The train slows before the bridge so that they can flag the conductor. I see no reason why it can't be done before dawn."

Sister Jane reached down and traced the proposed route on the map with the bitten nail of her forefinger. When she reached the rail bridge into the Bronx, she stopped and stood erect. "Just about seven miles, is it? It could still be done tonight, I suppose. Yet, if there are miscreants about before they reach Central Park, how do you propose to hide the boy's identity with that mass of hair?"

Ben returned to the bench where the pair's baggage was piled and opened his haversack. He removed a large wad of cotton dressing he's worn since Gettysburg then returned to the sergeant's desk.

"Perhaps this will work?" The bandages still evinced the dry blood from Ben's wounds.

Sister Jane looked askance as she inspected the material. She brought it to her nose but then instantly shoved it back into Ben's hands. "I believe that will fool anyone who might search for the boy. They might even think he has gangrene. All right, MacDonald, I'll need some time. When you've got them ready, have them wait at your alley door. Margaret will take them to the park; beyond that James will lead them." She turned to Ben and Seamus. "No talking to my assistants, or to each other for that matter. You'll need to walk quickly without stopping. For their sake, say nothing about the orphans downstairs, not to anyone." She paused for a moment before she took Ben's hand. "Thank you for what you did at the orphanage. Not many people would put themselves into such danger. I wish you good luck in your travels."

With bony fingers, she lifted the boy's chin until their eyes met. "Remember what your catechism teaches you about God's forgiveness. Please seek out a priest along your travels to make your confession. Complete your contrition and then accept the Lord's grace. I'm sure it will be no easy thing to learn to forgive yourself as well." She gave the boy a final hug, then she swept out the front door and disappeared into the night. A copper locked it behind her.

MacDonald smiled as he watched her go. "There goes the smartest woman in all of Manhattan. Nice enough, too, once you get to know her. Otherwise, she can be something of a, well, I guess she's helping us tonight. Come on, now, let's get the boy's head wrapped."

CHAPTER 19

*B*en kept watch through the small guard hole in the rear door of MacDonald's precinct. Seamus rested nearby. The boy's head was now swathed in the bloody wrappings. Nearby the children from the orphanage appeared huddled in sleep. A copper walked a frequent round to check the back door and the jail cells full of orphans.

Before midnight came a light knock at the door. At the peep hole, Ben found a young woman peering back at him. "Are you Seamus?" she asked.

"No, the boy's right here. Who sent you?"

"Sister Jane."

Ben removed the wooden bar across the door frame? "Are you also a nun?"

"No, not yet. I am just a novice at the Sisters of Charity of Saint Vincent du Paul. You may call me Margaret."

"Seamus, would you call up that we're going out? They will need to close up the door behind us."

The boy shuffled to the stairwell where he called out for help. Soon another of the coppers appeared. "Ready to go, are you? Best of luck to you then."

"Thank you. Thank the sergeant as well," the boy said. "I hope this tempest of anger will blow away by morning."

"You're from the Kitchen, aren't you?" the policeman asked Seamus. "Then you know these things can go on for days. I pray there won't be much carnage."

Ben watched Seamus turn toward the sound of the copper's voice and extend his hand. "Saol fada agus breac-shláinte chugat."

The policeman took the boy's hand and shook it warmly. "Go raibh míle maith agat."

Seamus turned around and came back toward Ben, feeling his way along the steel bars of the jail cells. Ben found this reversal of roles amusing. After a week stumbling about at the mercy of the lad's direction, now he was the escort. He hoisted their baggage onto his shoulder, then lifted the Enfield. The young novice looked surprised that Ben carried a weapon.

"Sister Jane didn't mention you'd bring a gun," she said.

"We carry three," Ben replied. "I have two pistols in my knapsack. Is that a sin?"

The novice hesitated, staring at the rifle a few moments. "No. I suppose tonight it might be a very good idea. I'm sure you can be trusted. Sister Jane told us about events at the orphanage. Shall we go?"

Ben took Seamus by the shoulder and led him toward the alley. "What did you say to the copper?"

"I wished him a long life and good health. And he wished me many thanks."

"You're quite a scholar," Ben said. "Speaking English, Gaelic and a little German."

At the threshold, Margaret turned and put a forefinger to her lips. She quietly shushed them before stepping into the alley. The earlier rain storm had calmed to a continuing drizzle. She led them in silence west through the darkened alleyway. Ben did his best to keep Seamus from stepping in deep puddles of rainwater. He saw few people outdoors. He did not hear any screaming mobs or see any flames, but the smell of smoke lingered in the air. After several blocks, they turned north and went along the sidewalk. Margaret and Ben walked on either side of Seamus, as if escorting a patient to or from a hospital.

At the entrance to Central Park, Margaret stopped and quietly instructed the pair to wait there for their next escort. She made the sign of the cross toward them and turned back down Seventh Avenue without another word. Within a few minutes, a young black man emerged from the park and motioned for Ben and Seamus to follow him, saying only, "Sister Jane sent me." When they were in the shadows, he whispered that they must follow him in silence. Even at night, he said, there were plenty of people in the park, including thugs who might rob them of all they carried. Like Sister Jane, he wore only black clothing as if to be invisible in the park at night. As with Margaret, they walked in silence, stopping only twice when they heard disturbances in the nearby woods. Crossing Central Park took several hours. When they emerged, they went east across Manhattan, still in silence. When they reached the train tracks, the man positioned Ben and Seamus where they could flag the conductor. Then he left them as wordlessly as Margaret had.

An early morning carriage of the New York and Harlem Railroad carried them out of the city as far as Chatham Four Corners, where they transferred to the Albany and West Stockbridge line. During the train rides, Seamus kept up a steady thumping with his hands. This tapping supported Ben's story to the train conductors that the lad, whose head was wrapped thoroughly in Ben's former bandages, was a regimental drummer badly wounded at Gettysburg. Perhaps Ben's face lent an air of credibility to their yarn. The tale evoked sympathy both in the stations and on the railcars. Ben could barely get a dollar from his pocket before the steward or conductor pushed his hand away. They did not pay for passage on a train or a meal in a station over two days. Not once in the course of their rail travels across New England did anyone mention struwwelly hair.

They arrived in Boston before dinner Tuesday evening. There Ben had an idea that he telegraphed to Rockland for only two dollars, with instructions that the message should be delivered to his brothers waiting on Sorrow Ledge: *"Coming now. Arrive Rockland Thursday on horses. Meet mid-morning. Take horses to Augusta and train to Bangor. Stop."*

To Ben's pleasant surprise, this plan came together nicely. At least in terms of timing. In Augusta Wednesday afternoon, Seamus doffed the thick bandage wrapped around his head. That evening, they knocked at the rectory of St. Mary's Church on State Street where the priest agreed to hear the boy's confession. On the following morning, they hired a pair of horses at a livery near the station. Seamus was at first hesitant at his first time on horseback, but he soon demonstrated true enthusiasm for riding. Ben felt a surge of emotion as they galloped toward Rockland. Still he was not ready himself for the emotional reaction of his brothers when they stepped ashore from Noonan's packet boat. Both Stan and Val together wrapped their arms around Ben, as if he had been missing at sea for many years. Ben could not remember a time when the twins had been so effusive. They expressed concern about his injuries, while he explained Meade's orders that they were to serve under Chamberlain. They wanted to hear all about the battle of Gettysburg, which had been a great source of gossip in Maine. They eagerly welcomed Seamus to Rockland. They asked the boy questions about life in New York City. When their eager questions subsided, Ben finally inquired about the condition of the light station. Abruptly the twins decided to pack their gear on the horses and be on their way to Augusta. Ben thought they acted like a pair of skedaddlers, although running toward military service rather than scurrying away. Given their sudden departure, Ben thought he might need to resupply the quarters with victuals, but Noonan was already anxious to get his boat underway.

"Your brothers sure seem nice," Seamus observed as he watched Valcour and Stanwix ride up Bear Street toward Rockland proper. "Kind of in a sudden rush to join up, aren't they? In all your letters home about the army, you never mentioned a little thing called war?"

As he passed their baggage down to Noonan at the bottom of the pier's ladder, Ben chuckled at the lad's observation. "Right at the moment, I suspect the boys are more afraid about how they left the light than any welcome that Bobby Lee might arrange for them."

A northerly breeze enabled Noonan to run up a square canvas on the mast, and the little boat chanced along at good speed across Penob-scot Bay. Ben put up his nose and inhaled the sea breeze, feeling he was home at last. As the boat sailed farther southeast from Rockland, he sensed that Seamus grew increasingly uncomfortable with the distance they traveled from dry land to reach Sorrow Ledge.

"Are you feeling seasick?" Ben asked.

"No. At least not yet," Seamus said. He glanced over his shoulder toward the receding coastline. "I thought lighthouses were on shore. Not in the middle of the ocean."

"Sure, some are coastal, but there are lights on islands, too. That's Sorrow Ledge straight ahead there."

"I just wasn't expecting to be so far from real land."

"Understood," Ben said. "I expect you'll find it peaceful. And safe."

Once ashore, Ben found the condition of the light station alarm-ing. The pantry was virtually barren; he found only a bag of flour, a half-pound of sugar and two jars of home-cooked ketchup on the shelves. There were no coffee beans, tea, canned vegetables or even fresh eggs to be had. As he surveyed the pantry, Ben realized that they had all the ingredients required to make more hard biscuits. Leaving Seamus in the kitchen, Ben climbed the tower to discover that only a minimal supply of kerosene remained to light the lens through the coming night. As to the lantern itself, Ben was appalled that Stan and Val had allowed the glass to fall into such poor condi-tion. He marveled there were no cracks in the thick glass lens of the light optic. He would need to spend hours each day polishing away the grime on both glass and brass, courtesy of his brothers' combined sloth.

Resigned to these conditions, Ben descended the iron stairs of the tower. In the storage room at its base, he found the lockers there empty as well. Taking the hand-carved wooden yoke from the wall, he set off for the fuel house on the far north side of the ledge. Dismayed as he was by the failure of his brothers, Ben was not totally surprised. They had never received nearly the same rigorous training as Ben at light keeper's duties. In the fuel house, he was relieved to discover that the ordering of kerosene, black powder and cleaning agents had not been neglected. He assumed their mother completed this work before she departed Sorrow Ledge for Portland. Emerging from the squat granite structure, Ben heard the voice of a woman calling his name.

"Bennington Grindle, you come out and face me like a man, do you hear me? Right now, damn it!" Neither reason nor manners tempered the shrill anger in Rebecca's voice.

Ben stepped out from behind the blast wall around the fuel house. Rebecca stood 30 feet away, near the large stone cairn. She had no way to know two corpses were encased within. She faced away from him. She wore a knitted shawl over a brown cotton dress; her auburn hair fell almost to her waist. He walked slowly toward her.

"Please don't hide from me, Ben," she pleaded loudly.

"Hello, Rebecca," he said quietly.

She spun toward him in surprise. He watched her face closely. She hesitated, yet her expression betrayed no shock at seeing his face. No horror. No revulsion. To Ben's great relief, he saw no pity in her eyes. She strode toward him. "Bennington Grindle, who do you think you are to come out to this desolate rock without stopping ashore to see me after all this time?" She stopped when she stood about a rod away from him, her hands planted squarely upon her hips. "What do you mean by this?"

"You didn't receive my letter, then?"

"Oh, I did. Just who do you think you are? Giving the mitten to me? That won't happen. Not so long as my father is alive."

"Rebecca, we were never betrothed. You've no obligation to me at all."

"Hush. I won't hear any more. You'll marry me, or I'll tell father about the terrible things you've done against me so he'll make sure that you become my husband or a convict."

"You cannot lie to your father, no more than you could be cross with him," Ben said simply.

"I don't understand why you don't want me here with you any longer."

With both hands, Ben pulled his shirttails from within his trousers and began to unbutton his shirt slowly from the neck down. He watched her eyes follow along, button by button, as he gradually exposed the scars across his chest and abdomen. A long ridge of raised flesh from his chest downward across his stomach evinced the slash of a Confederate officer's saber. Scars from two gunshot wounds marred his torso, though fortunately neither had harmed a vital organ within. When he had shucked his suspenders from his shoulders, he allowed the shirt to fall off his arms and drop at his feet, exposing an ugly star-shaped lesion left on a shoulder by the passing of a Minie ball. A bit of shrapnel had left an ugly weal in his forearm. Last of all, he doffed the 2nd Maine's cap, revealing the full extent of the burnt flesh across his cheek, forehead and scalp created at Gettysburg. She had a clear view of his butchered earlobe. Only his trousers remained in place, concealing from her view half a dozen more scars, including where Jackson's artillery at Groveton Heights had disfigured his thigh.

From a distance, Ben heard a young girl's voice call out. "Rebecca, I haven't found Ben anywhere, but there's a queer Irish boy in the kitchen. He's drinking ketchup."

"That's my little sister Anna," Rebecca said.

"I recall. Does she still imitate everything you do?"

Rebecca tittered. "Constantly." She called out, "Anna, leave that boy alone and go back to the boat. Ask Mister Noonan to wait for me just ten minutes more."

Ben knew that Jacob Noonan would wait ten hours if it meant he might row Rebecca back to shore.

"I'm not the same man as I was, Rebecca. Not just on the skin. The old timers said once you see the elephant, that you're a changed man forever."

"You saw an elephant?" Rebecca asked with a measure of incredulity as she stepped slowly toward him.

"No, not the real animal. I suppose they mean that once you see something like an elephant or war, you can never forget it ever again. I still see it. Hear it. Smell it. Dream it." Ben picked up his shirt and cap. "I swear that I saw things that surely God never intended to exist."

She moved slowly toward him until he could smell the rum she used to rinse her hair. She came so close that it would be awkward for him to get dressed again. With a forefinger, she traced a few of the white ridges across the skin on his chest that marked an earlier path of a bullet or bayonet. "Ben, would you please turn around for me?"

He hesitated for long moments. Unlike the relics of war, he was not yet prepared to let her see what marks he bore upon his back. The scars on his chest he felt were earned in honor; across his spine were marks of dishonor left when he had been whipped with baleen rods like a rabid mongrel.

"I want to say something… Ben, I need to say something to you that I don't believe I could say looking into your face. Please. Turn around."

So he did. He looked northeast toward Vinalhaven. Rebecca gasped when she saw the cross-hatched pattern of scars across Ben's back. "My God, the cruelty that evil bastard did to you," she whispered. Ben did not correct her. Better now to blame the responsible than to accuse the accomplices. Suddenly he felt her cold, trembling fingertips touch the welts across his shoulders. She rested her hands on his arms as she stepped up close against him, then laid her cheek against his neck. He felt her warm breath and heard her inhale sharply when she began to cry. He was puzzled at how her cool tears coursed down his back along the furrows of the scars there.

"We all knew, Ben. Everyone in Rockland knew how that monster treated you. My father said it was even worse when he was in the boozefuddle. There was a day when I watched him whip you on the street outside our store. But you never flinched." She let go her hold on his arms and began to hug him around the chest. "I heard folks say that every man in town was afraid of him, so they dared not speak against him. Don't you see? You were braver than anyone in Rockland. Father said it was the best thing that could possibly happen when that terrible man fell into the ocean."

"Is it courageous to do nothing?" Ben asked. "He always said it was for my own good. Make me tough so I'd be a great man."

"Your own good?" The outrage she felt sounded clearly in her voice.

"He said I should be like Old Dan Morgan. During the French and Indians War, the British lashed him 500 times…"

Rebecca interrupted him abruptly. "Ben Grindle, I did not come to this barren rock to have a history lesson from you." Her exasperation was obvious in her tone. "I came here because I got your letter, and I disagree with everything you wrote. Do you think I'd want to go to Boston and marry a pretty stage actor? Do you really think so little of me as that? I want to be married to you, the bravest and strongest person I've ever known since you were just a boy. And the war didn't change that. These scars don't take your courage away. They prove it." Her arms hugged around his chest all the tighter.

"You must see at me as I am now, not when I was a boy. This is how I'll look forever."

She released her embrace but grasped his shoulder and spun him around hard. She thrust her face up close to his. "Well, then get a good look at me now because this isn't how I will look forever. Oh, I'm pretty enough now. Men come into the store to flirt with me. That makes my father happy. Ben, I don't want to be a mannequin in a mercantile forever." She suddenly pulled away from him and cackled harshly. "Good God, my mother would be horrified if she saw me now. How dare I throw myself at a man? I must be some terrible adventuress."

A sea breeze caused Ben to shiver as he stood, still naked from the waist up. "I don't know what to say."

"Say nothing. Please don't say another thing." Her voice came as a whisper. She stepped up against him. "There will be plenty of time for you to tell me all about Old Dan Morgan and the elephant." She laid her hand flat against the long scar across his sternum created by a Confederate saber. "Someday you'll tell me how you came by each of these. Every march. Every battle. Every wound. Please not now."

"What should I do?" he asked.

A gust of wind splayed long strands of her hair across her face, which she brushed back with her fingertips. "Kiss me," she whispered.

"Are you certain?"

"Do you want to disappoint Anna? She ignored my direction. She must be spying for mother."

"I've never kissed a woman," Ben admitted. A long pause followed.

"Just so you know then, I've been thinking about what it will be like to kiss you since you first started coming into the store."

"You never said."

"You never threatened that you wouldn't marry me."

"Are you sure this is what you want? To be a wickie's wife? To live out here on this barren rock?"

"Kiss me before I change my mind," she said, sounding impatient.

Ever dutiful, Bennington did as he was told. No sooner had their lips touched than Rebecca abruptly pushed Ben away. She held him at arm's length, her blue eyes affixed on his own.

"Ben, why is there an Irish boy eating ketchup in your kitchen?"

PART III

MAINE
JANUARY 1880

We watch'd her breathing thro' the night,
Her breathing soft and low,
As in her breast the wave of life
Kept heaving to and fro.

So silently we seem'd to speak,
So slowly moved about,
As we had lent her half our powers
To eke her living out.

Our very hopes belied our fears,
Our fears our hopes belied –
We thought her dying when she slept,
And sleeping when she died.

For when the morn came dim and sad
And chill with early showers,
Her quiet eyelids closed—she had
Another morn than ours.

— *Thomas Hood*

CHAPTER 1

*B*en watched intently as the young doctor manipulated Rebecca's skull. His long fingers twisted her head on her neck as though it was mounted on the gimbals that keep a ship's compass level. He parted her hair in a dozen places to peer intently at her scalp. With his thumb and forefinger, he held her eyelids apart to peer beneath with a magnifying glass. Next, he raised each hand and foot, in turn, to flex and twist her joints. At last, he leaned forward and placed his ear on her chest while motioning with one hand for quiet in the room. Throughout Satterlee's examination, Rebecca betrayed no more sign of life than one of the girls' old dolls.

Next Satterlee questioned Hortense Russell on what she had observed throughout the previous night. How warm was the patient's fever? How long did it last? What time had transpired while she was unconscious? Did Rebecca suffer any seizures or paroxysms? Had she responded at all to smoke, smelling salts or hartshorn? Were any medications administered?

"Nothing at all," Ben said. "We thought it best to let her simply rest."

After acquiring this knowledge, Satterlee led Ben downstairs to the parlor but then retreated alone to a corner with only a thick medical tome. The doctor sat hunched over the book in solitude for nearly two hours, seemingly oblivious to the tumult of activity that Missus Skevold directed in the kitchen. She and Elizabeth had fallen into a routine of chopping and slicing that made quick work of each bird carcass. All the while, Molly and Phoebe dashed about carrying and fetching in a more orderly fashion than a well-drilled regiment on the parade field. Ben himself settled at his small desk and began to write out his report to the district Superintendent of Maine lighthouses, detailing the events of the prior 24 hours. Explosive events, to be sure.

As Ben scribbled out his account, Captain Swett reclined nearby in the rocking chair where he had slept the night before. Once again, his gray-bearded chin rested firmly on his chest. A snore rasped in his throat. Professor Russell had settled near the Franklin stove, reading a dog-eared book that Ben recognized from the Light House Bureau collection. These libraries were meant to create a little diversion from the tedium of living at a remote station. Ben thought that fewer volumes by James Fenimore Cooper might attain that goal more readily.

Myrick had already returned to his cutter for the evening, accompanied by Tommy. The lieutenant planned to introduce the *Gideon's* young crewman to the boatswain's mate on the *Dallas*, and perhaps the captain as well. Ben and Swett agreed that Tommy needed just precisely such a change to help move him past the day's trauma.

"I write to inform you of a series of incidents that have occurred of late at Sorrow Ledge. I accept full responsibility for any damage that has occurred to the light station and the reputation of the Light House Bureau or the Treasury Department." As Ben wrote these words, he wondered how to best phrase the description of the storm, the blind flight, the wreck, and Mr. Green so that the report did not sound like a long series of excuses or sheer fantasy. *"I will describe these events with the utmost veracity and attest to the truth of this statement of facts. During the midwatch of January 16 this year, I observed that the barometer fell markedly. The temperature had declined nearly 30 degrees overnight from the prior day. Predominant winds came increasingly from the southwest."* Ben stopped and penned a short chronology on a separate sheet of paper to ensure that he did not skip any significant detail in his narrative. He was well into the third page

of his report when the doctor tapped his shoulder and motioned for Ben to join him in a remote corner of the parlor.

"Have you reached a diagnosis?" Ben asked quietly.

"Perhaps a better word is suspicion. Absent an injury or wound, it is sometimes difficult to name a malady with complete certainty."

Ben found that Satterlee's manner of speaking with eyes closed to be an irritation, though perhaps that was how the young man avoided distraction in his thoughts. Still, the habit seemed somewhat rude, even condescending at times.

"And though I could not find any sign of injury, I feel certain that the fall on the icy rock has caused two separate injuries. Her initial period of insentience was likely the result of the blow to her head, which would account for her deep sleep when you brought her in from the storm. No doubt in the army you had an opportunity to observe men knocked out by a blow to the head."

Ben simply nodded.

"When she swooned this evening, I believe, that was the result of either swelling or bleeding within the brain itself."

"Did we cause that by getting her out of bed too soon?" Ben asked. "Or the turn of a dance?"

The doctor shook his head slowly, eyes still closed, as if pondering this possibility for the first time. "No, I wouldn't think so, no. I believe the fall itself caused the injury. It merely took some time for this pressure on her brain to manifest itself."

"Will she recover?"

Abruptly the doctor opened his eyes and stared intently into Ben's face. "Here is where we enter the realm of suspicion. Because I cannot see inside her skull, I cannot tell what damage has occurred or even whether it continues to worsen. If the harm was mild, she might have a headache when she awakens. If somewhat worse, I would expect her to slur her words and stumble. That she is now cataleptic makes me fear that the brain has suffered a hidden trauma."

"And is there nothing more that can be done?" Ben's gaze went beyond Satterlee to where the girls bustled about in the kitchen. Ben was just about Molly's age when his father died suddenly.

"That decision will be up to you. There is a possible treatment, but there is no guarantee."

Ben waited in silence for the doctor's prescription.

"Are you familiar with trepanning?"

Ben was not.

"Trepanation is an ancient practice of opening the cranium to reduce stress by removing blood or other fluids."

Ben was somewhat dumbfounded to learn this was an actual medical treatment. During the war, he had many opportunities to observe a man's skull opened by a Minie ball without any beneficial result to the new corpse. "How exactly is that done?"

"With a drill."

"A drill?" Ben asked in loud astonishment.

"Yes, a steel drill."

"A drill? As in drilling a hole into her brain?" Ben was incredulous as Satterlee described his proposed treatment in more detail.

"No, not into the brain itself. We pierce just the cranium to allow any liquids to drain. We may need to puncture more than one site until we find where the gore has pooled."

"Have you done this often?"

"I understand the practice dates back to ancient times."

"No," Ben said firmly. "Have *you* done this treatment yourself?"

"Once before. On a boatswain who was struck by a spar. I relieved him of nearly a cup of blood."

"And that man's condition today?"

"I'm afraid he's dead. He survived my treatment well enough, but the unlucky bastard fell from a yardarm on a later voyage." Satterlee paused and studied Ben's face intently. "I assure you that I take the greatest caution when I operate. I cleanse all my tools in carbolic acid, just as Professor Lister recommends, to prevent infections at the surgery sites. I am not a surgeon who cuts into a patient all willy-nilly."

Another thought struck Ben. "Will she be disfigured?" Rebecca's vanity was not an issue with which a husband could safely trifle.

"The holes are small themselves. I will need to shave small areas of her scalp, so her hair does not tangle the drill itself. However, that should all grow back in good time."

"If you do this thing, drill into her head and drain these excess fluids, then you are certain she'll live?"

"I'm sorry, Mister Grindle … Ben, but there are no guarantees in medicine. I've no doubt you saw many men with seemingly mortal wounds return to service while others who barely breathed a complaint went off to the hospital but never returned."

"Are you telling me you cannot predict the outcome? You're asking me for permission to punch holes in Rebecca's brainpan without any certainty she'll recover from it?"

Satterlee sat silent for a long while, his eyes again closed in reflection. "Yes, I am. I believe she'll have a greater chance to live if we do this than if we do not. I cannot give you precise odds, only my belief. I would not suggest this if I did not believe that it – that I – could help her."

Ben imagined there were many more questions he should ask. Other details to explore. First, he had to reckon with the notion of puncturing his lovely wife's skull. "I'll need a few moments, Doctor Satterlee. Just a few moments, please."

Ben went upstairs to where Rebecca lay in a second coma in as many days. Molly had just come up the kitchen steps to relieve Missus Russell, who was also reading a book from the station's lending library. Hortense began to speak but stopped abruptly when she saw Ben's face. Instead, she rose and went downstairs, the trail of her skirt rustling against the steps behind her.

"Father, I was wondering if we might ask Aunt Anna to stay with us and help care for Mother after the ladies from the *Gideon* leave us?" Molly asked. "I thought that she might come out on the *Katahdin*. If she cannot take passage on her, I am certain Seamus would be happy to row into town to bring her out. I believe it would be good for Phoebe to see her as well."

"An excellent idea," Ben said. "Perhaps we could persuade one of the guests to carry a message to her. Would you please write a short note to Anna? The next time you see Seamus, ask if he wishes to include a message to Anna as well."

The girl left to complete her assignment, and Ben knelt next to the bed. Rebecca's hands felt cold to his touch, so he pulled a quilt up to cover her extremities. When he stroked her cheek with his fingers, she felt feverish. He leaned forward to whisper. "I wish we could talk this over, though I do not doubt as to what you would say," he told her, brushing a stray lock of hair from her forehead. "You know I'm not much given to prayer. He's only answered my prayers one time." He rested his face in his cupped hands, eyes closed. He could not fathom this house, this island, this life, not one thing without Rebecca. "I'm not ready to ... the girls won't ... we can't go on without you."

Thinking back over his conversation with the doctor, Ben remembered a time he sat outside an army hospital tent, listening to the conversations between patient and surgeon as they discussed the recommended treatment, most often amputation. These talks were often followed by the patient's muttered prayer as the anesthesia took hold. Later, when the amputees woke, their conversations with God were often more accusatory and profane. Ben wondered how Rebecca would respond when she awoke if Satterlee proceeded with his proposed surgery. Would she curse God? And Ben? Would she retain her wits and humor? Or ever wake?

Of the wounded men Ben helped on the battlefield, those most likely to survive were those who reached the hospital. The men beyond the reach of the stretcher bearers and surgeons were usually the ones who died on the ground in the arms of their comrades. Ben had held many such men as they crossed the bar, beyond the reach of medical intervention. Kissing Rebecca's forehead, Ben rose and turned to go downstairs.

From the parlor stairs, Ben observed that women from the *Gideon* were seated about the dining table, sipping from coffee mugs. His girls were still at work in the kitchen; Phoebe was plucking birds like shucking corn while Molly adeptly carved off the breast meat from the carcass. They seemed to have a rhythm to their process that perhaps precluded the other women. Swett rested in the rocking chair while Mister Russell appeared to be losing in a game of chess against Doctor Satterlee. Ben tapped the doctor's shoulder and leaned toward him.

"Would you please try to help her?" Ben asked.

CHAPTER 2

"Father?" Phoebe called from the boathouse doorway. "Are you up there?"

"Yes, I'll be down in just a few moments," Ben responded. He was standing by the workbench on the second level, overlooking the boat and the equipment lockers.

"Oh, I guess this can wait, then. It's just that neither Molly nor I recall when Bosun has eaten last," Phoebe said.

"All right. I'll check on him when I come inside." Ben struck an awl hard with the wooden mallet. He punched two additional holes in each strap of his leather suspenders to keep his trousers from falling below his waist. After he buttoned the straps back into place, he pulled on his jacket and climbed down to the main gallery. He was surprised to find Phoebe waiting for him.

"He was eating after the *Gideon* folks left, but we can't recall any time after that," she said.

"So, what have you set down for the dog today?"

"I gave him what you left from breakfast. He had the chance at eggs, some ham, a flapjack, maybe half a biscuit, I think. As well *as* all you left of lunch, so most of a bowl of chowder. I thought the smell of haddock would entice him, but he would have naught of it."

Ben looked around the interior of the boathouse. Even two months later, Ben remained unsure whether any rodents had managed to elude the Great Safari on Sorrow Ledge in the aftermath of the *Gideon's* grounding. If so, he hoped that the wire rigging he had constructed would thwart any rats from reaching the canvas sarcophagus hanging overhead. For more than a month, the freezing temperatures on Maine's coast had kept the corpse wrapped within frozen.

Phoebe and Ben walked together toward the keeper quarters.

"No reason a dog can't feel under the weather, I suppose," he said. "He'll probably mend in a day or two."

"Molly says our dinner will be ready soon. Shall I carry something up to Seamus?" the girl asked as they reached the kitchen door.

The wickie pondered over this question for a moment. "No. I think this evening we will invite him to join us for dinner. He's spent a great deal of time in the tower lately."

"Father, is there anything I can do to help you tonight?"

"Nothing I can think. Thank you kindly." Before turning toward the light tower, he paused and kissed her forehead. "Please let Molly know that I'm going to go up to fetch Seamus."

As he walked through the passageway between the quarters and tower, Ben reflected upon all the work the girls had done since the wreck of the *Gideon*. In their mother's absence, they had helped feed the stranded passengers. Over the past seven weeks, the girls had assumed responsibility for the housekeeping duties in the keeper's quarters. Molly had become cook and laundress, while the younger girl appeared to have accepted the scullery work, cleaning, and the literal dog watch. How they had negotiated these roles was unclear to Ben. Little squabbling arose between them, and the girls finished the work consistently and thoroughly. They took turns sitting with their mother during the day, while Ben kept the vigil overnight. And when the end came, Molly and Phoebe helped Ben prepare Rebecca for a final voyage to shore.

Throughout the afternoon, the sky had cleared, and the temperature had warmed. When he went up the tower to relieve Seamus for the midwatch, Ben planned to keep a close eye upon the barometer. If the weather continued to moderate through the night, tomorrow would be a hectic day. The station's small boat was outfitted to run down the ways from the boathouse to the waterfront in preparation for the voyage. Ben had many reasons to dread this crossing to Rockland; however, the duties this journey entailed could fall to no one else.

In the base of the tower, he stopped to retrieve a can of mineral spirits from the storage locker beneath the steel stairway. Closing his eyes, he climbed upward, following his usual cadence: From the landing at Bull Run he climbed ten steps to Yorktown; then upward through Hanover Court House; Beaver Dam Creek; Chickahominy River; Malvern Hill; Groveton; Second Bull Run; Antietam; Fredericksburg; Chancellorsville; Gettysburg; then those fateful ten steps to New York. In the watch room, Ben opened his eyes and placed the cleaning fluid on the workbench.

"Hello, Seamus," he called up through the hatchway in the ceiling that led into the lantern room. "Would you like to join us below for some dinner?"

After a few moments, the Irishman poked his head down into the watch room. "You mean something formal, maybe eating from plates at a table with a knife and fork like genteel folks, then?" He laughed. "Please give the ladies my regrets, but I don't believe I have had my waistcoat cleaned since our last soiree." While waiting to be rescued from Sorrow Ledge, Missus Russell and Elizabeth had taken a great interest in the reddish hair that once caused so much consternation to the German immigrants residing in Pennsylvania. The ladies had begged permission to crop the cowlick and reduce its bulk until Seamus now looked more like a Bangor lawyer than a young sailor on a lengthy Arctic expedition.

"I believe our lovely hostesses will overlook such trifles," Ben said. "Besides, your dining companions this evening will include a drooling idiot."

"So, you're planning to join us at the table, then?" Seamus asked as he climbed down the ladder from the light cupola into the watch room.

"I was thinking of the dog, thank you," Ben said.

"Well, of course, you were." The assistant keeper smiled at his boss to indicate he was jesting. "You know, I've only rarely seen you drool. Hardly at all since Pennsylvania."

Even knowing Seamus was joking did not completely assuage Ben's sentiments. "Perhaps you'd be happier cooking for yourself in your quarters?" he asked.

The young assistant cackled. "And who do you suppose would help you keep the light after I poison myself? You imagine that big dog will be climbing up all these stairs to lend a paw?"

Without any purpose, Ben began moving tools and cleaning materials about on the workbench. "Listen, that's the reason I want you to come eat with us. Bosun seems listless the past weeks, and the girls say he won't eat. He hasn't seen you in a few days, and I think it might cheer him up a bit if you come in." When he stopped speaking, he realized he'd been holding a mallet and chisel for no reason at all.

Gently the younger wickie took the tools away from his boss. "Here, you should let me take those before you hurt yourself." His smile suggested that he was only mildly concerned about Ben's safety. "Of course, I'll come down. Seems we've all been a little morose. Do you think you might get off for Rockland in the morning if the weather holds? Tomorrow looks to be a downright Irish hurricane."

Ben chuckled at the ironic slang for good weather. "Yes, if the seas remain calm, that's my plan. The boat is ready to run out."

"And the girls?"

"I've told them that they would stay here tomorrow. There'll be a church service come summer, I expect. I hope to arrange with the district office for someone to come stay so we might all go ashore overnight at that time. It's been ages since the girls have seen their grandfather."

"Ben, would you object to carrying a letter for me?"

"Three cents due, I suppose?"

Seamus chuckled again. "I suppose I owe you much more than that. Far more."

CHAPTER 3

$\mathcal{W}$hen Ben and Seamus came into the quarters, the girls were nearly finished cooking dinner. Molly had prepared pheasant preserved after the blind flight. The girl had neatly carved a plate of succulent breast meat. In two weeks spent at Missus Skevold's side, the girls had learned to cook the variety of game birds that never before appeared on the menu of Sorrow Ledge. Molly had seared the birds in a skillet with thick slices of salted bacon laid over top. In a bowl were boiled potatoes, courtesy of the cutter *Dallas*, which had recently called upon the light station. Phoebe was cutting open the spuds to cover them with butter, salt and black pepper. While the girls laid out the plates and utensils, the men took turns cleaning up at the wash basin.

To Ben's disappointment, Bosun's greatest exertion upon seeing Seamus was to move his eyes and flap his large thick tail exactly twice. In other times, the dog would be on its feet to rub those slobbery jowls on whichever diner made the mistake of standing too close. The Newfoundland's newfound lethargy was near as total as General McClellan's unwillingness to chase the rebel forces after Antietam. When they had finished eating, Ben set his half-full plate in front of the dog's snout. Bosun turned away his face as if offended.

"No, he doesn't seem to have much of an appetite," Seamus observed.

Ben knelt and lifted a piece of the bird that he waved slowly before the dog's big nostrils. Bosun responded by merely closing his eyes. Ben stroked the Newf's huge head gently.

"Daddy, Bosun has been spending a lot of the days sleeping at the foot of the stairs in the parlor," Molly said. "Do you think he might be waiting still for Mother to come down?"

Phoebe began to weep gently. "He always loved her best," she said. Suddenly her soft crying erupted into a wail. "He did all he could to save her." After a moment, she jumped up from the table and ran upstairs. She had said similar things before. Ben worried that her words were meant to accuse him of failing to do all that he could have done or done so sooner. Yet he did not question her. He could not endure hearing her say outright what he suspected was kept in her heart. If Phoebe said the words aloud and Molly agreed, how would Ben go on living on this rock with them, surrounded as they were by all the sad reminders, large and small, of Rebecca?

The remaining three sat in silence for several long minutes. Ben noticed that Phoebe's cries did not seem to affect the dog. After another moment, Seamus rose and suggested that he was needed in the light tower now that sunset had passed. Molly quietly gathered the dishes and put them into a tub in the kitchen. "I'll go check on Phoebe now," she said before going upstairs.

As Seamus prepared to climb back to his duty in the light tower, he took Ben's elbow and whispered, "I see what you mean about the dog. I don't know what feelings an animal can have, but for that beast to forgo food seems wholly unnatural."

"Nothing I should do that you can think of?" Ben asked.

"Nothing you could do that I can imagine," Seamus replied. "You can see for yourself that the dog is morose. I'm no expert, but it appears he has coiled his last line."

At the threshold of the passageway, Seamus agreed to remain on watch until midnight, and Ben assured him that he would arrive on time. Ben went into the parlor and sat in the same rocking chair where Captain Swett had slept so many nights from the time the *Gideon* grounded until his passengers were rescued by the steamship *Katahdin*. Seamus had hailed the ship as she was bound into Bangor. Ben was surprised to discover that Frank Garnsey, who had been a captain in the 2nd Maine, was now serving aboard the old *"Katy."* After a bit of reminiscing about the war, Garnsey happily agreed to carry Swett, Missus Skevold and the Russell family on to Bangor. Ben had taken Garnsey aside to suggest to him that Captain Swett did not need to imbibe any more alcohol than what polite society would require.

Garnsey smiled and nodded. "Won't be the first sailor I've met drowning his aches in a bottle."

As Ben began dozing off to sleep, he felt Bosun's big square head settle upon his knee. The dog's brown eyes looked up at him, and Ben scratched his fingers behind the beast's big floppy ears. Bosun leaned heavily against Ben's legs and let out a cough that sounded to have two separate parts: "Hel—fth." Ben had no idea about how to help the creature. He simply hugged the dog around the neck and spoke calmly, "You're a good dog. You'll feel better if you eat something. Surely you must be starving by now."

The Newfoundland rose and walked around the living quarters before settling back upon Ben's feet. "Hel—fth," the dog whimpered. "Hel—fth." Ben went into the kitchen to rinse the dried slobber from the dog's bowl and refill it with fresh water. He then tried again to interest the hound in the remains of the earlier dinner. All this came to no avail as Bosun just settled next to the rocking chair and made his plaintive hack, "Hel—fth." There seemed little that Ben could do for the dog, so he simply sat and petted the dog's head and neck so far as he could reach. At times, the animal again perambulated the first floor of the living quarters as if on an inspection tour before coming back to lean against Ben's legs. The dog repeated this walk again and again over several hours. On one excursion, the dog stood at the bottom of the parlor stairs and barked fiercely into the dark. On other rounds, Bosun seemed almost aimless, as if unsure of what he sought or even where he was. Yet each time he settled back near Ben, the dog made the same complaint, "Hel—fth." Just before midnight, the dog sat again with its head resting on Ben's lap.

"I guess I know now," Ben said, quietly. "You've been a good dog.

But you go on now. You go watch our girl over there. I know that you loved her. I'll stay here for Phoebe and Molly." Ben finally understood that Bosun was crossing the bar, just as so many men he had watched on the battlefields on both sides of the Potomac. "I'm so very sorry I did not come to find you both sooner that night."

Bosun continued to exhale that same harsh, "Hel—fth." The dog settled on the floor of the parlor; his head laid out flat between his front paws. After a long moment, the Newf again made the distinctive "Hel—fth" sound in his throat.

"Bosun, I am going to go check on our girls. I'll come right back down to you." Ben stood and stretched the many parts of his body that had stiffened from sitting so long. He walked through the kitchen and climbed the same creaking stairs up to the bedrooms. He expected that he would find both girls deep in slumber, exhausted by their many chores. When he reached the top balustrade, he heard no longer the dog's rasping breath from below.

CHAPTER 4

*en closed the upstairs doors so that the girls would not hear any noise. Back in the parlor, he moved aside Rebecca's rocking chair, as well as the small table where she had left her knitting kit and *Little Women* from the lending library. She had been reading the dog-eared copy before the *Gideon* wrecked upon Sorrow Ledge and their lives. Next, he draped the shorter edge of the woven mat over the dog and began to roll the corpse down the remaining length. First, he tried to scoop the rug-wrapped carcass in both arms only to discover that the dog's weight was much more than he expected, likely heavier than Ben himself.

In the boathouse, Ben searched through the storage shelves for a large bit of canvas. With difficulty, he laid a wide sheet out across the stone floor. The material did not spread smoothly because it had frozen over the winter. In a corner, he found a pair of old worn oars that he laid on the floor and wrapped into the canvas. In illustrated magazines, he had seen pictures that showed the Indian tribes of the Great Plains dragging something called a travois behind their ponies to transport the young, the old, or the infirm.

He returned to the quarters and walked into the parlor where the dog's corpse laid. He concluded the best approach would be to drag the bundle out through the kitchen door and then onto the canvas travois. Perhaps the thin coat of frost crystals on the rocky ledge would help him skate the dog's body down to the boathouse. Ben felt bad about treating the dog's body no better than cargo, but he also realized he had no choice under the circumstance. Already rigor mortis had begun to claim the animal's remains. Ben worried he would be unable to navigate the cadaver through the doors of the living quarters. He handled the carcass as carefully as he could – almost reverentially. At the kitchen threshold, Ben halted, recalling all those mornings when he opened that same door for Bosun to go out on his daily constitutional, just as trained. The dog always seemed at its happiest when he returned to the kitchen, perhaps knowing that some remnants of the family's breakfast awaited him inside.

After maneuvering the steps, Ben turned so he could drag the travois behind him. He stopped to admire the swirls of light overhead as a blind flight of meteors burst out of the night sky. With little effort, he picked out the principal stars of Perseus and Pegasus. He turned his attention back to his shuffling stride with which he proceeded down the slick slope, dragging his sad freight behind him. Finally, in the boathouse, Ben laid out a broad swath of canvas, then pulled the bulky roll of carpet on to it. Wearing a leather sail palm to force the thick needle through the heavy sail cloth, he stitched a second cist closed using waxed twine. He then hoisted the bundle into the air with a line and pulley.

Returning to the keeper's quarters, he was surprised to find Molly kneeling on the floor of the parlor. She scrubbed the surface with a holy stone, just as Tommy had done weeks earlier. She wore only her nightgown over bare legs, with her sleeves pushed up past her elbows. Strands of her long dark hair fell willy-nilly from the ribbon tied around her head. Beside her sat a jar of vinegar and a tin of baking soda. With these she made a thick paste that covered the large spot on the wooden floor where Bosun had died. Ben knelt beside her.

"Molly, please stop. Let me finish this. I did not know that I had woken you."

The girl did not miss a stroke of the stone. "Captain Swett made Tommy scrub and scrub at the floor for hours. The captain said, 'piss and blood stink on wood, like the mud of Noah's flood.' He said it so often that Missus Skevold finally demanded that he be quiet."

"I'm sorry, Molly. I thought I moved Bosun before this happened. Weren't his fault; dead bodies can't hold it in." He took a hunk of sandstone and began to scrub at the wood floor near where she was busy with her own holystone.

"I understand. I know that was why you dragged out the new feather mattress after Mother died. I was just happy she was comfortable at the end."

"You know, your mother always wanted a feather pallet. She told me more than once that she could die happy if ..." Ben stopped himself.

"I'm glad Missus Skevold was gone by then; she would have been so upset after we plucked all those birds. Here, Father, let me finish this work. Seamus said he thinks that tomorrow's weather favors you making way into Rockland. You'll need some rest if you're to get back to the ledge tomorrow evening."

"Not to worry. I hardly sleep these days," he said.

"Nor eat, so far as I can see."

"It's not because of your cooking, I promise. I have no desire left for food." Ben reached out to put his hand on her wrist to stop her scrubbing. "Molly, I fear asking this, but after what Phoebe said at the table, I think I must. Does she blame me that I did not save your mother?" He wished that neither daughter blamed him, because he already held himself responsible. For weeks he had maintained a vigil over his unconscious wife. Then one fateful sunrise, he woke to find Rebecca's hand had slipped from his own during the night. Was his grasp all that kept her tethered to this world?

The girl settled back, resting on her heels. She shook out more baking powder from the tin onto the floor, then sprinkled vinegar over it. With the back of her hand, she pushed stray hairs away from her face, which was flushed and sweaty from the work. She did not raise her eyes to meet his own. "I wish I knew for sure. Phoebe's never been so withdrawn from me. Like she's locked her thoughts away in a secret place and won't share any more than prattle now. I hope that Aunt

Anna can come stay for a few weeks this summer. Perhaps Phoebe will talk to her."

"Thank you, Molly. I think you've got a smart idea about asking Anna to come for a visit," Ben said. "But now a harder question for you. What of you? Do you blame me for what happened? For... for your mother dying how she did?"

Molly stopped all scrubbing. Her head drooped low on her shoulders; her chin almost touched her breastbone. Ben heard her weeping quietly. When she raised her head, her cheeks were streaked with tears. "I don't know how to feel because I don't think I understand just how she died. Was it falling on the rocks? Catching the death of cold out there? The doctor's drilling into her skull? Were there but one clear cause, I might answer that question. However, I can't say. I'm sorry, but I can't." When she sobbed, her tears fell into the mix of vinegar and baking soda on the wooden floor. "I don't wish to blame you at all. I don't." She shook her head once, then leaned forward to resume her scrubbing, erasing the evidence of her tears left in the baking soda on the floor.

"Thank you, Molly. I'm glad you told me that. I promise I know no more than you. I think the doctor did his best with what he knew then. Were she in a Portland hospital, perhaps more could be done. I hope God chose what was best for her."

Molly raised her head and looked up at Ben sharply. "I have never before heard when you gave God credit for anything. Or the blame."

Ben knew this to be true. He was not a man given to either prayer or profanity. After a year of his father's floggings, Ben surrendered any hope of divine intervention. Nor did he see the face of God in war. He was left to find his own answers.

They worked on together in silence, crouching over the cleanser and scrubbing the wood floor with holystones that rasped against the wood with each pass, sounding to Ben's ear much like the churning gravel on the southwest strand of Sorrow Ledge.

CHAPTER 5

Throughout the midwatch, Ben wiped down the big windows around the tower's cupola with cotton rags dipped into water mixed with vinegar. Cleaning the Fresnel lens itself was performed only during the days because the glass was too hot to touch at night while the lamp's wick burned. The lens might crack if rubbed with a linen rag doused in mineral spirits. Because the southwesterly breeze warmed after midnight, he had propped open the door at the base of the tower and that of the cupola, hoping to air out the musty scents of the long winter and the lingering odors of the explosions. He had sent Seamus below to get whatever sleep he could before Ben departed in the morning. Ben could not predict when he might return to Sorrow Ledge. He could not postpone his visit any longer. He felt he had a duty to both Rebecca and her family.

During the night, Ben completed the duties that the Light House Bureau called the "second department;" work usually assigned to the assistant keeper such as sweeping and dusting the remaining spaces and stairs of the light tower, including the workroom. The Light House Board listed the necessary daily chores in a manual titled *Routine Duties* so detailed that it left little to the imagination.

While working, Ben maintained a watch on the barometer, which continued to rise while the mercury in the thermometer remained stable. When he stepped out on to the catwalk wrapped around the cupola, he was again surprised by such warm winds in March. During the intervals when the Fresnel lens directed its light away from him, he could see *Polaris*, the bright North Star, as well as the constellations *Ursa Major* and *Ursa Minor*; mother bear and little bear. The clear night sky further suggested that Ben would not have a challenging voyage across Penobscot Bay the next morning.

Ben struggled with how he could achieve all that his civic and familial duties required and still return to Sorrow Ledge on the same day. The Instructions from the Light House Bureau read: "You will not absent yourself from the Light-house at any time, without first obtaining the consent of the Superintendent, unless the occasion be so sudden and urgent as not to admit of an application to that officer; in which case, by leaving a suitable substitute, you may be absent for twenty-four hours." Although Seamus would remain on Sorrow Ledge in his absence, Ben hoped that if he was delayed that the Superintendent would be sympathetic, given the circumstances of his travels.

False dawn illuminated the island and surrounding waters as the chronometer ticked quietly toward six a.m. The tower's elevation gave the wickie a vantage from which he spotted, to his surprise, a big male harbor seal stalking a raft of ducks in the waters off the rocky southwest shore of the ledge. He rarely saw the mammals so early in the year. The seal pods typically arrived ashore upon the island's northeast beach in April to bear their pups and then molt almost immediately. One encounter with an angry female was all that was needed to convince a young Bosun that seal pups do not make good playmates; thereafter, the dog rarely ventured beyond the stone monument before the summer months.

At six minutes after the hour, Ben turned his attention to the eastern horizon in time to observe a bright flash of green light as the dome of the sun crested the ocean surface. In his years on Sorrow Ledge, he had witnessed the phenomenon most often on clear mornings when the ocean was warmer than the night air above. Perhaps this weather condition explained the arrival of the harbor seal. Had the unseasonable water temperature fooled the seal into a premature migration or merely an early hunger? Ben saw no other seals in the surrounding ocean. With his father's long glass, he scanned the snowy peak of Mount Cadillac to the northeast of Southwest Harbor.

At five bells, Ben extinguished the light. On a day as clear as this, there was no need to expend the fuel. Vessels with a proper lookout would have no problem discerning safe passage into the bay. Ben intended to push off in the station's boat no later than two bells so that if he were forced to stay ashore overnight, then he would have a few hours remaining to row back to Sorrow Ledge on the following day. The times of his departure and return would be carefully recorded in the light station logbook, and woe to any wickie whoever falsified that document.

Though he wished to depart without any grand leave-taking, Ben found when he entered the keeper's quarters that he could not get away quietly. He had learned over time that the fewer people who lived together meant less privacy for each. On an island with four residents, no one's prayers, griefs, or travels are entirely their own. In the kitchen, he found Molly at the stove with a fry pan and spatula in her hands. Nearby Phoebe was pumping fresh water into one of Ben's old army canteens. On the main table, Seamus was allocating items for Ben's trip such as a tin of crackers from the Ladies Relief Association closet, an abundance of toffee, and handfuls of horehound. Ben didn't wonder but that the horehound was the last remnants of their march from Gettysburg. When the apportionment was complete, Seamus packed the supplies in the same haversack they had carried home from the war.

"I appreciate all that everyone has done this morning," Ben said loudly.

As he prepared to leave, Phoebe pulled him aside. She drew a wide ribbon of black cloth from the pocket of her apron. "I thought you might want to have this while you're in town." She wrapped the mourning shroud around his left bicep and secured it in place on his jacket with a safety pin. She stood on tip-toes to kiss his cheek.

"Thank you, honey. I hadn't thought of it." As he leaned forward to kiss her forehead, he noticed that her eyes were rimmed with red, as if she had been crying all night.

In the kitchen, Ben kissed Molly goodbye and asked that in his absence the girls assist Seamus with all wickie duties. Seamus followed Ben out to the boathouse and helped him load the Quoddy boat with their supplies. Next they loaded the two canvas cylinders into the small boat. Although they were about the same size, the shroud containing the dog weighed nearly twice as much. As Ben maneuvered the first bundle toward the small boat, Seamus lowered away on the hemp cordage. When the dog's canvas was secure athwart the keel of the boat, Ben cut the line loose with his pocketknife. The two men treated the second parcel with greater care, as Seamus lowered it into Ben's arms. Seamus cut the rope that had suspended the bundle from the ceiling for three weeks, and Ben carefully stowed it in the boat atop Bosun's corpse.

"I intend to return this evening, but if not tonight then no later than noon tomorrow unless a storm arises," Ben explained as the two men guided the small boat down the steel ways from the boathouse to the water's edge. "I left the *Routine Duties* on the workbench in the tower if you aren't certain how to proceed."

Seamus laughed aloud. "What do you suppose I could learn in an instruction book from the Light House Board that you haven't already taught me a dozen times over?"

"I trust you completely," Ben said. "My concern is that the Board has not yet responded to my report about the *Gideon* or any damage to the tower. Were there another incident in my absence, I do not believe the Board would look favorably upon my fitness as a keeper. Worse, I would not be shocked to learn that an inspector is already en route here aboard the cutter *Dallas* as we speak."

"Understood. I shall do my best to maintain the watch," Seamus replied.

"Thank you kindly. I have no doubt but that you will; however, do not hesitate to ask the girls to assist you. They are quick and smart."

"You said that you would carry a letter for me." Seamus extended a small envelope.

The wickie tucked the packet into a shirt pocket inside his wool jacket, away from the weather. "Of course. Seems a fair exchange for you watching over all of Sorrow Ledge. And my girls." He climbed into the small boat and set the primary oars into the oarlocks.

Manning the stern, Seamus gave a mighty shove at the aft end of the wooden craft. "Fair winds and following seas," he called to Ben.

Ben allowed the vessel to drift out from the ways before he began stroking with the oars. He stood facing aft so that he could put the greatest thrust into each sweep. When they had sailed into Rockland together for supplies, his father would scream at young Ben to "put your back into it." After he entered the main channel into Penobscot Bay, he laid up the oars while he rigged a single mast at the center of the boat and hauled up a small bit of canvas to catch the capful of southerly wind. Then he took up the oars again to propel the boat as quickly as he could through Two Bush Channel. At times, he set the oars aside to handle the tiller, so the boat remained on a northeasterly course for Rockland.

Beyond Alden Rock, Ben laid aside the oars and put his arm over the tiller to steady the rudder while he opened the satchel. Near the top was the egg sandwich that Molly had prepared and enclosed in wax paper to keep it from mixing with the other contents of the haversack. Over recent weeks, the girl had learned to flavor the fried egg with black pepper just as Ben liked. The breakfast reminded him of the meals Rebecca had sent up the towers with the girls when fog or gales would prevent the wickie on watch from coming down to the quarters for a regular meal. When he finished eating, he wedged a chunk of horehound between his cheek and gum. Ben did not need nautical charts or a compass; he knew the light houses and landmarks of Penobscot Bay as well as any lobsterman Downeast.

Not far from the rocky ledge he left behind, Ben saw that he was no longer traveling alone. Forward of the small boat's starboard bow swam a large harbor seal, likely the same old male as he had observed from the light tower. Ben wondered if this was an omen or just an odd coincidence. Despite the surging winds that strained the sail, the gray seal kept apace with the boat, occasionally surfacing to exhale a snort of ocean spray. When Ben moved the tiller to a more northerly heading, the big seal seemed to sense this change because it maintained a steady interval ahead of the small boat, with the regular pace of a color guard marching at the fore of a regiment. Bringing up the rear of this little flotilla were a pair of seagulls following along lazily to claim any edible morsel that might churn up in the dory's wake. Ben knew there was little chance the birds would strike upon food in this manner because his boat had a shallow draft by Maine standards, but there was just no reasoning with any relative of the coot.

Ben thought that perhaps this old seal's escort was in some manner a sign of gratitude or respect for the past welcome its pod had received at Sorrow Ledge. Over the years, Ben had shared the small fry of his daily harvests from nets or traps with the harbor seals that summered in the waters and on the ledges around the island. This thought of charity to animals drew Ben back to a remembrance of Rebecca. She had nurtured the small clutch of chickens and a rooster kept on the island despite the constant threat of harsh weather and waves that might overtop the rock. She disposed of the remains of any fish or lobster chowders out on the northern slope of the Ledge so that birds and seals could pick over the refuse. Rebecca was the favorite of their dogs, Bosun and his predecessors. She had nursed the two Newfs from puppy to potential rescue animal. Bosun and their prior Newfoundland had mastered the art of towing a rigged lifeboat as a result of Rebecca's determined and repeated training. Ben was grateful the worst had never come to pass. Until he lost her.

As the wind relieved him of the effort of propulsion and left him only to attend to the boat's navigation, the wickie reflected upon the many hundreds of occasions when he had made this transit during the past quarter century. In the early years, he was merely a passenger on the inbound trip but pilot and propulsion on the return voyage, as his father slept drunkenly in the boat's bow, rousing only to scream some inexecrable command. On those occasions, Ben would gamble that his father would forget any grievance before he next woke; losing that bet meant the boy returned to the light station at the end of the day with new welts on his cheeks or chin. After his father's death, Ben learned to make the regular voyages for foodstuffs as efficiently as possible, departing just after sunrise and returning before twilight to resume his watchstanding duties. With the addition of Seamus to the watch rotation after their return from the war, along with Rebecca's occasional assistance in the tower, Ben was free to reach the ways in the twilight of a clear sunset – a leisurely pace of travel he thought was nearly lollygagging.

The wind easily carried Ben on a northeast course through the Two Bush Channel, with Metinic Island to the south, as well as the Northern Triangles. Local mariners knew the shallow route through the rocks and shoals that lined the channel to starboard and port. Once he made the turn off Halibut Rock, he would enter deeper waters all the way into port.

From off Andrews Island to Monroe Island, Ben maintained a northerly course. As the boat came abreast of Owls Head, he brought his heading to bear north-northwest toward Rockland. This adjustment of his tiller seemed to give the dory a greater urgency before the wind. Abruptly the harbor seal expressed great annoyance as the boat's bow swept over its hindflippers. The beast raised its head and snorted a cloud of seawater at the lone mariner as he passed. Yet soon the seal was back at the boat's bow again, leading the way toward Rockland as if it could predict the course Ben intended to travel.

If the wind held, he might reach Rockland by noon. He began in his mind to prepare an itinerary for the afternoon, identifying those whom he must call upon and chores he must complete. First, he would need to pay respects to Rebecca's parents, then visit the sexton who cared for Achorn Cemetery; before the postmaster; the telegraph office; the Lime Rock National Bank; Lovejoy's Grocer and Dry Goods; and finally, the rector of St. Peter's, the Episcopal church in Rockland. Rebecca's father had retired from the mercantile trade a few years earlier to devote his days to local and state politics. Now Ben was forced to buy from Lovejoy's on terms that were much less favorable. More troubling to Ben was that her father had foregone a last will and testament on the advice of a Bangor lawyer and put his wealth into a tontine that would bestow everything upon his last surviving child. That meant Anna would now inherit all, leaving nothing for Rebecca's children. Ben understood little of such legal matters but knew that Molly and Phoebe would likely not benefit from this arrangement.

To pass the time on these voyages, Ben often gave air to a tune, either singing quietly or humming along but never with such gusto that he became winded. After years of reflection, he had concluded that the Confederacy had won the musical war, producing such jaunty ditties as *The Bonnie Blue Flag* and, of course, *Dixie*. The most rousing song among Union troops was *When Johnny Comes Marching Home*, although the men of the Maine ranks often marched singing a variation of *John Brown's Body* with the lyrics, 'We'll hang Jeff Davis on a sour apple tree." Ben's cousin Frank had fulfilled the duties of the chantey man for Company B of the 2nd Maine, singing loudly the rhythmic songs that kept cadence for the marchers. On this day, Ben could not shed the final stanza of the ballad *Lorena* from his thoughts:

"*Our heads will soon lie low, Lorena.*

Life's tide is ebbing out so fast."

In the waters off Rockland, Ben saw an increasing number of vessels, many of them lobstermen still pulling up their pots in the late morning sun. From those crews close aboard, he received a friendly wave. Far to the northeast, Ben detected a ship coming on a southerly course, with only its superstructure and deck rigging visible. Even though she was hull down on the horizon, Ben easily identified her as the steamship *Katahdin*. The *Katy* sailed a routine schedule from Maine ports to Boston and back, nearly as regularly as the flash of Ben's light.

"*There is a Future! Oh, thank God!*

"*Of life, this is so small a part!*"

Sighting the *Katy* reminded him how her recent port of call had changed life on Sorrow Ledge. With the *Gideon* women gone ashore, Ben sat a vigil over Rebecca every night. Molly and Phoebe spelled him during the day, taking turns between themselves. The girls also helped with bathing Rebecca, as well as the other conveniences. At each mealtime, Molly warmed a haddock chowder in which she had cut the fish, potatoes, and onions into small bits no larger than the slivers of wood in the tinder box. They spooned the watery chowder into Rebecca's mouth slowly to ensure she did not choke. After these meals, Ben administered the small measure of laudanum that Doctor Satterlee had recommended to help Rebecca rest comfortably. At night while Seamus stood the midwatch, Ben read to Rebecca selections from *The Library of Choice Literature*. Night after night, he watched her complexion gradually change from pink to pale, then white before an ashen gray.

"Tis dust to dust beneath the sod;
"But there, up there, 'tis heart to heart."
"Tis dust to dust beneath the sod;
"But there, up there, 'tis heart to heart."

CHAPTER 6

*a*s Ben maneuvered the small boat toward the pier, Jacob Noonan himself came down the wharf that had borne his family's name since the turn of the century. The Noonan's were renowned as shipwrights and sailors in New England. They fought alongside the British in the siege of Louisbourg in 1758. Later they built and sailed privateers, fighting then against the British in both the War of Independence and the War of 1812. More generations later shipped as merchantmen, whalers, fishermen, and lobstermen. Maine lore claimed that there was nary a vessel afloat from any port Downeast not baptized in either the sweat or blood of a Noonan.

"Hallo, Ben," Noonan called. "Throw me your line, and I'll tie you off."

Ben tossed over first a bow line that Noonan secured to a bollard on the pier. Next, he pitched a stern line with which Noonan lashed the small boat securely to a cleat on the dock. Unlike his sea-going kin whom Ben knew to be rather tall and lanky, Jacob's stature was stunted by an unfortunate twist of his spine. Most of Rockland's women blamed his affliction on an overly eager midwife called to two other births that same night. The woman's reputation suffered further from rumors that she had been imbibing cheap gin earlier on the afternoon of Jacob's birth. For a man with such a pronounced deformity, Jacob faced no challenge hauling the small boat to the moorings. "I see you have a bit of cargo to unload," Noonan observed. "I'll swing out the cargo hoist if you think it necessary."

"Hello, Jacob," Ben said as he put up the oars and hoisted the rudder. "It's good to see you again. Would you mind if I left the boat tied here for a few hours? I have several errands to run while I'm ashore today."

Noonan extended his hand and helped Ben step from the Quoddy boat onto the dock. "Of course, Ben. You're always welcome here." Noonan lowered his voice and said, "Since the *Katahdin* docked at Bangor, word of the *Gideon* is all the news along the coast." He paused for a long moment. "The passengers expressed great concern about Rebecca's health."

Ben stood on the pier for a few moments, looking out at the seagulls dipping and reeling over the waterfront. "I fear that Rebecca has passed, as well as our dog. They are there in the boat. Perhaps you could help me sway them up and loan me a cart. I must tell her parents this terrible news. Then I'll need to see about interment."

Noonan rested his gnarled hand on Ben's shoulder. His years of hard work and constant exposure to the weather left his skin as wrinkled and craggy as Maine's rocky coastline. "I'm sorry to hear this. She were a true flower of Rockland. Anything you need, Ben, anything at all. Just ask. I'll do whatever you need. But let me deal with this. I'll have my boys hoist your cargo and treat it gently. I promise they'll be as careful as I would myself, or they'll feel the wrath of my belt."

"Please, Jacob, I'm sure there will be no need of the strap. Surely not on my account, I beg you. I'll be glad of your help, but for now, please say nothing to anyone. I need to speak to her parents. I'd rather like to talk to them before the gossip reaches their front door. For now, I'd be grateful if you could see these two great parcels are delivered out to the Achorn Cemetery. Let the sexton know that I'll go by later today."

"Sure, I'll hold my tongue. And, Ben, I do apologize for my remark about the belt. I ain't forgetting what your father did many times right out on Main Street when we were young."

"No offense taken," Ben said.

"Will you be having a load of supplies going home with you as well?"

Ben fished from his shirt pocket and handed over a folded sheet of paper that contained his list of supplies necessary to keep the inhabitants of Sorrow Ledge fed in the coming weeks. "Aye, I'll have the usual vittles. If all goes well, I hope to be getting underway a few hours before sunset."

"Understood. If this is your full list of provisions, I'll have one of my boys take it to Lovejoy's. You still keep a credit there? We'll get the cargo stowed aboard and ready when you're set to go."

Ben shook Noonan's hand and thanked him. As he turned to walk up the pier, Noonan placed his hand on Ben's arm. "How are your girls, Ben?" he asked.

"Tolerably well," Ben said.

Noonan lowered his voice a second time. "Ben, if you approve and when you think the time right, my son Daniel would like to call upon your elder girl. He's an earnest boy and works hard around here. He's my oldest, so he'll have this business and a share of interests in the family's fleet. If he's ambitious, he's got a good start to go far."

Ben nodded. He hadn't thought of Molly with suitors, though she was already several years older than Rebecca when her father had put her to work in the family's general store. "Sure, I know Daniel. He's carried our mail out to the light. Has the boy broached the subject with Molly? She's not mentioned it to me, though perhaps she spoke with her mother in the past."

"That I don't know. I'll ask. I'll tell the boy not to speak with Molly again until he has your blessing."

"Jacob, you and I go back a ways. I believe we're friends. If Molly is happy, I'll have no objection. I'll ask her when I return."

They walked side by side up the pier and climbed the steps to the wharf in silence. Apart from a few wagons heading down to the lime kilns, there was little other traffic along Bear Street when Ben turned west toward town. As he reached the Thorndike House, he turned north on Main Street and crossed the street in front of the Masonic Hall. Beyond the Glover lumberyard, he passed the Lindsey House at the corner of Main and Lindsey Streets. Opposite the Torrey Brass Foundry, he walked between the Baptist church and the Congregational church sitting on opposite corners of Summer Street. This arrangement always bemused Ben, as though believers might shop between the two faiths for one that better suited their needs, like choosing between the haberdashers downtown. Rebecca's family lived on Cedar Street in Ward 1, nearly a mile from the center of town and well away from the bustle of the wharves. A tree nursery to the west shielded their house from the noise emitted by the lime quarry and the odor of Whitney's tannery farther west in Ward 7, near Blackinton's Corner.

Ben stood at the gate to Rebecca's childhood home for several minutes. The Barrows' house was a large, impressive structure, even by Rockland standards. A veranda flanked either side of the front porch, shielded from the sun by vine-covered lattice works. Two great brick chimneys towered over the house. Atop the roof sat a widow's walk, though Ben was uncertain whether a wife would be able to watch for the return of a seafaring husband given the distance from the house to the harbor. Ben thought the primary purpose of these features was to impress visitors, an objective he thought was supremely crucial to Mister Barrows.

Ben felt unprepared to deliver the news that he must. Although he knew many soldiers killed during his two years at war, he had never been called upon to bear the sad tidings to the family back home. With so many tasks still waiting for him that afternoon, he finally went up the porch steps and rapped the door knocker.

CHAPTER 7

*L*eaving Rebecca's family to their mourning, Ben continued northwest on Cedar Street until he reached the burying ground. He hoped her family did not blame him as he did himself. As he suspected Phoebe did, too. He was unsure of Molly's feelings, but he felt enough guilt without any further aid.

He wandered through the lanes between rows of headstones, looking for any of the workers. Low walls constructed of fieldstone or cement separated the individual family plots. The most striking memorial was a statue of Major General Hiram Berry erected atop a granite pedestal. Ben once met Berry, who was mayor of Rockland before the war. Berry was promoted to brigadier general for his efforts at Second Manassas in 1862 but was killed by a sharpshooter at Chancellorsville soon after. In a letter that reached him months later, Rebecca had described to Ben how the principal dignitaries of Maine marched in the funeral cortège, including Vice President Hamlin, Governor Coburn, a regiment of State Guard, a drum corps, delegations from several Masonic Lodges and the Major General's battle horses. From the engraving on the pedestal, Ben saw that when Berry died, he was just a year younger than Ben's current age.

At a distance, Ben noticed several mounds of fresh dirt in nearby family plots. Finally, he saw two heads appear above the surface of the ground. The men were shoulder deep in a grave, busily shoveling sod onto a brown heap. He walked toward them and called out a greeting.

"I'll be with you presently," one of the men called out. "Give me a moment to get myself up out of here." The man climbed from the pit. His shirt sleeves were rolled to his elbows. Back on the surface, he tucked his shirttails into his waistband and snugged his suspenders. As he came toward Ben, he buttoned his sleeves back at his wrists and struggled to pull on a jacket. He stopped to brush dirt from his trouser legs, but his hands were equally filthy. "I apologize for my appearances. We've been a wee bit busy with the warmer weather." He wiped his hands on a handkerchief before extending his right hand to greet Ben.

"Has there been a fever or ague about town?" Ben asked. "Seems a lot of fresh digging."

"No, sir, not at all, thank God. Just these past two days was our first chance to dig since winter froze the ground." The man stepped toward Ben and lowered his voice to a conspiratorial tone. "I've got nine waiting in the icehouse now. With burying services and putting up headstones, I've got two full weeks of work ahead. Assuming the good weather holds." The gravedigger absent-mindedly mopped his brow with the same handkerchief with which he had cleaned his hands, leaving a broad dark streak across his swarthy forehead. His thick arms and chest suggested a man who would have no trouble digging nine fresh graves.

"Oh, then I should apologize for adding to your burdens. I'm Bennington Grindle, the keeper of Sorrow Ledge Light House. One of Jacob Noonan's boys will be bringing a cart carrying my wife."

"I'm so sorry for your loss. I'm the sexton here. Henry Pelletier." He offered his hand again. By his complexion and hair style, Ben assumed the man was an Abenaki, likely down from the Old Town settlement. Below the edges of his cap, his hair was trimmed close to the scalp, but a long braid trailed down his neck onto his back. "Do you have a family plot here or a special location in mind?"

"I do. Let me show you." Ben walked south down the graveled lane. The trees in the cemetery were leafless, and drifts of snow still sheltered on the north face of the stone walls. "Could you proceed with the burying now? I fear we won't be able to hold a funeral until May when I can bring my daughters safely off Sorrow Ledge. However, I have a special request to ask, for which I will pay for your additional labor."

Pelletier coughed a little as though embarrassed by the offer. "I always try to accommodate the grieving family." Ben was certain that was true; no doubt that grave digging was one of the few occupations available to the remnants of the native tribe. In his perhaps tenuous position, the man could hardly afford to ignore a request from an aggrieved family.

They stepped over one of the low walls and walked toward a far corner near a line of white pine trees. "Noonan's lads are also bringing you the body of our dog. My wife and the dog died from the same incident, so I'd like to have them buried together."

The sexton seemed to ponder this idea for a few moments. "I don't suppose my current tenants would object, but you know how families can be."

Ben nodded in understanding. "I was hoping that no one would know apart from me, you and your assistant. Perhaps dig a foot deeper and lay him beneath her. Certainly no mention on the tombstone." Ben extended his hand to confirm the deal, with ten dollars cupped in his palm. "I'd like them to go here next to this grave." In a secluded corner, Ben knelt to brush snow and leaves from a small granite headstone. The inscription read, "Catherine Anna Grindle." There was only one date: April 8, 1864. Below that was the simple inscription, "A New Voice Has Joined His Choir of Angels."

"I'd like my wife to lie next to our daughter."

CHAPTER 8

as Ben emerged from the post office with a thick parcel under his arm and began walking back toward Bear Street, he heard a voice loudly calling his name. When he approached the corner of School Street, he saw a one-legged man frantically waving his cap in the air.

"By God, Bennington Grindle, as I live and breathe!" the man shouted.

Only when they came within about five rods apart did Ben recognize Enoch Veazie, another enlistee in the Castine Light Infantry and a fellow "three-year" man. Veazie replaced his hat and extended his left hand; his right hand held a thick walking stick carved of gnarled wood that supplanted his missing limb. Ben gripped the proffered hand and clasped the man's shoulder.

"I wouldn't have recognized you, but Jacob Noonan told me you were in town," Veazie said. "You have my deepest sympathy on the loss of your wife. I dread the time for myself and hope to go first."

"Thank you, Enoch," Ben said. "What took you down to the wharf this afternoon? I recall that I'd heard you work out at the quarry. Clerical, is it?" He wasn't surprised that Noonan had shared the news of

Rebecca's death despite Ben's appeal. Gossip in Maine has the same currency as air.

"Indeed. I was there for twelve years, but there was a recent change of ownership. The new owners are Democrats." Veazie forced a laugh; his open mouth revealed that several of his front teeth were broken or missing, perhaps from close combat when the battle lines clashed. "I think they were embarrassed to have me there. I can hardly hide what I did in the war. Say, I was heading over to Thorndike House to tap the admiral. Why don't you come with me, seeing that it's on your way and all?"

"Sure, Enoch. I wouldn't mind a drink. I've been walking about town all day, like chasing Bobby Lee's ghost. I'd guess I'm about as parched as when we were pinned down before Fredericksburg, and the pioneers couldn't raise their heads much less bring us water." Ben accepted Veazie's offer despite the disgust he felt at hearing again the common Maine invitation to "tap the admiral," a crude reference to the fact that John Paul Jones had been embalmed in alcohol.

In a block, the two men passed the Commercial College and crossed Main Street, where they entered the front entrance of the Thorndike House, just at the corner of Bear Street. Off the main lobby was a small tavern with a bar discretely offering rum and beer for the guests. Ever-changing state laws variously prohibited the sale of alcohol except for specific purposes, though there always seemed to be a source for those with a thirst. They sat at a table in a dark corner away from the bar and a small cluster of tables where a few older gentlemen were seated to play card games.

"Here's to Admiral Jones." Veazie dropped onto his chair as though he had been carrying the world on his shoulders. He doffed his hat and raised his glass. "And to all needs artistic, medicinal and mechanical." Veazie's complexion was ruddy, except for a white scar that seemed to trace his jawline.

"So, how be you?" Ben asked. "I suppose I haven't seen you in 17 years now, since we joined the 20th Maine."

"That long, already?" When Veazie settled back, the dim light in the tavern created shadows over the man's gaunt eyes. "Does it ever seem to you that the days since we returned are just a blink? We expended our youth marching or hunkering down under rebel guns. Now we'll expend what time we have left to us getting ready to hang up our boots."

At a nearby table, several men in starched collars and silk ties exchanged stories of their days drilling with the Home Guard during the war. Rebel pirates had seized the cargoes of several ships Downeast for many months, which prompted the erection of earthworks mounted with artillery for the defense of ports like Rockland, Belfast, and others. The theft of a revenue cutter that General Meade described at Gettysburg was merely the Confederates' most brazen attack.

"Sometimes I wonder but that the whole war wasn't fought back here on the homefront, based on what I hear," Enoch said, nodding his head in the direction of the other tables. "There was sure a great amount of money made from government contracts to build all these coast defenses to keep the *Chesapeake* and the *Tallahassee* from stealing a lobster pot. They built a bulwark over that eel rut that runs into Belfast and mounted it with big guns. So far as I know, they only fired their cannon once, when word of the rebel surrender reached Maine. So you know what the Home Guard did? They fired that cannon right into the Maddocks' brothers who were standing at the muzzle. Think of that, Ben. The only men to be called aft on Maine soil in the whole war died of a celebration."

Ben saw that other patrons were starting to stare in their direction. Ben's appointment as lightkeeper was mostly political. Having Ben dismissed might be as easy for an affronted veteran of the Home Guard as a brief visit to the Customs House, just a short distance away. He couldn't easily hide his identity; the residents of Rockland had been seeing his scarred face since the war.

"Tell me. Remember when we sat around the campfire after supper, talking about which limb we could most easily live without?"

Ben chuckled. "Sure. We talked like we had a choice. Really it was always a matter of windage."

"We was all foolish back then. We should have known we were headed for trouble when they loaded Company B on the *Sandford* and sailed us up to Bangor. Then we waited around at Camp Washburn while the army found buttons for our uniforms and enough rifles for everyone."

Ben chuckled at this memory of the earliest days of Company B, 2nd Maine. "What I recall best was bobbing around on that steamship outside New York for two days with nothing to eat but crackers while they figured out where to put the men with measles into quarantine. We should have known then we wouldn't eat well for two years. Hardly anything but hard biscuits."

"And that was when we were lucky." Veazie leaned forward. "Now look at us; it's not quite so funny on this side of the war. A few years back, I wrote out a list of all the men I remembered from the company who were killed or crippled. More than fifty names, just in our company." His voice betrayed a wave of surprising anger that Ben had also heard in the words of other veterans he had met around Rockland from time to time. Ben no longer felt this resentment and had not for some years. Recent events had reminded him that tragedy was not limited to war and might lurk as well on an icy ledge in a blizzard.

"Did you apply for a pension?" Ben asked.

Now was Veazie's turn to snicker. "I did. Every month I receive thirteen dollars from the office of the adjutant general, the same pay we received during the war."

"I talked to a couple of the men who received a lump sum last year from the Arrears Act. I guess Congress decided to pay back to the date they were discharged, not when they applied to the pension office. Seems like common sense that a man was disabled during the war, not when he posted a letter."

"I don't complain. Only took them two years to review my case. I've met some who are still waiting." Veazie straightened himself in his seat and sipped his drink. "No, the ones I pity are the wives. I'll tell you what. I dread each funeral now, with the grieving widows not having two pennies to put on the dead man's eyes. Their husband didn't have the decency to die before mustering out."

"Do you have any prospects for work now?" Ben asked.

"Not in Rockland. I tried to work a lobster boat, but couldn't keep my footing in any kind of a swell. I need to convince my wife to move up to Bangor. Quite a few of the men from the 2nd there, so I figure to have better chances. I'm going to try my hand at the law. If not, I might teach school"

Ben shook his head in sympathy. "I'm sorry that you have to leave home."

"Well, we can't live on just thirteen dollars a month. Not with two little ones to feed."

The wickie reached across the table and put his hand on Veazie's wrist. "I'm sorry for your troubles. I wish I could stay and talk more, but I must get underway if I'm to get back to Sorrow Ledge before sunset." He stood and draped his jacket over his shoulder before removing his wallet. He laid two dollars on the table. "Please stay and have another ale on me." The amount was far beyond the price of an ale; neither man spoke of it.

Veazie stood and shook Ben's hand. "I'll gladly take you up on that offer. I hope to see you again before we go up to Bangor. Thank you kindly."

Ben went out into the warm afternoon and walked east on Bear Street toward Noonan's wharf. The southerly wind that had filled his sail coming north from the ledge had freshened since noon, blowing perhaps 10 knots stronger. He walked into the wharf's warehouse and found Noonan in his office.

"Sorry to interrupt, Jacob, but could I borrow your long glass?"

Noonan stood and reached to a shelf over his window. "Worried about sea conditions for the way home?"

Ben nodded. "Seas were choppy on the bay this morning, but the breeze and following seas gave me good speed coming in. Could be quite a struggle going back against them in this wind."

Noonan followed Ben to the end of the wharf, and they discussed the events of Ben's day. Noonan offered a slightly different version of how Veazie came to lose his employment at the quarry. "I think he would have been better served if he hadn't defended Chamberlain back in January as strenuously as he did. I know you served with the general, so I mean no disrespect, but the position he was put into made everyone angry at him: Republicans, Democrats, Greenbacks, Fusionists. Hell, stray dogs probably pissed on his shoes. There were people calling him a traitor. Well, you can't defend a traitor without being tarred as a traitor yourself. Enoch would have done better shaving a pig."

When they reached the far edge of the waterfront, Ben raised the telescope to his eye. As far as the eye could see down Penobscot Bay, the waves wore frothy white caps. The breakers coming ashore looked to be as high as eight feet, nearly half the length of the station's small boat. Such sea conditions did not portend a safe transit home. "Looks like I'll be staying in town tonight. Could you ask your sons to stow my cargo in your warehouse for the night?" The two men started back in the direction of Noonan's office.

"To be honest, Ben, we never loaded your boat this afternoon. When I saw the wind blow our pennants out straight, I figured a prudent sailor like yourself wouldn't attempt that crossing."

"You think Enoch's right that he won't find work here?" Ben asked, handing the long glass back to Noonan. "He should pack up his family and go off to Bangor?"

"I wouldn't tell a man what he needs to do, but enough people in town heard his gorming talk during the Twelve Days. Maybe if he holds his tongue in Bangor, he can convince someone to give him a try."

Ben responded with a soft chuckle. "Before today, I'd not seen the man since '63, but if my memory serves, that may be a greater challenge for him than you can imagine. We were both considered three-year men in the 2nd Maine, so when the two-year men came home, we were transferred together to the 20th. He bellyached so much that some of the others thought he might get us all shot or sent off to prison on Dry Tortugas. Myself, I was never certain which would be the worst outcome. But a few of the men thought it might do the remaining hundred well to cut Enoch's throat in his sleep one night."

"They say the child is father to the man, so maybe that explains Veazie," Noonan said, nodding. "He's not a man given to holding back an opinion. For his sake, I hope he learns soon. I suppose you haven't met his wife. She's a fine woman, but my wife says she is a woman who has just about reached the limit of her patience. Enoch might find considerable interest in Bangor for a lady of her quality, children or no."

Ben stopped outside Noonan's office so that his sons did not overhear this gossip. "Why do I suspect Enoch is not aware of his wife's discontent?"

"Because, Ben, the child is father to the man," Noonan repeated as he opened the door and started inside.

"I plan to get an early start tomorrow morning, so I hope it won't it be too much of a burden for you," Ben said, extending his hand through the doorway toward Noonan.

Noonan shook Ben's hand firmly. "We're always here early. I'll have the boys get your load secured aboard and ready to ship when you arrive. Again, Ben, my deepest sympathies to you and the girls. You know, it's all the talk of the town, what you did for those survivors and how you stopped a madman, whatever his plans were."

Ben reflected on the events of the past few months. "Well, I wouldn't say it was all that heroic. Weren't really any choice in the matter."

"I can't agree with you there. Sure, many men like you and your brothers raised your hands to serve and look what that earned you. But many other men had other priorities, so to speak, just when the cause needed them. And not just the Democrats and copperheads. There were the skedaddlers who skulked off to Canada. Hell, I heard of men who hacked off their trigger finger so they would be deemed unfit to serve. I wish to heaven I could have passed muster with this wretched spine, so that I could spit on those bastards today. Instead, I'm lumped in with them as just another shirker."

Turning toward Noonan, Ben placed his hands on the man's shoulders. "No one could think that, Jacob. Any man can see the challenge you have. Now I'll take my leave and see you in the morning."

"Thank you for your kind words. Good night, Ben," Noonan said. "We'll be ready to see you off in the morn."

The wickie walked up the wharf back to Bear Street and then west toward Main Street. Without any prior plan to stay in Rockland overnight, he turned north toward Cedar Street and went back toward the home of his in-laws, hoping that he would still be welcome. On the front door of the Barrows home as he approached, he saw a large black bunting to signal mourning.

CHAPTER 9

$\mathcal{T}$he Barrows' home seemed to Ben unusually busy, with a steady stream of visitors at both front and back entrances. Social callers rapped on the big oak door facing Cedar Street, most often a mother and daughter bringing a plate covered with wax paper or a full Mason jar so that the grieving family would not need to cook during their time of mourning. Still, more food went directly to the kitchen, delivered in pots carried by servants who tapped at the rear entrance. Ben sat with Mister Barrows in the parlor, ready to greet and thank each visitor to the front door. Missus Barrows conveyed the food back to the kitchen after carefully listing the name and dish of each donor. Rebecca's sister Anna performed the same function at the other door. Within a week, the ladies would write meticulous "Thank You" missives to all.

While Ben was busy with chores during the afternoon, both Mister and Missus Barrows had changed their clothes to black mourning suits. Apart from a white shirt, Mister Barrows wore all black; necktie, vest, jacket, and trousers. He was a stout man who wore his bushy mutton chop whiskers in a fashion that evoked for Ben the image of General Burnside, whom Ben had glimpsed once on the eve of the Mud March and resulting donnybrook. Since retiring from business, Mister Barrows seemed to affect the demeanor of a grand politician in both attire and comportment. Ben assumed the man was waiting for someone in the Republican Party to invite him to run for one office or another. Missus Barrows was dressed in equally somber black, from neck to boot. The elegant gray brocade on the bodice of her dress betrayed the slightest hint of color on her garb. Only Anna had not yet dressed befitting bereavement; she seemed to have spent the afternoon with other chores.

When they were not busy greeting visitors and accepting condolences, Mister Barrows held forth on politics to the small audience in the parlor of Missus Barrows, Ben and Reverend Nash from the Episcopal Church. The good reverend took Ben's hands into his own and offered a brief prayer in Rebecca's memory. Nash cut an imposing figure, standing several inches taller than Ben and dressed impeccably in a gray woolen suit that matched the well-coiffed gray hair combed back from his forehead.

Mister Barrows expounded at length on Chamberlain's treachery after the election, then moved onto local issues of which he had a seemingly endless supply. Atop a credenza, Mister Barrows maintained a stack of the local newspaper – which he disdainfully referred to as "The Rockland Bellyache." From these he drew a stream of new topics for his lectures. After he had politely sat through this oration for an hour, Ben collected the teapot to get hot water from the stove, as a pretense to cover his escape.

In the kitchen, he found Anna thanking a servant from the Cobb household. After closing the door, she lifted the pot lid, and the aroma of trout chowder filled the kitchen. "Oh, that smells so wonderful," she said, placing the pot on the stove. "Maybe we should have that with dinner this evening. Chowder and bisque are always best when freshly cooked."

Ben held out the teapot. "I've come on a quest for hot water."

She accepted the pot and motioned toward a chair. "You can't fool me, Bennington Grindle. You came looking for a bit of quiet." She moved a kettle from an iron trivet on the table to the stovetop. "I often do the same myself in the evenings."

"You won't betray me?" he asked, as he sat down. "I mean no disrespect to your father, but I weary so."

"And reveal myself? No, Mother and I both feel fortunate when the reverend pays a call."

Ben nodded in agreement. "Yes, he seems to have the patience of a saint."

At this Anna snickered aloud. "Well, he's not strictly a saint. His persistence is in the pursuit of a more earthly reward, I fear. He has given hints to my father about the need for a new organ in the church. He has his hopes set on hiring the esteemed Hook and Hastings company from Massachusetts. Apparently, they employ special reeds imported from France. I cannot say just how that will elevate our worship in God's eyes."

"Anna Barrows, you shock me," Ben said playfully. "I have no doubt the reverend could clarify any questions you have."

"Oh, yes, that's true enough. The good Reverence Nash readily shares his knowledge on the subject." She chuckled again. "Readily and constantly. Trust me."

"Then I suppose I won't be much missed." He settled back on the chair and crossed his arms. When his hand touched his shirt pocket, he remembered that he carried a message from Seamus. "Here, I almost forgot I had this for you." He extended the letter, which she took and placed in a pocket of her apron just as her mother entered the room. Ben had brought these letters to Anna on his frequent visits to Rockland over the years.

"Well, there you both are," Missus Barrows exclaimed as she came into the kitchen. "You'll need to come bid goodnight to the reverend soon. He's about halfway through his usual sermon on the new organ. Your poor father must sit through it all again." She peered into a mirror on the back of the hallway door and moved a few stray strands of her silver hair back into place.

"Oh, yes, poor father," Anna said while giving Ben a sideways glance.

"Though I suppose turnabout is only fair play. Reverend Nash listened patiently to your father for more than an hour."

"Mother!" Anna said in mock indignation.

Missus Barrows came to stand next to Ben and hugged him about the shoulders. "Please don't think any worse of us. We haven't forgotten Rebecca. If I were to dwell upon it too long, I believe my heart would break."

He stood to embrace her. "I understand. When I find myself thinking upon the matter too long, I try to find a different subject around the lighthouse that requires my attention. Come summer, Sorrow Ledge may be the cleanest station in all of New England."

"Ben, I thought that perhaps you would allow the girls to spend a week or two here with us," Missus Barrows said. "They might enjoy the distraction. And perhaps I could come visit, as well, if you feel that will work well for you."

"I will ask them about coming ashore. Molly thought that perhaps Anna could come to stay with us for a few weeks. She thought it might cheer Phoebe."

Anna spoke up quickly. "I'd be happy to come out any time Mother can spare me."

Missus Barrows cocked her head to one side. "Oh, I heard your father's chair. We must go say goodnight to the reverend."

Anna and Ben followed Missus Barrows into the front hallway where Mister Barrows was helping Nash into his overcoat. The reverend's face looked chiseled from stone, and he sported an exquisitely trimmed mustache. He bid each of them a warm good night. When he came to Ben, he leaned into their handshake. "Ben, might I speak with you outside for a few moments?"

Out on the big veranda, Ben found the evening air surprisingly warm still, as though Spring had arrived early Downeast, although he knew that the weather at this time of year was nearly as fickle as an Augusta politician. Reverend Nash came out behind him and placed a hand on Ben's shoulder. "So, Bennington, I think this evening that you met nearly every eligible young woman in Rockland. What did you think?"

"I thought the outpouring of sympathy and kindness toward the family was quite remarkable."

"Oh, fiddlesticks. I mean the ladies. Didn't you notice that the young ladies wore their Sunday best on a Wednesday night? Your in-laws couldn't eat that quantity of food in a fortnight. I may stop by tomorrow to see whether they might agree to send some of the preserves and canned items over to the veteran's home in Togus."

Ben scratched his chin and reflected on the evening's queue of visitors. Upon consideration, he could agree with the reverend's observation, but he didn't understand its significance. "Don't decent folks dress nicely when they come calling to pay their respects?"

"Tell me, Ben, did you see any husbands or sons this evening? Any men at all?" Reverend Nash seemed a little irritated with Ben's failure to grasp the significance of the evening's events. "These women came to see you!"

"Me? Look at me. I can't imagine why anyone would want to see me." Absentmindedly, he touched his scarred cheek.

"I overheard a widower asking Mister Barrows whether he thought it would be possible to land a piano on Sorrow Ledge. I don't think it was a purely academic question because I know she practices daily."

"Goodness, don't they recognize me? I've been coming into Rockland almost every month for nearly thirty years. I'm not a handsome actor from Boston."

"Perhaps we could sit for a moment," the reverend said as he motioned toward a settee that faced Cedar Street. "You see, I think the ladies of Rockland recognize you just fine. You've been a good husband and father. You came back from the war with all your limbs. You've a position of responsibility. You're a sober, God-fearing man, and I fear that's increasingly uncommon these days."

Ben did not answer. The reverend also remained quiet for several minutes. At last, Nash leaned forward and fixed a steady gaze with his dark eyes on Ben. "Let's suppose God makes a man for every woman; an Adam for every Eve. Then along comes Mr. Lincoln's war."

Even 15 years after Appomattox, Ben stiffened at what he perceived to be copperhead talk.

Reverend Nash did not seem to notice Ben's reaction and continued. "How many men from Maine joined the army?"

"I have no idea," Ben said honestly.

"You were 2nd Maine, correct? How many men were with your unit when you left Bangor?"

"A few more than twelve hundred, I believe."

"How many mustered out in 1863?

"I guess more than three hundred fifty, although some joined up with other regiments."

"And then how many were transferred to the 20th with you in that awful business?"

"Some one hundred and twenty," Ben answered, realizing the point the reverend strove to make. He turned away.

"That was your regiment alone. So how many regiments did Maine offer to the Great Cause?"

"Between infantry, cavalry and artillery, I suppose about forty all told."

Reverend Nash reached to where he could put a hand upon Ben's knee. "That would mean a lot of Adams lost in the war who will never come home to their Eve. Also, with our busy harbor, many ships and fishing boats never find their way back across our horizon."

Ben nodded in agreement.

"I don't wish to intrude upon your affairs, but I feel I should ask this because when I see these women about town in the coming weeks, I know they will ask me. Do you think you will remarry soon? Your daughters could certainly benefit from having a woman in the household. My wife expressed her concern that it might hurt the girls' reputations to be raised on an island by a widower and a bachelor, such as yourself and the Irishman."

The wickie struggled with how to respond. Ben felt insulted that anyone would suggest he was unfit to raise his children alone. He also grew weary of the continuing aspersions against Seamus for the accident of his birth. "No. I don't believe I could ever love a woman as much as I love Rebecca."

"I certainly understand how you feel now, but your marriage vows said only till death do you part." Nash now spoke more quietly, "Of course, you need not expect the same relationship just as you experienced with Rebecca. No doubt many of these women would be amenable to companionship. Now, I know you're no nullifidian. Even God does not expect a man to remain faithful to a woman he'll never see again." The reverend sat back in his seat as though he had delivered the final coup de grace in a theological debate.

Ben nearly shook in anger at the man's sanctimonious speech. "Reverend Nash, each night I climb 100 steps to light a flame to guide ships I may never see across the ocean. People I will never know. My life is a constant vigil for strangers. How can I do any less for Rebecca? Good night, sir."

Ben stood and walked inside the Barrows' house, then climbed the front stairs to a bedroom in the back of the house where he would spend the night.

CHAPTER 10

*W*hile Maine turned from day to greet twilight, Ben sat on the edge of a narrow bed to unlace and remove his brogues, wondering as he did whether he had been too forceful with Reverend Nash. Would the minister perform still a service for Rebecca in the Episcopal Church when better weather permitted her entire family to gather? A ceramic pitcher on a small dresser held water, and someone had laid out a washrag and towels. Ben unbuttoned and removed his shirts. As he did, he revealed the weals and welts on his skin, both front and back. He wondered whether any other woman could view this anthology of his wounds from youth and war with the same compassion as Rebecca. Reverend Nash's suggestion that he might find another wife seemed absurd. These marks on his skin were simply physical disfigurements. The greater trauma, he knew, were the scars carved upon his soul. What woman would tolerate his continuing nightmares of the elephant?

Ben had come to believe that people start as a whole at birth, but they are slowly whittled down by the sum of their losses. Like a block of marble carved by the chisel and mallet of a sculptor. Or the craggy shoreline of Sorrow Ledge sculpted by the ceaseless tide. While a boy still, Ben learned of the death of Lieutenant Clough, a man he had come to admire. He then had lost his father in a tragic accident, followed by comrades and his brothers to the war, his mother and sister to small pox, and now his Rebecca. Each of these hurts carved another small notch from his heart. He had believed at Gettysburg that he had outstripped his capacity for grief, only to be proven utterly wrong during the past weeks. For the first time in the years since that earliest strike of his father's hand across his cheek as a child, Ben wept.

Ashamed still, he splashed water across his face and reached for a towel. As he stood upright, he was shocked to see in the mirror that Anna stood in the doorway just a few feet behind him. She gave out a little cry of surprise.

"I am so sorry, Ben," she said. "I did not hear you come upstairs. I thought you were still outside with Reverend Nash. I have hot water." She held out the kettle from the kitchen.

"Then I should apologize for coming up without alerting anyone. I wanted to evade the reverend's marital advice." He held a towel across his chest and stomach as he turned to face her.

"Oh." She seemed to pause to think about this for a moment. "What did that horrid man say to you? I swear that if he dares tell me one more time how I must hurry to find a husband before I am a spinster that he will preach his own eulogy from inside his coffin."

Ben hooted heartily. He had not heard Anna speak so forcefully before on any subject. "I fear he has similar designs on my future. I must disappoint the man."

"Oh, dear," she said. "I'm sorry that I barged in on you like this." She paused, seeming to search in her mind for the right words. "Rebecca told me about the harms you endured, but I never imagined the extent of … Does it still bother you terribly?"

"Not so much, really," he said. "The outside hardly hurts at all these days."

"I'm so sorry. I never imagined the scars you've carried all these years." Turning, she pulled the door closed behind her as she went out but stopped abruptly. "Will you join us for dinner?" she asked.

"No, thank you kindly. I have not had much of an appetite of late."

"Alright, I'll inform Mother. Good night, Ben." She closed the door, and Ben heard her going down the back stairs.

Ben sat in the chair for several hours, just as he had done at Rebecca's bedside. He had held her hand as he waited through each night until dawn. Without her, he would watch now alone as first Molly and then Phoebe moved ashore to pursue their own lives. Soon Seamus would be offered his own light station. Ben could not guess how much longer he must wait before he could be laid down at Rebecca's side. Instead, he could only wait and hope.

Although he had drawn closed all the shades and curtains in the room before he laid down, Ben was still surprised by how brightly illuminated the room remained from the streetlamps and other homes along Cedar Street. Even late into the evening, the fires at the lime kilns brightened the eastern horizon. He drew a handkerchief from his trousers and knotted a blindfold over his eyes. He lay awake for hours in his darkness, recalling in detail the incidents by which he had proved to this world that he was no more than his father's son – maiming and murdering rebels across miles and months with little remorse in his heart. His skin was scarred by the scourge of war, but he always gave as good as he got. Yet he never knew the tally of dead or wounded he left in his wake. Edmund Dantes went to the Chateau d'*If* an innocent man; Ben could make no such claim. Worse, he felt a remorse for Rebecca's death that lashed his heart like the raging tide of a nor'easter against Sorrow Ledge. Perhaps the isolation of sorrow on his own Chateau d'*If* was the punishment Ben deserved most.

CHAPTER 11

For the first time since the morning after the wreck of the *Gideon*, Ben woke knowing just what he must do.

No one could mistake the scents wafting upstairs from the kitchen for anything but breakfast. Ben detected biscuits baking in an oven, while bacon, sausage, and eggs fried in a skillet, alongside coffee boiling in a pot. He rose and dressed completely, from his brogues to necktie. Lastly, he pulled on his jacket and adjusted the black mourning shroud that Phoebe had pinned to his sleeve.

When he went downstairs, he was surprised to discover the parlor empty. Instead, the family was gathered in the kitchen. Mister Barrows sat at the head of the table with a small pile of newspapers at his elbow while his wife stood at the stove prodding the cooking food with a pair of spatulas. Mister Barrows sat in his shirt sleeves; his wife and daughter both wore formal black dresses, covered with aprons. Anna sat at the table across from her father; her head bent over a sheet of paper that Ben assumed was the note from Seamus. The way Anna tilted her head reminded him of her sister. Even the curve of her neck was identical to Rebecca's.

"Good morning, Ben," Mister Barrows said. "Have a seat here. I want to show you some of the things that the Bellyache wrote about your beloved Chamberlain." Mister Barrows had rolled his sleeves halfway up his forearms to avoid brushing his shirt against the newspaper ink.

"Peter, please let the man sit and eat something before you lecture him on politics. He's probably starving," Missus Barrows said. "Ben, were you too tired to join us for dinner last night? I imagine rowing in from your island must make a man rather hungry."

Ben did not sit at the table but stood apart so he could easily see all three Barrows at once. "I apologize. I've had a lot on my mind. I have a question to ask that involves each of you, but especially Anna." He stopped to clear his throat, aware that all eyes were now focused intently upon him. Ben coughed then began, "I don't suppose many men have come to a father to ask for the hand of a second daughter in marriage."

CHAPTER 12

*F*or a long minute, the only sound in the kitchen was the sizzle emanating from the skillet.

"However, I have known Seamus for 17 years since he walked me back from Gettysburg. We have worked together each day of every one of those years. I can vouch for his character; he's been a good dory-mate." Ben paused to look at the faces of his audience. No one seemed more surprised than Anna herself, so he spoke to her directly. "I don't think it's any secret how he feels about you. Two letters or more every month for the past ten years? There simply isn't that much to say about events on Sorrow Ledge." Ben turned to face his own father-in-law. "And Mister Barrows, I hope you won't hold his Irish against him. During the draft riots, he helped at the Negro orphanage. When the *Gideon* shipwrecked, Seamus helped rescue those people, and he helped deal with that Irish lunatic. I've heard you say it's not a man's birth, but what station he attains that matters most."

More silence followed when Ben finished.

No one spoke for several minutes until finally Missus Barrows asked, "Would you like that coffee now, Ben?"

Anna stood and brought two trays loaded with breadstuffs to the table. Ben politely ate a buttered biscuit but declined the offer of any other foods. He hoped no one would be offended, but he had felt little desire to eat over the past few weeks. When he asked for milk to add to his coffee, both Missus Barrows and Anna jumped from their seats to bring it to the table.

At last Mister Barrows spoke. "I have no objection to Seamus because he's Irish. But we cannot forget he was raised Catholic. Is he still a Papist? Just what are his prospects? He's been an assistant wickie all these years. What are we to expect of him?" His face appeared to redden as he listed his objections.

Ben smiled and tried to tamp down any resentment he felt at this slight; after all, he had been a lead wickie 'all these years' and what did anyone expect him to achieve? Was Mister Barrows still disappointed in Rebecca's choice? Perhaps Ben received some dispensation for his war service or, perhaps worse, what he had endured at his father's hand. "Sir, I have told Seamus that I am ready to nominate him for a position as lead keeper any time he is ready; however, so far he has declined my offer." He looked at Anna. "I think I know why. He is certainly the keen candidate to succeed me on Sorrow Ledge. Perhaps Owls Head Light might become available. Or he could apply to become a district inspector. Those are political appointments; however, I believe the letter of recommendation General Meade gave him might seal the deal."

"From General Meade?" Missus Barrows asked.

"Yes, after the war, Seamus did a personal favor for the general regarding those Fenian renegades planning to invade Canada," Ben explained. "If you will consent, I thought that Anna might come with me this morning. She would stay in the main quarters with the girls, while I bunk with Seamus in his quarters. I am certain the skipper of the cutter *Dallas* would be willing to perform a civil ceremony when Anna is ready, and then this summer we could all come ashore for a blessing by the church at the same time we hold a service for Rebecca. If I have not insulted Reverend Nash too greatly."

Mister Barrows sat back in his chair and crossed his arms. "There are many things to be considered here," he said. "General Meade's letter aside, what do we really know of the boy's character? What of his family? This papist thing is still troubling. Anna will someday

KENNETH ARBOGAST

inherit a sizeable fortune. Is he the right man to manage her funds? Would he give her money to the Pope?"

Anna rose as if to leave the kitchen but turned and put both hands on the kitchen table as she leaned forward. "Father, I love you, but why do you insist upon treating me this way? Finally, when a good man suggests an interest in me, you question whether he meets your standards? Isn't Ben's word good enough? Doesn't a letter from General Meade account for his character? Father, I've nearly lost my chance. You paraded Rebecca around the store to drum up business, but you always kept me hidden in the storeroom like a leper. How do I embarrass you so much? At last, I have a chance to be happy. If you don't trust me, then take the damned money; let Reverend Nash buy his grand organ. I don't care what you do with it. I will be going out to Sorrow Ledge with Ben. Today. Whether you approve or not. I will marry Seamus, and there is nothing you can do to stop me."

Missus Barrows rushed to Anna's side and hugged her tightly. Mister Barrows did not stir from his seat. Ben was uncertain whether he should say anything at all. Clearly to Ben, this dispute had already been years in the making. At last, Mister Barrows stood and gripped his suspenders with both hands. As he inhaled deeply preparing to speak, Missus Barrows spoke sharply, "Peter Barrows, I want you to stop this minute. If you say one word, I will leave today with Anna. Every word she said is true. For years now, I haven't understood why. How could you love one child more than another? Well, it no longer matters. You have broken Anna's spirit. Do you want now to break her heart, too? Anna, go up and gather what you need. Take the black trunk from the foot of my bed and dump the contents on the floor. I'll deal with it all later."

For his part, Mister Barrows sat back down on his chair and wrapped his hands around the coffee mug in front of him on the table. The grease remaining in the skillet on the stove began to burn and smoke. Missus Barrows removed the pan from the open flame, then came around the table to where Ben stood.

"You'll take good care of her? She's all I have left. So, you promise you'll contact the *Dallas* at the earliest convenience? I don't want her reputation to suffer from any delay. May I come visit for a few weeks

420

this summer? I would like to spend time with my granddaughters now."

"Of course, ma'am. You're always welcome out on Sorrow Ledge. You are both welcome in our home."

Anna swept out of the kitchen, and soon footsteps could be heard upstairs. Missus Barrows turned back to the kitchen and filled a plate with eggs, bacon, sausage and a muffin that she placed before Mister Barrows without comment. Ben pushed the butter dish toward him but then begged off any further breakfast with the excuse that he needed to complete one last chore before returning to Sorrow Ledge. As he left through the kitchen door, he worried over what discord his visit had wrought.

Ben walked down Cedar Street and made his way east over to Camden Street. He trudged north past the Baptist Church for another mile until he came to a narrow lane that led east toward the waterfront. Where the rutted drive ended at the bay, he found a weathered, two-story house and dilapidated barn. When knocking at the front door yielded no answer, Ben walked around the cowshed, looking for the farm's inhabitants. There he found a man and boy trying to corral a small herd of roly-poly puppies to feed them. Both wore threadbare clothes, and the boy was shoeless.

"Henry," Ben called. "I'm Ben Grindle. I bought one of your dogs some years back." For Ben, the moment was bittersweet because his last visit had been to purchase a rotund ball of fur that his wife dubbed Bosun.

Walking toward Ben, the man extended his grizzled hand. "Sure, I remember. You're the keeper on Sorrow Ledge. He was your second dog from me, wasn't he?"

"Yes, we had a female first. You remember back that far?"

"Well sure, each litter are like children," he said. "I'll bet this last boy grew big, didn't he? I remember his sire was big as a pony."

Ben nodded in agreement. "Oh, yes, Bosun could tow a small boat in the water."

"He's what now, seven years, maybe eight? How's he doing now?"

"I'm afraid he crossed the bar a few nights ago."

"Oh. I see. I'm sorry to hear of it. He were too young. I've had sires live to ten years or better. What happened to him?"

Ben sensed the farmer was worried there might be an accusation forthcoming. "I'm afraid that he just stopped eating after my wife died."

"I'm sorry. You know, I've heard Canadians say that anyone a Newfoundland sees while their eyes are still blue the dog is bound to love forever." The man seemed relieved that there would be no allegations that he bred bad stock. "Maybe it's true."

"I suppose so. He sure loved Rebecca best. After she passed, I think he died of a broken heart. I need a pup to keep a lookout for my girls for as long as they stay on the ledge."

"Well, I'm sure sorry to hear about your missus passing away. Were you looking for a boy or a girl this time?" Henry asked.

Ben leaned forward to rest his arms on the fence as he surveyed the puppies in the yard. "Well, it looks like you have a new litter now. Do you have any that aren't spoken for?"

"Not really, I'm afraid," the man said, waving his arm toward the puppies in his corral. "The bitch only birthed six this time. There's three to homes in town; two for lobstermen, so I've only the small boy runt. One back leg seems a crooked, but my wife won't let me finish him off. She doesn't understand that a broke dog is no use to anyone."

"Would you bring that one to me?"

"Well, I wouldn't want word to get out that I sell dogs that aren't fit."

Ben tried to smile in a cajoling manner. "I promise I'll be discrete."

The dog owner turned and yelled at his son. Soon the boy approached with a prone puppy slung over his shoulder. Ben took the dog and laid the young pup on its back in the crook of his left arm. He placed his right hand on the dog's belly to assure it that it would not fall.

"See what I mean about that back leg?" the man asked. "He don't favor it or limp, but you can see it just don't seem true like the others.

"Yes, I see just what you mean. Any other problems with him? He isn't afraid of water, is he?" The puppy did not wiggle away from Ben's hold. When Ben looked at the dog's face, he found blue eyes fixed upon his own. The Newfoundland did not whimper or squirm but seemed to trust Ben not to drop it.

"I am very sorry. I do not like to hawk faulty dogs. Perhaps I can give you one of the others from this litter. I will tell another buyer that their pup did not survive and promise another from her next brood."

"No, that's not necessary," Ben said. "This one will do. Sorrow Ledge is small, so a dog doesn't need to walk far in any direction."

"Well, if you are sure, you may have him. Free. I suppose it is better he goes with you than get drownded in the bay."

CHAPTER 13

*W*hen Ben reached the front of the Barrows' home, he tied the twine that was looped around the puppy's neck to the front fence. The black furball instinctively sat on its haunches. As Ben opened the gate, Anna came out the front door pulling on a large black trunk. Missus Barrows followed behind, holding up the rear end of the luggage. They both remained dressed in their black mourning garb, with black veils draped across their faces.

"I'm so sorry, Ben," Anna said. "I wasn't certain when I might come home again, so I brought what I thought I might need."

He chuckled. "We're not going to Africa in search of Doctor Livingstone, you know? You may come home whenever you choose."

"I tried to explain that to her," Missus Barrows said. "Rebecca spent half her summers ashore. We could have fed all Rockland with the food we canned each fall."

"Ben, I hope you don't mind that we summoned up a cart from Noonan's wharf," Anna said. "I just thought it would be easier for the baggage and mother."

"Anna Barrows, how could you equate me with baggage!" Missus Barrows said indignantly. "If I am not afraid to challenge your father, how dare you suggest I am too frail to walk down to the wharves?"

Abruptly Anna asked, "Bennington, who's your little friend?" She knelt to greet the Newfoundland puppy sitting at the gate.

"Oh, the girls' new best friend, I hope. When he's smart enough to piss outside, we can train him for rescue. He may be a little lame, but once he's in the water, I don't think that'll matter so much."

The puppy leaped into her lap. "It's cute. Have you thought of a name?" Anna asked.

"Well, I'll need to await the girls' approval, but I was thinking of 'Joshua.'"

"That seems a splendid choice," Missus Barrows said, though she added quietly, "Could we please not be in a hurry to tell Mister Barrows? Seeing how agitated he became during the Twelve Days, I fear that might cause him apoplexy."

"No, ma'am, I don't see any reason your husband should know," Ben said. "I don't foresee any occasion when the dog will ever be so close to your home again in its lifetime. He's bound to live out his days on Sorrow Ledge."

"Well, Ben, didn't you say that the dog also belongs to Molly and Phoebe; that they get a say in his name?" Anna asked in a mischievous tone. "So, wouldn't they be able to bring their dog to town when they come for canning in the Autumn?"

"That is a discussion that I will leave for the four of you," Ben said. "A full-sized Newfie can be a bit of a challenge." When young, Bosun would accompany Ben on his morning rounds of the family's nets and traps. Once the dog reached full size, Ben was no longer able to lift the dog into the station's Quoddy boat without risking serious harm to both wickie and animal.

Within a few moments, a cart hauled by a haggard-looking horse arrived from Noonan's Wharf. "I'm sorry, sir," the boy said. The driver was a young man, dressed in worn clothes that may have been handed down from one of his uncles who was in the family's sailing ships. He pointed toward the flat rig intended for hauling cargo with no seats to accommodate people "My father didn't say I needed to carry passengers." Before Ben could reach Anna's luggage, the boy had hoisted it from the ground with ease and placed it on the bed of his cart.

"No worries," Anna said. "A walk in the morning air will do us good, but could you arrange a carriage to bring my mother home?"

"Yes, ma'am. I'll see to it myself." The boy bowed slightly from the waist.

Ben suggested that the two ladies walk at the head of the procession to avoid stepping into anything that the horse left behind in the street. He walked alongside the Noonan boy who carried the horse's lead. "You're Daniel?" Ben asked.

"Yes, sir. I've been out to Sorrow Ledge with parcels a few times when my dad was laid up. There are days that the pain in his spine lays him out flat. My mom gives him laudanum to help him rest."

"I think your father is a very strong man to deal with that every day."

"Some people in town call him a lazy cripple," the boy said quietly.

"Some people in town are morons and cowards," Ben replied. "Did you know that when the war started, your father went up to Bangor to see about enlisting. Some people around here sniggered at him, but you didn't see the lot of them joining the war effort. Moreover, I think you'll find some people in this town are just jealous."

"Jealous of my dad?"

"Oh, sure. You know the waterfront. How many wharves do you suppose Rockland has?"

"Twenty, I guess?"

"Easily twenty. And think of all of them: Abbot's, Spear's, Pillsbury. Also, Crockett's has two. You go past them all nearly every day. And which of them is the busiest? I'll tell you. Noonan's. That's because of how hard your father works. You hear anyone in this town criticize your father, you think about what they've done." They were now walking down North Main Street, approaching the school beyond Rockland Street. The chubby puppy had no trouble keeping pace with them. "Listen, your father told me that you'd like to call upon Molly."

"She's always been so nice to me whenever I see her." The boy smiled as if the mere sound of her name delighted him.

"All right. I'll tell you what. I will talk to her and ask what she thinks. We'll let her decide. Fair enough?"

"Yes, sir. Thank you," the boy said. "If I may ask, is Miss Anna going to stay on Sorrow Ledge with you?"

"Yes, Molly thought Phoebe might like the company." Ben did not wish any rumors to get out into the town until the engagement was confirmed. Prior to shocking everyone in the kitchen at breakfast, Ben had discussed his idea with neither Anna nor Seamus. He knew that playing matchmaker in this way was nothing short of felony meddling in their lives, even if it resolved so many of the concerns on Sorrow Ledge that arose in the wake of Rebecca's death.

Soon they were on Main Street proper, passing the limestone kilns clustered around Brown's Wharf. Missus Barrows and Anna walked together ahead still. Anna's hand held her mother's arm, and their heads were close together so they could speak in whispered voices. Ben wondered how Anna had left things with her father. Had either apologized? He regretted causing any riff, but it hardly seemed a fresh matter.

"Tell me, Daniel, what are your dreams for your future? Will you stay in the family business? Either on the wharf or do you think you will go to sea?"

"Mister Grindle, I must confess this to you because of Molly. I want nothing to do with any of this. Please don't tell my father. Or Molly yet."

"Your secret will be safe with me until you want to reveal it. What do you plan to do instead?" Ben had to walk carefully because the puppy tended to weave back and forth in front of his legs.

The boy's voice lowered to almost a whisper. "I want to build things. Buildings, bridges, railroads, ships. I want to be able to point to something and say, 'Look what I created.' I don't want to cart other people's things around for them." Despite his quiet tone, he sounded excited as he described his dreams.

"That sounds ambitious. I'm impressed."

"It can't happen," the boy said. Abruptly his delight turned to woe. "Why not?"

"I don't have enough schooling for that. I would need to go to college. However, I'm expected to take over the wharf business."

Ben stopped and took the boy by the arm. "Don't you have younger brothers who also work on the docks?"

"Sure, Matthew and Mark. But I'm oldest, so it's my responsibility." The boy seemed crestfallen.

"I think I know how you feel. I kind of inherited a family business as well." Ben smiled at the young man, feeling happier about Daniel calling upon Molly now knowing that the boy had such aspirations in mind. "My father was a lighthouse keeper, but before that my family was whalers for two generations. And before that my great grandfathers fought in the Revolution and the wars with the French. I never wanted to be a soldier or a whaler either, for that matter. I had my war, as did my brothers." As he said these things, Ben realized that as a boy he held no great desire to be a lighthouse keeper; the duty was simply thrust upon him after his father's accident. Once he returned from war, the duty once again devolved to Ben as his brothers went off to join the 20th Maine.

"Mister Grindle, I didn't know you had any brothers. Where are they now?"

"Both dead. Stanwix died in a Confederate prison, a hellhole called Libby. Valcour was carrying the regiment's colors next to Colonel Chamberlain during the assault on Fort Mahone outside Petersburg, when a rebel bullet killed him where he stood."

"I'm sorry. I didn't know," Daniel said.

"No need to apologize. How could you know? You were barely born then. My point is that you don't always need to follow a family tradition. You know, I met a civil engineer who teaches at the Maine College. Perhaps I could send him a letter for you." No one had ever expressed any interest in Ben's vocation. Instead, there was an expectation he would carry on at the Ledge in order to provide continued support for their mother and Saratoga.

"Would you? If I had an introduction, I could learn what I need to get a start."

"Of course, I will," Ben said, hoping Jacob Noonan would not be angry with him for encouraging the young man. He wondered whether Molly knew of the boy's secret ambition. Ben then thought that perhaps she had no romantic notions of Daniel at all. On the chance that Molly might have an interest in the young man, any ambition that took Daniel away from the waterfront would spare her a life of hardship and struggle that cursed so many Maine women widowed by the sea.

They reached the Noonan wharf at mid-morning, and Daniel took the cart down to the pier where the light station's boat was moored. Ben walked to where the two women stood murmuring together. The elder Noonan emerged from his office and joined the group. "Ben, the bay looks much calmer than yesterday. I believe you'll have smooth sailing this morning."

Ben extended his hand. "Thank you, Jacob. I appreciate you sending your son to help us this morning. He's a smart young man. I will speak with Molly when I reach home." As they shook hands, Ben made another request. "Do you think you could arrange to have Missus Barrows taken back home?"

"Of course. As soon as the boys are done with the cart, I'll have Daniel harness the horse to the carriage. It will be just a few minutes before he's ready to go. My other horses are hauling freight to the rail station this morning." Noonan left them to walk toward the dock.

Ben turned to Missus Barrows. "I hope Mister Barrows won't be angry that I am taking Anna away, just as I did Rebecca. However, I will try to bring her ashore as often as we can. She can come to visit with the girls or with Seamus." As he took her outreached hand in his own, he leaned forward and brushed his cheek against hers. He whispered into her ear, "I believe Seamus has set aside money for them to set up a household in his quarters once they marry and even to visit Boston after the wedding. I hope your husband will learn to accept Seamus as a good man." He kissed her cheek.

"Not to worry," she said. "I will work on bringing my husband around. I can be rather persuasive when I need to be." She gave him a warm smile as she patted his arm. She then turned to hug Anna as one of the younger Noonan boys arrived with the horse and carriage. "I expect to hear from you each time Ben's little boat sails into Owl's Head Bay. And when summer arrives, you can expect me to visit you there. I will bring whatever you need from home." She gave her daughter a final hug before turning to climb into the coach.

As Anna watched the wagon carrying her mother drive off toward Bear Street, she wiped a tear from her cheek. "I realized as I was packing my nightgown that tonight will be one of the very few nights in my life when I have not slept under the same roof as my mother." She turned toward Ben and smiled. "I so love Mother, but I am delighted this day has arrived at last. Though I do hate to deprive you of your bed. Perhaps I could stay with Molly and Phoebe in their room."

As they reached the small boat, Ben replied. "I do not want your parents, or all of Rockland, to fret about your accommodations during the next few weeks." He stepped from the pier into the boat then turned back as Daniel handed down the puppy. Then Ben helped Anna climb aboard. Once Daniel was out of earshot, Ben added, "I don't mind bunking with Seamus. And if you stay in the quarters with the girls for a few nights, I'm sure you will hear all of their gossip about Seamus. Perhaps you will want to know these things before you marry. And I can let you know if he snores."

She chuckled as she settled onto the forward seat. Almost immediately the dog climbed up to sit next to her. He laid his furry head on Anna's lap. "I promise you that no man's snores could trouble me. There are nights when my father's snoring sounded like the Knox and Lincoln Railroad came right through our parlor. She never talks about it, but I know my mother sometimes sleeps in Rebecca's old room just to put more walls between them."

Daniel cast off their mooring lines, and Ben pushed off from the dock with the starboard oar. With a few hard sweeps, Ben maneuvered the boat out into the harbor. Away from Noonan's Wharf, they could see the activity around the busy bay until a steamship departing from the Steamboat Wharf belched a cloud of thick black smoke from its stacks that enveloped the waterfront from Commercial Wharf at least as far as Snow Wharf.

"I will not miss the stench of the constant exhaust in this town," Anna said. "Our home was situated just about halfway between the stink of the tannery and the belching kilns, so we were inundated whether the wind blew from the west or from the east. There were evenings when the house reeked so badly that Mother did not force Father to take his after-dinner cigar outside; his tobacco was preferable to all the industrial smells."

Driving the small boat forward with both oars, Ben maintained an easterly heading until they were abreast of Shag Rock on the starboard side before changing to an east-southeast course that would take them past Owls Head, where he would turn to pass Monroe Island. Once in the main body of West Penobscot Bay, he expected to find adequate wind to raise the sail. He explained his plans to Anna.

"Ben, I have been puzzled by two sailing terms for several years, but I never thought to ask you before. When we get out onto open water, we'll be heading south, but you'll put the sail up because you think there will be a good northerly wind. So, we'll be sailing south with a northerly wind?" By now, the dog had climbed completely onto her lap; his face burrowed into the folds of her jacket. "Why not just call both by the direction where they're going?" Anna asked as she stroked the dog's fat flank.

"In that case, the boat's heading is south, but the wind is coming out of the north."

"Yes, but the wind is going south, in the same direction as the boat," she insisted, as if she had not been understood.

"Well, the wind and the boat are two different ..." His voice trailed off when he saw the puzzled look on her face. "Oh, I get your question now. You know, I have a book called the *Bowditch Practical Navigator* at home. It's the sailor's bible. We'll see if Mister Bowditch has any thoughts on the topic."

The puppy was snuggled firmly up against Anna. Ben wondered if he was warming to her in the same way Bosun had taken such a fancy to Rebecca. He hoped that Anna would not be too upset when she discovered all the fur and drool the puppy would leave behind on her nice clothes when they arrived upon Sorrow Ledge. A Newfoundland can easily thwart even the most fastidious dresser.

"Ben, may I ask another question without being too annoying? In all the years that Seamus has worked for you, he has only rarely come ashore. I was wondering why you usually come into town instead."

"Anna, I will tell you why but I must swear you to complete and total secrecy. I asked the same of Rebecca. You may not tell even your mother. Do you promise?"

With a look of alarmed concern on her face, Anna nodded slowly. "Lord, has Seamus murdered someone?"

"Some might consider what he did for the country worse than murder. You may have been too young at the time to remember, but after the war, there were a lot of Irishmen who had served in the army. A large group wanted to invade Canada to create a Fenian nation. They gathered up the coast in Eastport and Calais. Do you recall hearing about that?"

"Oh my, and how." Anna giggled, disturbing the dog's repose. He raised his head to look for the cause of this disturbance. "How could I forget my father every night railing about the Fenian fanatics until he was blue in the face?"

Ben took a deep breath before he continued his recitation. "At the time, General Meade was in command of the army. He was responsible to keep the fanatics from starting a war with Canada and England. I had met him at Gettysburg, so he sent a telegram asking me to get him information about their plans."

"Meade asked you to spy for him?" she asked in a hushed tone, sounding both impressed and intrigued by this turn in the story that she did not know.

"Well, yes, he asked me," he explained, "but I could not sneak into a camp full of Irishmen. For one thing, I fought alongside quite a few Irish, especially New York troops. There was a chance they might recognize me. And of course, I do not speak Gaelic at all, so I might not understand all the conversations. Pardon me for a moment." Ben paused his storytelling to lay up the sweeps so that he could rig the short mast and hoist a canvas sail to catch that northerly wind to propel them south, chuckling as he reflected on Anna's conundrum. He affixed the rudder on the small boat's stern and then settled where he could easily keep a hand on the tiller. "So, I recruited Seamus to go in my stead. He spent a few days there and learned how the leaders planned to get the boats they needed to carry seven hundred Fenians across to Canada. There was a chance that someone may have recognized him, with his eyes and all. But Seamus stayed. With what he learned, Meade arrived and prevented the attack."

"General Meade himself came all the way Downeast because of

what Seamus reported?" Her astonishment at the lad's exploits was obvious.

"Well, yes. Gave Meade the chance to seize a ship carrying a load of weapons as well as some small boats the Fenians needed for the attack. Took the wind right out of their sails."

She wrapped her arms around the Newf puppy and snuggled him against her bosom. "Wow. I had no idea about any of this. Rebecca never said word one." She affixed an intense glare on Ben. "And you? I suppose you went back to Pennsylvania to help round up the Molly Maguires?"

Ben shook his head ruefully. "No. I have remained here, polishing glass and trimming a wick. You should know that I had no business asking a boy to do such a thing, but he understood that the British would never have tolerated an attack on Canada. There would be hell to pay back in Ireland. We came very close to war, with British warships and American gunboats lined up on either side of the St. Croix River. And Anna, it was a very dangerous thing for Seamus to do. When he brought me home from Gettysburg, we came into New York during the draft riots. He helped me rescue a fireman from the micks. If anyone of the Fenians had recognized him, they might have murdered him where he stood. Seamus was a true hero; I'm just a wickie."

As they reached the main channel of Penobscot Bay, the wind quickened, and the small boat chanced along quite nicely. Instinctively Ben reefed the sail so that the breeze did not outrun the boat's ability to carry the speed. They were making good headway without putting too much strain on the jury-rigged mast. He brought the tiller over slightly to adjust their course. If the wind held, they would arrive at Sorrow Ledge soon after the noon hour.

"That's not how Father describes you; now he tells anyone who listens that you were instrumental in winning the war. But it wasn't always that way, you know. He doesn't remember that I was the one Rebecca sent ashore the day you returned home and she had decided to stay on Sorrow Ledge. That night he didn't have many nice things to say about you."

Ben nodded in understanding. "I suppose I'd be just as unhappy if

Molly or Phoebe sent a message that she was moving into a man's house before marriage. Those two weeks while we waited for the *Dallas* to pay a call were the last time I bunked with Seamus in his quarters. I can at least vouch that he didn't snore back then."

Ben opened the bag at his feet and fished out one of the horehound candies. He offered it to Anna. "Here, this will help keep away any queasy feeling." He took a deep breath before he broached the next subject. "Anna, I was thinking that you might wait a bit before marrying, just to be certain you'll adjust. It's a lonely life on an island."

She did not answer immediately, but instead looked away to study the waters toward Vinalhaven. When at last she turned her head toward him and spoke, Ben saw a tear glistening on her cheek. "I suppose I should have no troubles if Seamus has in him for me the love that you have for Rebecca."

"I meant only that you might find life dreary out here, away from people."

"Oh, I've considered that notion thoroughly, all the time I've been waiting to hear from Seamus. I know all the whispers around Rockland about how I'm just an old maid. Rebecca was the better one. I look forward to being away from the gossip of such nasty people. Even the disapproval of my own father."

They were now within about 100 fathoms from the northernmost point of Sorrow Ledge. To mark this occasion, a large harbor seal collided with the hull of the boat. The puppy rose from his place on Anna's lap and went to stand at the edge of the seat. With its front paws placed firmly on the gunwale, the dog barked fiercely at the seal. The seal did not demonstrate the slightest concern. Ben then lowered the sail and shipped the rudder so that he could maneuver up to the boathouse ways with the oars. As he did this, Seamus and the girls came around the corner of the boathouse and began to wave. Upon seeing Phoebe and Molly on shore, the Newf jumped into the water and swam toward them, his small head bobbing just above the water.

"Good to see the pup swim so well," Ben said.

As Seamus prepared to throw over a line to winch the boat up the ways, Anna turned to Ben. "Thank you," she said simply. "This is all a wonderful gift."

CHAPTER 14

*A*fter dinner, Phoebe cleared the table while Molly filled a kettle at the pump to heat water and wash the dishes. Anna followed Seamus up the tower so that they could speak together in private while he prepared to light the lamp inside the Fresnel lens. All the while, the puppy roamed freely around the quarters, exploring all the smells in his new home. So far, he had only one accident that prompted Phoebe to scoop him up and carry the squirming creature outside while Molly doused the spot with vinegar.

Ben walked out onto Sorrow Ledge, carrying one of the Colt revolvers he had taken from the Pennsylvanian officer during the Mud March. He still feared the possibility that a rat, or perhaps more than one, had survived the massacre by the *Dallas'* officers. In the coming weeks, he would begin to bring barrels of soil from the mainland to create a new vegetable garden. He hoped to be sure that no rodent population would steal the harvest just as it sprouted.

Under one arm he carried the second volume of the Dumas books that he had inherited upon the death of Lieutenant Clough some 25 years earlier. He thought of the officer often, remembering how the lieutenant dealt with the lingering pain of the wound suffered in

Mexico. Certainly Captain Swett relied upon a daily dollop to find dreams. Ben wondered if the occasional laudanum was enough for Jacob Noonan or did he keep his own flask in a bedside table, ready to ease his suffering from a birth gone terribly wrong. Or did Jacob resist that relief, knowing that the cause of his pain was a drunken midwife? Was pain or drink the reason Veazie could not refrain from complaining loudly about copperheads still, 15 years after the cessation of hostilities? Despite Ben's physical aches and scars, his sharpest pains were most often from other sources.

Secreted inside the leather cover of the Dumas book was the last letter he had received from his young sister. He removed the pages gingerly from the envelope and unfolded the well-worn sheets.

1873 Jan. 10

 Gallops Island, Boston Harbor

Dear Ben,

 I hope this letter finds you and all your family both healthy and well. I was astonished to discover only recently that Mother has not sent you any correspondence since your return to Sorrow Ledge after the war. I heard of your marriage from cousins while we lived in Portland, but nothing since we came down to Boston.

 I regret to tell you that our Mother passed away just yesterday. We have been at quarantine since October. At Thanksgiving, I thought we might both come through this horror alive, but she began to wane three weeks ago. I believe at the end she had no further desire to live here a single day longer.

 The quarantine is on Gallops Island in Boston harbor. When I walk along the shore, I can easily see the old Boston light house. The staff here says it is the elder to any other in the country and once Ben Franklin himself wrote a poem about the first wickie's death by drowning. Fancy that. In the other direction lays the great city of Boston. I will not miss it, as I so miss the good Maine air. No matter where I walked in the city, I never escaped the smells of fish, molasses, soot and men. Even this island is different. I miss the solid rock of Sorry Ledge – remember how Poppa fumed when we called it that? This island is all gravel and sand, which even now is being dug out and hauled away for Boston's streets.

Thank you for your tithes these past years. We lived on the wages I earned from cleaning private homes and the sums you sent from your earnings. Mother never mentioned these amounts to me, but after she took ill, I discovered a ledger book with her notations going all the way back to when we left the Light-house for Portland. I have arranged with Mother's banker to have any sum that survives me returned to you post haste.

I do not believe I will come home to Maine again. I would very much have liked to see Rebecca once more and to meet any children you may have had together. One of the young doctors says that I look better each day. I think he may be sweet on me. The nurses do not tell me such pretty lies. My corset no longer binds, and my skirt hangs from my waist like an old curtain. I often feel they should give those of us imprisoned here a choice, either hemlock or an opiate, so to end this suffering. An old woman across the way said she would rather be a horse with a broken leg — at least the end could be hastened with a pistol shot. I don't wonder but what you saw many men in the war who were at the same juncture of life and death. The one regret I carry is that our family shall never be united in death upon one parcel of ground.

I often thought these past months to write to you that we both had taken sick with the smallpox, but Mother forbade it. Just as she forbade any correspondence in the past. For my part, I am very sorry for whatever happened when we were young. Mother never spake of it to me. I have no doubt it was about how Poppa treated you boys. I can say he never struck me even one time. I still wonder why. But it was hard to watch what he did to you especially. I hope you will forgive me if you feel that I am in any way complicit in Mother's hard feelings toward you. I have never understood why she harbored such animosity. She refused to speak of it even at her end.

I have little strength to write more, and I do not know what more I should say. If you feel it needed that I should for anything that happened, I promise that I forgive you. In that same fashion, I beseech your forgiveness for what has transpired in these years since, particularly any feeling which you may harbor that I am ungrateful to you.

Please tell Rebecca and your family that I have loved them in absentia. I know now just how much you have done for Mother and me. I hope that you still bear some love for me after all these years.

Goodbye Bennington, and farewell to you.

Your loving sister,

Sara(toga)

Each time Ben read Saratoga's letter, he paused when he reached the passage where she wished to find a way to hasten the end. Many men with whom Ben had fought in the war expressed the desire to die of the "one shot" that soldiers claimed the victim never heard. That was far preferable to the agonizing death of the men who lingered in the Union hospital on Point Lookout, where the Potomac and Chesapeake converge. Or perhaps even more terrifying, to perish of dire hunger within the confines of the rebel prisons Libby or Andersonville. Ben thought about the different deaths that had claimed the two corpses entombed in the stone monument where he sat. The English sailor was likely shipwrecked with other crewmembers from some anonymous vessel. Ben assumed the others made it off Sorrow Ledge alive because no other bones or skeletons were found there, but any other remains may have been swept into the ocean by storms or high tides.

The other enclosed corpse suffered a much different fate. One cloudy day on Sorrow Ledge when Ben was 14 years of age, he was standing watch in the tower while his father went below to lunch and nap. Stanwix and Valcour were playing in the cupola so that Ben could keep a watch over them as well, and their noise would not disturb their father. The boys were imagining that the lantern room was the gun deck of an American warship sailing into the harbor at Tripoli during the Barbary Wars. While pretending to fire one of the imaginary ship's guns at the Bashaw's palace, Val reached for the pull lever connected to the alarm in the quarters. Ben was unable to stop him in time. When their father reached the tower's lantern room, he was in a lather, angered by the false alarm and the disruption of his sleep. Ben stood firm to explain what had happened while the two younger boys hid out on the outer catwalk. The elder Grindle always carried a length of right whale baleen with him, a souvenir from his days stalking the great beasts. He employed the staff for a variety of purposes, mostly related to punishment. He directed Ben to join the two boys on the catwalk, where he forced Ben to kneel at the railing. Then their father snapped his baleen rod in half against the railing of the catwalk, before handing a length to each of the twins. Their father felt that all three boys were complicit in raising a false alarm, but as Ben was on watch, he deserved the harshest punishment. Young Ben had failed in his duty that day.

Their father instructed the younger boys to each thrash Ben across his back fifteen times, on pain of getting the same count themselves. And woe if they held back. Tears streamed down their faces as they finished. Ben knew, however, that if he cried out his punishment would be doubled. When they finished, their father next took one of the rods and gave it to Ben, with instructions to lash each boy fifteen times in return. The younger brothers cowered in fear. Ben refused, even as his father grew angrier. In a rage, their father lunged at Ben, but the young man ducked away. Their father's fury carried him over the railing. Only Ben saw their father fall even as he leapt with hands outstretched to reach for the falling man. It was too late.

At his mother's direction, young Ben wrapped his father's shattered body in a swath of old canvas and dragged it to the stone monument. He carefully disassembled the ancient cairn to lay his father's corpse next to the skeleton of the long-dead sailor. While the other children remained in the keeper's quarters with their mother, Ben worked through the afternoon and into the evening. His toil was then lit by the regular flash from inside the Fresnel lens. Sometime after midnight, he finished reconstructing the tomb before climbing the tower to assume the midwatch. This ruse had allowed the Widow Grindle to be appointed as keeper of the light station. She had reported to the Superintendent that her husband had stumbled over the south-facing cliff of Sorrow Ledge in a dense fog and his body washed to sea in a high tide. To prevent a similar tragedy from ever occurring again, the Light House Bureau mounted a chain strung on stanchions across the edge of the precipice. Years later, Sara still believed their mother's story of their father's drowning, hence the *"Fancy that"* comment in her final letter.

Ben sat atop the tomb encasing the British sailor and the American whaler. With no rat sightings, he placed the pistol on a rock next to him and tucked Saratoga's letter back into Clough's book. How many times had his father struck Ben a blow between his face and eyes? Yet he still held deeply the same guilt over all those years since that day on the lighthouse catwalk. Now he had failed to do his duty yet again, this time at Rebecca's bedside when he had fallen asleep on the midwatch, allowing her hand to slip silently from his own.

With Rebecca's death, Ben was the last survivor who knew of his father's fate. This knowledge gave Ben some comfort, realizing that any strain of brutishness in the family blood would end with him. Rebecca and Ben had been careful so that Phoebe and Molly were never exposed to the malevolence young Ben had endured in private and public. The girls never heard the stories of Ben's suffering or observed the scars. Though decades had passed, he felt still the shame of a little boy being whipped on Main Street because he had dropped a burlap sack of dried beans. Never again would that evil man's rage shame the Grindle family.

From his jacket, Ben removed the package delivered to him the previous day at the post office. Inside he found a parchment wrapped around a sealed envelope. In the light of the early evening, Ben read the letter from the Superintendent of the Customs in Portland.

March 10, 1880
Portland, Maine

Light Keeper Grindle,

By this letter, I transmit to you the determination of the Light House Board regarding allegations of your culpability in the grounding of the vessel Gideon *and subsequent events at Sorrow Ledge Light House on or about January 16th, in the year of our Lord One Thousand Eight Hundred and Eighty, as well as the Board's decision regarding your continued incumbency in your current position. The gravity of these matters has caused an urgency in adjudication which I find unprecedented in my career. I wish to assure you that I did include with my report to the Fifth Auditor the correspondence from the former Commanding Officer of the United States Army, the late General George Meade, pertaining to your loyal service during the Irish threat of 1867. Said letter has been in the custody of each successive incumbent in the position that I am now honored to hold. I assure you that I have also informed all relevant parties of your valor during the Great War.*

I ask that you not refrain from contacting me in the future should your circumstances warrant.

Enclosed in the packet from the Commissioner of the Customs was the envelope, postmarked in Washington, that Ben now sliced open with his pocket knife to learn his fate.

EPILOGUE

Pennsylvania
July 1863

$\mathcal{W}$hen Lieutenant Colonel Joshua Chamberlain returned from brigade headquarters, he found his younger brother standing in the middle of Taneytown Turnpike. Together they watched a wounded man, his head wrapped in linen and covered in a straw hat, hobbling away. He traveled with another of the mutineers from the 2nd Maine and a young boy with a shock of red hair. Chamberlain wondered aloud if he might ever learn whether the blind man completed his journey home to Maine.

Captain Tom Chamberlain shook his head slowly as he watched the trio shuffle southbound down the dusty road. "Tell me, Joshua, if you were back teaching at Bowdoin, would you call this tragedy or irony?" Tom asked.

With an eyebrow raised quizzically, the colonel looked at his brother.

Tom smiled broadly. "You do appreciate, don't you, that you're sending a man who may never again see daylight to be keeper of a light house? His duty will be to guide mariners in the dark. Aren't you sending a blind man to lead the blind?"

The colonel looked toward where Ben Grindle trudged along, with his hand resting on the Irish lad's shoulder. "Well, Tom, when I saw him in the hospital last night, they'd removed his shirt to make certain there were no more powder burns. He had at least four bullet wounds and many other scars."

"Sounds like the man's quite a lead mine."

"Brother John thinks he was lashed as a boy." Colonel Chamberlain flexed his left hand tensely around the hilt of his saber. "Tragic or ironic, you ask?" Chamberlain halted again and drew a deep breath that he exhaled slowly. "No, Tom, I hope what we've done today is justice."

The End

AUTHOR'S NOTE

In his 1938 anthology, *Trending into Maine*, Kenneth Roberts described several stories from the state's history that he wanted to write. These included the exploits of two Maine infantry regiments in the Civil War, the 2nd Maine and the 20th. Regrettably Mr. Roberts did not pursue these stories; his published historical novels spanned the American Revolution through the War of 1812. As a result, I began reading about these regiments in other books and novels, including Michael Shaara's excellent *The Killer Angels*.

In the course of this reading, I discovered many interesting historic events in Maine during the 19th century that I thought might make a compelling yarn. Any author of historical novels relies upon the essential fact-gathering of historians and other writers. I am indebted to many authors, diarists and historians who thoroughly documented the Civil War era and the maritime history of Maine. Some of those include:

Joshua L. Chamberlain, General, U.S.A., *Through Blood & Fire at Gettysburg*

Barnard L. Colby, *For Oil and Buggy Whips: Whaling Captains of New London County, Connecticut*

Henry Steele Commager and Eric Bruun, Editors, *The Civil War Archive*

Stephen H. Evans, Captain, U.S.C.G., *The United States Coast Guard 1790 – 1915*

Clyde H. Freed, LL.B., *The Story of Railroad Passenger Fares*

John Gould, *Maine Lingo: Boiled Owls, Billdads, & Wazzats*

Jeremiah E. Goulka, Editor, *The Grand Old Man of Maine, Selected Letters of Joshua Lawrence Chamberlain, 1863-1914*

Harry Gratwick, *Penobscot Bay: People, Ports and Pastimes*

Francis Ross Holland, Jr., *Great American Lighthouses*

Francis Ross Holland, Jr., *America's Lighthouses: An Illustrated History*

Austin M Knight, *Modern Seamanship*

Glenn W. LaFantasie, *Twilight at Little Round Top: July 2, 1863 – The Tide Turns at Gettysburg*

Edward G. Longacre, *Joshua Chamberlain: The Soldier and the Man*

Basil Lubbock, *The Down Easters: American Deep-Water Sailing Ships, 1869-1929*

H.L. Mencken, *The American Language and Supplement II*

James H. Mundy, *Second to None, The Story of the 2nd Maine Volunteers, "The Bangor Regiment"*

Francis T. Palgrave, *The Golden Treasury of Songs and Lyrics*

Kenneth Roberts, *Trending into Maine*

Richard A. Sauers, *Meade: Victor of Gettysburg*

Mason P. Smith, *Confederates Downeast*

R.H. Stanley and Geo. O. Hall, *Eastern Maine and the Rebellion*

Stan Tekiela, *Birds of Maine, Field Guide*

Willard M. Wallace, *Soul of the Lion, A Biography of General Joshua L. Chamberlain*

Geoffrey C. Ward with Ric Burns and Ken Burns, *The Civil War, An Illustrated History*

Readers with questions about the historic characters, events or language may contact me at sorrowledge@arbogast.com

I wish to thank several people who have helped me understand maritime history, including Coast Guard historians Dr. Robert Scheina and Dr. Robert Browning, as well as Barbara Voulgaris, research assistant in that office. That office preserves a wealth of maritime history; there I learned which Revenue Marine cutter patrolled Maine in 1880, where it was built and who was its skipper when this story is set. I am appreciative of the work of Wayne Wheeler and the U.S. Lighthouse Society to preserve American lighthouses and their rich history.

I am extremely grateful to the late CWO4 Ken Black, a retired Coast Guard warrant officer who started the Maine Lighthouse Museum in Rockland, Maine. He generously gave his time to help me understand the mechanics of lighthouses and the daily lives of the lighthouse keepers. A portion of the proceeds from the sale of this work will be donated to the Maine Lighthouse Museum.

I was encouraged to pursue my writing by the first Coast Guard photojournalist, Chief Petty Officer Alex Haley.

All authors benefit from "experiential research," by going and doing whatever activity relates to the topic of their book. My knowledge of nautical customs was derived from 17 years with the U.S. Coast Guard. My knowledge of certain canine customs benefited by sharing a home for 17 years with two Newfoundlands, first Bailey and then Bosun.

Editorial advice provided by Kate Arbogast, Marguerite Arbogast, Mari Dattolo, Rose Ingram, Brooke Shaffer, Ed Wendover and RTF Communication. Publishing assistance from E.A. Kafkalas.

Cover art by Mariah Washburn. Cover design by Rita Kogler Carver. Nautical chart of Maine by the First District of the U.S. Light House Board.

Thank you kindly.

ABOUT THE AUTHOR

Kenneth Arbogast was a writer and editor for the U.S. Coast Guard and U.S. Forest Service for 35 years. He served as editor of the Coast Guard's national magazine and an instructor at the Defense Information School. His fiction and nonfiction have appeared in journals, magazines and newspapers from Maine to Alaska.

Made in the USA
Columbia, SC
31 May 2021